REALIZATION

AN AGRIPUNK THRILLER

THE MARTINIERE LEGACY BOOK THREE

JOYCE REYNOLDS-WARD

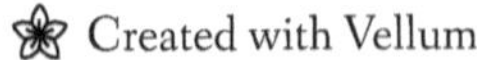 Created with Vellum

A SINGLE RAY OF EARLY MORNING SUNLIGHT SUDDENLY illuminated an elongated rectangle on the dark soil of the freshly watered arena footing. As the chestnut mare Casey approached the lighted rectangle, Ruby Barkley kept an eye on Casey and her rider, Ruby's husband Gabriel Martiniere. Ruby vibrated the lunge line slightly to remind Casey that she was watching.

Casey flicked her ears and arched her neck to eye the spot of light suspiciously as she trotted over it, but showed no other reaction.

Gabe laughed and raised his arms from his sides where he'd dropped them protectively. "Wasn't sure about that one."

He spread his arms wide, swaying slightly as he sought to find his balance in the dressage saddle. Casey twitched her ears back to focus on Gabe, and halted due to his unsteady seat.

Gabe growled and clucked Casey back up to the trot. "Mare, I don't need *that* much babysitting!"

"It's good for you, Gabe!" Petra Marks, Gabe's physical therapist, called from the arena gate where she and Gabe's doctor, Amy Caruthers, watched. "Work that core! You need it."

"She's pickier about my weight shifts than she was a week ago," Gabe grumbled.

"Casey is very reactive to rider balance," Ruby said. "And a week ago you were in my old barrel racing saddle with the extra-stiff fenders to keep your legs steady. Plus, she was only walking. You want to be pushed? I'll switch the dressage saddle out for my close contact jumper."

"No, this saddle is enough of a challenge. Even with knee and thigh blocks." Casey started to slow as they approached her palomino daughter, Legacy, who was tied to an arena post and fussing. Gabe's legs tightened on her sides to urge her back into the steady two-beat jog. "Though it would be nice to lope."

"Not yet. You need to be stronger."

Ruby bit her lip as she watched Gabe's face tighten with the strain of keeping himself upright. He was working harder to stay steady than he wanted to admit, and it hurt her to see the struggle. When younger, Gabe had been a saddle bronc rider capable of dancing with the biggest, boldest, craftiest bucking horses, using a deft mix of balance and strength to stay aboard until the eight-second buzzer sounded. But the G9 virus—and the relapse just three weeks ago triggered by an enemy's injection of weaponized G9—impaired that mixture of skill and strength.

Luckily the Chan Protocol for G9 treatment appeared to be working. Gabe had gotten back on his feet within a week. According to their son Brandon, who had cared for Gabe during his initial attack, this recovery progressed much faster.

Wherever Brandon is now.

His visits to Ruby and Gabe's home ranch, the Double R, were furtive and quick, between his appearances as the public face of the indentured labor reform movement. Rebellion stirred in the assorted indentured labor pools around the US. Brandon's girlfriend Kris Markey and her sister Pat, leaders of the rebellion, were in hiding. An underground indentured freedom organization operated by Ruby and Gabe's business partner Jeff Swait and Jeff's sister Carrie had taken over protecting them from pursuit.

Kris was a freed indentured already, but Pat had been held long past the expiration of her contract. Gabe, Ruby and Brandon had collaborated with Kris to free Pat from an indentured research compound where she had been slated to undergo a protocol which would have turned her into a mindless cyborg. Her now-former owners aggressively sought Pat. Not only did she know details about their interdicted research, but other indentureds with illegally extended contracts had also bolted from the research compounds and were now publicly revealing their experiences.

"Won't get stronger if I don't push," Gabe said, breaking into Ruby's grim thoughts about Brandon and Kris.

It had been his idea to substitute horseback riding for some of the exercises that Petra had him doing. Petra had agreed easily with his suggestion, since her hope was that muscle memory would help Gabe progress faster.

"There's pushing and then there's overdoing." Petra slipped through the arena gate. She hesitated until Casey had passed, then joined Ruby, standing out of the way of the lunge line. "You're working plenty hard right now. Let's focus first on working with trot until it's easy."

"Perhaps we should try posting trot," Ruby said, glancing at Petra for her opinion.

"Let's see how that goes," Petra said.

"Gabe. Posting trot. You cue it."

Gabe nodded. His lips tightened along with his legs. Casey's trot extended from the easily-ridden slow jog to a faster version of the gait, her legs reaching out further in diagonal pairs as Gabe started to rise and fall in the saddle, following the motion of Casey's outside shoulder.

He lasted for half a circuit. Then he swayed and dropped his hands to Casey's neck, collapsing into the saddle and blowing hard as the chestnut mare halted. Beads of sweat lined his forehead.

"All right. You win. I could probably do it in a Western saddle."

"Maybe," Petra said. "But you need to build up your strength in this saddle. And this is plenty of work for this morning."

Gabe sighed as Ruby called Casey to her and unhooked the side reins. "It doesn't feel like I've ridden long enough," he said.

"It's been a good ten minutes."

Ruby led Casey over to the mounting block. Petra waited by the block to steady Gabe as he dismounted.

"Oh, you'll feel the burn in a little bit," Petra said. "A more difficult saddle, and you added three minutes today."

"Only ten minutes. God." Gabe shook his head.

Ruby held Casey as Gabe slowly and carefully slid his feet out of the stirrups, then stepped onto the block. He wobbled a little but recovered with Petra's help, then cautiously made his way down the steps and to the gate. Once there, he unstrapped his helmet and pulled it off, setting it on the ledge that held other helmets. Amy Caruthers unfolded his walker and handed it through the gate.

Gabe leaned on his walker, head down for a moment, then looked up.

"I've *got* to get back into shape. Need to take you to Donnagran's so you can learn more about how to use that ring, Ruby. Need to help you with the haying. Need to get moving with—" he waved his right hand. "—everything to help Brandon and get my fucking father Philip out of the Martiniere Group leadership. God damn it, we did not need me to be sidelined like this!"

"Right now you need to focus on getting stronger, and strategizing just how you're going to take care of Philip," Ruby retorted. "You're well enough to do that. As for the haying, it's *under control.* How the hell do you think Charlie and I took care of things before you came back to the ranch? We'll be able to meet up with Donna-gran soon enough." She patted the chain around her neck to make sure the emerald ring and the silver locket were still there.

Gabe sighed. "I know." He smiled at Ruby. "I'm sorry. Just frustrated by my damn body. Things would be so much easier without the G9."

"I understand." She slipped in close. Gabe reached for Ruby and pulled her to him, kissing her, then resting his forehead against hers. They lingered together, savoring the moment. "And the last three weeks have been a whirlwind."

"I'll say. But I still owe you that honeymoon," he grumbled.

She snorted. "We didn't have much of one the first time around. Why should it be any different when we remarried?"

"Because I *wanted* it to be different," he said. "I wasn't planning to get nailed by weaponized G9 less than forty-eight hours after the ceremony. I really wasn't. You deserve better."

"Stop beating yourself up." She squeezed his shoulder. "We didn't have a choice. Not really. Not if we were following through on our plans and promises. All three of us—you, me, and Brandon—are committed to beating Philip. I'm a part of it. That's why I wear the Martiniere emeralds."

"I still feel guilty. I've a lot to make up for."

"That you do."

But she kissed him to soften the edge in her voice. Their divorce twenty-one years ago had been nasty as hell. Even though she had recently discovered the degree to which mind control techniques used by Philip and his associates had played a part in their split, they both still had a lot of *who do we trust? How can we trust?* issues to work through.

"I'll get breakfast started while you school Legacy," Gabe said. "I can do that at least. About an hour or so, you think?"

Ruby glanced at the golden mare, now standing quietly. Much as she would like to ride longer, today was not that day. All she had time to do was a quick catch schooling of bending and flexing under saddle. The ranch's third cutting of grass hay to feed horses and cattle was baled and still in the field. She wanted it all stacked under cover today, if possible. The weather had been in their favor while cutting, curing, and baling. No need to tempt fate any further. If she and her crew put in a long day, it could happen, barring equipment breakdowns.

"Forty-five minutes to an hour," she said.

"Okay. Ride." He kissed her forehead. "It'll make you happier." He gave her a gentle shove away. "Go work with Legacy. You both need it."

"Oh Gabe."

But he's right, she thought as she walked over to Legacy. *Knows me way too well.*

Ruby liked working with the young horses she raised. Bringing green-broke horses along carefully and slowly so that they made good saddle horses well into their twenties kept her grounded through biobot development, the ups and downs of ranching, divorce, and now the craziness of being remarried to the primary Martiniere heir—with all the insular, corrupt craziness that went along with that family—and the mother of another.

Legacy and Casey were descendants of Sunshine, the palomino mare that Ruby had ridden in barrel racing competitions and her year as Miss Rodeo Oregon. Ruby didn't keep all of Sunshine's descendants. But select ones like Legacy, Casey, and Casey's latest foal, the yearling colt Dancer, stayed on the ranch.

As Ruby gently encouraged the golden mare to lightly collect and accept contact between her hands and the bit, her worries about Gabe and Brandon faded away. She was astride one of the best mares she had ever bred, and that felt pretty damn sweet at the moment. And at least Legacy didn't feel like she needed to tear around the arena or take off bucking today. A nice gift.

But all too soon her timer buzzed. It was time to let Legacy walk a couple of arena circuits on a loose rein, then untack and turn her into a pen with Casey. The rest of the herd was on range turnout and would be out there for a few more weeks, with only a handful of saddle horses kept at the home place—Legacy, Casey, Red, Pard, Cisco, and Blaze.

Ruby hesitated long enough to assess the rising sun and the sky around her. Clear. Bright. Blue, not a puff of white in the sky. The faint chill in the air that warned her that summer was almost over.

A perfect day for finishing this round of haying.

As the sun dipped behind the Blue Mountains to the west, and the violet haze of dusk hovered over the prairie and distant mountains to the east, Ruby parked the big farm truck and flatbed trailer next to the truck and trailer they had rented for hauling hay. With her ranch manager Charlie Thompson running the tractor at the hay shed to stack the bales, and an assortment of rented equipment run by local day laborers, they had managed to get the rest of the hay in from the fields.

She plugged her truck in to charge, then stretched and

placed her hands on her hips, surveying the now-full hay barn before her.

It wasn't often that haying worked this well. But harvest weather was just about the only thing that had run smoothly this summer. This late-September third cutting could be a struggle if the fall rains came early. They hadn't this year. No rain during cutting, drying, or baling. None during the three days it had taken to stack it in the barns, this big barn here being the last.

Charlie parked the big tractor and joined her, shoving his weathered straw hat back from his forehead as he rubbed it. One of his heelers, Rusty, jumped down from the cab, galloped over to Ruby and nudged her leg. She bent to scratch Rusty's head as he leaned against her, his stub tail wagging and tongue lolling happily.

"Mighty nice hay crop this year," Charlie said.

"Yeah, it's the one thing that seems to have gone right," she said, giving Rusty a final pat before straightening up. "Now I'm worried about the grains."

Charlie snorted. "One thing at a time, Ruby. We can feed stock this winter, and at least this year we don't have loan payments hanging on the harvest." His other heeler, Crimson, dropped a ball at his feet and Charlie threw it for her to retrieve.

"True," she conceded.

Between her winning the Superhero AgInnovator reality show contest last spring (along with Gabe and Jeff Swait), Gabe gaining access to his Martiniere trust fund, and investments in her RubyBot biobot line, the Double R was doing well for once. Even with the additional expenditures in security, housing, and lab expansion that came along with the Martiniere connections, she was securely in the black for the first time in years. They could lose over half the grain crop and still be doing well—not that she wanted to see that happening. But the RubyBot was finally, *finally* starting to pay off after years of struggle.

"The data feed from the RubyBot fields sure makes things simpler," Charlie said. "It's matching the ground observations." He threw the ball again, Rusty and Crimson vying to reach it first, then squabbling over possession. "Hey! Knock it off!" he yelled at the dogs. Crimson snatched the ball as Rusty hesitated.

"We'll do them all with the RubyBot next spring," she said.

"Any chance you can just sleep the bots over the winter and revive them instead of turning them off?" Charlie asked, ignoring the ball that Crimson dropped at his feet.

Ruby shook her head. "Not for the basic RubyBot. Maybe the Defender, especially in milder climates."

She clicked up her comp and made a note to herself to discuss the issue with Jeff Swait, because his Arkansas location might be a better development site for that mode. The Defender was part of the collaboration between herself, Gabe, and Swait. It was a biobot with aggressive defense capabilities intended to protect fields against intruding bots that would sabotage a grower's operations. Unlike the basic Ruby, the Defender was still under development.

"Just seems like a waste of resources," Charlie said. "Yeah, I know we grow the mediums over the winter, but still. Be nice to have it reusable."

"The way the bot's designed, it breaks down into essential nutrients once it's switched off. That's why it took so long to perfect the design—allowing for breakdown without contaminating the field."

"Yeah, I know, I've heard about it from Martin," Charlie said. Ruby's lab manager Martin was Charlie's husband. "And I suppose that creating a bot that lasts for several years cuts into profits."

"It's more complicated. I think we can go that route with the Defender. It would be nice to have a bot that you could command to reload itself into the growboxes at the end of the year, though, wouldn't it?"

"Yeah." Charlie rolled his shoulders. "Well, that's done for the year. See you in the morning. Or not. You have a meeting, right?"

"GMR Group. Will probably eat up most of the morning." Ruby frowned. "I'm just glad I was able to pitch in with the haying. I have to spend more time dealing with Martiniere and indenture reform issues for the next few weeks—months, even. This was just a quick break."

"Well, if it needs to be done, it needs to be done," Charlie said. "I've known too damn many good people caught up in the indentured system, even before Rick and Beck moved here. If you, Gabe, and Brandon can change that, then *good*. Guess I won't be seeing you in the morning, then. I'll clean up the rental equipment and get it back to the co-op. Good night, and good luck with your meeting. C'mon, you two," he said to Rusty and Crimson, picking up the ball that Crimson dropped at his feet.

"Good night and thanks."

Ruby headed for the house. Her skin itched from the day's work, her body sticky with half-dried sweat, and her face, hands, and hair dusty. At least it was cooling off fast tonight, with a faint damp chill that meant September. She slipped off her boots while sitting on the back porch steps, shook them out, then brushed off what she could of the hay chaff before going inside, leaning her elbows on her knees for a moment to breathe deeply and let fatigue wash over her. Her body ached. She sure wasn't getting any younger. Fifty-one in a few weeks. Some days she felt older than that.

Voices rose and fell from inside, along with the clatter of

dishes. Ruby couldn't make out the words, but recognized the speakers as Dr. Amy Caruthers, on the ranch to supervise the early stages of Gabe's Chan Protocol treatment for the G9, and Gabe. The enticing scent of beef curry wafting made Ruby's stomach rumble, reminding her that she hadn't eaten lunch.

Gabe was at the stove when she entered, while Amy washed dishes. "How'd the haying go?" he asked, hobbling across the kitchen to grab bowls.

"All done and in the barn. Only a couple of easily-fixed breakdowns."

He grinned at her. "Good. Dinner in ten minutes."

"Enough time for me to get showered, then."

"I'll keep it warm. Bran sent a message that he has another show running tonight."

"Another show?" She halted at the hallway entrance. Brandon and Kris had production experience from their work on the AgInnovator. They had been quick-releasing interviews with escaped indentureds over the past two weeks, irregularly and from different locations. "Kind of close to the GMR meeting, isn't it?" Her skin prickled and not from the hay chaff.

"I have no idea what it's about. I'm hoping he and Kris are using adequate judgment. His message was just that this one was too hot to sit on." When Ruby hesitated, Gabe frowned at her. "Go get cleaned up. They posted it about midday, and I cued it up in our room. You look exhausted. I'll bring up the food while you're showering."

"How are you gonna carry it?"

"He's already enlisted me," Amy said. "With bribes of sharing huckleberry crisp." She patted her stomach. "Three weeks on the ranch and I'm putting on weight. You two are good cooks."

"Part of ranch life," Gabe said.

"Darn, should have put you on the hay crew," Ruby said, grinning. "If the weight gain is too much."

"Eh, I'll work it off once Justine finds another clinic for me to work out of," Amy said. "But I've appreciated the time working in the lab here, when I'm not doctoring Gabe or helping out at the hospital. Your Dr. Sheri would sure like me to set up shop in Lakeside. But it's just too small a town. Too visible for me to be pulling indentured hormonal tags. Too hard for those who need my help to get here."

"We appreciate what you have done."

Amy shrugged. "It's been a good place to lay low for a few weeks. Justine messaged that she's negotiating another site."

"So you'll probably be leaving soon?"

"In a week or so."

"We'll miss you."

"Thanks."

Ruby left the kitchen and headed up the stairs to their bedroom. Earlier in the year there had been more people living in the house. She and Gabe had adopted the habit of eating dinner in their room to have private time. Now that Beck O'Toole and Rick Keysing had moved out of the main house and to a prefab small house next to the lab, Amy was the only other regular occupant, while she supervised Gabe's recovery. Brandon and Kris still had a room of their own, and Gabe's sister Justine did as well.

But Justine had joined Brandon and Kris in their exile, moving from place to place to keep ahead of Philip Martiniere's private security. Ruby was surprised that Justine wasn't already here for tomorrow's meeting, but perhaps she would arrive later. Brandon would probably come only for the duration of the meeting, then leave. Gabe had mandated that it was too dangerous for both of them to be in the same house for very long. Especially now that he was jockeying to challenge Philip for leadership of the Martiniere Group.

Both of my men are too easy a target.

Ruby sighed as she entered the bedroom. New realities, new concerns, now that she was part of the Martiniere Family. She pulled off her clothes and dropped them in the hamper, then undid the silver chain to take off her two most precious pieces of jewelry—her old silver good luck locket that held a picture of the grandparents who had raised her, and the emerald Martiniere wedding ring that was much more than it appeared to be.

She held the ring for a moment, studying the green flickers within the stone. It wasn't just a gem. The cultivated, lab-created, and hardened stone had electronic circuits grown within it that accessed mind control programming devised by the Martinieres to control not just their indentured chattels but other members of the family. Only Ruby and Brandon were free of that programming.

Gabe had been in hiding from his family when she had married him the first time. He had testified against the man he thought was his uncle, Philip Martiniere, in an attempt to shut down mind control programming forced upon unwilling inden-tured workers. When Philip discovered Gabe's location and his family, he locked Gabe down so he couldn't say who he was, and demanded that Gabe divorce Ruby.

Oh, that had been an ugly time. It hadn't been until seven months ago that Ruby and Gabe had communicated more than the minimum required for raising Brandon. She had said farewell to Gabe when Brandon turned eighteen, and they hadn't spoken for years—until they returned to compete against each other in the agtech funding game show, the AgInnovator.

And then the revelations spilled. Gabe's connection to the Martinieres, that had brought about their divorce. The discovery that Philip was Gabe's father, not his uncle, part of a complex agreement between him and the man Gabe had thought was his father in order to protect the family. Learning that Martiniere mind control coupled with covert psychotropic drug administration had been used to manipulate both Ruby and Gabe, so that she would reject his attempts at reconciliation twenty-one years ago. The intent had been to push Gabe to suicide, to rid Philip of an inconvenient, rebellious, unacknowledged son.

Philip's attempt failed—but from Gabe's accounts of that era, just barely.

And then meeting Gabe's grandmother. Donna-gran, who had negotiated that devil's agreement between Philip and his brother Saul. The Martiniere Matriarch—*former* Matriarch since she had passed that role on to Ruby—who knew the patterns programmed into the ring. Had apparently been part of the development of those control structures.

Ruby's fingers closed around the ring. How far dared they trust Donna-gran? It wasn't a question she could ask any of the Martinieres, not even Brandon, who had been enthusiastically accepted by his newly discovered relatives. Definitely not Gabe or Justine, who appeared to idolize their grandmother.

As long as we go along with her aims, as long as our goals coincide with the best interests of the Martinieres, we can trust her.

At least right now they all appeared to agree on the need to restrain the growing movement of converting indentureds into actual slaves. But she didn't dare forget that Donna-gran had been part of the program that had led to the creation of the indentured class. Had devised those control structures.

How do I keep us safe?

Ruby exhaled. That was a question she couldn't answer

yet. She released her grip on the ring and set it down gently on the vanity before going into their bathroom.

When Ruby came out of the bathroom, her long silver-streaked red hair combed out and left loose to dry, a soft green silk robe that was a gift from Gabe wrapped over matching pajamas, she stopped short. The room lights were dimmed, their small dinner table set with battery-operated candles, already-dished up bowls of curry and huckleberry crisp for dessert, champagne glasses and an ice bucket with an opened bottle in it.

Gabe sprang up from his sleep recliner as she eyed the table.

"It's not fancy," he said as he took her in his arms again. "But you're tired out from haying and I thought you'd like a small celebration since third cutting's done. And it's our three week anniversary."

She half-chuckled, leaning her head against his chest. "Official or ceremonial?"

"Does it matter?" Gabe delicately lifted Ruby's chin with a forefinger, keeping his contact light because he knew she didn't like being touched there, and kissed her. "Given everything that's going on, I'll take any excuse for celebration."

"Timing's right for ceremonial," she said. "But I agree. Celebrate everything and anything, because who knows what's going to happen."

After all, within forty-eight hours of celebrating their remarriage with family and friends, she had been holding Gabe, screaming at him not to die on her while he spasmed and puked his way through a G9 attack,

"Come and eat." He guided her to a chair. "Might not be able to help with haying but I can at least feed you."

Ruby laughed and dove in. Gabe was a good cook, always had been. The curry followed by a bowl of huckleberry and apple crisp filled her up, enough that she finally dared to sip her champagne.

Gabe raised his glass. "Three weeks on our second marriage-go-round. And a successful third hay cutting."

She saluted him and drained her glass. "What's the story on Brandon's latest show?"

"I don't know." He refilled their glasses. "To be honest, I've been on the comp all day crunching numbers for you. We've been getting a lot more interest in the basic RubyBot *and* Moondance Microbials ever since Brandon and Kris went public. Been answering inquiry after inquiry. Martin, Rick and I had to talk about lab production capacity because we're almost at our cutoff point for next year. If you could check my numbers in the morning, that would be great."

"Thanks." She sipped her champagne. "I wouldn't have anticipated more orders because of Brandon and Kris."

"Me neither. I have to wonder if today's jump in orders is connected to whatever it is that they posted. The timing's right."

"One way to find out." She stood up and gathered the bowls. "I'll take these downstairs. Then I'll be ready to watch Brandon's show."

When she came back, Gabe had moved the candles to their nightstands ,and put away table and chairs. He sat in their adjustable bed, the head set to its highest position. A fresh glass of champagne waited on her nightstand, and a projection on hold shimmered at the foot of the bed. She tossed her robe onto her rocking chair and joined Gabe, delicately balancing her glass as she snuggled in next to him.

"Ready?"

She nodded.

Gabe snapped his fingers and the projection firmed up. Brandon sat in an armchair, leaning forward with his elbows resting on his knees, fingertips pressed together as his dark brown eyes stared toward the camera, a faint smile curling the corners of his mouth. Despite the position he appeared sleek, professional, and earnest. One lock of his dark wavy hair curled rakishly over his forehead, and his fitted dark blue suit accented his pale brown skin.

"This is Brandon Martiniere with another report from the Indentured Freedom Coalition," he said, straightening up. "Patricia Markey will join us with another testimony from a former indentured whose contract was extended past expiration date. But first, an announcement. As of noon today, the Biobot Producers Alliance has unanimously voted to reject all use of indentured workers in every stage of agricultural production, and has joined the Indentured Freedom Coalition."

Ruby raised her brows at Gabe as Brandon continued to speak. "Did we vote?"

"Yes. And I cast your proxy vote."

"Good." She settled back against him. Not that she had any doubts about the correctness of this action. The BPA was Brandon and Gabe's creation, and while this step hadn't been written down, nonetheless it had been one of their agreed goals.

Gabe nodded as the screen changed to Pat. "But there's more going on here. I wouldn't think that Bran would want us to watch this just for these announcements."

"Yeah, you'd think this wouldn't be big news for us."

She turned her attention back to the show. Pat was interviewing a gaunt, balding, long-faced white man. Something about him looked familiar. He raised a quivering hand to display the blue and green diamond-shaped AgI tattoo between the thumb and index finger of his left hand.

"I call on President Stephen Tolliver to listen to the Indentured Freedom Coalition." He drew a ragged breath. "Stephen, you may not remember the circumstances of my indenture."

Ruby elbowed Gabe. "What's this?"

"I don't know."

They focused as the man continued. "My name is Colin Fields. I am—I *was*—married to your cousin Laura, Stephen." He choked for a moment. "We—Laura ran up a raft of medical bills when dying of cancer fifteen years ago. I couldn't pay them after her death, and AgI bought my indenture. It was supposed to be for five years." He paused. "My indenture actually ended three weeks ago. Ten years overdue. Thanks to the brave actions of Gabriel Martiniere, Ruby Barkley, and others in freeing not just me and you, but twenty other indentureds whose contracts had been illegally extended."

Ruby gulped.

Which one was he?

She peered closer at him. Colin resembled the medic that had helped her and Brandon during those first frantic moments after Gabe had been injected with the weaponized G9. He turned his head and the profile made it definite.

The medic.

"I thank you, Gabriel. And Ruby. And Brandon. And Pat," Colin continued slowly. "And to all of you who are watching this 'cast. None of us are immune from being forced into indenture. *None of us.*"

Gabe whistled. "Holy crap. The President's cousin," he breathed. "That's got to roil things up."

"He's the medic who helped you," Ruby said.

Gabe raised his brows, but before he could speak, Brandon came back on screen. "And that was the testimony of Colin Fields, married to a cousin of President Tolliver." He leaned forward again as the camera's focus tightened on him, only showing his upper body in profile. "And he is right. *None of us are immune to indenture.* Colin is just the first of several former indentureds with high profile connections that you'll see in our reports. That includes *me*. Less than a year ago *I* faced the prospect of lifetime indenture. Me. Brandon Martiniere, the grandson of Philip Martiniere. You'll hear my story later, but just remember *this*. *Not even the Martinieres are safe from indenture.*"

Pat broke in from off-camera. "But Brandon, you didn't know about your Martiniere connections then."

"True. But the people who sought to indenture me knew —*including my grandfather*." His voice harshened. "I have proof. It is publicly available online at the Indentured Freedom Coalition's site."

"Fuck," Gabe murmured. "He's playing with fire now."

Brandon's gaze became harder and more intense. "Indenture was a flawed attempt to solve a crashed economy in the late '20s and '30s. It didn't work. It is not a policy that should be around as we enter the '60s. End indenture now. View the Indentured Freedom Coalition proposals at our site. And remember. Message President Stephen Tolliver. Petition to end all indentured contracts NOW." His face faded, replaced by a screen with contact information.

Gabe snapped the projection closed and slumped back against the mattress. "I am really surprised we haven't heard anything about Fields before." He drained his glass and set it down on the nightstand. "But perhaps that explains the swarm of orders this afternoon. All the same, Philip isn't going to ignore this challenge."

"Bran's good at handling it, though," Ruby said, thinking about the presentation. "And if they've uncovered more high-status indentureds whose contracts have been extended—"

"You would hope that starting with the President's cousin means they have higher level testimonies to come." He ran his fingers through his hair. "I just hope our son knows what he's doing." He dropped his hands and turned onto his side, reaching for her. "After this it makes me wish I was still capable...." His voice trailed off. The G9 had left him impotent, a known side effect that didn't respond to the usual treatments for that condition. "Not just as a reaction to news. A three week celebration." He sighed. "Oh well."

"Does Amy have any idea if the Chan Protocol will reverse that side effect?" Ruby asked.

Gabe's lips tightened. "I've been kind of afraid to ask. Stupid guy thing."

She stroked his cheek. "She may not know. I've done enough reading on post-G9 syndrome to find out that there's still a lot of unknowns."

"That's why I've hesitated about asking. Even the Chan Protocol has its issues." He shook his head. "It's stupid of me. But I'm afraid to ask for too many details. I'm just—I'm just getting stronger faster than I did after the initial G9 attack. That's promising, All the same, the Chan is experimental. I'm a guinea pig."

She nodded. Five years of grace was what they had been told, if the Chan Protocol worked. Five years of nearly complete recovery—and then a crash, with who knew what level of disability afterwards. Possibly even death.

But in five years, perhaps there would be another treatment that would work even better. It was a gamble, and Gabe *was* reacting well to the Chan Protocol. Amy had ruled out death in five years as a possibility in Gabe's case. It was just a question of how disabled he would be.

"Let's just go with what we have now," she said softly, taking his face in her hands. "Take it day by day. Who knows what could happen next?"

"Very true," he said.

CHAPTER 2

Early morning rustling in the bathroom woke Ruby. Gabe was still in bed next to her and the shared bathroom door was closed, so—*Brandon.* She slid out of bed quietly and padded over to the door, tapping lightly on it.

"Bran?" she whispered.

"It's all right, Ma. You can come in," he said quietly.

After a quick glance to see if Gabe had roused, she eased into the bathroom. Brandon still wore the suit he had on in the video clip, but his hair was disheveled and his face heavy with studio makeup. He took off his jacket and hung it on a hook.

"Didn't mean to wake you," he said.

"I'm a light sleeper."

"I remember." Brandon undid his tie and stripped off his dress shirt, leaving on a t-shirt. He fumbled in his shaving bag and groaned. "Forgot to grab my cleanser from the last place. Can I borrow yours, Ma?"

"Sure." Ruby pulled her good facial cleansers out and gave them to him, then leaned against the counter as he washed off the heavy studio makeup. "Kris going to be at the meeting, too?"

He reached for a towel to wipe his face and shook his head.

"She and Pat have gone on to our next location. They dropped off me and Justine."

"You need to take that with you?" She gestured to the cleansers.

Brandon handed them to her and she put them away. "No. Mine are probably in Kris's bag—if not, I can borrow hers after our next recording tomorrow afternoon. And it'll be easier for me to get more than you. Thanks for saving me tonight." He gestured toward his room. "If you want to talk, we can go in here."

"Less likely to wake your dad for sure." She hesitated. "I probably should get back to bed."

"Eh, I had a question to ask you anyway."

She followed him into the room, now curious.

Brandon flopped on the bed. "How's Dad doing?"

Ruby shrugged. "Amy's talking about leaving soon, and Petra seems to think he's progressing nicely. He did half a circuit of posting trot in the dressage saddle, and he talks about feeling stronger a lot faster than he did after his initial illness. Amy *has* ruled out death as a possibility when the treatment fades."

"That's good to hear. Though I wish I could have been around more when he was going through the worst of it."

"We got him through. And you have other things to do."

"Yeah, well, I still feel like I should have been here. Which reminds me. I brought a batch of booster vax for all of us except him, cleared by Dr. Chan." He grimaced. "Serg has found evidence that the weaponized G9 Joseph hit Dad with is not the only one out there. We all need to be up to date on our broad spectrum G9 vax because he suspects that Philip may try to use it as a weapon against us again. Dad will need boosters later. All of us will on a regular basis."

"Crud." Ruby's lips tightened. If anyone would know about

this possibility, it would be Serg Vygotsky. He and his father Piotr were the security experts for the splinter Martiniere factions who opposed Philip.

"Yeah. We'll do the vax as part of the GMR. Justine also has a clinic set up for Dr. Amy to work at. We're getting a lot of indentured women who need their implants yanked. Chan had to shut her clinic down so she's on the run now."

Ruby nodded. Justine and her ex-husband Donald had been operating underground reproductive clinics for the last twenty years. In the past ten years their services had extended to removing hormonal implants not cancelled out when indentured women had finished their work contracts. As long as the implants were present, the women could unwillingly be called back into indenture. Removal of the implants by the former indentured woman herself was highly illegal—and the existence of the implants was unknown to most non-indentured.

"I don't think we'll need Dr. Amy's services on a daily basis, now that your father's just doing his rehab," she said. "Check with Amy in the morning, but I think Dr. Sheri and Petra Marks can cover his needs."

"That's good. We really need her to get back to work for the clinics." Brandon yawned and she got up. "Anything else? Early morning tomorrow."

"Your dad says that RubyBot orders shot up after your 'cast went live yesterday. I wouldn't know—was finishing up the haying. I haven't looked at numbers yet."

Brandon grinned. "Now *that's* some good news. Didn't think it would be one of the effects, but glad to see it all the same."

She hesitated. "One last thing. That man in your latest 'cast."

"Colin?"

"Yeah. If you could get in contact with him—tell him

deepest thanks from us. He was the medic amongst the indentureds who helped your father."

Brandon nodded. "That's good to know. I'll get a message to him."

Ruby yawned. "That's all for tonight. I'll see you in the morning."

"Night then."

Gabe snuggled up to her after she got back into bed. "Whassup?" he mumbled.

"Bran's here," she said. "So is Justine. I heard him and went to check."

"Mmm. Kay." He nestled in, throwing an arm over her side.

She closed her eyes.

Colin Fields.

Connected to the President, but still swept up in indenture. And he had helped save Gabe. Thanks weren't enough. Did Fields have a job, a place to stay? Might be worth investigating —but he was only one person.

How many others like him were in the ranks of the indentureds? Like Kris and Pat? Until the past year, she hadn't been all that aware of the plight of indentured workers, because Thunder County was too small to support a labor pool, and she had too many other things to worry about.

She wondered how many other people shared her lack of knowledge.

Until they face indenture themselves.

That had to change. All of it.

THE WELCOME SCENT OF REAL COFFEE WAFTING FROM THE kitchen was a signal that Gabe's half-sister Justine was definitely at the ranch. As Ruby entered the kitchen, focused on the coffee, Justine was settled at the old Formica and chrome table, glowering at her screens. Her usual perch when she was at the Double R.

"Hey Ruby." Justine leaned back from her screens with a sigh, closing them down with a snap.

"You brought coffee. Thank you. We ran out of the last real stuff you brought." Ruby grinned at her sister-in-law—who up to three weeks ago had been thought a cousin, not a sister.

"Hey, I figure I need to pay for the use of a room here in some way."

"Oh, you've more than paid for it. The airstrip. The prefab security residences—heck, the security. Gabe's treatment and Dr. Amy for this round of the G9."

Justine shrugged. "It's my contribution to GMR. They're tools for what we're trying to do. The coffee is one small personal thing that I can pitch in."

"And we are grateful." Ruby poured her coffee and sat across from Justine. "Things going okay? Hardly seen you since everything blew up."

Justine scowled. "Daddy-fucking-dearest is outright *pissed* about your killing Joseph." Joseph was her other half-brother, who had attacked Gabe with the weaponized G9 during the raid where they'd freed Pat, Colin, and twenty other indentureds. "Especially since he can't get the prosecutor in LA to file charges against you. As a result, he's going after me and Brandon as best as he can for theft of property."

"Theft of property? Sheesh."

"Yeah. That's not going over very well with the courts and prosecutors. Every single one of those indentureds we sprung along with Pat was being held illegally. We have all the documentation. Your lawyer did such a good job keeping you out of trouble, I've asked her to give us a hand with the Indentured Freedom Coalition cases."

"Remy should eat that up." Ruby's lawyer and long-time friend Remy Trask had once worked as a prosecutor in LA. Remy didn't talk about the reasons why she had left LA and returned to Thunder County with her wife in tow, but Ruby now suspected that threats from Philip Martiniere had played a part.

"She insists on doing it pro bono. I'd like to find a means to repay her."

"The Trasks are old County money. Remy doesn't need it. I can get you a list of her favorite charities. That would mean a lot to her—and there are some that could use the boost. I give, but donations from another Martiniere would be a big deal. Possibly even endorsements."

"That would be great." Justine got up and poured herself more coffee. She waved the carafe invitingly at Ruby.

She shook her head. "Too much real coffee gives me the jitters. Even though it is so, so good. The fake stuff just doesn't have the same level of caffeine."

Gabe and Brandon's voices echoed in the hallway.

"You mean to tell me that *every* single one of those indentureds that escaped with Fields was in the same position? Not just one or two years past contract expiration, but five or more years?" Gabe shook his head as he made a beeline for the coffee pot.

"Yeah. Every single one of them had been kept in indenture at least five years if not seven or eight years past their original contract terms. There have been no grounds for the extension in any of the records we've recovered so far. Fields was just the most extreme example." Brandon handed Gabe a cup and got one for himself.

He wore jeans and a t-shirt, both items Ruby recognized as coming from the small stash of clothing Brandon had left at the Double R years ago. The jeans were a little short—Brandon had gained a couple of inches of height in college, and the gray shirt read *Thunder Valley Wrestling All Star*. Definitely left behind.

Brandon's lost weight.

That shirt had been tight on him a few months ago, and it had been ages since Brandon had fit into those jeans. Life on the run and not eating right, or more self-defense training?

"Good luck getting Stephen Tolliver to do anything about that," Gabe said bitterly, leaning against the kitchen counter next to the refrigerator. "I've been really disappointed in his Presidency—not to speak of his re-election campaign so far."

Brandon shrugged. "At some point he has to pay attention if he's going to beat Philip for the Presidency. Kris messaged me the post-'cast positive click numbers this morning. Philip's losing ground, but support for Tolliver is still on the fence. Good reviews on the 'cast itself, strong negatives on indenture. If we can keep getting the stories out, the history of what's really happened with indenture since 2028, and the role that Philip played in creating this situation, well, sooner or later Tolliver's going to have to do something." He leaned against the kitchen sink, opposite Gabe.

"Why should Tolliver do anything? You're handing the election to him. Who's going to support Philip when this all comes out?" Gabe furrowed his brows, studying Brandon.

Brandon took a sip of his coffee. "Because if Tolliver doesn't do a damned thing to remedy the indentured mess, he'll get primaried in the spring. The Classic Democrats are also making noises about a coalition candidate between them and the New Democrats for the first time since they split. After the next 'cast we'll run Tolliver-specific numbers. People are uneasy about him, and we *think,* based on the same strong negatives toward Philip, that indenture is the issue. We'll know more once we query further."

"Numbers don't always translate into political action. Who

amongst the power brokers are going to support a challenger to a middle-of-the-road incumbent? Who can challenge Tolliver?"

"We-e-l-l," Brandon said slowly. "Perhaps a former indentured who is not only speaking for the rights of indentured, but has been approached by Tolliver's own party to run against him if he doesn't do something about indenture."

"Who? Fields?"

Brandon shook his head. "Pat. And it's legit. I was there when the pitch was made to her. Some of the New Dems's biggest money people contacted her through the Indentured Freedom Coalition. If Tolliver doesn't do something and soon, they're willing to run her against them. The Classic Dems are also interested in her as well." He grimaced. "We have to get her voting rights back. And a permanent address."

"Well, that's interesting," Justine said. "Because there is also a movement amongst the Real Truthers to yank the nomination away from Daddy-damned-dearest."

"Really?" Gabe said. "And who is pushing that?"

"Oh, I don't know," Justine said. "Rumor might just have it that certain...*interests*...connected with a particular grandmother of ours might be in play. Donna-gran's not been obvious about it but for those of us in the know...she has her sock puppets running. And she is so very not happy with Daddy-poo, especially since you and Brandon now provide an alternative, and Joey is no longer a consideration—thanks, Ruby. He was my brother and I should feel something, but—he was an ass all his life and he would have killed me if he could."

Gabe rolled his eyes. "All right. Are we having this GMR meeting now or what? Who else is coming this time? I'd really like to have a non-businessy breakfast."

"Me too. I'd like some down time before the meeting," Brandon said. "Ma, can I run a load of laundry?"

"You know where everything is," Ruby said. "Go right on ahead."

"Serg and Piotr will be here about nine," Justine said. "We really can't meet until they're here."

Ruby pushed herself up as Amy came into the kitchen. "So how about breakfast and *then* the meeting."

"Works for me," Brandon said. "Amy, I brought the booster vax. It's in one of the lab fridges."

"I'll need time to set it up," Amy said.

"Let's get breakfast going." Gabe pulled out eggs and bacon. "Eggs from Vickie Chandler, and the *good* bacon from Winged Pigs Farms on the other side of Thunder. Do you want individual eggs or a baked omelette? We have green onions, peppers and more to throw into one of those."

A chorus of "Omelette!" echoed around the kitchen. Ruby pulled a paring knife out of the block, lay the big chopping board down on the counter, reached in the crisper for the green onions that she had pulled from the garden yesterday, and started slicing. Gabe joined her with the peppers as Brandon left the kitchen. As they worked, each anticipating the other's moves, it almost seemed as if the twenty-one years they had spent apart had never happened.

Almost.

Ruby had a hard time focusing throughout the GMR Group meeting in Gabe's office. The injection site for the G9 booster ached, and her head hurt. She kept seeing flashes of light, and sometimes objects she looked at were doubled. A quick shake of her head and her vision settled, but in a few minutes the flashing and doubling returned.

"Ruby?" Gabe's voice caught her attention at one point. "Something wrong?"

"Just tired from all the work yesterday, I think," she said. "What was it you just said about security?"

Gabe frowned but repeated what he'd said about increased security including drone surveys and stationing watches on the Double R and Moondance boundaries.

"Sounds good," she said, pressing her lips together. Now her gut was roiling and she felt nauseous.

What on earth?

The G9 booster? Something in their breakfast? But the booster was tested and reliable—just wasn't readily available yet because of the expense in producing it. And no one else appeared to be having problems with the food.

Then the world spun around her, as if she had been drinking hard and fast. Her gut churned, and she knew she was going to puke.

Ruby stood up suddenly, knocking over her chair, swaying as she tried to find her balance. Flashing bright colors joined the spinning around her. She clapped her hands to her mouth to hold back the sick sourness rising in her throat as she staggered away from her chair.

The door. Where was the door? She had lived in this house all her life. Why couldn't she find the door?

"Ruby!" Gabe's voice, more insistent, but coming from far away.

"Mom!" Brandon's hands grabbing at her as she reeled in the opposite direction.

"Sick," she groaned, *finally* finding the door and lurching through it.

Now where did she go?

Her breath came short and fast. Ruby swallowed back sour bitter liquid as she swayed, trying to remember just which door led to a bathroom. This was her worst drunk ever, worse even than the epic night she decided to drink herself sick when her divorce from Gabe was finalized.

But she couldn't remember the drinking. How much had she drunk? So much that she couldn't remember it? She was too old to be doing this.

When was this? Where was she?

Her knees buckled and she slammed into the wall, unable to walk straight. Ruby fought to stay on her feet, fought to keep back the foulness in her throat.

But it overcame her. She collapsed to hands and knees as spasms wracked her whole body.

"Ruby! Oh God, Ruby! Branny! Get Dr. Amy here now!"

She couldn't keep the puke back as Gabe grabbed her.

"Sorry," she mumbled.

And then it hit her even harder. Sharp, piercing pain that lanced through her joints and head, accompanied by bright flashing lights. Muscles spasming hard, then blackness.

"*Oh Ruby no, not you too. No.*" Gabe's groans were the last thing she heard before the darkness shut out her awareness of everything else.

BRIEF SURFACING. NOT ABLE TO SEE ANYTHING. DISTANT voices. Gabe and Brandon. Body burning where it wasn't aching. Moan. Gabe fussing, words she can't understand. A slight touch that sends her screaming into pain, until darkness blanks everything out again.

AWARE AGAIN. BRANDON WITH HER.

"Ma. I'm sorry, but I have to go. I'll be back soon. Too much going on—" his voice catches, chokes on a sob for a moment. "Please get better. Please."

Trying to move, trying to make a sound to let Brandon know she hears him. But gray cotton chokes her voice and vision. Instead of the abrupt shuttering of senses like before, a slow fading as he keeps talking. She can't make out the words but worry stands out by the rhythm of his speech and the tone of his voice. She wants to kiss him, warn him to be careful.

So grown up is her last thought before gray cotton wraps around her and muffles her awareness.

Momentary fading of the grayness around her.
Sobbing. Gabe sobbing. Why is Gabe sobbing?
"Oh Rubes, Rubes, it's all my fault."
Grayness wraps around her again.

The gray cotton thins into fog, and she can push some of it away, fan at it until it keeps thinning.
Almost clear.

The fog twists away in gray wisps. She's surfacing at last.

A sensation of *heaviness*, followed by a dull ache throughout her entire body, as if she had been beaten hard, was Ruby's first awareness free of the gray. Muffled sobs came from the side of the bed. Gabe. Faint memories of rousing just enough to hear him crying earlier drifted back.

What the hell happened to me?

Bad enough to make him cry. But was she getting better?

She hadn't hurt like this since childhood. The beating that had been the final straw, when the Big People had taken her away from Mother and Father, left her with Granma and Gramps. The stern hard look on Gramps's face as he scowled at Granma, holding Ruby tight in his lap as he rocked her through the first night when she couldn't sleep, for fear of the nightmares.

This is it, Ruth. They're gonna kill Ruby if we don't put a stop to this.

And they *had* put a stop to it for two years, until Father climbed into her window and stole her away. But he paid for that, after beating Mother to death. This time, when he turned toward Ruby with tire iron in hand, ready to do the same to her, she raised the .38 steady with both hands, just like Gramps had showed her in shooting practices over the past two years. Aimed for his nose. Pulled the trigger. Even as he laughed that she wouldn't dare, and raised the tire iron high to kill her.

I did it, Gramps. Just like you showed me.

But she wasn't little Ruby anymore, was she? Even though she'd done the same thing not that long ago, to a man who'd dared hurt someone she loved.

"My fault. My fucking fault. Oh God, Ruby. I've done nothing but bring you pain."

No you haven't, she wanted to say.

"This G9. This motherfucking G9."

Ah. The booster vax. She must have reacted to it. God

damn, this was a nasty awful bug. Gabe was going through what she had experienced just a few weeks ago after Joseph had injected him with the G9 accelerant. Only now he was the one waiting to see if she lived or died.

Fuck. This damn thing is awful.

No wonder he was crying. She had done the same thing at his bedside, his fate in doubt until he woke. And now she knew damned good and well what it felt like on the other side. But at least this was reality and not a hallucination. Right?

She needed to let him know she was going to be okay. He had done the same for her. Ruby strained against the heaviness weighing her down, trying to give Gabe some clue. But the effort to open her eyes was still too much.

At last she managed to twitch her little finger. It brushed against one of Gabe's index fingers and she gasped as the contact sent waves of pain rushing through her, enough that her eyelids popped open at last.

Gabe's breath caught, choking off his sobs in mid-gulp. It hurt to move her head, but she could glance just sideways enough to see his tear-reddened eyes, his disheveled hair, the hope mixed with dread as he stared at her.

She forced her lips to move in the slightest of smiles.

But oh God, the joy in his face as she did it. He *glowed.*

"Ruby. Oh God," he gasped.

She kept the smile on her lips and shifted her head a little so she could see him better. He bent over her. She inhaled deep, cherishing that spicy musk that meant Gabe and blinked hard, tears welling up.

"I know you hurt like a sonofabitch despite the meds and you can't talk yet," Gabe said softly. "At least that was how this damn virus hit me. But when I was sickest, just having you next to me really helped. Do you want me to lie down next to you?"

She nodded, wincing as the movement sent pain ricocheting through her. Some movements hurt. Others didn't. She needed to figure out which was which—but she remembered going through this process with Gabe just three weeks ago.

Gabe smiled and eased himself onto the bed next to her.

"I know touch hurts, at least it did me," he said. "But it also helped me realize what was and wasn't real. You'll have spells of that for a day or so. Would me touching you be a help? Don't move your head. That hurts. I remember. Blink once for no, twice for yes."

She blinked twice. He *understood*.

Gabe delicately stroked her cheek with the tip of his index fingernail. "That all right?"

She blinked twice.

He followed the fingernail with the first joint of his finger, then the knuckle. Everything seemed to snap back into place. An explosion of sensation followed that first touch. It hurt at first, but the tender delicacy of that contact left her wanting more. Ruby shifted her head to push against that finger, that *feel* that wasn't her, that feel of Gabe.

"It's good?"

She blinked twice again.

"You're feeling again? No numbness? Once for numbness, twice for not-numb."

Twice blink.

"I could hold you if you want. But it might be overwhelming."

I don't care.

She tried to speak but a sobbing gasp was the best she could do, along with blinking twice. Gabe nodded.

"I'll try not to make it hurt," he said.

He delicately slid one arm under her shoulders. Touch. So much contact. But it was *good* contact, with careful, precise, measured movement and just enough pressure to ease the sharp fiery pinpricks racing through her body. *Safety* along with *pain* and *joy* flooded through her as he shifted his weight and pulled her against him. Ruby gulped again, eyes wet with tears as she pressed her head into his chest. She felt his sobs matching hers as he murmured into her hair.

"You're feeling, you're feeling, you're oriented. Oh God, Rubes, you're past the worst of it. Oh God, if I could have spared you this..." His voice trailed off.

Movement seemed to be easier now. She hitched herself closer to him. Refuge. Safety. She could fall asleep in his arms without fearing that the gray fog would wrap around her once more.

Safe.

<hr>

GABE STILL WAS HOLDING RUBY TIGHT WHEN SHE WOKE again. This time she could open her eyes without fighting against the heavy weight. A slight movement of her head didn't send pain reverberating through her body. She twitched her right hand and shifted her weight.

"Gabe?" she whispered, voice raspy, harsh and rough.

His eyes flew open. "Ruby. I'm here. How are you feeling?"

She paused, assessing. She no longer felt like she had been beaten nearly to death, but her limbs still were weighted and sluggish.

"Doesn't hurt to move," she said finally. "Throat hurts."

He grabbed a cup with a straw in it. "Drink. I'll hold it for you."

The cool water soothed the ache in her throat. She coughed and sipped some more. When she spoke again, it didn't hurt. "How long?"

"Five days," Gabe said. "Five fucking days of hell. You had

one of those rare damn stupid redhead medication reactions of yours to the booster. It was just as severe as getting the illness in the first place." He pulled the cup away. "Little bit at a time. Your reaction was worse than either my initial attack or the one brought on by the accelerant." His voice caught again. "I called Branny back once because we thought you were dying."

"Oh shit. Gabe, I'm sorry for putting you through this."

"Don't be. I've done it to you. My turn to be on this side." He kissed her forehead. "Amy says that there's measures we can take for future boosters—both of us will need to pre-medicate. And we don't dare lapse with the boosters."

"Which treatment?" As far as she knew there was only one G9 treatment where booster vaccinations were indicated.

He sighed. "Chan. Same as me."

Five years, then.

She drew a ragged breath. "So we're both on the same timeline."

He nodded grimly. "I'd have spared you this if I could. You might end up recovering more quickly than me, since you don't have partial impairment from a previous attack," he said. "At least that's what I am hoping."

"What's happening with GMR? Branny? The ranch?"

He stroked her brow. "There's time enough for you to worry about it tomorrow."

She tightened her lips. "You wouldn't let me run that excuse by you when you were sick."

He sighed. "Yeah. I know. Okay. Short version. Charlie's identified several fields with grains dry enough to harvest. Started that yesterday. We used the RubyBot data to make the decision and boy is it ever a help. Measures are accurate."

"Good to hear."

Gabe nodded. "There's been three arson attempts since we set up the extended security. Two here, one at Moondance.

Beat them all down fast. And Bran—" he hesitated. "He's supposed to have a meeting with Tolliver in three hours. He wanted to know when you woke up—insisted that I call him right up to when that meeting starts."

"Guess we'd better do it. And Justine?"

"Busy. She checks in. She's managing her clinics. Amy's been flying in and out once we determined you weren't contagious. The booster acted like accelerant on your system, and she's consulting with Chan about that process, sharing data with her."

Ruby nodded. "Okay. Call Bran?"

"Might as well." Gabe snapped up his comm.

Brandon was in one of Justine's jets. Ruby recognized the layout from her own travels.

"Dad?" And then he spotted Ruby, and his tense expression relaxed. "Ma. God, am I glad to see you're awake and oriented. I'd heard that you had already wakened but—yeah. Seeing you this time is much better."

"You're being careful?"

"Absolutely. Kris and I are talking to Tolliver soon. Private location." He shifted in his seat. "I will come see you as soon as possible. Okay?"

"Okay. I understand if it takes a while."

"It won't." His voice was firm. "Got to go now. Damn, it's good to see that you're past the worst of it. Wish I could be there. But—"

"What you're doing is more important."

"Equally reimportant. Family counts too. Love you both, but I've got to run." He clicked off.

Ruby yawned. How could she already be feeling so tired?

"Sleepy?" Gabe asked.

"Yeah. Just hit me all of a sudden."

"It's normal," he said. "Amy just messaged that she likes

your stats, but that she'll wait to check until your next waking. There is *some* advantage to having another recovering G9 patient around the house. I know when to call for help, and when to tell them to let you sleep."

"Thanks." She snuggled into his chest. Sleep came quickly.

CHAPTER 3

THE NEXT FEW DAYS WERE A FLURRY OF TESTS AND SLOW easing into physical therapy. Brandon popped in for a short but intense visit, nearly in tears as he stared at her. Ruby discovered that she couldn't do her usual work on the comp for more than an hour before her head hurt. Gabe resurrected an old printer and scrounged paper to print out reports for her. Physical therapy dominated the early mornings, followed by a rest, then switching between comp and paper to monitor the grain harvest reports from the RubyBots.

Five days after Ruby first woke, it was her turn to be lunged on Casey while Charlie, Petra, and Gabe supervised. It was surprisingly hard to sit upright as Casey walked around and around. A couple of times Ruby grabbed the chestnut mare's mane as a wave of pain washed over her and made her momentarily dizzy.

The second time she swayed off balance and Casey halted, Ruby burst into tears. She nearly fell off when she tried to rest her head on Casey's neck. She was *tired*, too damned tired for just five circuits at a walk, and her muscles *ached*.

"That's enough," Gabe said. Instead of calling Casey to him, Gabe strode out to the chestnut mare and wrapped his arms around Ruby. "Let go, Ruby, I've got you." Gabe steadied Ruby as she slid off and buried her head in his chest, shaking with sobs as she leaned against him.

"It's so damn hard!" she wailed. "Why is it so hard? God, am I ever going to be able to ride like I used to?"

"Hey," Gabe said soothingly. "It's your first time back in the saddle. Remember mine? The swearing? The tears? It'll come back. Right, Petra?"

"Right." Petra rested her hand on Ruby's back. "You're making progress faster than Gabe did. Trust yourself, Ruby. It's coming."

Instead of reassuring her the words triggered more tears. Gabe held her tight.

"It's okay, Rubes. It's okay," he repeated over and over.

"And why am I crying so much?" she gulped as the sobs eased off.

"It's the medication and the aftereffects of the virus," Gabe said. "I've been through the same damned thing. Come on." He scooped her up in his arms.

"Should you be carrying me?" she gulped.

"I'm getting better. Just like you will. Maybe I can't hold you all the way to the house but I can at least make it part of the way."

He almost reached the back steps of the ranch house before having to ease Ruby down.

"You okay?" she asked as he breathed hard, not quite gasping for breath but clearly winded.

Gabe nodded and took another deeper, shuddering breath. "I couldn't have done that before this second round," he said quietly. "Not before the Chan Protocol. And—Rubes, you've lost a lot of weight. Makes you easy to carry but you have no reserves. No strength. Trust me. I've been there. But I'm tired out too. Let's lie down for a while."

"I don't know how many stairs I can manage."

The biggest problem with their bedroom was that it was on the top floor of the old farmhouse. They had a lift floater that could carry one person up the stairs, but both of them? Maybe they *should* go to Gabe's Moondance Ranch with both of them in recovery. Everything there was on one level. But Moondance's horse facilities were lacking compared to the Double R, and it wasn't *home*.

"I'm thinking living room," Gabe said. "We have a recliner and we're not gonna bother anyone."

Ruby choked out a sharp laugh. Until she had bought them adjustable beds for both the Double R and Moondance, Gabe had slept in a recliner. He had been doing that since his recovery from the initial attack of G9, a result of persistent sinus drainage caused by the virus.

Gabe rubbed her shoulder. Then he wrapped an arm around her waist. They leaned on each other as they went to the living room. He settled himself in the recliner, then held out his arms. She eased herself onto Gabe's lap and he pushed the chair back, shifting until they both lay on their sides, facing each other. She snuggled into his chest and he held her tight.

***

"*JUSTINE MARTINIERE.*"

Gabe's comm chime roused them.

Gabe sighed. "Accept." Ruby blinked, trying to figure out from the light in the room just how long they had been napping. An hour, perhaps?

Justine's projection appeared next to the chair. "*Gabie. Ruby. I am so sorry to bother you. But I don't have a choice.*"

Gabe tensed. "What's going on, Tine?"

"*Fucking Donna-gran.*" Justine scowled. "*She's demanded*

to see you two. At the Double R. She used a compulsion on me, damn it! I thought all of that had been wiped out when you and Ruby went through the Martiniere Ritual!"

"What the hell is her game?" Gabe demanded as a chill prickled through Ruby. At the family wedding ceremony, Donna-gran had activated the circuits in Ruby's ring that *should* have wiped out any control she would have over Justine.

Justine shook her head. *"She wouldn't tell me. Just insisted that she needed to see you two personally, and soon. I'm on my way to pick her up in Montreal."*

Ruby pressed her lips tightly together, trying to push her lethargic brain into action as Gabe and Justine continued to talk.

Donna-gran. Here. Where could they put her? Brandon's room was on the third floor next to theirs. Wouldn't work. Donna-gran was wheelchair-bound and somewhere around her hundredth year.

Wait. Rick Keysing and Beck O'Toole, the principals of AgSystems Inc, who grew her stem cell seeds and had relocated to the Double R, had recently moved out of their first floor room into a small house of their own that was even closer to the lab. But where had she put Dr. Amy? Justine's room was on the second floor, and there were two spare rooms there. Amy could move into one of those if she was on the first floor.

Hold it. She'd already put Amy into the second floor room.

Ruby shook her head wearily, annoyed at the sluggishness of her thoughts. How on earth had Gabe been able to function so well when recovering from the G9?

"We have space," Ruby said. "First floor room for Donna-gran."

"I just told Tine that," Gabe said.

"Sorry. G9 brain," Ruby said. "I couldn't remember."

Justine glanced away, then turned back. *"Coming into approach now. I'll ring off. Message you once I have an ETA."*

"Thanks," Gabe said.

"I'm just pissed about this," Justine said before her image faded.

Gabe sighed. "So. Donna-gran. Here. And she wants it so bad she forces Tine into it—which does take a lot."

"I figured as much." Ruby started to sit up but Gabe pulled her back down.

"No. We don't need to rush around for special preparations, and I'm not inclined to do it anyway. I wanted all family business to go through Moondance. If Donna-gran's decided to throw her weight around for some reason, then she can damned well learn why I wanted it that way." He sighed again. "I love my grandmother, but damn it, when she starts getting pushy—" he shook his head. "Other people can get her room ready. Resting is a much bigger priority because we both need to be as strong as possible to deal with her. But damn it, I wish she had held off for a few weeks."

"She was pretty insistent about me learning the uses of the ring," Ruby said, reaching up to her neck where she had hung the ring from her silver chain while riding and doing physical therapy. She fumbled with the chain and slid the ring off, then put it on her finger.

Gabe stroked her forehead. "It's too soon, Rubes. I don't know much about the ring's processes, but I am aware enough to know that you've got to be a lot stronger to manipulate it. Especially while learning. What is she thinking?"

Despite her worry, a yawn forced its way out and Ruby had to admit that she really wasn't ready to get up. She snuggled back against Gabe's chest, the steady beat of his heart lulling her back into sleep.

AIR CONDITIONING WAS THE ONE THING LACKING IN THAT first floor bedroom, and even though it was autumn, the daytime temperatures were still hot. Ruby had two of their security force members, Reed and Karen, move one of the older window units from the basement and install it in the first floor bedroom.

Reed drove their crawler down to the airstrip while Karen piloted a second crawler for Donna-gran and Justine. After they got out, Ruby used Gabe's extra cane to steady herself as Justine's small jet taxied to the hangar. Rick and Reed waited with the cargo lift to help Donna-gran and her wheelchair out of the plane.

The plane stopped. The attendant opened the door and waved off Rick and the lift.

"The stairs will work better," he called.

"What the—?" Gabe muttered as Rick parked the lift and Reed drove the stairs over. "How on earth is she getting a wheelchair down the stairs?"

Once the stairs were set up it became clear. Donna-gran, leaning on Justine with a cane in her opposite hand, appeared in the doorway. No sign of a wheelchair.

Justine and Donna-gran slowly negotiated the steps. Once they reached the ground, Donna-gran released Justine's arm and steadily hobbled toward them. Ruby frowned. Did she actually look younger? Ruby hadn't realized how tall Gabe's grandmother was until now.

Had Donna-gran's need for a wheelchair been a sham, meant to lull her opponents into complacency?

Donna-gran stopped in front of them. "Whew. Steps are complicated when you haven't been on your feet for a while." She eyed Ruby and Gabe. "You two look like hell."

"G9 is no easy walk in the park," Gabe said sharply. "Donna-gran." He gestured at her. "What the hell? What is so damn urgent that you had to come *here*?"

"You two need to get off your feet," Donna-gran answered. "And so do I, pretty quickly. Walking is hard when you've been in a chair for several years. Once this treatment kicks in fully, I will have a rough forty-eight hours. I'll explain when we're all sitting down." She marched past them to Karen's crawler and managed to scramble in.

"This is fucking weird," Justine snarled as she paused by Ruby and Gabe before joining Donna-gran. "I saw her use it in the plane and damn, the changes started happening right away. *Visibly.*"

"Use what?" Gabe asked.

Justine's face went tight. "Anti-aging serum, Gabriel. It exists, and she has the last doses ever made from that formula. Fuck." She continued on to the crawler with Donna-gran.

Gabe paled. "Oh fuck. Anti-aging serum."

"What the hell?" Ruby glanced at Gabe as he took her arm and guided her toward their crawler.

"Anti-aging serum is not supposed to exist. Nearly impossible to achieve. It's been one of Philip's obsessions. He's been looking for a formula for ages—was doing that even before I left the family. If Donna-gran has some...." His voice trailed away as Reed started up the crawler. "It's been his Holy Grail for years. From what Brandon has said, it's been a significant part of his indentured research goals."

She shook her head. More Martiniere complexities. "Let's go to the front door. Shorter staircase and we don't have to walk so far to the living room. Reed, please pass that message to Karen."

"Will do, Ruby."

Gabe wrapped his arm around her shoulders as she leaned into him. They rode silently.

Anti-aging serum. What the hell does that do to everything? And why would Donna-gran use it now? What does that have to do with us?

Donna-gran seemed stronger and less wobbly as they stopped at the lesser-used front of the house. She eyed the old farmhouse, then marched up the steps, stopping at the top to look back at the mountains.

"Well, you said the Double R was pretty, Gabriel," she said tartly as Ruby and Gabe joined her. "I see what you mean."

"Welcome to our home," Gabe said, a sharp note still in his voice. "Our *private* home. Donna-gran, I would have preferred this meeting happen a few days from now, and at Moondance. I want to keep Philip's attention as far away from this place as possible. He knows where it is, but I'd just as soon it not come to his attention."

Donna-gran patted Gabe's cheek. "I know, Gabie. But we do not have the luxury of that sort of time, and your labs are better here than at Moondance. We will need them." She turned and hobbled toward the door, pausing. "Well? Are you coming? Someone needs to show me where to go."

Donna-gran stepped aside as Ruby led them into the house and into the living room. Gabe took the recliner and waved Ruby over to sit in his lap. She leaned against him gratefully as Donna-gran surveyed the living room, hobbling around and peering at pictures, knickknacks, and the china cabinet with Ruby's old pins, buckles, and sashs from her rodeo days. Justine sighed and sprawled on the couch.

Napping was a tempting idea. Fatigue still pulled hard at Ruby and she was beginning to ache again. She was supposed to be starting to wean herself from pain meds today. But the way everything just *hurt* was going to make it hard. Nonetheless she was *not* going to yield. She didn't like how fuzzy-brained the pain meds made her. Gabe had fought through his initial stages with minimal painkillers. Surely she was capable of doing the same thing.

Donna-gran stopped in front of Ruby and Gabe. "When was this house built?" she asked.

"1880. My family has added upgrades to the place over the years. Unfortunately, central heating and air hasn't been one of those changes. We live with it."

Donna-gran nodded sharply. "It is in good shape for the era. And mostly authentic."

"Not had a lot of money to throw away on new furniture," Ruby said.

Donna-gran snorted. "But you have recovered and maintained it." She selected a straight-backed armchair and sat. "A good thing to see."

Ruby snorted, too tired to soften the sharp tone that slipped out. "Ranchers don't have a lot of money to throw around, and it was a heck of a lot easier to do our own upholstery than hassle with buying new. At least that was the way my grandparents did things. I never saw a reason to change it. The one big luxury was expanding the house to rent out tourist rooms before the C-19 came through."

Donna-gran chuckled. "Oh, I wish my Louis had lived to meet you, Ruby. You truly do have the mindset of a Martiniere Matriarch. Frugal. Determined. Strong." She fixed Gabe and Ruby with a stern look. "But both of you are a mess. How on earth do you expect to challenge Philip while coming back from this illness?"

"How did you find out about Ruby?" Gabe challenged. "Me, yes, that's public, as a result of helping Pat escape and Joseph's death. But Ruby? We've kept her illness private."

Donna-gran arched a brow at him. "Not as private as you

think, Gabriel. Ruby maintains a fairly steady social media presence with her RubyBot promotions and ranch updates. For them to suddenly stop was a signal that something had gone wrong. Brandon missed a couple of production dates. I know from his AgI history that he just doesn't do that without a good reason. The two together suggested to me that there were issues, perhaps with Ruby. I have too much invested in your success to ignore a danger signal, and I had to see your condition for myself." She sighed. "Yes, I still have some ability to force a compulsion. I cornered Sergei. He was quite reluctant, until I explained my specific concerns to him. And I used another one on Justine to make her bring me here."

"And those concerns of yours would be?"

"Pressure is being brought to bear on Stephen Tolliver. But the Real Truthers—oh, there are a number of reasons why I have been a part of their organization for years, and a situation like this is the major one. They are seriously discussing replacing Philip as the nominee. In return, Philip is agitating to make Joseph a martyr, and targeting Ruby as responsible for his death. You can't ignore that."

"That's why we have security," Justine said sharply.

"And you and Sergei do an excellent job of putting it together," Donna-gran said. "All the same, even from Montreal, I can see the currents stirring. I hear things from my own connections. There is a lot of concern that the Indentured Freedom Coalition is going to create a revolution. I am concerned about the reaction. Philip will exploit that to promote his campaign. You two need to be fully functional, *fast*. How long before you are both fully able?"

"Another couple of weeks and I'll be at nearly optimal function," Gabe said.

"It has been—what—four and a half, almost five weeks since that poor damned fool Joseph injected you? Given the typical eight week recovery on the Chan Protocol, you have three, three and a half weeks more to go?"

"More or less," Gabe admitted.

"And Ruby still has around seven weeks of recovery ahead." Donna-gran turned her attention to Justine. "My dear Justine. Do you have either Dr. Caruthers or the admirable Dr. Chan on site right now?"

"Amy is monitoring Ruby while flying out to clinics," Justine said. "She's here."

Donna-gran exhaled. "I apologize for compelling you into bringing me to the Double R, Justine. And to you, Ruby, Gabriel, for imposing on you in your private home. But circumstances force my hand. We cannot afford for the two of you to be incapacitated for weeks. Not with the way events are moving."

"I don't see any other options," Gabe said. "The Chan Protocol is the fastest treatment with the best recovery odds. You have anything better to suggest?"

"Justine, would you please bring the esteemed Dr. Caruthers here? I do have a solution," Donna-gran said. "But we need to talk about it quickly. I can feel the next stage of the anti-aging serum coming on fast. I must tell her what to expect."

Justine slowly rose. "The so-called anti-aging serum," she said, her voice sharp. "That you so blithely shot yourself up with in the jet."

"Yes. That." Donna-gran's hands tightened on the arms of her chair. "I've used it before. I know what to expect, both good and bad."

"It's real, then?" Gabe asked.

"Oh yes," Donna-gran said. "But the price paid for it..." Her voice trailed off. Then she continued. "Two doses remain of the last three in existence, that I kept safe all these years. I have given myself one of those three because from all I see, you are going to need my knowledge to defeat Philip." She waved at Justine. "Please go get Dr. Caruthers, and quickly. I have data to share with her so that she can evaluate the probable outcomes of giving Ruby and Gabe those last two doses. I would prefer to only explain myself once—and she needs to know what to expect for me, because I will be in this next stage far too soon and will need her supervision."

"All right." Justine left.

Donna-gran pulled a bioplast-wrapped bar out of her pocket. "I assume you reuse?"

"All the time," Ruby said. "Hand wash." She rested her head back on Gabe's chest as Donna-gran ate the bar delicately, then folded the bioplast and put it on a side table.

"You will need to eat more than usual while the serum is taking effect for optimal success," Donna-gran said. She scowled at Ruby. "The G9 has taken a lot of weight off of you. You will need to double your calorie intake."

"Both the G9 and the Chan play havoc with appetite," Gabe said.

"I know," Donna-gran said as Justine and Amy returned. "I have read the details about the G9 and the Chan Protocol. Doctor Caruthers. I'm pleased to make your acquaintance. I've been a donor to Justine's programs and have been following your work for some time. I am Donna Martiniere."

Amy reared back. "*You're* Donna Martiniere? Then I am very pleased to meet you, and thank you for your support over the years. Justine says you have an—*anti-aging serum?*"

Donna-gran gestured toward the couch. "Go ahead and sit. As for the serum—well, you could call it that. A side-effect from pursuing a full-body beauty treatment. It provides a short-term rejuvenation effect, which wears off over the course of four to five years. Not really a life extension protocol, and the number of doses a particular patient can take over a lifetime are limited. The final dose is a killer. Literally. Oh, it takes one to three years for that to happen after it's taken. One to three years of rejuv, followed by a swift decline and death." Tiny sweat beads broke out on Donna-gran's forehead as her face flushed. "I can give you Louis's and my notes on the serum, how it works, everything, Dr. Caruthers. I have recently added some observations on how it might interface with the Chan Protocol for G9. You will need to know that when Gabriel and Ruby take those last two doses. I'll message it over to you."

Amy nodded and popped up her screen. "I appreciate this —" she hesitated. "Ms. Martiniere?"

"Call me Donna." Donna-gran pulled up her screen and sling-protocoled files across the room to Amy, her hand quavering a little. "You will want to look at the red highlighted second stage administration response, Dr. Caruthers. I can feel my temperature rising even now. Soon I will need to be in a bed. You will find past treatment notes in that file."

"Got it," Amy said, studying the file. "And call me Amy or Dr. Amy. *Doctor Caruthers* is a bit formal for this situation. So. No fever reducers? Not even with that high a temperature?"

"Reduces effectiveness. Same for painkillers. We discovered that one the hard way. And this is my final dose. We have to do everything by the book. I can't afford to lose any time."

"Your final dose," Gabe said slowly. "Then that means you have one to three years?"

"Depending on how long it takes you to put things right, Gabriel. One to three years, then a six-week final decline." Donna-gran grimaced. "Note for you, Dr. Amy. Stress shortens the effective period of the serum. And the course is progressing. Besides fever, joint aches are starting now. This round is going to be the most difficult one for me, I'm afraid."

"All right, Donna-gran," Justine said. "Your plan is—what?

You take the final dose of this elixir and do what with it besides die in a few years?"

"Short term—the last two doses should speed up Gabriel and Ruby's recovery so that they—plus you and Brandon—can deal with this indentured situation and put things right before it blows up even worse than it has already." Donna-gran coughed. "Mistakes were made too many years ago, and not remedied when they should have been. I was a part of those mistakes. I was silent when I should have acted. This is my atonement."

"There aren't any details on how this serum is created," Amy said, looking up from her comp screen.

"That is because all that information has been destroyed," Donna-gran said. "I made certain of that years ago. The two remaining vials in my possession are the last of it. Thank God."

"But why? This knowledge could be useful," Justine said.

Donna-gran's face tightened into a scowl. "Because Peter and Louis created that serum using the bodies of indentureds as the growth medium. It *can't* be cultivated in anything other than an adult human woman. And it kills her in the process."

"And you want *us* to take it?" Gabe shuddered. "Donna-gran. Really."

"The women who died for that serum are long gone, Gabriel. Ending the evil awakened by its creation makes this last use of it worthwhile. It honors their memories—and yes, I *do* know their names and histories. I learned that information for each and every vial, as part of my own atonement for using the serum. I can tell you about the women who died for my doses. About the ones who died for yours, should you choose to use them." Donna-gran leaned her head back.

Ruby thought she could *see* her skin smoothing and plumping up, filling out the wrinkles and fading the age spots.

"Jesus, Mary and Joseph," Justine murmured. "I thought

things were bad enough now with the indentured. But Grand-father and Peter—that means Daddy-fucking-dearest *knew* it existed for certain. And explains his obsession. Oh shit. This explains a lot. Some of the files we've come across."

"Exactly." Donna-gran closed her eyes. "Headache now. I'll need to be in bed shortly. I'll be down for around forty-eight hours. But this is what I can tell you for the moment. Twenty doses were made, no more than that. Louis and I used them. So have Louis's nephew Artie and Artie's wife Nora—it kept her cancer under control but she's on her final dose, too. The decline phase."

"This is supposed to do—what—for us?" Gabe asked.

Donna-gran opened her eyes again. "Rejuvenation. Dr. Amy will need to review the files, but it *should*—if my reading is correct—not only work with the Chan Protocol to reset your condition to pre-G9 status within forty-eight hours, but offset the problematic pieces of the Chan. I *think* I spotted the possi-bilities of interacting with the Chan in that manner. Dr. Amy should be able to confirm it."

"And at the end of five years?" Gabe said, arching his brows and pursing his lips skeptically. "Back to post-G9 syndrome? Complications of the Chan Protocol?"

"No, not that severe. A slow decline that fits the norms for the age at which you originally took it. But it's not a life exten-der, Gabriel. Especially given the impact of the G9 on your body, and the interface with the Chan. The most the serum can do for you and Ruby is to improve your physical health to what it should be for your age, and as the serum wears off, you'll revert to age norms. That means no more post-G9 syndrome. Period." Donna-gran started trembling. "And so it begins. I'd best go to bed now. Have Dr. Amy review the files, and go by her recommendation. But I would highly encourage you to use those last two doses. If not, I want you to destroy them. Promise me. You will either use or destroy them, without analysis. *Promise.*"

Ruby *felt* the compulsion in that last word, even though it only made her ring finger prickle.

She still has that ability.

Justine scowled and Gabe shivered.

"You don't need to force me," he said.

Donna-gran slowly pushed herself up as Amy joined her. "I thought not. But best not to take risks. You will promise to use or destroy them?" Even though stronger tremors wracked her body, she fixed her gaze on Gabe.

"On my honor as the Martiniere," Gabe said, not looking away from her. "We will either use or destroy those doses without analysis. Tine?"

"I agree with Gabie," Justine said.

Donna-gran slumped against Amy. "Thank you."

Justine hurried to Donna-gran's side and helped Amy guide her out of the living room.

Gabe exhaled, long and slow. "The more I learn about my family's history...." His voice trailed off. "God. What the hell are we supposed to do now, Ruby? Fuck. This is *so* damn tempting. Back to my old self in forty-eight hours—well, as much of my old self as I can be at this age. But shit. Someone died for it to happen."

"Yeah," Ruby said. "I—yeah. What the hell are we supposed to do?"

"Donna-gran clearly thinks we need to use those doses."

"I want to puke at the thought that my well-being happens as a result of a woman who died to make that serum." She shook her head.

"Me too, Rubes, me too." Gabe sighed. "And yet—if it gives us more strength to take the fight to Philip. If we can stop him sooner, if we can free more indentureds—is it worth it?"

Ruby buried her head in his chest again. "I have to think about this before I say yes or no, Gabe. I want to stop indenture but—knowing someone died to make me better—"

He rubbed her back. "It doesn't look like it would be a comfortable forty-eight hours, either."

She raised her head. "As if G9 and the Chan Protocol weekly infusions are comfortable."

"True. And just the first-stage changes—Donna-gran walking. Standing straight. I guess we now know why she's lived so long. And Artie."

"Yeah," Ruby said. "It is tempting. But—the price."

"And yet." He sighed. "Maybe this is something to discuss with Bran and Kris. Make sure that we aren't making a publicity mistake that will offend indentured people should we use the serum and—worst case—it goes public."

"I agree."

"Agree to what?" Justine said as she returned to the living room. She sprawled on the couch again. "Are you two going to do it?"

"We're not sure," Gabe said. "The ethics of the damn serum. Women died for it to happen."

"Do we want to honor their sacrifice or do we not exploit their deaths? Which may lead to a greater tragedy because we were unable to respond in time to move along the cause of indentured freedom." Ruby shook her head. "That's what we face."

"Donna-gran insists that they would be honored by your use of the serum," Justine said.

"Well, that's her interpretation. I want to have it vetted by freed indentureds," said Gabe. "Like Kris. Or Pat. Or Colin Fields." He shook his head. "All those years. I thought the unwilling mind control experimentation was bad enough. To have this happening as well—God."

"Why do you think I became the Rescue Angel?" Justine said in a low voice. "Our family has done some bad shit, and it wasn't just our father. Nasty bad shit."

"Agreed." Gabe cleared his throat. "Which is why Ruby and I are going to talk to Brandon and hopefully Kris. Besides. Amy has to review the files to make sure it *is* safe for us. I'm not about to endorse putting anything into me or Ruby that's going to give us more problems."

"Makes sense." Justine quickly pulled up a screen. "I can have him, Kris, and Pat here in two hours. That work?"

"Perfectly," Gabe said. He stretched. "Meanwhile. Let's see if the two of us can choke down some food, Rubes. Donna-gran *is* right on that front. You've lost too much weight."

Ruby eased out of the recliner and steadied herself. It helped when Gabe put an arm around her, but from his slight sway, it was more than clear that he needed her support as well.

CHAPTER 4

"This is beyond wild," Brandon said as he sat in one of the living room chairs, shaking his head and leaning forward, resting his forearms on his knees. Once again, he wore his studio suit and heavy makeup. Kris and Pat sat in the chairs by his. Both were dressed for filming as well—from what Justine had said, they had just finished recording another 'cast when she contacted them. "Anti-aging serum cultivated in the bodies of indentured women? This sounds like a bad science fiction movie."

"I wouldn't have believed it if I hadn't seen the changes in Donna-gran," Gabe said.

"The changes are legit," Justine added. "But it's not an easy process."

"What about the ethics of using the serum?" Ruby asked. She felt better after dinner and taking meds. It was a transitory moment of strength, but right now she'd take any whisper of improvement.

"You said that she knows the names and the stories of each of the women," Pat said, kicking off her shoes. She wriggled her toes before tucking her feet underneath her, sighing with relief.

Ruby eyed Pat. She hadn't really met Kris's sister before

now—she'd only gotten a glimpse of Pat during the rescue, and that had been just before Joseph injected Gabe with the weaponized G9.

Like Kris, Pat was slim, her brown skin a couple of shades darker than Brandon's. Her dark hair poofed in frizzy tight curls unlike Kris's neat cornrows. But while Kris's body was proportionately slender, Pat looked like she had been starved into thinness. *Broader shoulders, heavier bone structure*, Ruby decided. But no mistaking that they were sisters, from the similarities in their brows and cheekbones and jawlines. Or the identical way their hands moved to emphasize points when talking.

"Yes," Justine said. "When Amy and I were getting Donna-gran settled into bed and a saline drip set up, Donna-gran started reciting names, contract length, and date of death. Beginning with the victim who provided her first treatment. She named all of them. Said that she did this every night the first week after using the serum, so she wouldn't forget them." She shivered. "Amy *says* that the serum is harder on her because of age and it being her final dose. But damn, if going through that level of fever and pain is required for it to work... there is a price to be paid for it."

Pat nodded. "She knows the names. It might be possible to find their relatives when this is all settled. If any escaped indenture and still survive."

"God!" Brandon exhaled. "Just when I think my Martiniere heritage is bad enough...something like this comes along." He glanced at Ruby. "Makes me think the Barkleys weren't so bad after all."

"Oh, if the Barkleys had the opportunity, don't fool yourself. They would have glommed right onto the serum and used the heck out of it," Ruby said tartly. "The Ryders of the Double

R were different. Even if we do descend from a bank robber and rustler."

Brandon rubbed his face. "I know. But this." He shook his head.

"All right, then. From an ethical point of view," Gabe said. "We have this tool, obtained through an unethical process. If Ruby and I take it, then our recovery happens faster. We can act instead of sitting here and being acted upon for another month or so. The question is—should we do it? And if we do use it, then how offensive is this choice going to be to those we intend to help?"

"Do you intend to honor those who died for this serum?" Pat asked sharply.

"Privately," Gabe said. "I'd prefer that the knowledge that such a thing is possible never gets out. An impossible hope, I suppose. But the longer we can keep it a secret, the less of a temptation it is for someone else to try to recreate it."

"If it started as a beauty treatment, then similar research may be further along than you think," Justine said softly. "I've had some questions about a couple of people on the society circuit. We joke about them hiding a painting in the attic. Gabie, it may already be too late to hide this information."

"There are ways we could honor the victims publicly," Brandon said. "A foundation for the victims of medical research. These twenty women wouldn't be the only ones who lost their lives due to medical research on unwilling indentureds."

"A foundation that goes further than that to make conditions better for former indentureds left disabled," Ruby said. "Not every freed indentured person is going to be able to support themselves. Older indentured. Medical research victims. Others who are psychologically unable to transition from indenture to freedom."

"That would work," Kris said. "At least in my opinion. Pat?"

"There is a need," Pat said. "All the same, I don't envy you two this decision."

"Another piece. How much time *do* we have? How far do you think we are from a nexus where movement one way or another could change the situation?" Gabe asked. "Brandon, is President Tolliver going to act on indentured reform of some sort? If we have time, then perhaps I just have the serum destroyed."

"That's the problem," Brandon said. "Tolliver talked a good line to me when we met. But the follow-through is not happening yet. No bills proposed. No executive orders. I'm not hearing anything from my people in Congress or the courts that he's considering an action."

"In other words, he's blowing you off," Gabe said.

Brandon nodded. "We're upping the ante as best as we can, but—even with the Biobot Producers Alliance coming out in favor of reform, even with the polls supporting the ending of indenture, he's not acting. My suspicion is that we haven't yet pulled down the heavyweight support from non-Martiniere sources that we need."

"There *are* small revolts happening that aren't being publicized," Pat said. "Sooner or later the workers at one of the food processing plants are going to blow. That's the sector where we're seeing the most indentured workers escaping and becoming one of the Freed. Food processing. Agricultural labor. Some manufacturing. But not transportation. The Loyals have a strong lock on that sector. Lower-level research is Loyal as well. Entertainment too."

"Loyal?" Ruby asked.

"Indentured supporters of the current system," Brandon said.

"How close are we to having that kind of blowup happen?" Gabe asked again, a weary tone in his voice.

"Six weeks to six months," Pat said. "No longer than six months."

Gabe rubbed his face, then looked at Ruby. "Do you think we have time to recover without using the serum? It's your choice as well. If you won't do it because you don't think it's ethical, then I won't either. I can't make up my mind—help me, please."

Ruby chewed her lip thoughtfully. Forty-eight hours versus seven weeks for their recovery. The possibility of an indentured revolt breaking out sooner than that.

One—no, two lives, taken years ago. Two lives long dead against setting things right for many still living. Two lives that might save others if we can stop the coming war. But God. It feels so wrong.

"The odds don't sound good. If we destroy the serum and something happens that we could have prevented if we'd used it—then that's a problem," she said.

He nodded slowly. "Are you willing to use the serum, then?"

She sighed and met his gaze. "I don't like it," she said slowly. "I really don't like it. But if Amy says that the serum will work like it is supposed to—and we can take it—then, reluctantly, yes. I am willing to use it, because we will hopefully be able to save many more who are still living. And may God have mercy upon us for making that choice."

Gabe exhaled long and slow. "Then I agree. You're saying the same things I've been thinking, but my doubts—and the reluctance—and the weight of the family history—thank you, my love." His hand wrapped around hers. "Brandon. Get me the names of Tolliver's major supporters and the contact people in the New Dems and Classic Dems who are willing to support

Pat. Once I'm back on my feet, I'm going to push for concrete commitments. I want a campaign ready to roll should it be clear that Tolliver isn't going to act. And I plan to make it clear to Tolliver's supporters that Philip is on his way out. That I am the Martiniere, and *things will change*. If Tolliver won't take action to reform the indenture system at the very minimum, then I will throw what I control of the Martiniere Group to support Pat."

"I could do—" Brandon started.

Gabe interrupted him. "No. You can't. You're not the Martiniere yet. *I'm the one who has to do this.* You have your 'casts, and your role with the Indentured Freedom Coalition. That should be your focus—that, and you and your mother need to spend time with Donna-gran learning the ins and outs of the Family, so that you two can go to all the branches that didn't show up for our wedding, and have them swear loyalty. For what it's worth, I *am* the Martiniere according to Donna-gran, and I *will* act to stop indenture. Even if it ends up killing me."

"All right," Brandon said, exhaling slowly. "Dad, for the record, I don't completely agree but I understand your point. I'd prefer you'd not kill yourself doing this, and I'm sure Mom agrees with that as well."

"I'm in agreement with your father—to the same degree," Ruby said softly. "It's all or nothing time, Bran. That includes us."

"I *would* like to have you two around longer," Brandon said.

"Point duly noted, Bran," Gabe said dryly. "But your mother's right. It's all or nothing. We made that choice months ago during the Superhero. Pat. Starting now, we're prepping you for the primary against Tolliver. Period. Maybe Tolliver will come around, but even if he does, I want you ready to roll in case he backs out or screws us over. We need to get you registered to vote to start with."

"Good luck with that," Pat said. "I don't have an address, and as a recently Freed indentured—"

"You have an address," Ruby said. "Here. Or Moondance, whichever would be more preferable. And we'll get Remy Trask to work on reestablishing your rights."

Gabe nodded. "Tine. Six months ago, you said that Donald had installed a dead man's switch poison pill in the Martiniere accounts should something happen to you, and that Philip and Joseph had taken similar measures. Have you had problems since Joseph's death?"

Justine shook her head. "They tried. Donald disabled their switches as part of that raid to rescue Pat and the others."

"Can he activate your worm in a targeted fashion? I want to keep some accounts active while disabling others—and gaining control of what I can. When it's time. I need the ability to shut things down fast."

"That's something you'd best discuss with him," Justine said. "It sounds possible to me, but...I'm not certain. It's not my area."

"That's another meeting I need to have, then." Gabe solemnly looked at each of them. "Once Amy gives us clearance to use the serum, Ruby and I will be down for forty-eight hours. Let's count on us being out of play at least that long—and whatever needs to happen for recovery afterward, because I'm *not* going to assume that we're going to be back at full strength immediately once the serum's done its work. Then it's time to finish this fight. I had thought to wait until we're closer to next year's election. However, it doesn't look like we have the luxury of that leisurely a schedule. So." His voice took on a greater intensity and urgency, and Ruby felt the pull of a compulsion that tugged at her before releasing. "Indenture is going to end. And we will take control of the Martiniere Group to eliminate it there as a beginning. *We're going to eliminate indenture. Now.*"

Silence fell.

Brandon finally looked up from his interlaced fingers. "All right, Dad. Pat. Kris. Since the Chicago condos aren't an option any more, I would like to establish ourselves at Moondance. It's close to the Double R, and I want to be nearby. Just in case things go weird with treatments. Justine, what's the security status at Moondance?"

"Locked down as tight as the Double R, if not more so," she said.

"Dad. Can we appropriate the lab at Moondance for a media post-production facility?"

Gabe shrugged. "I told you I wanted it to be your center of operations as well as for Martiniere Group functions. I don't see a conflict."

"We'll need room for staff."

"Talk to Tine to set it up. That's her area." Gabe yawned and stood up. "Sorry. Tired. Tine, has there been any more information about the condo fires?"

She shrugged. "Other than arson by person or persons unknown...not a thing. Serg has been pushing for more information from the police. I'm in no hurry to reestablish a place in Chicago, at least not until we know what happened."

"What about labor pool access?" Ruby asked. Originally Kris's ability to slip camouflaged into the central labor pools in Chicago had been Brandon's justification for locating there rather than at Moondance. But when their condo had been fire-bombed, along with Justine's, that option no longer existed.

"We have workarounds," Kris said. "And since the raid in LA, I'm not exactly anonymous. Swait Secure—Jeff Swait's security organization—is helping us access the labor pools, along with recoding tattoos. Moondance isn't perfect, but neither are Chicago nor LA at this time."

"In any case I don't want you risking going back into the pools in your condition," Brandon said sharply. "We have other, less visible people who can gather information. Time for you to step back from that role—we need you to coordinate and set up post-production at Moondance."

Condition?

Ruby took a sharper look at Kris. No, it couldn't be a pregnancy, could it? Not so soon after her surgery to remove hormonal tags in her former indentured tattoo as well as the preliminary implants to prepare her for body mods.

Probably aftereffects of the tag and implant removal.

Beck had gone through tag removal plus a complete hysterectomy at the same time. She was only now starting to be able to work at full strength with Rick in growing stem seeds and expanding the capacity of their part of the lab. Justine had said the process would be harder on Kris since she'd kept her reproductive organs. Maybe that was what Brandon meant.

Kris frowned at Brandon. "It's not a matter of my condition, it's a matter of security," she said. "You're being overprotective again."

Gabe cut in before Brandon could respond. "I'm afraid overprotectiveness is a male family trait. Right, Ruby?" He gave her that slow smile that always sent her heart pounding.

"Looks that way," Ruby said.

"And with that—Donna-gran said that we have to increase our food intake. Ruby and I need to eat. We'll leave the rest of you to your planning. You know what we want you to do. Any questions?"

"I'll check in before we leave," Brandon said. "You'll be upstairs?"

"After we eat, yes," Gabe said.

"I'll make sure that Amy and Justine know our travel schedule," Brandon said. "I'll be dropping in until you're through this treatment."

"All right." Gabe rose. "I don't think you need us at the moment. Come on, Rubes. Let's see what you can choke down."

After they left the living room his hand reached for hers again. As they walked by Donna-gran's room they heard her voice droning. Ruby paused to listen, Gabe swinging back to face her, his face tightening as they made out the words.

"Monica Marie Everhart. Indenture number 398547. Divorced. Mother of Valerie Ann Everhart, indenture number 440592. Indentured with Valerie Ann Everhart due to credit card debt. Vial lot number eighteen. Date of death...." A moan.

Ruby shuddered. She hurried away, dragging Gabe with her. She couldn't hear any more. She didn't dare hear any more. Not right now. Not risk changing her mind about taking the serum.

It had to happen.

Gabe paused when they were in the kitchen and took her other hand.

"Are you still all right with this, Ruby? *Really* all right? I know you said you were back in the living room—but now. Privately. Your doubts. Sounds like they mirror mine."

She lifted their linked hands to her face and rested her forehead on his knuckles.

"Oh God, Gabe." She gulped, then took a deep breath and raised her head to meet his dark brown eyes. "I don't think we have any real options. Not without backtracking on plans and promises we've made. I meant what I said. I'm reluctant, but if we can save more than those two lives that were sacrificed to make the doses we take—if Amy thinks it will work like Donna-gran says—then I don't see any other choice."

Gabe sighed. "If you want to walk—it's not too late."

"No. Absolutely not. I remarried you, remember? I vowed to support you as the Martiniere." She turned her left hand so that the emerald in her wedding ring was visible. "You put the Martiniere emeralds on me. I'm not leaving, Gabe. The time when leaving could have been an option for me is long past. We're committed. Whatever turns up—I'm here. Are you here for me?"

"*Yes.*" He slipped his hands free and wrapped his arms around Ruby. "I was stupid enough to underestimate you over twenty-one years ago, Ruby Barkley. Never again. Now that you're back in my life, I'm going to do whatever it takes. But this—" He swallowed hard. "God. I don't know what kind of price we're going to have to pay for using this serum."

"But if it enables us to end indenture—as awful as it is, maybe, just maybe there's a little bit about it that's right," she said, her voice quavering.

"I just wonder about the price," he repeated.

"It's not as if we haven't already suffered a lot," she said. "Perhaps we've already paid it. Maybe this serum will give us a better life together, free from the G9. A longer, less painful life without the specter of relapse, once the Chan Protocol wears off."

He half-gulped, half-laughed. "Oh God, Ruby, I hope to hell you're right."

She rested her head on his chest.

I hope so, too.

By noon the next day Amy was ready to administer the serum. She set Gabe and Ruby up in their bed with slap-on monitors and saline drips to begin with, waiting for half the plain bag to drain before opening the line with the serum.

Hydration is an issue in getting through the first stages, she had said that morning. *Injecting it directly like Donna did is less than optimal. Hopefully using an infusion process will ease the first three stages for you two.*

Ruby watched Amy as she flipped the switches that added the serum to the saline first for Gabe's infusion, then hers. The red-gold liquid trickled from the bag into the tube, paling as it reached the port in her elbow.

Fiery pain blazed up Ruby's arm as the serum entered her system. Gabe's hand tightened on hers.

Oh God, this hurts worse than the Chan.

Ruby took a deep breath. "Deidra Alison King. Indenture number 300754. Student loan debt for a master's degree in education. Vial lot number twenty. Date of death 2028."

"Janet Elizabeth Ingram. Indenture number 495774. Medical debt caused by an automobile accident. Vial lot number nineteen. Date of death 2028," Gabe said.

She burned. Her breath came short and quick, almost panting, almost like childbirth. Almost like the G9 itself.

What is being born by our actions?

"Deidra Alison King," she repeated, chanting along with Gabe.

She must never forget Deidra. Must never forget Janet. Monica, and all the other names.

Never.

Was this what Donna-gran felt?

CHAPTER 5

Hours. Hours of burning heat with excruciating pain. Sometimes it felt as if she were being whacked with a baseball bat. Other times the pain came in white-hot little needles that danced up and down her body. Ruby was barely aware of Gabe moaning in bed next to her, their hands clasped.

And yet she endured, panting through the worst of it, staring up at the ceiling, mumbling Deidra's name and stats whenever she had breath enough to do it.

You died so that I eventually received this. I have to honor your death.

Occasionally she dozed, only to jerk awake when another wave of pain washed over her, barely aware when night gave way to day, and day became night again. Or when Amy or one of the nurses now back on the premises helped her out of bed and to the bathroom. Or when Brandon appeared, sometimes in studio makeup, sometimes not. She wasn't sure how many of his appearances were real and how many were fever dreams. Surely he wasn't coming by that often, was he?

But there came a time when she roused, shivering. The bedroom was dark except for a small watchlight on her dresser. No pain. Ruby held her breath and wiggled her fingers against

Gabe's suddenly clammy palm. No dull thud, no march of white-hot needles running up and down her spine.

"I'm cold," Gabe said softly. "How about you, Rubes?"

"Yeah."

Amy appeared on Gabe's side of the bed. "Looks like you two are through the sequence." She gently spread a blanket over them before she checked his vitals and disconnected the port that had been feeding saline solution. Then she did the same for Ruby.

"What happens now?" Ruby mumbled. She didn't hurt, she wasn't burning up, but damn, she was drained and exhausted. And still cold, despite the additional blanket. She just couldn't stop shivering.

"Sleep," Amy said. "For now, you need to sleep and finish your recovery. Do you need another blanket?"

"Yes, please," Ruby said.

"I'll help," Gabe murmured. "You've lost so much weight from being sick, Rubes. That doesn't help with the chill. I'll keep you warm." He pulled her close, her back to him, wrapping himself around her. She nestled into his warmth as the weight of another blanket settled over them. "Better?"

"Yes."

Her shivering eased as she finally got warm. Now it was easy to fall into sleep.

This time Ruby dreamed. Wild, colorful dreams mixing up past and present, combining her confrontation with Philip just weeks ago with the first time she spotted Gabe Ramirez at a rodeo.

A small-town rodeo. He was riding broncs and she was barrel racing. Sunshine was reacting to everything instead of settling and calming, as if she hadn't been to a much bigger rodeo just the weekend before. A bad heat cycle, and no money for meds to ease it. Ruby didn't scratch her from competition, though, even when the big palomino mare decided to buck her way through a pattern and knocked over a barrel. She wasn't going to quit, and by God, sooner or later she'd get this behavior figured out and managed. Even with disqualifications.

Once done with that run, she headed for the warmup arena, determined to ride it out. Sunshine bucked harder than ever before finally settling into a hard gallop. Ruby let her run, until she felt the mare relax under her. She should have done this before the race. Oh well.

Someone chuckled from the fence, and she realized that one of the bronc riders had been sitting there watching her.

"Damn, lady, you sit a bronc better than most men on the circuit." A slow smile spread across his face.

And then the scene changed, and she was facing down Philip at the Real Truthers banquet just weeks ago. Only this time he had a gun and she was unarmed. He raised the pistol. Fired. She saw the bullet coming toward her.

Ruby roused with a gulp, gasping for breath. Gabe's arms tightened around her.

"You all right?" he whispered in her ear.

"Bad dream. I was at our first meeting—and then Philip was shooting me at the Real Truthers. I *saw* the bullet coming at me—and woke up."

Gabe pulled at her gently until she turned to face him. He stroked her cheek and kissed her. "I'm sorry. I'm here."

"The sudden switch. Dream logic, but still not comfortable."

"Yeah. Dreams. Mine have been more pleasant, but still pretty damn realistic." He kept stroking her cheek. "But our first meeting, hmm? I was impressed by the ride you gave Sunshine that day. Followed you over to the warmup arena just in case you needed a hand. And to see if you were a horsewoman and not just a rider because damn, I liked your looks."

"We were still learning about each other. I got Sunshine for cheap because she had such intense heat cycles and would blow up like that at shows and rodeos. Well-bred, flashy and colorful—but inconsistent. I knew if I could find a way to channel that bucking energy that I'd have something. It was just—raspberry leaves and other herbals weren't working, and I didn't have the money for anything else because I was still in college. Thought about breeding her that next spring but needed cash for a stud fee."

"Well, you two did succeed." He smiled. "And I was definitely interested in an intelligent hot redhead who was a damn fine horsewoman. Whose field of study was so damn close to mine. Damn, it was hard not to tell you who I was sometimes. When Dr. Green assigned you that paper on microdrones, it was all I could do not to point to my name on the paper and say *see, I did some of the work on this.*"

"You've never said anything about working on a Masters degree."

"I was just the lowly grunt on that work, and I didn't finish. Philip demanded that I return to the US from the University of Paris and work in the Los Angeles labs."

"What was he afraid of?"

"Who knows?"

She startled at the feel of sudden pressure against her leg —*oh*. Ruby giggled in surprise and raised her brows.

Gabe's brows raised in equal disbelief. "Um. Another party heard from. That's...wow. I hadn't got my hopes up—so to speak. Not after the G9. It's been a while."

She stroked his cheek. "Even longer for me."

"No one else after I left you?"

"At first I didn't have the time. Then I just—I didn't want to. Didn't want to deal with learning another person, didn't want to let anyone close again."

"I was such a shit to you. I'm sorry." He kissed her forehead.

"Do you want to make love to me?" she asked, tentative.

"Oh God, yes. I have wanted to ever since we got back together. But I'm afraid. Okay. Maybe *afraid* isn't the right word. But concerned about things working right." He swallowed hard. "Things had started to get—challenging—with Rachel even before the G9. Blood pressure meds. She found it frustrating and didn't want to even try. How much of it was her cancer and how much of it was—I don't know."

"You've seen what my libido is like. Practically nonexistent."

So Gabe's second wife Rachel hadn't been perfect, either. There were times when Ruby knew that Rachel's death haunted him. Rachel had been the trophy wife Ruby could never be, social, at ease throwing parties, dazzling others with her careful beauty. Ruby frowned. She still had the occasional qualm about that difference between them. Yes, she could sometimes play the part. But from all she had seen and heard, that trophy wife role had come easily to Rachel.

"I know." He pressed small kisses on her forehead and cheek. "Damn. I see that look on your face. You're comparing yourself to her again. I'm sorry I brought Rachel up. Especially now."

"Kind of hard to talk about *it* when you don't. And—no matter what, it's you and me now."

"True," he conceded.

On the other hand, both Justine and Donna-gran had dismissed Rachel as *too nice*. Not someone who could have handled the demands of being a Martiniere wife. Rachel's death had happened before Gabe reclaimed his Martiniere heritage. So perhaps she needed to stop worrying about the past and focus on now.

"If you want to try...." Ruby let her voice trail away. "We both might need some practice," she added after a pause, catching her breath. Was this really happening?

"I'm all for practicing," Gabe breathed, before bending his head to kiss her, his hands sliding under her pajama top. She gulped, quivering with anticipation? Fear? She wasn't certain.

Please let everything work. Please.

IT WAS SLOWER THAN WHEN THEY WERE YOUNGER, BUT everything worked.

"IS IT BAD OF ME TO SAY THAT MUCH AS I'D LIKE TO cuddle afterwards, I'm also starving to death?" Gabe murmured as he held Ruby close.

She laughed. "I was thinking the same thing. But if we can stand up to get food, I'd like to get a shower first. I *stink*."

"I'd better come along. Just to make sure you don't fall." He leered at her and she shoved his chest.

"Gabriel!"

"Don't be silly. It is a good idea."

"True," she conceded. She extracted herself from his arms and carefully sat up. "Not dizzy. You?"

He sat up. "No dizzier than I should be after making love to a hot redhead." He lunged and pinioned her in his arms, kissing her again. She laughed as they fell back to the bed.

"I guess the serum worked," she said finally.

"Yeah," he said, suddenly somber. "Fuck. I feel the need to get stronger—bet the serum hasn't done much for cardio and stamina. But I feel like my old self again otherwise. Like I haven't felt for two years. Maybe longer."

"There's a niggling ache in my lower back that I've had to see the chiropractor for regularly. It's not there now."

"Oh God, Rubes. I know. Those little aches and pains that I'd just plain overlooked for years. But the price."

"We have to make it worthwhile. For Deidra. For Janet."

He nodded.

"For Deidra. For Janet," he repeated.

THE SUN HADN'T MADE ITS WAY OVER THE HORIZON YET, but it was getting light outside by the time Ruby and Gabe entered the kitchen. There was just enough ground coffee in the tin to make a pot of real coffee, not the substitute.

Gabe pulled a bioplast-covered plate out of the refrigerator labeled GABE AND RUBY—Eat all this. Amy.

"Huh," he said softly as the coffee started brewing. "Cheese. Meat slices—looks like roast beef and ham. Lots of cheese and meat slices."

"Don't gobble it all." She slipped a hand in to snatch a chunk of cheese.

"Putting it on the table." He set it down and grabbed a cup.

Ruby fixed her coffee before sitting down and helping herself to the food. Gabe joined her and they ate silently, bite after bite, hardly pausing even to drink coffee until it was all gone.

"This is where you've gotten yourselves to," Amy said as she came into the kitchen. "Came in to see how you were doing since I know you're both early wakers and—not there. So. You've eaten. Let's check vitals." She pulled her scanner out, examining Ruby, then Gabe. "All looks good. How are you feeling?"

"Oh," Gabe tried and failed to smile innocently, the corners of his lips twisting into a smirk that made him look like a kid who had just been caught with his hand in the cookie jar. "I'd say...just fine."

Ruby choked at his expression, then giggled.

Amy raised her brows. "Oh. I see. I *did* spot that mutual spike on the monitors and wondered. It's time I gave you two some privacy and pulled them. Don't think you need that much observation any more. Let's try this again. Fatigue? Odd mental state? I noticed some elevated cardiovascular activity before that mutual spike, Ruby."

"A nightmare."

Amy typed into her scanner. "Need to monitor those. If they keep up for more than a couple of days, let me know. What about fatigue?"

"I think cardio and stamina will need some work over the next week or two," Gabe said. "Just going by what I'm feeling this morning."

"Me as well," Ruby added.

"Aches? Pain?"

"Noticeable in their absence," Ruby said. Gabe nodded.

"Good. Well. We'll assess where your strength levels and therapy needs are this morning. From what I'm seeing, you two won't need as much help as Donna. We have to get some more weight on you, Ruby. Both of you need to eat regularly—small meals six times a day but also eat whenever you're hungry. The serum takes about a week to take full effect, and it gobbles up energy."

"Listen to her," Donna-gran said as she walked to the coffee pot and pulled a cup out of the cupboard. After pouring herself some coffee, she rummaged in the refrigerator and came up with another plate of pre-sliced meat and cheese, labeled DONNA. "Focus on protein for the first twenty-four hours. Then transition to a more balanced diet." She joined them at the table.

Amy turned her attention to Donna-gran, running her scanner. She frowned. "Results aren't as good as Ruby and Gabe's, Donna. How are you feeling?"

Donna-gran wrinkled her nose. "I can stand up straight and walk without assistance. From my perspective, that's a big gain. What you're seeing is the difference between an initial dose and the final dose. The treatments decline in effectiveness, and with our limited sample of twenty doses, the rate of decline varies from person to person. My heart attack thirty-some years ago occurred when that dose was wearing off due to stress. A lot of stress."

"All right. I'll run data on your strength and endurance levels this morning, and take Ruby and Gabe's baselines. Then I'm all right leaving you in Dr. Sheri and Petra's hands for PT and continued monitoring. Unless you anticipate further problems?"

"Shouldn't be any," Donna-gran said. "But don't tire Ruby out too much." She gave Ruby a stern look. "Let's start training this afternoon. Vocalizations and basic theory. And if Brandon shows up again this evening, then we'll have a review of Family history. The sooner we can get you two talking to the rest of the Family, the better."

EVEN THOUGH SHE WASN'T ALLOWED TO RIDE YET, RUBY slipped out to the corrals after her morning tests. Cisco, Blaze, Red and Pard snuffled her hands and lost interest once she was done feeding treats in their pen, but Casey and Legacy hung out with Ruby even when the treats ran out. She scratched each mare's neck under the mane in their favorite itchy spots. After that she hugged first Casey and then Legacy, burying her nose into their necks to draw in that deep scent of *horse* which had always meant comfort and reassurance.

As long as she had a horse to hug and—hopefully soon—ride, the world was in its right place.

"Beautiful horses," Donna-gran said, leaning on the wooden fence.

Ruby straightened up, still keeping one arm over Legacy's neck. "Mother and daughter, third and fourth generation of my breeding program."

Donna-gran pursed her lips, nodding. "You have an eye for sure. May I meet them?"

"Certainly."

Ruby watched as Donna-gran slid through the rails neatly. She approached Casey first, holding out the back of her hand for Casey to sniff. The chestnut mare inspected her hand, blowing softly. Donna-gran reached up and gently scratched her cheek, working her way up to Casey's poll. The chestnut mare dropped her head, ears sagging slightly as her facial muscles relaxed, her eyelids half-closing.

"You know horses," Ruby said.

"I put Gabriel on his first horse when he was just three," Donna-gran said. "I used to have eventers. Gabriel and Justine were my only grandchildren interested in horses, and Gabriel more than Justine. She was my show jumper. Gabriel wanted to be a cowboy, not event." One corner of her mouth quirked into a wry smile. "Looks like he fulfilled his dreams. Complete with marrying the rodeo queen."

Ruby didn't know what to say to that so she focused on scratching Legacy. Donna-gran finished with Casey and repeated her introduction to Legacy. Casey flicked her ears back jealously and Ruby growled at her. But she also reached out to scratch Casey.

"So, your mama is jealous of you getting all the attention, hmm?" Donna-gran said. She scratched the big white star that topped Legacy's blaze—always a spot that itched. "What a gorgeous girl you are. Both of you. So. Third and fourth generation of your breeding program. Who's the foundation?"

"The palomino I rode in some of my queen competitions as well as barrel racing," Ruby said. "Barn name of Sunshine. Miss Sparkle Chex, from old foundation and reining lines."

"Quarter Horse, then." Donna-gran stepped back to study the mares.

"Yes."

"I had warmbloods, and a lovely Connemara that Gabriel and Justine rode when they were first learning." Donna-gran's smile turned wistful. "I would love to ride, but I don't think that climbing up on a horse is necessarily a good thing at my age."

Ruby shrugged and moved away from Legacy. "Depends on the horse. We've been using Casey for our rehab work."

"Well, maybe I'll think about it."

"I've jumped Casey a little bit, and she is a respectable dressage horse."

"All around rider, then?" Donna-gran raised her brows. "Not that common these days."

Ruby shrugged. "4H competition, and I liked low-level jumping." She moved to the gate, Donna-gran with her. "We've never done any big shows. Once Gabe and I married the first time, and we took over the ranch after my grandpa died, there was no time or money to spare for extended campaigning. Especially after we divorced. But I've always been a sucker for a good horse. Casey's yearling son moves like he could be an English-type horse under saddle—either jumping or dressage.

We'll see what Dancer does." She paused, wondering how to phrase her question.

Did you really come out to see the horses?

"Ah." Donna-gran turned around, taking in the surroundings. The mountains, the ranch, the ridges of the big upland prairies to the north. "A beautiful place." She exhaled. "And it helps me get a better picture of who you are. You use your voice quite a bit in horse training, don't you?"

"Yes," Ruby said as they walked to the house.

"I thought so. Then to some extent learning how to use the compulsion tones with the ring will be easier for you than most people."

"You know, I'm not quite sure how this vocal tone training works—especially with the use of the ring. It doesn't match anything I've ever learned or studied."

"For best effectiveness, using the tones requires that your subjects have either early imprint training or a link to a wireless chip," Donna-gran said. "That early imprinting requires light doses of psychotropic medications."

Ruby winced. "On *children?*"

"Much less crude than the methods used by earlier generations," Donna-gran said drily.

Ruby shook her head. "But. Children. That's awful."

"The Martinieres have done many things to be ashamed of in the name of survival over the years," Donna-gran said. "Ever since they fled the French Revolution."

"I won't be complicit with programming children," Ruby said firmly.

Donna-gran sighed. "I have a lot to atone for. Which is why —all of this with you. Gabriel. Brandon. Justine."

Ruby didn't respond to that. They silently climbed the stairs to the back porch and kitchen.

Why didn't you stop the problems with the Martinieres earlier if you have so much influence?

She wanted so damn desperately to ask the question...and yet, did she really want to know?

Donna-gran had power then. Didn't she? Or had it been a slippery slope, with breaches like the one she and Gabe had committed in accepting the serum? Minor violations in hopes of preventing a bigger problem?

Did she really want to know the answer to this?

At least she and Gabe had Brandon, Kris, and Pat's influence to keep their priorities straight.

"Eat," Donna-gran said. "Before we work."

Ruby nodded. She pulled out sandwich makings as that sounded good to her. "I'm making myself a sandwich. You want one?"

"Heavy on the meat. I need to set up some things for your training. Where should I do it?"

"Take a look in my office to see if it works," Ruby said. "That should be sufficiently private." She decided to make a sandwich for Gabe as well. "If you need a bigger space, then the living room."

"I don't require that big an area." Donna-gran left.

Ruby tightened her lips as she made the sandwiches, hacking off slabs of roast beef with more pressure than needed.

The ethics of this. The ethics of all this.

Why did the mention of psychotropic use on kids to program them make her so much angrier than everything else? Was it just *one more thing*? Something she couldn't justify for the sake of bringing about reform? Another long-ago injury to Gabe? Or her own past?

She finished the sandwiches and picked up the plate with the one she'd made for Gabe, adding a handful of cherry tomatoes from the garden to the dish. She needed a moment with

Gabe before she went into this training with Donna-gran. She needed—something. Reassurance? This had rattled her, *bad.*

Gabe had *three* screen projections up and running as she came into his office, typing in front of one screen and spinning to finger through data projected on the second and third screens. Shades of the old days. How he had worked when they were younger.

He paused and smiled at her.

"Rubes. Perfect timing. I'm starving and I need a break from this approach to Tolliver. Thank you...." His voice trailed off as he took in her expression. "What's wrong?"

Ruby set the plate down and shook her head. "Just—Donna-gran mentioned the use of psychotropic drugs. On children. As part of early imprint training." She choked. "God. Gabe, I don't even do that with *horses.* It just—it hit me—" She swallowed hard. "She was *so damned casual* about it."

"Come here. Please. Let me hold you—looks like you need it." He opened his arms. She hesitated, then yielded and sat in his lap because it was true—she wanted the contact. He held her tight and stroked her head reassuringly.

"This is why I testified thirty years ago," he said finally. "All of this stuff that you're just now learning. I knew I would have to leave the Family once I was done. Worse. I knew Philip would come after me. And you've seen what that's caused." He sighed. "I didn't know the half of it then. I just saw the pattern. What Joseph was doing. A new indentured girl on his arm at every social event. And then—the woman—girl, really, like all of Joseph's victims, she wasn't even eighteen—that I found beaten nearly to death on the lawn after one of Philip's parties. I reported it to the police but she didn't have standing to press charges. Nor did she want to for fear of punishment."

Ruby raised her head. "All of this. I just...."

"I know, hon. *I know.* And that is why we are finally going to do something about this whole goddamned mess. Donna-gran is doing her part as well."

"She said she had a lot to atone for." Ruby swallowed. "I just don't know why this one hit me so hard."

"It piles up and then it clobbers you."

"Yeah." She sighed. "And now I'd better get to work doing my training. For my part."

"Damn right. I want you to be able to exploit that fucking programming to the fullest extent possible, and cram it right down the throats of those members of my godforsaken family who dance to Philip's exploitative tune." He kissed her slowly. "Ruby, you are my avenging angel. And I love you for it."

"I love you too." She extracted herself from his arms. "And now—you'd better eat."

"You too. You have food?"

"Made sandwiches for me and Donna-gran."

"Good. Go eat."

She pointed at the dish. "You, too."

Gabe rolled his eyes but obediently picked up the sandwich and took a bite. Ruby smiled as he continued to hold it, contemplating his third screen. Hopefully he would remember to eat the sandwich and not just hold it as he got drawn in by the screens. Another pattern from the past.

She went back to the kitchen, exhaling long and slow to release her tension. This was just one more thing to overcome, like doing a run-in during a downpour in an outdoor arena with footing she didn't trust.

Donna-gran was back at the kitchen table, eating her sandwich.

"Is Gabriel eating?"

"He is now." She sat and pulled the plate with her sandwich on it over to her. She took a bite.

Donna-gran sighed. "I am sorry. But you have to learn the

mechanisms of early imprinting in order to use your tones most effectively with the family. I have a list of the various psychotropics used on different family members, along with who performed the conditioning. That will help you emulate the needed tones more accurately."

Ruby swallowed and forced herself to take another bite of the sandwich.

I have to eat. I need to eat. It's the only way I can do right by Deidra. Janet. Everyone else.

"Before you look, you need to know. You and Brandon are on the list."

Ruby set her sandwich down and forced herself to swallow that bite before resting her forehead on fisted hands. "How? Why?"

She knew it had been possible, the way she had been manipulated during the divorce, but to hear it confirmed...and Brandon, too?

"Twenty-one years ago. Yours was completed. Brandon's was partially administered, and Piotr cleared it from him shortly after it happened." Donna-gran reached over and rested her hand gently on Ruby's arm. "I am sorry. You already knew that Philip and his associates used compulsions on both you and Gabriel to force your divorce. This explains why the compulsions worked on you. No idea how they got access. It could have been so simple as a meal eaten away from home."

"Or the hospital, though if that was where—then why wasn't Brandon also given it? Not that it matters. Doesn't make the fact that it happened any better." Ruby exhaled hard, shaking her head, then lifting it. "And Brandon—"

"Not administered. That means he has never come under influence."

"Except when I commanded him." Ruby fixed her gaze on her sandwich.

"When?"

"In LA. After Gabe—before his treatment. Brandon and Justine both. I rubbed the ring."

"It wasn't the ring, Ruby. For Justine, yes. For Brandon—you're his mother."

"I hope you're right."

"You are his mother," Donna-gran repeated. "Brandon is *not* under any influence, but you know as well as I do that you as his mother have an effect. Nonetheless. When he becomes the Martiniere, he will be the first leader in several generations who is free from that horrible, horrible blight of childhood manipulation to force him to conform to Martiniere goals."

Ruby gulped. "You're not just telling me this to make me feel good?"

Donna-gran fixed her with a stern look. "I don't say things like that. Especially when it comes to a woman and her child."

"Oh God. Oh God." To her embarrassment she choked out a sob. She buried her head on her hands again, shaking as the tears broke loose.

Donna-gran murmured reassurances Ruby couldn't hear through her cries.

At last Ruby gasped and raised her head, wiping her eyes. "I'm sorry. I don't know what came over me. Just—psychotropics on kids. That clobbered me."

"It was an awful, awful business. And yet it was better than what was done to Louis and his siblings," Donna-gran said with another sigh. "That was—physical. Electroshock. Other techniques."

Ruby gulped again.

No. I am not going to cry any more. No. This is ridiculous.

"If I had been given a choice, the practice would have ended with my children," Donna-gran said softly. "But Louis was unwilling to risk it. His brothers Antoine and Alain demanded we do the imprinting, or risk family war. And Philip demanded it for my grandchildren. Psychotropics were the gentler choice, and my other objections were overruled."

Another sob forced itself out of Ruby's throat as a memory surfaced. Something she had long forgotten. Pills that made her feel funny after...what happened with her parents. Pills the Big People had given her, until at last Gramps *was there.*

Just a fleeting fragment of her past, but....

"You have to understand how these compulsions work and what was done to make them work," Donna-gran said. "Not every branch of the family used psychotropics. There were— harsher means." Her voice tightened. "I don't know for certain if psychotropics or these harsher means are what has been used on the programmed indentureds. There are differences in dealing with them based on the methodologies. I reviewed the recordings from your rescue of Pat. My suspicion is that the harsher means were used on them."

"I need to know both, then," Ruby said, her voice choked and tight.

"Yes." A world's weight of heaviness in Donna-gran's voice.

"Will this ever stop?"

Donna-gran pushed herself up. "Ruby, I have asked that question of myself so many times over the years. All I can say is that you need to do your best to stop what you can in this generation." She patted Ruby's shoulder. "And as for the tears...that also comes along with the serum. It will settle in a few days. Eat your sandwich. I'll see you in your office."

"Okay." Ruby heaved a sigh and picked up her sandwich.

Another bite. Chew. Swallow. Another.

She had to get through this.

CHAPTER 6

A STEADY FALL RAIN STARTED UP AROUND DUSK. IT WAS damp and chill enough that Ruby kindled a fire in the living room's blue and black colored soapstone wood stove for the comfort of it—not yet sufficiently cold to start up the solar-charged furnace to heat the whole house. But the faint chill was a reminder that she needed to check the storage batteries dedicated to the heating system. The mechanics of fire starting, along with dinner preparations, was a welcome distraction from the information and concerns roiling from this oh-so-busy day.

A lot for the first day back on my feet.

And, serum or no, she felt it by now.

But she suspected they all did. After a big dinner, the three of them retreated to the living room to bask in the warmth. Ruby settled on the couch with one of Gramps's old Western novels, feet propped up on an ottoman. Gabe stretched out with his head on her lap while he read text on a screen. Her casual glimpses when she looked up from her own book suggested it might be one of Ivan Doig's books, from the references to Montana that she glimpsed, and the phrasing of the writing.

Doig had been one favorite of Gabe's during their previous

marriage, and she thought hard copies might be in the attic somewhere.

Might be worth digging them out.

She had enjoyed reading both Doig and Norman Maclean years ago, a shared pleasure with Gabe that she had discarded after the divorce. The quality of writing was certainly better than the book she was reading, though it *was* one of the better non-Longmire books in Grandpa's collection.

Donna-gran sat in one of the upright armchairs near the fire under a brighter light, embroidering what looked to be a sampler or small quilt square. She was working on text right now. Ruby had caught a glimpse of the decorations around the text when Donna-gran had first taken it out of her bag, surprised at the mix of guns, pansies, and roses.

Donna-gran's deftness with the needle reminded Ruby of Granma before the arthritis in her hands had gotten to be too bad. The whole scene tonight was comforting, reminiscent of both the life with her grandparents, and the early days of marriage the first time around.

Gabe sighed and snapped off his screen. He shifted to rest on his side and closed his eyes.

"Ready for bed?" she asked quietly.

"Not yet," he murmured. "Just enjoying the fire and the quiet. And being with you. Brain doesn't want to process text any more and I don't feel like vids, that's all. Maybe I'll nap, but this feels too good to leave."

She smiled and rested her free hand on his shoulder, occasionally lifting it to turn the page.

About the time she was ready to add more wood to the stove, but was debating whether she wanted to disturb Gabe as he napped, his comm chimed.

"Brandon Martiniere."

"Aw, fu—dang," Gabe groaned, sitting up. "What's gone wrong now? Accept call."

Brandon's image in tight focus appeared, showing only his head and shoulders. From what Ruby could see of the background, he appeared to be on one of Justine's jets.

"Dad. Mom. Donna-gran. Sorry to disturb you. But this is urgent. The Defender bots at Swait's have killed an intruding indentured that appears to be the next stage of cyborg."

"What?" Ruby snapped. The Defenders weren't supposed to be *this* aggressive...though she did remember that they had gone after a couple of problematic indentureds just a few weeks ago.

Another attempt?

"Get your people out of there before the authorities show up," Gabe said.

"In process." Brandon ran his fingers through his hair and sighed. "Got out just before the authorities arrived. Keeping this short. On our way to our place. Pat IDs the corpse as a prototype cyborged indentured from the LA labs, with Loyal characteristics. Martiniere Group identification. Not a fake, not conflicted, like it's been in the past. I scanned the chip and verified it was a good copy before Swait called the authorities. On his part he's clearing out all but immediate adult family. I'll drive over with more data in the morning. Sorry. Need to go. Too much going on."

His image winked out.

Gabe groaned and stood up. "Holy fu—" he shook his head.

Donna-gran scowled. "Gabriel. It's not going to hurt my ears to hear you swear. You're an adult now. And besides—" She held up her embroidery. IT'S TIME TO FUCK SHIT UP was outlined in bright red, the letters of the first three words filled in with orange. "I use those words myself. And I'd say this situation calls for it."

"Philip's making his move. I wish Brandon could have spoken longer so we know more about what's going on." Gabe started pacing.

Ruby put another chunk of wood in the stove. "We'll know in the morning. Right now, I'd much rather our son concentrates on getting everyone out safely than keeping us up to date."

"I'm still worried about it."

"So am I. But Gabe, it was pretty darn clear to me that reporting details to us is not a priority, at least compared to getting out of Swait's as fast as they can. Plus it's best they can't track him through a call."

"God damn it, Ruby, we need to know what's going on! Tempted to call Jeff Swait and find out what happened. Or Justine or Serg."

"It's an evolving situation, Gabe, and we don't know what's going on at Jeff's place." Ruby frowned as she eyed Gabe. Why was he being so reactive and not considering why Brandon wouldn't want to stay on the comm? The serum's emotional effect? "The authorities may still be there, and then what? How do we explain our knowledge of the situation? *Think*, Gabe, *think*."

"And what if that Loyal indentured was the first wave of attacks on us? On Jeff? We're in trouble."

Ruby called up her comp and flicked through stats. "Gabe, it looks like Brandon's already called for maximum security here and at Moondance. Additionally, if Jeff's evacuating everyone but immediate adult family, that tells me he's worried and he's taking care of his own."

"Martiniere Group ID. Philip's not even trying to hide it now!"

"Actually, that is a good thing, because we can publicly tie him to misuse of indentured workers." Donna-gran inserted. "Let's see what data we get from Brandon's scan."

"I'd feel a lot better if I knew what was going on."

"All we'll achieve by calling someone right now is distracting them from what they need to be doing," Ruby said firmly. She took a deep breath. *Use a vocal tone on him or not?*

He's locked into an emotional loop and if he doesn't break out of it....

Donna-gran *had* gone into more detail about why they needed to be careful about overdoing these first few days after the serum. With her, not both of them.

"Gabe, *stop.*" She punched the *stop* lightly, barely emphasizing it as she ran her thumb over the emerald in her wedding ring, wincing as a sharp quick pain lanced through her forehead.

Gabe halted abruptly, a mixture of emotions flooding over his face. He shook his head and tightened his lips. "Ruby. Really." He glared at her.

"This is our first day back on our feet. We need to be careful with ourselves. You already said your brain didn't want to process text. That's a sign of overload. And since you're working yourself up, you're damn right I'm going to clobber you with a control tone. I don't want you having problems with the serum."

"We have to talk about this."

"And we will. I judged that it was best for your mental and physical health that I snapped you out of this fit you're winding yourself up into. I'm your *wife.* I'm *supposed* to watch out for you. I'd much rather use a tone than a fist to snap you out of this, okay?"

Gabe exhaled slowly, tension deflating. "When you put it that way...."

"Gabe. I don't intend to use this tool casually. I mean it. But the best thing we can do right now is sit tight, wait, and not get in the way of what Brandon, Jeff, and probably Kris and Justine are already handling. It's our turn to sit and wait, even though it drives me crazy, too."

"You're right," he said finally. "Should have realized myself that calling would be a distraction. You shouldn't have needed to remind me. But I'm worried. And brain's still not processing fast—pushed myself too hard today. I'm exhausted, but now—no way I can sleep."

"Which means you need to disconnect. You're not the only one hit with an adrenaline jolt from that call," Donna-gran said sharply. "We all need to settle down. Getting upset won't help the serum's working. It heightens emotions. As you're noticing."

"I just—I hope Bran checks in with us when he gets to Moondance."

"Have Tim call or message us when they get there," Ruby suggested. "You know he'll be up and waiting, and we won't get in anyone's way."

The tension in Gabe's face eased slightly at Ruby's mention of the Moondance ranch manager. "Good idea. I'll message Tim—entirely possible there's a lot of things happening there right now with Brandon coming in fast like this. A call's going to be distracting." He pulled up a comm screen. "God, I hate this fuzzy brain. Donna-gran, does it get better?"

"It will," she said. "It just takes a couple more days."

Ruby stretched as Gabe left the living room, dragging the screen behind him, noticing that Donna-gran had put away her embroidery. She certainly was too restless to pick up her book again. A vid? Her head ached at the thought of screens. She sat back down with a sigh. How long would it take for Brandon to reach Moondance?

"Well-handled," Donna-gran said softly. "Having those horse trainer vocal skills makes a difference. You possess a nice subtlety to how you use the tones. But it still needs work. You need to soften your tone a little bit more with Gabriel. His reaction was a bit more than you want."

"The only difference between Gabe and Legacy when it comes to vocal tones is that I'm more likely to use *quit* rather than *stop* for Legacy." Her words came out sharper than intended.

"Not that great a difference. Just think about it, though, especially the words you choose to use. For you, any command you stress is going to have an effect on anyone subjected to Martiniere conditioning."

"All right," Ruby reluctantly conceded.

"So where is Brandon going?" Donna-gran asked. "Swait's in the South, right?"

"Arkansas. And they're flying to Moondance—straight flight would be maybe three, four hours if they're not stopping."

"Arrival about eleven, then. If they don't stop."

Ruby nodded.

Gabe sighed as he came back into the living room, and flopped back onto the couch, next to Ruby. "Tim says he's been given an ETA of 1 am, so they're stopping somewhere. God. I'm tired. But I'm also too roiled up to sleep."

"Not the only one," Donna-gran said.

A faint smirk touched Gabe's lips. "Cards?"

"As long as we don't have to leave this nice fire."

"Oh, I'm sure that can be arranged," Gabe said. "Which table, Ruby?"

She nodded to a maple drop-leaf side table and got up. Bigger than the usual side table, it had once been used for jigsaw puzzles and card games. They moved the table to the center of the room. While Gabe got chairs, Ruby fetched two decks of cards, one poker, one pinochle, and poker chips from the game cabinet. That should cover most possibilities.

"*Two* decks?" Donna-gran said, brow raised.

"Choice of poker or pinochle."

"Oh, I think poker will do quite nicely."

Ruby replaced the pinochle deck in the cabinet, then counted out chips while Gabe went to the kitchen and brought back a pitcher of water and glasses.

"Gabriel, why don't you get us something to nibble on," Donna-gran said, deftly swiping the box of poker cards. "I'll do the first deal."

Gabe paused in the doorway. "And the game?"

Donna-gran smirked. "Texas Hold 'em."

"Waaait a minute," Ruby said as Gabe went back to the kitchen. "Why do I have the sudden feeling that I'm in a game with two card sharks?"

Donna-gran laughed. "Who do you think taught Gabriel to play and lose at poker?"

"Now, now, now," Gabe said as he returned with nuts and dried fruit. "Donna-gran, you only *introduced* me to the game when I was ten. I took a grad course in poker while riding the rodeo circuits."

"We'll see," Donna-gran snorted.

An hour later Ruby was cleaned out, and watching grandmother and grandson swap chips back and forth. Not surprising. She had never been that good a poker player.

First the majority of chips were with Donna-gran. Then they switched to Gabe. But after that his pile went down, bit by bit, until he had only a few chips remaining—and it was his turn to deal.

He dealt the first two hole cards, face down. Both players looked at their cards.

"Five," Donna-gran said, sliding a red chip to join the two white chips between her and Gabe.

Gabe glanced at his cards again, and winced, almost *too*

much of a wince. He eyed his chips, three whites, two reds, a blue, and a black. He tapped his fingers on the table, then shoved a red chip to match hers.

"Here's the flop." He slowly laid out three cards between them, face up. Ten of spades. Nine of spades. Jack of spades.

Donna-gran pursed her lips and studied her cards again. "Ten," she said, dropping a blue chip onto the pile.

Gabe matched her. "Fourth street," he said.

He discarded the next card, then dealt a fourth card next to the three spades. Another spade, this time the ace.

"Do you need change for the next bet, Gabriel?" Donna-gran asked.

"I'm fine."

"Ten." She pushed another blue into the pile.

Gabe cocked his head thoughtfully, then shoved his remaining two reds into the pile.

"Fifth street." Final community card. Ace of hearts.

"Ten. Are you sure you don't want change?"

"I meet your ten and raise you. All in," Gabe said, slowly pushing the black one hundred chip and the three white chips into the pile.

Donna-gran's eyebrows arched, and she matched Gabe's bet. "Call."

A smirk spread across Gabe's face as he revealed his hole cards. King of spades. Queen of spades. He laid them next to the community cards. "Royal flush in the spades. Ace, King, Queen, Jack, Ten."

"Pssh!" Donna-gran shook her head. "I had the other two aces."

Gabe snorted and shook his head ruefully. "Never got this kind of hand while playing for real money. Honestly, it's one of the few times I've gotten one of these."

"Which is why you don't do this for real money," Donna-gran scolded. "Gabriel. I thought I had taught you better years ago. For you to get into *gambling trouble*—" she shook her head.

"That was the past," Gabe said. "Got plenty of other things going on to stir up my adrenaline now."

"I should hope so. But that's enough for me tonight. I'm off to bed. Looks like we'll have a lot to discuss in the morning."

Donna-gran collected the dirty dishes and carried them to the kitchen while Gabe and Ruby returned the chips to their case and gathered the cards to put into the game cabinet. They moved the table back to its place, then went upstairs.

Once they were in the bedroom Gabe turned to her, frowning, crossing his arms. "Ruby. I'm still pissed about you using a tone on me like that."

Ruby bristled at the sudden sharpness in his voice. "I get it. But you were looping. I needed to find a means to break the cycle—and this was the fastest way I could think of to do it without getting into a bigger fight. You can get fixated sometimes."

"All the same, I don't like it. I don't want you using tones on me." His scowl deepened.

Ruby slapped her hands against her thighs, frustrated.

First he wants me to have this tool. Then he doesn't like it when I use it on him because he's not thinking and needs to get snapped out of a loop.

"Look. I don't intend to make a habit of using a tone on you. But if you're making a mistake, I need to let you know, and sometimes using a tone is going to be the fastest and best way to do it."

"How about just plain words?" His arms tightened against each other. Her hands squeezed into fists.

Ruby couldn't read Gabe's expression. Anger, for certain, but there was something else that she couldn't quite identify. God, were they going to have another one of *those* fights?

At least I have the tones. Ruby forced herself to relax her clenched hands, ease her posture. *God damn it, you wouldn't get this confrontational with a horse. We can't afford this shit. Not now.*

"That would work if you were listening to me," she said softly. "But you weren't listening right then. You get hyperfocused, and it's not always good when you do that. Damn it, Gabe, you could potentially work yourself up into a heart attack like Donna-gran did!" She let the quaver in her voice break through for a moment, allowed her worry to show. "Even with the serum in you—especially in these first few days. Gabe. I don't want to lose you! Didn't Amy tell you anything about taking care of yourself?" Despite her attempt to control her voice it broke.

"She probably did and I didn't listen," Gabe admitted, his posture softening slightly. "But all the same. I don't want you resorting to using tones on me very often."

"How about only when I'd use a fist instead?" she snapped.

"I'm not *that* bad—am I?" He winced.

"Sometimes," she acknowledged, softening her voice. "And I'm probably less patient with you getting difficult with me now than I was when we were younger."

"I'm sorry," he said slowly, unfolding his arms. "I can be a butthead, I guess."

"You *guess*?" She relented as he gave her a pleading puppy-dog look. "All right. You can be a butthead some of the time—but when you are, boy are you ever one."

"Okay. I'll grant you that." Gabe paused, then continued, quieter. "It's just that the tones—do weird things in my head when they come from you. Especially now. It's like my brain's run into a brick wall and everything freezes for a moment. My brain locks. It was bad enough when I was a kid. Joseph used to use my words on me as part of his bullying until I learned how to beat him to it. But this is worse."

"Because it's me, or a change in the programming from the ring?" Ruby winced.

Joseph used tones to bully him.

She shuddered at that thought.

"Husband and wife thing through the ring, I suspect." Gabe heaved a sigh. "And you're *good* at the tones, Ruby. Maybe a little too good, as hard as they hit me. Seriously. Philip never affected me like this, and my parents—I could blow right through their control tones." He paused. "Maybe that's it. Your voice hit me like a sledgehammer. I couldn't move, couldn't catch my breath for a moment. It scared me."

Ruby blew out the breath she didn't know she was holding. "I didn't realize it was that—intense."

"It was." His shoulders sagged slightly. "I mean—it could be dangerous if you lock me up like you just did and—something's coming down. That momentary pause could make the difference between success and failure."

"That wasn't what I intended at all." Ruby swallowed hard. "I'm sorry. I'll save it for emergencies where freezing up isn't going to be an issue."

"Thanks. Don't get me wrong. If strength like that is a result of just one afternoon's coaching from Donna-gran, then damn, woman, I definitely want you on my side." Gabe reached for her hand. "Rubes. I was being an ass. I admit it. Still, we have to find some way for you to get my attention without going nuclear when I'm being problematic." He shook his head. "It's something we never did figure out—before. Working through our difficult moments without resorting to angry words and fists. But with the serum and—well, everything ahead of us if all goes right—we can't afford to lose it with each other. We're leaders. We have to act like leaders."

She looked down at the emerald ring on her hand. "I was thinking I wouldn't get in a horse's face like I do with you sometimes."

He tightened his hand on hers, raising it to his chest as he also stared at the ring. "There's a time and a place for that level of confrontation. But not between us. We have to channel our energy, our rage in the right direction. Outward, not inward. Not against each other."

"You're right." Ruby sighed. "I'm quick-tempered except with the horses, for the most part. We're both strong-willed. But it's getting over the secrets and the shadows."

Gabe stroked her cheek, then gently took her face in both hands and kissed her. "We've both led hard lives. Said things to each other that we shouldn't have. Maybe it's time to leave that baggage behind us. Step forward into our future as the Martiniere and the Matriarch."

"We have so many ghosts." She blinked back wetness in her eyes.

"Both Martiniere and Barkley ghosts." He delicately used his thumb to wipe away the tears.

She blinked hard. "No kidding. So how do we move forward? Exorcise them?"

"This is a start. We're talking."

"I need to use a softer phrase to get your attention. The words *stop* and *quit* are easy to make hard. Snap them out. Growl them. That's why they're so useful in training." Ruby paused, thinking. "*Drop it* still has that hard p sound. Perhaps *leave it*? Not something we're necessarily going to say in one of those heated moments."

"Leave it," Gabe mused. He dropped his hands. "All right. Try it. Use a tone on me like you would if you're trying to break me out of a loop."

"You sure?"

Gabe nodded, tensing.

"Gabe. *Leave it.*" One swipe over the emerald, an almost weary note in her voice, going for *unhappy with you* rather than *angry.*

Gabe winced. Then he exhaled. "That got my attention but it didn't lock me down. Say it more firmly."

She repeated with a firmer note, letting anger creep in. A small ache started up over her right eye.

"A bit more of a sting. But still not a lock down. Now. The full dump. When you want to take a swing at me but we're in the middle of a situation where it wouldn't do for us to break out the fists."

Two swipes of the ring this time, and a push. She winced as a quick bolt of pain lanced through her forehead, almost as bad as when she'd snapped out *stop* to Gabe earlier.

Didn't feel this when practicing with Donna-gran.

He jolted. "Edging into locking me up. But it doesn't have the freeze. Ruby, I think it works. I just—I'm roiling a little bit."

"If it works then I'm happy. I don't think we need to practice it any more." She fumbled for words. "I—my head hurts, Gabe. It didn't do that when I was practicing with Donna-gran."

"Did it hurt when you used *stop?*"

"Yes. Maybe it's some sort of feedback. Tied to us as husband and wife, like you said earlier? That linkage that Donna-gran did when reprogramming the ring?"

"I wish I knew more about this part of the Family tech stuff," Gabe said. "But it makes sense to me. Maybe it's a feedback mechanism to keep us from verbally flaying each other."

She shivered. "If so, it's pretty damn effective. My head still hurts a little."

"Then let's not do this to each other anymore."

"I agree," she said.

CHAPTER 7

BRANDON STILL HADN'T APPEARED BY THE TIME THE three of them finished the morning PT with Petra. The persistent shadow of worry loomed larger in Ruby's thoughts as she stared at the RubyBot seasonal summary reports in her office. The data confirmed past suspicions she had about the hydrology and the soil profiles of particular fields. Only she hadn't possessed this degree of detail before. Normally, she would be fascinated about learning these factors, but her thoughts kept skittering away.

Brandon had said he was driving over, not flying. But there were places where he could be intercepted. If he were really that concerned, shouldn't they be going to him?

Then she heard the faint barking of Crimson and Rusty outside. As she hurried to the kitchen to see who was parking at the charger, Gabe shot out of his office.

"I think that's Branny," he said.

"I hope that's Branny," she said.

"He'll be all right, Rubes."

But she wasn't ready to relax until she recognized Brandon plugging the truck in to charge, waving off his guards. She sighed with relief.

Gabe rested his hands on her shoulders, massaging them gently as they waited. Brandon bent to pat Crimson and Rusty before heading toward the house. A second, older man left the huddle of security around the truck and followed a few steps behind Brandon. She frowned, trying to place him, then realized.

Colin Fields.

The medic. The President's cousin-in-law.

"Hey," Brandon said as he came into the kitchen. "Mom. Dad. Sorry it took me longer to get here than I thought. Things coming up and—well, I took the long way around. Still had to drive through the canyon but other than that...the long way, at least until I got to Thunder County."

"Probably smart," Gabe said.

"Security wasn't thrilled about some of my road choices." Brandon half-grinned at that. "But I told them I'd been driving some of these roads in a lot worse conditions since I was old enough to have a license." He shrugged. "We got through. No snow, no mud. Easy-peasy." He sighed. "Good way to burn out a few of my frustrations and the adrenaline from last night. Some of those roads are pretty eroded from the last time I went over them. Had to get creative in a couple of places. That slowed me down."

"Everyone all right?" Ruby asked as Colin Fields came into the kitchen.

"Yeah," Brandon said. "So far. I checked in with everyone I could this morning, including Jeff. And so. Mom. Dad. This is Colin Fields."

"We've met," Ruby said, stepping forward and extending her hand. "Thank you for your help, Mr. Fields. I wish we could do more for you."

"Thank *you*," Fields said. "I wanted to thank both of you for what you did. Getting us free."

"You helped save my life—I'd say that's more than repayment," Gabe said.

"We'll call it equal, then," Fields said with a grin. "Brandon said you wanted to say thanks face-to-face. I wanted to do the same."

"I'm glad you came. I'd like to talk to you later, but first the three of us need to take a look at these files, by ourselves," Gabe said. "Coffee cups are in the cabinet over the coffee pot. Creamer in the fridge. Feel free to settle down here in the kitchen. Bran. Ruby. Which office?"

"Let's use mine," Ruby said. "More space. And let's get Donna-gran in on this as well."

"Sounds good," Brandon said.

Brandon and Gabe went into her office while Ruby tapped on Donna-gran's door.

"Brandon's here," she said when Donna-gran opened it. "Meeting in my office."

"I'll be right there," Donna-gran said.

After they were all settled in Ruby's office, Brandon clicked up his screen and expanded it to show a gray-colored body lying face down in stubble at the edge of a field. Ruby recognized the field from their visit to Swait's farm in August. Only then the field hadn't been harvested.

"The Defenders called it in to the main farm office," Brandon said. "This was what we saw when Carrie and I went out there. Jeff was handling—shipments."

Ruby nodded. Carrie Swait, Jeff's sister, managed his farm operations, and had impressed Ruby with her level headedness. "Was there a reason they hadn't pulled the Defenders from the fields yet?"

"Data collection and extra security," Brandon said. "Part of Jeff's defensive screen, given the current events. You think we're paranoid and cautious—the Swait family is even more so, for damn good reason, given their history and their indentured rescue operations. Which are more extensive than Justine, Kris, and I realized."

Second photo. In closer range, the gray was a form-fitting bodysuit with a hood and something shiny on the person's back. Tiny lines of the teal-colored Defender bots wrapped around the person's neck and upper body.

"Same bodysuits that we saw in the research compound," Gabe said. "Didn't Artie say something about them having limited use before the wearer had to recharge?"

"Something like thirty minutes," Ruby said.

"That sounds right," Donna-gran said thoughtfully. "And Artie would know." Gabe's cousin Arthur had worked with those suits in Europe before discarding their use as problematic. She leaned forward. "What are those blue-green lines?"

"Defender bots," Ruby said. "All of the RubyBot-based applications look like very tiny colorful ladybugs, depending on what variant is being used. Defender is teal."

"Ah, got it." Donna-gran sat back.

Third photo. Gray-suited body lying on its back. Shiny covering on face and chest. The mask-like face covering appeared to have a filtration system.

"Pat identified this as one of the cyborged indentured." Brandon pointed to the face mask. "This is metallic bioplast. I took samples from it—it has programmable nanos in it meant to protect the wearer from inhaled chemical or biological agents."

"Agricultural application that also works for military uses," Donna-gran said.

Brandon nodded. "The chest shield has similar usage. Solar cells on the back in an apparent attempt to extend use time." He exhaled a ragged sigh. "From what we were able to put together last night using the scans, the Defenders killed that indentured in three modes. First, they clogged air filters.

Second, they blocked the solar cells which interfered with oxygen and cooling systems. Third, they shut down the cyborg links, which effectively finished the person. And triggered an alert to whoever it was reporting to."

"You sure of that?" Gabe asked.

Brandon nodded. "That was our second warning, right on the heels of the Defender's alert. Couldn't stop the alert, but Jeff's monitors caught it. We started evac right away while Carrie and I whipped out there to investigate—that's what I meant when I talked about Jeff handling shipments when I called."

Ruby tapped her chin thoughtfully. "Was there a clear progression of the Defender attacks?"

"As I described," Brandon said. "Showed up with clear time stamps. Air filters. The cyborg switched to a short-term solar-powered oxygen tank, so it kept going. The Defenders switched to blocking the solar cell links. That cut primary oxygen and cooling support. But the cyborg kept going, so—the Defenders went to the cyborg links. They burrowed through the suit to reach that implant, or so Pat thinks."

"*Really.*" Donna-gran perked up at that. "Those suits are pretty damn hard to break through."

"That's what Pat said." Brandon nodded. "The suits have redundancies upon redundancies, from what we were able to make out from the scans. But the Defenders beat all of them. Mom, the Defenders showed a clear and escalating learning pattern."

"I want Beck and Martin to look at this data," Ruby said. "That shows a process we didn't anticipate with the Defender. The programming wasn't supposed to be that sophisticated."

"That's an interesting new development," Gabe said, leaning forward, resting his arms on his knees. "The Defenders discarded the redundancies and went straight to the next level, then." His eyes met Ruby's. "That could be useful for non-ag applications."

"I agree. Brandon, do you know if Swait has any leftover Defenders?" Ruby asked.

Brandon grinned. "Every single group we dropped off last night got a small box of Defenders. We have them at Moondance as well. Jeff—officially doesn't know about those Defenders going off-site. And. Um. Carrie and I harvested the Defenders on the cyborg before we beat feet and I hopped on the plane. I brought samples here, but sent the rest along with the spare Defenders. Figured if there was a learning curve, it might be a good idea to have some of those on hand to teach the others."

Gabe mirrored Brandon's grin. "Good job. But." He sobered. "The Defenders can be tied back to Jeff."

Brandon shook his head. "After I called you, I hacked the origins file on the Defenders, and added a hard wipe and self-destruct command should anyone probe for sourcing. Not entirely fail-safe, but it was the best we could do before dropping off our first group. I've ordered folks not to be reckless in their usage of the Defenders, because the supply is limited."

"Pretty good programming on the fly—in what, an hour or so?" Ruby said. "Bran, did you keep copies of the programming changes?"

"It's all in the copies I'm leaving with you. That includes not just the copies of the cyborg programming and the pix but what I did to the Defenders," Brandon said. "And Ma, it was the hardest piece of coding I did. In a half hour."

Ruby whistled. "That's damn good."

"Doable only because I knew how you and Martin code," Brandon said. "And growing up with the RubyBot didn't hurt, either."

Gabe's comm chimed. *"Philip Martiniere."*

"Fuck!" Gabe snapped. "Taking it. Brandon, Donna-gran, *get out of here.* At least out of sight range, and *be quiet.* Ruby. With me."

They scurried around. Gabe sat behind her desk and pulled Ruby into his lap.

"Play along," he whispered in her ear. "Have the ring prominent. I want to come across as relaxed, calm, and decadent as possible. If I fondle you, don't jump. Part of the game that he'll understand, contribute to his underestimating you—I hope. Got it?"

She nodded.

"God, I love you." He cleared his throat. "Accept call. Record call."

Philip's image glowered at them. "Gabriel. Took you long enough to answer."

"Father. Or should I call you Daddy-dearest, like Justine does?" Gabe's tone was playful, edged with malice. Ruby stifled a shudder at the sharpness and rubbed her chin against Gabe's chest in an attempt to be—what? She wasn't sure, but Gabe could use any little bit of encouragement. He squeezed her arm.

"God damn you," Philip snarled. "You have no right to call me that."

"The DNA scans and IVF certifications that Donna-gran provided me say otherwise." The malice edged closer to the surface.

Philip shook his head. "That's not what I called about." He thrust a finger at them and it was all Ruby could do to keep from slapping it away—not that it mattered, it was nothing more than a projection. "Your son—"

"*Our* son," Gabe said, kissing Ruby's cheek. "Your grandson."

Red spots flushed on Philip's cheeks. "And that—that—murdering bitch—"

"Careful there, Father. You *are* talking about my wife and the mother of my son, who acted in self-defense." Gabe stroked her cheek.

Ruby glanced at him and he smiled at her. She met it. An impulse made her kiss his ear lingeringly before shifting slightly to give Philip a coy smile.

Want to see your ideal Martiniere woman, Philip? You're looking at her. And she is not the sweet little thing you probably fantasize about.

Philip gritted his teeth. "Your son was in close proximity to an incident involving one of our indentureds. Don't deny it. We have evidence."

"It's easy to make assertions—" Ruby started.

"Shut up!" Philip snapped.

"No. *You* don't tell *me* to shut up. I am the Matriarch. *I* tell *you* to shut up." She pointed her left hand at Philip, thumb resting near the emerald. "Shall we test my ability to lock you down remotely? We know I can do it face-to-face, after I did it at the wedding."

"You wouldn't dare—even if control tones worked through comms."

"I wouldn't push Ruby," Gabe said mildly, before Ruby could react. "She's quite strong. I wouldn't discount the possibility that she can do it."

"*Fine,*" Philip said through gritted teeth. "Here's what I want. We know that your son copied data from our indentured."

"Definitive proof?" Ruby lowered her hand and leaned back against Gabe. He turned his head to press soft kisses on her temple.

"Bitch. Yes," Philip growled.

"Ain't any good unless you show it," Gabe said, curling a loose strand of Ruby's hair around his finger.

"Here you go." Philip snapped his fingers. A second image appeared, a fisheye lens view of Brandon squatting, scanner in hand.

Ruby's wireless house system alarms flashed.

Image virus load.

She tapped in the code that nuked both the image and viruses, then cordoned that sector of the system off until one of them could investigate it further.

"Nice virus load, *father-in-law*," she said to Philip.

Philip pressed his lips together and glowered at her. "All right. Let's cut the bullshit. I want all copies of those scans that Brandon made. Tracking's enabled so I know how many there were. And whether further copies have been destroyed."

"Oh really? We can block that information," Gabe said. "Especially when it comes to second and third generation copies. Our algorithms are strong."

"That's what you think," Philip shot back.

Gabe shrugged. "I'll talk to him. No guarantees."

"You're his father. You can command him."

"He's not programmed and he won't be," Ruby said sweetly. "As the Matriarch, I'll make certain of that. No more programming of Martiniere children."

Philip visibly bit back a retort. "If you don't get those copies to me and shut the fuck up about what you've discovered about them so far, Swait's vulnerable." He bared his teeth in a feral grin. "And, well, given his race and his region's history, that could be problematic."

Ruby restrained a shudder at Philip's expression.

So like Gabe in that "don't give a shit, let's fight," mode. So like Branny. Now I know where it comes from.

If she had any doubts about the kinship before, she didn't now.

"Oh really, progenitor of mine," Gabe drawled, an affected, bored note in his voice. "The race card. Typical. How many times did I have to listen to your racist rants over dinner during those rare days at what was supposed to be my home during my teen years? Sorry. Times have changed, or did you miss that memo?"

"I seem to recall that the two of you are partners in a company with Swait," Philip growled. "A nice little lawsuit for deprivation of services might just change your tune."

"Bring it on," Gabe said, menace closer to the surface but still under a veneer of boredom. "I'd love to see the schematics on that indentured. And if you sue, we're going to have a lot of fun with the discovery process. If a lawsuit doesn't get thrown out of court first. I dare you."

"You haven't changed since you were an insolent teen," Philip snarled.

"I've always been a gambler, even if I was only gambling on what punishment you and Joseph would deal out to me," Gabe said. He kissed Ruby. "And I have a damn fine woman in my life who not only has my back but is a *true* independent Martiniere woman. I meant what I said. Go ahead and bring that lawsuit. If you dare. And as for Swait—" his voice hardened. "I seem to recall you're mounting a serious run for the presidency. Trust me. Any indication that you've brought about *any* harm to Swait and his family and friends, or *caused* it to happen, and this threat will go public."

"Nonetheless. Hand over those copies, *or else*," Philip snapped. His image faded.

Ruby pulled her scanner out of her pocket. "Check for new recording apps from that last call."

Brandon and Donna-gran re-entered the office from where

they'd been crouched in the hallway. Silence ruled until a mechanical simulation of young Brandon's voice droned, *"No new recordings, Ruby-mom."*

She sat up. "All clear."

Mother, Mom, Ma, Ruby, Ruby-Mother all meant different levels of intrusion. *Ruby-mom* was the one safe response.

"I remember recording that," Brandon said. "I was something like what—twelve?"

"Around that. About the time I started competing in the AgInnovator again and wanted to ensure no one was trying to steal our work." Ruby stood. "We'd better check the versioning tracker blocks."

"Already done," Brandon said. "Donna-gran and I ran them. He's lying. He can't beat them."

Gabe cocked a brow at him. "You sure?"

"Probably," Ruby said. "Let me run a second scan."

She opened her screen and Brandon flicked a file toward her. As a precaution she scanned the file first, then opened it. Her coding program was a modified version of BotLive, more sophisticated than the version they used for the RubyBots. Philip's file also used BotLive, which made her scan relatively simple.

Ruby found the "call home" routine quickly, and skimmed through. No replication tracking code capable of breaking their blocks. One highlighted section with Brandon's initials that was an attempt at a tracker, but fragmentary. Another section with Donna-gran's initials, also an incomplete tracker. Ruby probed further, then looked at both sections on the off chance that there might be a linking program. No. Nothing.

She looked up.

"So?" Gabe asked.

"Just what they found. Incomplete code sections. Running

BotLive, engineered for a more sophisticated organism than our agbots. No linkages."

Brandon nodded. "I'll be interested in hearing what Martin and Beck think of it."

"Sabotage from Philip's own people, perhaps?" Donna-gran suggested.

"I hadn't thought of that possibility," Ruby said. "But that could explain the lack of links."

"Okay. Then we're good now," Gabe said. "Donna-gran. How much more training does Ruby need?"

"Several days. Why?"

"It's time for her and Brandon to start lining up Family votes. Brandon, please share this with Justine and Serg. Donald and I have been working on a program today that will shift control of Martiniere subsidiaries from PJM Inc.—Philip's holding company—to GMR Group—my holding company. Starting with the subsidiaries managed by the Family branches who have already pledged to me and Ruby. " Gabe started ticking off names on his fingers. "Let me sum up where we stand. The branches headed by cousins Artie, Paul, Ken, and Piotr are already transferred since they've sworn loyalty to me. That leaves us with Uncle Gerard and his sons David and Vincent in France, Uncle Peter's sons Christopher and Thomas in Britain, Madeline's sons Adrien and Pierre, also in France, and Jeannette's son Marc—another French tie. I need to know where they stand. I want their pledges if it is at all possible. And the Canadians—Donna-gran?"

"Yves listens to me and the rest of the Canadian Family is solid. Vincent is not a good prospect," Donna-gran said. "I talk to Marc regularly, and while I sometimes have to kick some sense into him, he'll listen to me. Thomas and Christopher—unfortunately I don't know my British descendants as well as I should. They tend to keep to themselves. We will need to cultivate the sons as secondary heirs as well as the fathers. Paul's son Robert is close to Gerard, even though Paul has sworn to you."

"I want to know where all of them stand," Gabe repeated. "It's time. So Bran, you need to be ready to meet with them as soon as your mother's trained and we can get meetings set up—
"

"We can leave by tomorrow," Donna-gran said. "Ruby's training can happen as we're working. I'll set up the meetings today."

"So quickly, Donna-gran?" Gabe asked.

"You're right about the need to act, Gabriel. And yes, she's ready."

Gabe nodded. "Okay. Two more things and then I think you'd better get the hell out of here, Bran. First. We need to offer more protection to Swait. How can we arrange that?"

"Let's talk to Colin before we leave," Brandon said. "He's already been directing small groups of Freeds to be available to Jeff as a defense. I can relay the necessary defensive profile from the Defenders to them should more of those cyborgs show up. So we've started that action."

"Second, we need to devise a statement of basic principles for those Family members to swear to." Gabe leaned back in his chair. He ticked off one finger. "Principle One. All nonconsensual body and mind control research using indentureds within the Martiniere Group must immediately stop. Non-coercive consents must be on hand for all body and mind control research before any of it proceeds further."

"The consent issue is touchy," Brandon said. "How do we document that it hasn't been coerced by some means?"

"That's something that needs to be worked out, and until it is, nothing happens," Gabe said. "And we can be straightforward about that, because of Principle Two. All subsidiaries will either immediately release all indentureds or submit a five-year phaseout plan. Principle Three. All indentured contract expiration dates are to be reviewed and any over contract are to be released with compensation for every day they were held over their contract."

"Thomas isn't going to like that," Donna-gran said. "Going rate for the area and work?"

"I mean for this to hurt, Donna-gran," Gabe said. "Thomas's division is going to be one of the biggest offenders, if my company review is correct."

"It is," she said.

"Terms, definitions, anything else I haven't otherwise specified can be left to your judgment. Amongst the three of you I think something decent can be devised."

"I suggest that Justine go to Europe with us," Brandon said. "She will also have more security connections. They know that. Have me and Mom be the carrot—and you and Justine be the stick."

"Good idea."

"And let's work out a somewhat more formal statement from these principles and record you speaking them," Ruby said. "Yes, Brandon's your heir and I speak with your voice. But they also need to see you saying those words, even if it's just a recording."

Gabe tightened his lips. "Can you help me with that, Rubes?"

"Absolutely."

Gabe sighed. "All right. Last piece because I just thought of it. I really wish you could be with me, Ruby, when I talk to Tolliver tomorrow. I want witnesses, both with me and listening in."

"Take Pat," Brandon said. "That'll put him on edge. Her numbers are rising and there's that big New Dems donor dinner coming up." He frowned. "I *was* going to be there. But if I'm in Europe or Canada...."

"We can fly back in time to attend that dinner after meeting with Thomas and Christopher," Donna-gran said. "It's going to be important, and I want to be there as well."

"All the same," Gabe continued. "Ruby, you'll have the emeralds with you. Could you listen in to my meeting with Tolliver through the brooch? I don't know if you can record but if so—Donna-gran?"

The gold, emerald, and pearl brooch that was part of the Martiniere emerald set had been configured as a secure communication device between the Martiniere and his wife while at events. Ruby and Gabe had already used it when Ruby had attended the banquet where Philip had received the Real Truthers nomination for president.

"Not recording, no," Donna-gran said slowly. "We never set the jewelry up for that. But yes, listening. That's what Louis and I designed into it."

"Better than nothing, I guess," Gabe said. "All right. Bran, let's talk with Colin. Then I think you'd better get out of here quickly."

"Agreed," Brandon said.

Donna-gran turned to Ruby after Brandon and Gabe left. "If we're going to be meeting with Family members day after tomorrow, we still have a lot to do. I have more exercises for you to practice. And then I'll show you the basic psychotropics and how best to administer and conceal them. You may not need them for these visits, but it doesn't hurt for you to know how to handle them."

Ruby nodded, and settled in her chair as Donna-gran pulled one over behind the desk.

Here we go.

She just hoped she could live up to what being the Martiniere Matriarch required.

***

No cozy relaxing in front of the wood stove this evening. Ruby saved packing for the trip as the last thing she did before bed. Gabe sat in the rocking chair while she considered what to wear. Suits? Skirts or pants, or take both? Or a jacket over a nice dress? What did one wear when cracking the whip over Family members she hadn't met before? How cold was it going to be there?

"This is hard," she said. "How formal do I get?" She scowled at the options she had available.

"Business casual used to be the norm for this sort of family meeting," Gabe said. "What you would wear to a conference or presentation."

That was a help. "Thanks. You don't think slacks are going to be a deal breaker? After all, your family does run conservative."

"Rubes. Be who you are. That's why you're the Martiniere Matriarch. I chose you, was stupid enough not to trust you initially, and then became smart enough to recognize I'd lost a good thing and got you back. You're *my choice.* They can deal with it one way or another, but if the difference between slacks and a skirt is enough to make them stick with Philip, then they aren't gonna change. Period." He got up and took her hands. "You did a great job at the Real Truthers banquet, and you only had Justine for backup. Now you've got her, Donna-gran, and Brandon to support you. You'll do fine. Pack the slacks if that's what you want to wear."

She sighed. "All right. It's just that it's a different level of social class from what I'm used to handling. I'm a little nervous about coming off as a hick."

"To be expected. But this is what we're doing these days. You are classy, and nowhere near a hick. Will you be what they expect? No. Are you part of that social group they're accustomed to? No. Is that going to be a problem? If so, they can damned well learn to accept that things are different, because that attitude is part and parcel of what we're trying to reform in the Family. But I don't think it will be a problem. You code switch well." He hugged her and sat back down. "I plan to listen in via the brooch. If I have to, I'll speak through you."

"All right." She turned back to the outfits she had laid out on the bed and started packing them. Jewelry at least would be easy, since she would be wearing the Martiniere emeralds for the meetings and the freshwater pearl earrings that Gabe had given her years ago otherwise.

That done, she brought out the garment bag that held the formal dress she had worn at the Real Truthers, and slipped the dress out.

"It looks like we'll be flying straight back from Britain to the New Dems reception from the schedule that Donna-gran gave me," she said. "Gonna be a lot of changing on the plane, possibly even sleeping. Justine's handling those arrangements." Donna-gran and Justine had decided that staying more than one night in the same place was not advised. Ruby was still not quite clear what that meant in practice. "Do you think I should wear this dress—or a different one? I was pretty high-visibility in this one at the Reals."

"It's probably not a good idea to wear the same thing to the New Dems that you wore to the Reals." Gabe got up, took the dress, and went to her closet. After he hung it up, he fingered through the selection of formal dress wear Ruby had acquired with Justine's help over the past few weeks. He pulled out a long dark green dress with metallic threads that looked black from certain angles. "How about this one?"

Ruby eyed the dress. It was bespoke—Justine had taken her to the dressmaker—with long sleeves, fitted snugly over her torso then but probably would be a little loose on her now, and a full skirt.

"Might be a wee bit big on me with the weight I've lost," she said. "But let's try it."

The fit wasn't as loose as she feared, and Gabe's grin was sufficient endorsement. She studied herself in the mirror. It wasn't as striking as the other dress, but then again, she didn't have to be the center of attention this time around.

"This is the one," she said.

Gabe helped her out of it, and she slipped the dress into the garment bag, along with a pair of shoes specifically to wear with it and the undergarments she would need. It could stay on the plane and it would make changing simpler if their schedule changed. She hung the bag on a hook and rolled the suitcase next to it.

"Guess that's ready," she said.

"You'll do fine," Gabe said. He took her into his arms again. "But I'll miss you. God, Ruby. Here we really go, now."

"Worried?"

"Absolutely. Afraid for you. For Bran. Oh, I know he's grown up and all, but damn. Our son sometimes takes more risks than I'm comfortable with."

"He is our son in so many ways," she said.

Gabe laughed. "So very true." He grew more solemn. "And you. I've just gotten you back. I—shit, when you reacted to the vaccination, I thought you were dying."

"I know the feeling," she said softly.

"We've both been through it lately."

"You will take care of yourself, right?"

He chuckled. "I'll have both Pat and Kris nagging me when I see Tolliver. And Serg in the background."

"And I have support, too."

"I know."

They stood together quietly for a few more moments. Then Ruby leaned into Gabe and kissed him gently. The kisses grew more intense.

"It's going to be a couple of days," Gabe murmured. "Think we could try and see if things are still working again?"

"You bet."

This time their lovemaking was less tentative and more passionate. It temporarily drove away her worries, and even afterward, she was too tired to do anything more than lay quietly in Gabe's arms as they spooned together, his arms folded around her.

She would think about the challenges ahead tomorrow. Right now, she wanted to savor this moment.

Gabe's steady breath on her neck. The gentle pressure of his arms holding her. His warmth.

Together again.

CHAPTER 8

The atmosphere in the jet's cabin the next day was tense as they awaited Gabe's call. Then Ruby felt a sharp buzz from the brooch at the same time her comm chimed in her ear, quiet instead of its usual open announcement.

"Gabriel Martiniere."

Ruby tapped a code on the brooch. "Do you hear me, Gabe?"

"Loud and clear."

"Brandon's figured out how to project the audio from the brooch so we can all hear," Ruby said. "Unless the signal's blocked."

"Good," Gabe said, voice low and tense. "Can he record?"

"Yes," Brandon said. "You need to know this, Dad. Either the Secret Service or Tolliver's private security will do a security scan that will include active transmissions. Tell them before they scan. Stress that it's an FQR-certified network licensed to Serg Vygotsky. Went through this dance when I talked to Tolliver. Noticed that they relaxed when I told them it was FQR. That said, just so you know. They have FQR-level blockers."

Ruby's hands tightened on the arms of her seat. She had gone through this discussion with Brandon.

I'll do my best to keep the signal going, he had said. *If Tolliver chooses to shut things down, he can. He has military tech and we have corporate. Two different levels of security, and in spite of what Piotr and Serg can do, the government still has those damn backdoors that can block our comms. We're doing our best to work around it but that tech is interdicted to us. We've the best non-military tech there is, however....*

"Got it," Gabe said. "Going in now."

They listened as Gabe talked to the Secret Service. Buzzing intermittently blocked the conversation. A pause while clearance was discussed, referring the question to Tolliver.

Then the buzzing stopped.

"I'm clear," Gabe said quietly. "Said that you are listening, Ruby, and that I do the same when you're in a meeting without me as a GMR Group corporate policy. They have their own recording devices going—signing mutual disclosure agreements right now."

"Got it," Ruby said.

"Here we are. Going into the Oval Office now."

Gabe introduced Pat and Kris to Tolliver. They exchanged mild pleasantries and Ruby tapped her fingers on the armrest impatiently, wishing things would happen faster.

Tolliver coughed. "All right, Gabriel. I talked to your son Brandon not that long ago about indentured reform. I don't know that I can consider supporting extreme change in the laws related to indentured contracts. Indenture is a necessary evil. Philip Martiniere can spew all the reactionary bullshit he wants about expanding indenture and I'd tell him the same thing I'm telling you. I don't support any changes in the law, either to diminish or to increase its frequency."

"Eliminating indenture is the right thing to do."

"I can't support it. The impact on the economy is dire, plus I haven't seen sufficient evidence that doing so is the politically expedient thing to do. The situation really hasn't changed since Brandon and I talked. Has it?"

"That slimy son of a bitch," Brandon muttered, low enough that the mic couldn't pick up his words. "He *promised* me, the asshat." He continued swearing in a soft voice, hands clasped, staring at the floor between his feet.

"Actually, I believe the situation has significantly changed when it comes to political expediency," Gabe said. "I've had some interesting discussions with prominent New Dems fundraisers. Specifically, Dorie Sterling, Warren Davis, and Tara Schott, in my capacity as GMR Group president. And as part of my conditions for expanding my contributions to the New Dems."

"Oh really?" An edge sounded in Tolliver's.

"They *are* major contributors to the Indentured Freedom Coalition as well," Kris said. "Several million dollars apiece. I can show you their endorsements of our cause, if you would like."

"That would be interesting."

"Here's the file."

Silence.

Then, "Exploratory Presidential candidate committee. What the fuck, is the IFC running their own candidate?"

"Actually," Gabe said, "that committee has been exploring the possibility of supporting a different New Democrat candidate in the primaries next spring."

"You?" Tolliver snapped it out. "Your son's too young. Rabble rouser that he is."

"Oh no. I have no interest or inclination toward running for any office," Gabe said, voice slow and quiet. Ruby visualized him sitting in a chair across from Tolliver, slouching back in his chair, fingertips pressed together, doing his best to project nothing but relaxation. "I anticipate having my hands full with business, and in any case, my health is such that I don't want the added stress of the Presidency. No. The candidate of interest is a former indentured worker. She knows quite a bit about the abuses that indentureds have endured from personal experience, and has supporting documentation."

"*Who*?" Tolliver's voice rose.

"Me. I'm pleased to meet you, President Tolliver," Pat said. "My name is Patricia Markey, and I served in a research indentured compound along with a man named Colin Fields. I'm sure you recognize that name."

"*Damn* it." Soft but fervent. "All right. What do you want?"

"Justice for the indentured," Pat said. "My contract was extended by five years without renegotiating or payment options. I am only a minor case. But I was freed just before I could be subjected to a highly experimental cyborg implant that at the very least would have blanked out my personality and at worst possibly hasten my death. Colin and I were amongst the fortunate ones. There are at least two hundred people in that one facility who have gone through the cyborg process or will be put through a similar cyborg procedure in the next few weeks. They will never be the same."

"What does that justice look like?"

"Immediate review of all indentured contracts. No new contracts, and phasing out of old contracts over the next year," Pat said. "Reinstatement of all legal rights to people currently under indenture. An end to the use of indentured workers as nonconsensual research subjects."

"Damn, you don't want much," Tolliver said. "Do you realize the economic impact these measures will have?"

"Less than you think," Kris said smoothly. "Here's the research from the IFC."

"Honestly, Stephen, do you really place economics at a higher level than human life?" Gabe's tone was mild but there was no mistaking a faint note of menace in it.

"Economics is what wins elections."

"Hmm. You might want to tell that to Dorie, Warren, and Tara at the upcoming banquet," Gabe said. "I do assume you're planning to attend?"

"You *know* I am," Tolliver growled. "I am one of the speakers."

"Funny how that works," Gabe said. "So is Pat. And, I believe, my son, talking about how he was almost forced into indenture. By his grandfather, no less."

"You're walking a thin line," Tolliver said. "Indenture is not that important to voters."

"I don't know. After all, Dorie, Warren, and Tara have signed the Indentured Freedom Coalition pledge to end indentured servitude," Gabe said. "As has the Biobot Producers Association. GMR Group is also a signatory, along with BMS Associates."

"What do you want me to do?" Now Tolliver's voice was pleading, almost imploring. "I can't just abolish indenture overnight."

"It is my understanding that there's a bill in the House right now that's been languishing because the New Dems don't care to prioritize it," Kris said.

"That bill is a piece of—" As Tolliver exploded the sound suddenly cut out. They couldn't even hear the buzzing over voices that had happened before. This was empty, dead air, as if they weren't even connected.

"What the hell?" Ruby said. "Gabe. Gabe. You've cut out."

No response.

"GABE!" she bellowed, trying and failing to keep her voice steady. "God damn it, Gabe, *answer, damn you!*" Her voice caught.

Brandon enlarged the screen he'd been using to record the conversation. "Mom. The call's been dropped. Try reconnecting with him."

Ruby tapped the brooch to activate the private link.

Nothing. Not even the chime that signaled the call had gone through.

"Fuck! It's blocked," Brandon growled. He slammed his hands on his legs. "That motherfucker Tolliver...."

Ruby tried again.

Still nothing.

"I can't raise him," she said, voice shaking. "God. What does that mean?"

"Hopefully just that Tolliver hit the block button so we can't hear and record what he's saying about that bill," Justine said grimly, pulling up a screen. "Donald's been monitoring their scanners."

A pause.

"Shit. He says he's shut out too." She stared at her screen. "He's not seeing any unusual activity outside," she said finally. "But I'm activating Serg and his team so they can try a rescue if it looks like they're being hauled off somewhere. Sending Donald what we have from the meeting so that if necessary, we can push the recording out, embarrass Tolliver into letting them go."

Ruby shook her head, dread tightening her gut.

I should have insisted on going with him.

She moaned and buried her head in her hands.

"It was supposed to be a safe meeting," she whispered.

"That's why we took these precautions," Justine muttered. "Motherfuckers are afraid of what Daddy dearest might do?

About fucking time they learned to worry about us as well. *I'm not letting them have my good brother.*"

Hands gently took Ruby's, easing them away from her face. Brandon knelt in front of her, holding them in his. "Ma. Don't panic. Not yet. Kris is carrying a trouble button that *can* get past their blockers." A faint quaver in his voice as if he were trying to convince himself.

His love is there too, she reminded herself. *We're in the same position.*

Ruby squinched her eyes tight and took a deep breath before opening them and meeting Brandon's gaze, seeing his own fear and worry.

Donna-gran moved to the seat next to Ruby. She didn't say anything but rested her hand on top of theirs.

Silence except for the faint rumble of jet engines and Justine's occasional murmurs on her comm. Silence that extended into forever. Silence, and the icy shards of dread knifing into her gut, the terror of *not knowing.* Rediscovering that the terror of watching someone struggling with illness was nothing at all like this version of *not knowing.* She'd encountered this once before, when Gabe had been kidnapped six months ago. But this time the *not knowing* was somehow worse.

Brandon moved from kneeling to sit by her legs, hiding his face in his knees, one hand clenching hers in tight squeezes as the other one pounded on the floor in a steady four-four beat.

Silence. Silence. Silence.

She fought the temptation to check the time. That wouldn't help, would it?

"Outside movement," Justine said suddenly. "Looks like it's their car. Pulling up now."

Brandon's pounding stopped. Ruby dared to check the time. An hour since the meeting started. How much of that had been silent? She should have checked.

"Serg reports visual contact with Gabe—Kris—Pat." A pause. "All into their car. Pulling out. Escort front and back, not our people."

What does that mean?

"Bran?" she breathed.

"Don't know yet. Kris hasn't punched the danger button so...." His voice trailed off and he still wouldn't look at her, his one hand tightening and releasing on hers, his other hand irregularly tapping the floor with less force than before.

Silence again, never ending damned silence.

"Looks like they're heading for the airport," Justine said. "Our people following now."

More silence.

Ruby strained for the slightest sound, wishing for some means to watch what was going on.

"Airport. Their escort pulling away. Ours moving in."

Yet another unbearable silence.

"Serg says all clear. Everyone on the plane."

Ruby exhaled as Brandon sat up, releasing his grip on her hand.

Ping.

Brandon shot to his feet. "*Kris!* What the fuck just happened?" He strode back to the jet's bedroom, closing the door behind him.

"*Gabriel Martiniere.*"

"Accept—oh god Gabe what happened?" she exhaled as Gabe's image appeared.

His face was hard and set. "That motherfucker Tolliver. Tine, it's a good thing you and Serg had that network set up. Otherwise—" he shook his head.

"Gabriel Marcus Martiniere, what the fuck happened?" Ruby demanded.

Gabe sighed. "Tolliver had some heavies in there that sure

looked like some of those cyborged indentureds. No one of them up front and center to begin with, and they had shirts, pants, and jackets, so I had to look quick to see the gray suit underneath. There was some tension between Tolliver's personal guards and the Secret Service. I didn't hear it, but I think one of them wanted to keep the Service out, and their head wouldn't agree to it. We had Secret Service crawling all over us right after our contact cut out, alerted because their comms shut down as well. At first they thought it was our doing. Guns in our faces. A clear excuse to have us hauled out of there in handcuffs. I was able to talk us out of that situation."

"Oh, shit," Ruby said.

Gabe nodded. "Absolutely. It doesn't make sense, Rubes." He exhaled slowly. "Anyway. Once we got the assorted security groups settled down, Tolliver was willing to concede that he *might* support a modified bill calling for government auditing of indentured contract terms and release of indentureds on contracts of ten years or less in duration. But. He told me that in return, there will be a phase-out of short-term indenture contracts. Lifetime contracts will be the only existing ones in ten years. And all prisoners who chose indenture instead of imprisonment? Lifetime indenture. Crime severity not to be a factor."

"What the hell does he think he's doing?" Justine demanded as Donna-gran inhaled sharply through her teeth. "That's not a New Dems position. Not even the Classic Dems will go that far. Is he trying to win the Real Truthers over?"

"Tolliver also told us that if he wavered on this stance, he has been told that he will be responsible for the culling deaths of up to ten thousand indentureds," Gabe said flatly. "And that he is prepared to *privately* grant exceptions to free as many indentureds as possible."

"Who's making that threat?" Justine asked.

Gabe raised his hands. "He wouldn't say. But I think we could figure it out. Meanwhile, Pat's filing campaign paperwork for the New Dems nomination, and I'm going to have a little chat with Tara, Dorie, and Warren about this meeting."

"Should we turn around?" Ruby asked.

"No. What you're doing now is going to be more important than ever. Donna-gran. You're a certified proxy handler for the Family. I need you to deliver meeting notices and collect proxies if the Heads of Family you're talking to can't attend. I assume you have access to everything you need to send out meeting invitations to hold a formal vote of confidence about Philip's leadership of the Martiniere Group?"

"All but the details of when and where of the meeting, Gabriel. But you need a majority—"

"Donald is taking care of that right now," Gabe said. "By midnight Pacific time GMR Group will officially hold a 51% majority on the Martiniere Group Board. Enough to call a meeting."

"But not enough to vote for a change of leadership out of the usual cycle," Donna-gran said.

"No. Not yet. Getting those numbers is what you four have to do. The meeting will be October 15th. Noon. Moondance Ranch, Blue Bucket, Oregon. Ruby can give you further details. I'll get you a formal agenda and proxy ballot once I can officially make the call. Attendance either in person, online, or voting a proxy."

"Two weeks." Donna-gran nodded curtly. "I will send notice."

"All right." Gabe rubbed his face. "Thank you. I need to go private with Ruby."

"Brandon's in the bedroom talking to Kris," Ruby said.

"I know." Gabe sighed. "It'll have to be audio only."

"Doing it." She tapped off the video. "Gabe. Private now."

"Kris lost it once we were in the car and on our way to the airport. I didn't want to talk about this in front of Justine and Donna-gran yet," Gabe said. "That's why I didn't call sooner. Helping her keep from falling completely apart until she could call Brandon, getting her to calm down so she doesn't panic him. She did a good job of maintaining her cool throughout a rather exciting meeting, but afterward just let it all out. Tough kid, but scared shitless."

"That doesn't seem quite what I'd expect from what I've seen," Ruby said cautiously, not mentioning names. Gabe must have a reason for saying this privately. Could that mean...?

"Ruby, she's pregnant and was throwing up the whole way to the airstrip once we were in the vehicle. I was worried that that she had somehow gotten exposed to G9, so Kris told me what was going on. She and Brandon have been keeping her pregnancy quiet, but in the aftermath of that meeting the stress was just too much...." His voice trailed off.

"I—had wondered," she said, careful about what she said. "But it explains a bit about what's going on."

"Yeah," he sighed. "You might want to let Bran know that I told you. Pat's with her in back right now. It wasn't a planned pregnancy. An apparent consequence of everything happening around removing her indentured hormonal tags."

"Are they worried about problems?"

"Yes. That's also why Bran's had Kris working at Moon-dance, to reduce her exposure and risk. She found out right after we rescued Pat. They've not had the time to settle down and think much about this yet. But it's another reason to move quickly and resolve at least a few of the issues we're facing."

"Yes."

She must have been pregnant during the tag removal and the remote hormone manipulation before then. God. No wonder they've both been on edge.

"So, Grandma-to-be," he said, trying for a playful tone but sounding more tired than anything else. "Feeling old yet?"

"This is unfair to them," she said.

"I know. They want to keep the news under wraps for the moment. I don't think Kris would have said anything to me except the vomiting and—well, you know."

"Do I ever," she said ruefully. Morning sickness had been a regular feature throughout her pregnancy with Brandon.

"I love you. I wish you'd been there with me on the one hand but happier than hell that you weren't," he said. "I'm going to talk to Kris and Pat—and probably Bran too."

"I'll join Bran," she said. "Love you."

As she disconnected and stood both Donna-gran and Justine looked as if they wanted to ask her more. Ruby shook her head at them.

"Personal," she said. "Back in a bit. We're joining Brandon and Kris to talk further."

Donna-gran arched a brow but Ruby ignored it. She tapped on the door, then opened. "Branny."

He glanced away from the projection of Kris. Other than red and swollen eyes, and Pat firmly holding her hand, Kris didn't show signs of anything being of concern.

"Ma—"

"I know," she said, making sure the door was closed firmly behind her. "Your father told me. Congratulations to you two."

Kris gulped. "I—I—thank you, Ruby."

Gabe appeared behind Kris and Pat. "Yes. Congratulations. Welcome to the scary world of parenthood."

"We're not sure if we should keep the pregnancy," Brandon said quietly.

"Why?" Ruby asked.

"The timing—so close to the tag removal. There's terato-genic elements in those tags," Pat said. "We don't know yet how long it takes to clear those out of our bodies. And we don't yet have access to the counter medications."

"Have you talked to Justine?" Ruby asked. "She has the specialist contacts. They should be able to figure it out."

"Things have just been so crazy," Kris said. "I've not had the time to focus on it, much less be checked out...we just found out a few days ago. And at the time I—we—thought that those lingering traces from the tags would keep me infertile for at least six months. Not that I'd get pregnant before removal." She blinked, a tear running down one cheek. "It's just been so crazy," she repeated, her next words quieter and quavering as one hand rested low on her abdomen. "I'm scared. Not for me. And I don't know if I should be afraid or not because I may lose it anyway. Whether I should just bite the bullet and have it aborted. And yet—"

"We were going to wait to see if we make it through the first trimester before telling anyone," Brandon said softly.

"Why not get it checked sooner?"

"We would have, but...shit happened."

"From what we indentured know due to past experience, if you make it through the first trimester then there's unlikely to be problems," Pat said.

"And meanwhile you've got this worry hanging over your heads. One more concern that you don't need," Ruby chided softly. "You need to talk to Justine and get Amy in to check things out."

"But it's a distraction," Kris sniffled.

"So is dealing with G9 flares and vaccine reactions," Ruby said. "Don't stress yourself any further. Take care of yourself."

"I just...." Kris gulped, blinking her eyes.

"It's not something we tend to think about as indentureds," Pat said. "Either we take care of a pregnancy or not. If it survives the first trimester then it's viable."

"There are things you can do to help first trimester survival," Ruby said slowly.

Pat shook her head. *Not now*, her lips formed.

"I'll tell her the score once we're done, Pat," Brandon said.

"Anyway. We're here to support both of you," Ruby said. "No matter how it turns out. Okay?"

"Okay," Kris said faintly. She shivered. "Feeling tired."

"I gave her a med for the vomiting," Pat added. "One thing we learned in the ranks of the indentured. How to take care of each other. But Kris needs to sleep."

"I'll duck out," Gabe said. "Rubes. Love you."

"Love you too."

She went to the bathroom while she was back there. When she came out, Brandon still sat on the side of the bed, staring at nothing.

Ruby sat next to him. "Bran. Branny. It's going to be all right."

He shuddered and turned his head to fix her with that distant stare. "Ma. The reason for waiting until the first trimester is over before telling anyone. Some of the potential mutations are—monstrous if they survive. They generally miscarry in that first three months. Interventions may not prevent the mutations from happening if the fetus survives the first trimester." He swallowed. "We were so careful. Or so we thought."

"Bran. You two don't have to put yourself through this wondering and worrying," she said softly. "We have resources. *Think*."

Like father, like son. Both of them can get locked in their same circuits when it comes to their women. Understandable in this case but still....

"Come on," she said, pulling at him. "Let's talk to Justine.

Let's find out what's going on or not with Kris. Better than spending the next month and a half worrying, right?"

He gave her a weary smile. "I suppose, Ma."

"Well, come on. Let's give Tine some time to kick up some resources for Kris before we walk into our own hornets' nest. That way you two have one less thing to fret about."

Brandon stood and followed Ruby back into the main cabin. He stopped, eyed Donna-gran and Justine as they turned to face him, then sighed.

"Justine. I—we—need your help." He looked down, then back up. "Kris is pregnant. Discovered it after we rescued Pat. We're afraid of possible teratogens connected to those tags she had removed."

The smile that had started to spread across Donna-gran's face at Brandon's disclosure faded.

"Oh, *crud*," Justine sighed. "Is she going back to Moon-dance, Brandon?"

"Yes." He glanced at Ruby. "We wouldn't have said anything—were waiting to see how the first trimester went—and then she had a bad attack of nausea in the car after meeting with Tolliver. Dad found out as a result, and told Mom."

"Well." Justine straightened up. "Nausea is a good sign, Brandon. Means there's less likely to be problems. I'll contact Amy and send her to Moondance to run tests on Kris. It's not like Kris is still living in a labor pool with all of those nuances about keeping the pregnancy secret. There are things which can be done if there are—problems. It all depends on what the test results show."

"You'd wait until she's through the first trimester to do anything?" Donna-gran said, a horrified note in her voice.

"Kris wanted it that way," Brandon said, his voice strained. "I tried to convince her otherwise. We figured that maybe we'd be lucky, and if not, we wouldn't be distracting anyone when we need to be focused—elsewhere."

"It's a pretty standard mindset for indentureds, Donna-gran." Justine looked up from her typing, her face tight and angry. "They don't have access to good prenatal care unless the pregnancy is sanctioned by their contract owners. If they can make it to the second trimester, then they get care, approved or not. This isn't the first time I've encountered this situation."

Donna-gran shook her head. "Barbaric."

"Yes. It is," Justine said coolly. She rose and went to the bar, pouring a generous straight shot glass of real whisky, and handed it to Brandon. "Drink up."

Brandon stared at the glass, then took it from her. He drained it. "Whew. All right. Now what?"

"Now we prepare for our part of the game," Justine said.

"I can think of better games," he said.

Ruby had to agree with him. She buried her head in her hands.

We're doing this for Deidra. Janet. Everyone else.

And perhaps for an embryo that might just make her a grandmother.

CHAPTER 9

Ruby stared up at the brown-black centuries-old beams in the white bedroom ceiling, blinking as she slowly woke.

Paris. I've never been here before, and I won't be seeing much of it now.

What little she remembered of last night's drive from yet another well-guarded but nondescript private airstrip included narrow streets, a quick glimpse of the illuminated Eiffel Tower, circling the roundabout of the Champs Elysees and gazing at the huge French flag billowing in the middle of the Arc d'Triomphe, stopping at an unremarkable doorway, then finally making their way through multiple sets of Plexiglas doors before clambering into an ancient and creaky elevator to reach this apartment.

It's small and pretty plain, Justine had said last night. *But perfect for our purposes. Not at all the sort of place one would expect a Martiniere to be.*

All the same, this building was much older than the old farmhouse she lived in at the Double R. Made that place look like a baby in comparison. She rose and pushed the curtains aside from the narrow metal-framed floor-to-ceiling windows in her small bedroom. The spire of the Eiffel Tower was on the other side of the river—*the Seine,* she told herself. Creamy-shaded stone buildings surrounded theirs.

You can see the Louvre from here, Justine had also said. Was that the long building near the river? Ruby sighed and let the curtain fall. If they were lucky, if they succeeded—maybe she could come back with Gabe to visit.

Maybe.

What time would it be at home? She quickly checked. They were nine hours ahead of home, so it was late, the previous night. Should she call Gabe?

Might be worth a try. At least she could leave a message. He would be connecting with them in a few hours, to monitor while they met with the French Martinieres. Ruby crawled back into bed. Despite the pills Justine had handed out last night to help with sleep and jet lag, she still felt tired and confused.

But she wanted to talk to Gabe. Needed to hear his voice. Guilt nagged at her as she called—after all, he might be getting some much-needed sleep and she would be worrying him with the timing.

"Rubes." He smiled wearily at her—he was sitting in his office, she noticed, her heart sinking slightly. *Not getting enough rest.* "I was hoping you would call once you woke."

"You look tired. Are you taking care of yourself?" She frowned. How much rest was he getting if he was in his office?

"Trying." He shrugged. "I need to be up again soon enough to monitor your meeting. My office chair isn't my old recliner, but I dragged an ottoman in here to prop up my feet. It works. I've been napping." He grinned but it quickly faded. "Lots of experience sleeping like this after the G9. And—I tried lying down in bed. It's not the same without you there. You doing okay?"

"Justine handed out meds to help with jet lag and they seem to have worked, though I still feel tired and disconnected."

"Normal even with meds."

"I just peeked out the window. It's stunning. Different. I wish you were here."

"We'll go to Paris together," he said. "France. I'll show you places I know. Childhood memories. Once this is settled." He sighed. "Dorie, Tara, and Warren are on board with us. Tolliver is going to have one hell of a shock if he expects to get a positive reception at the banquet. That's part of why I can't sleep right now. Adrenaline hangover from that damn fiasco with Tolliver."

"That bad."

"Rubes, I didn't tell you the half of what happened earlier because we still had things to deal with. I was talking as fast as I could once the guns came out because—this came totally out of the blue as far as I knew. Not one indication of the possibility of this blowup based on Brandon's meeting with Tolliver. I was expecting some blowback but not a setup to make it look like we were going to assault the President. I talked to Colin after, and boy do I wish we had the opportunity to speak in more detail beforehand." Gabe rubbed his face. "Colin thinks that someone's got dirt on Tolliver. But that Tolliver's also scared shitless of indentureds and anyone who's gone through indenture. He won't communicate with Colin. Hadn't communicated with Colin's wife—before she passed away. Colin has no idea where his kids went off to."

Ruby shook her head. "Wow. That sounds—does he think that Tolliver has a hand in wherever the kids are?"

"They were adults. Kris is doing her best to track them down. They may have ended up indentured themselves." Gabe's voice was flat, bleak. "The more I hear about this whole fucking mess with indentureds, Ruby, the worse it sounds. We do not know the half of it."

"I've heard enough to turn my stomach." She swallowed hard. "And I know there's worse."

Deidra. Janet. Other sacrifices.

He nodded. "Much worse. I think Kris told Brandon everything that happened last night. You may need to watch him in that meeting if you get too much pushback."

"That bad?"

Gabe rubbed his face again. "Ruby, the fucking Secret Service shoved a pistol into my face and a stunner in my back while the private bodyguards started cuffing Pat and Kris. The privates were using a set of code phrases I recognized from Martiniere Family operations while I was growing up. They intended to take Pat and Kris to an indentured compound. No word on what was going to happen to me. Luckily I knew the right things to say to convince the Secret Service that we did not have bad intentions but that the heavies did—toward us. And I was explicit about how and why I knew of their intent. Told the Secret Service that both women were legitimately freed. That I couldn't work my comm any more because it had been blocked. That we had no weapons—thank God I left mine behind, expecting a more thorough search—and that we wanted to talk, not attack Tolliver."

"God, Gabe." Something struck her. "A more thorough search? But they made a big deal about your comm."

"The privates made the fuss. They also handed us off to the Secret Service as having been searched. But Rubes, if I had serious bad intent, I could have waltzed right into the Oval Office with weapons, especially with what we have access to through Serg and Justine. We were being set up."

"Shit."

I never expected things to be like this.

He nodded. "When Kris started throwing up in the car, at first I thought nerves. She would have been justified. Then I thought she had somehow been slipped a dose of weaponized G9. Scared the crap out of me because she was boostered and should have been safe. But she blurted right out that she was pregnant when I started checking her for fever and orientation."

"I hope she's all right."

"I do too." He paused. "Pat told me in gory detail what some of the problems could be. And those damn kids wanted to keep this news to themselves rather than worry us."

"Bran didn't give me details."

"Good." He grimaced. "You don't want to know though I bet you can imagine. Don't. That mindset, though...." He shook his head. "How the hell are we ever going to fix this mess, Ruby? It's not just financial. These people are doing an end run around all the anti-racist safeguards that came out of the '20s. They *want* to go back at least a hundred and fifty-some years. It's sickening. Horrific. The indenture system was supposed to operate on a strictly financial basis. Keep people from being thrown on the streets if they were broke. The racial bias stats that Pat is digging up—goes beyond the financial aspect."

"I wish I knew exactly what to do to make it all go away. More than what we're doing." She picked at the bedspread nervously. "It was bad enough for me to know that people in Thunder County didn't like you during our first marriage because you had a Hispanic name and brown skin."

Gabe snorted. "I wonder if me being a Martiniere would have made things different back then? Not that it matters now." He shook his head. "Oh Rubes, Rubes, Rubes. We're barely started and I already feel overwhelmed."

"One step at a time, I guess. Focus on what we can do now and worry about the rest later."

"Like you did with the RubyBot."

"I suppose."

"I did take half an hour to go out and visit the horses when I got back to the ranch," he said softly. "I needed that reminder of you. I love you and miss you."

"I love and miss you too."

"Be careful." He took a deep breath. "You shouldn't be facing anything like I did with Tolliver. Gerard makes a lot of noise but he's a straight shooter. He helped Justine elope with Donald. Philip may have leverage over him, and Gerard does not really want to become the Martiniere. And Artie messaged me that he planned to be at this meeting, unless Nora suddenly took a bad turn."

Her heart lifted. Gabe's much older cousin Arthur had made no secret of his support of Gabe from the first time she had met him. "That's good."

"Yeah. Uncle Gerard can be a stubborn old coot, but he's not irrational. What I really need readings on are the family members my age. Swear as many of them to us as you can. The elders of Louis's and Philip's generation have not been open to handing off authority to my cousins. I need my cohort on board because the dynamic is going to change quickly once their fathers die." He sighed. "And then there's Brandon's generation. Their kids. Bran seems to be the most ambitious of the pack. I'm hoping his example encourages his cousins to step forward as well."

"I'll do what I can, Gabe."

"Rubes. Do what is necessary to cut a deal. Use resources from Barkley-Martiniere Associates if you have to give them something. Can't do BMS without Swait's approval, and I don't want to bring him into this unless we absolutely need to."

"We haven't settled European testing, marketing, and

distribution for either the RubyBot or Moondance Microbials," she pointed out. "Do you have a priority?"

"Let's see what interests them, but I'd offer the microbials first. We don't get into the issues of the RubyBot programming with them. I don't trust anyone until they swear to me. Considering that programming was what Philip wanted to get his hands on, I think we need to be cautious with it."

"Oh, I agree. No testing variants. Locked down RubyBot versions only. Artie would be the one I'd trust to test the RubyBot in these local conditions. But we do have varieties that they'll need to have a BMA-trained tech to manage. Martin locked that down hard in our distribution lines," she said.

"Sounds like a strategy. All the same, I don't envy you dealing with a batch of grumpy Martiniere men."

She shrugged. "How is that different from managing you and Bran? Besides, Donna-gran and Justine will be there. And I have Bran to be obstinate right back at them. Plus the ring. I'm not very worried about managing them—it's more the whole formality of the situation."

"You'll do fine. You did so at the Reals, and you've done it as a rodeo queen. But remember that I'll be in your ear if you need it." He glanced to the side. "Much as I'd love to keep talking to you, I'd better sign off. Be careful. I love you—and go collect more support, my Matriarch."

"I love you, too, my Martiniere," she said. It was the first time he had called her that...or her to him. Somehow it didn't seem out of place in this ancient city.

FOG WAFTED AROUND THE LIMOUSINE AS THEY DROVE OUT into the countryside, a landscape vaguely reminiscent of driving through the Willamette Valley during a rainy fall day.

They pulled up in front of a huge, ornate building that never in a thousand years she could imagine entering other than for tourism even six short months ago.

Before she got out of the vehicle Ruby tapped open the brooch's private link to Gabe.

"*I'm here,*" he said, voice tense and tight, a reflection of the icy nerves in her gut.

Stay focused, she told herself as they walked up the wet marble steps. She led the others, Brandon a step behind at her right shoulder, Donna-gran on Justine's arm behind them.

Don't give into the desire to be a looky-loo. Treat this as just like another rodeo queen run-in. Or an AgInnovator performance.

Artie waited for them at the top of the stairs.

"Okay, it's showtime," she said softly to Gabe. "Artie's at the top of the stairs."

"*Good. Tell him hello. And good luck. No talking from me except for clarifications or corrections. Or commentary I can't help saying.*"

"Thanks."

Artie stepped back and bowed deep to her. Ruby acknowledged it with a nod.

Forget every damned one of your American egalitarian notions, Donna-gran had said this morning during their strategizing after breakfast. *You are meeting with the most traditional family members today. Ruby, you are the Matriarch. Brandon, you are the Martiniere-in-waiting. You must act like you are Martinieres by right and privilege. Both of you. Right or wrong, they will measure Gabriel by the actions of his wife and his son. Do not be shy. Do not demur. Be firm. They value strength.*

She offered her left hand with the emerald. Artie bowed over it, not touching her hand with lips or his hand, then straightened.

"Matriarch, we are ready to receive you and hear your words," he said. "I am G9 and C19 protected."

"Thank you." As he took her arm to lead her into the meeting room she whispered, "Gabe says hello."

Artie acknowledged her whisper with a curt nod. He guided her into an airy, bright, *huge* room with so much gilding including the ceiling that it would make a silver-studded pink or turquoise dyed-seat show saddle look tawdry and cheap.

Holy crap.

For a moment she wasn't certain whether to ignore it all or stare gap-jawed at the gaudiness of her surroundings. Ten people sat around a *huge* table with a throne-like chair at the far end—*her* seat, of all things—and slightly smaller ones to her left and right. And three regular chairs that were empty, one on the left, two on the right.

Focus. Act like you see this stuff every day. Don't behave like green-broke Legacy would at a show, eyes popping out and staring at everything. Chin up. No need to smile but move gracefully, don't rush it. They're waiting on you. You are setting the agenda.

"Ruby Barkley, Matriarch, wife of the Martiniere," Artie announced. "Brandon Martiniere, the Martiniere-in-waiting. Donna Martiniere, dowager Matriarch. Justine Martiniere, daughter of Philip, sister of the Martiniere."

Restive mutters at Artie's phrasing. She noted who grumbled. "Thank you," she murmured as he and Brandon went to the right, Justine and Donna-gran following her.

"*Artie's going for it,*" Gabe commented.

She couldn't answer, not without making it obvious, and she didn't know how aware those here would be of the private linkages within the brooch. Artie for certain, and probably Gerard.

Brandon waited by that big throne-like chair, and helped

her push it forward slightly before sitting down on her right side.

This thing is huge. At least I'm not on some crazy pedestal.

Justine helped Donna-gran into her chair to Ruby's left before sliding into her own seat next to Donna-gran's. Ruby rested her elbows on the chair's arms and interlaced her fingers, focusing on the faces and not the many shiny detailed things around them. It was beautiful and gaudy and absolutely the most elaborately decorated place she had ever been in her life, from the paintings on the ceiling and small sculptures in the ceiling corners, to the trim on the wall. She wanted to look at it all.

No time for letting her eyes pop out.

"So," she said, enunciating carefully and clearly, Donna-gran's warning words clear in her thoughts. *Your voice will resonate in that room. It's supposed to.* "You know who I am, but with the exception of my party, plus Arthur, and Nora, I am at a disadvantage because I do not know who you are. Perhaps we should start with introductions." She gestured to the man next to Artie.

No obscenities until absolutely necessary. Keep the contractions to a minimum. Formal language, she reminded herself.

He rose and bowed as deep as Artie had. "Matriarch, I am Charles Martiniere, son of Arthur, grandson of Louis."

One of their supporters, then, or so Donna-gran had told her.

Gabe whispered clarifications and relationships as each man introduced himself.

The next two men were Durands—Pierre and Adrien. Sons of Gabe's aunt Madeline. Adrien—one of the mutterers—sneered at Ruby while Pierre eyed her thoughtfully. Gabe had no clear idea who they supported.

Lucien and Robert Martiniere. Cousins, sons of Gabe's

cousin Paul. Lucien was said to be favorable to Gabe, while Robert was firmly allied with Gerard.

Marc Legarde, son of Gabe's aunt Jeannette. He smiled roguishly at her. An ally.

The last three.

David Martiniere, son of Gerard. No clear alliance. Gerard's eldest and next in line to be the Martiniere after Gerard, should something happen to Gabe and Brandon. He had been friendly to Gabe before Gabe's exile.

Vincent Martiniere, son of Gerard. David's younger brother, and a firm ally of his father, more friendly to Joseph than Gabe. Another mutterer.

And Gerard Martiniere himself, the next surviving son of Louis and Donna after Philip. The man who stood to inherit the title and control of the Group should something happen to Philip, Gabe, and Brandon. The *real* concern of this meeting. The man she most had to sway. Even though he had no apparent interest in stepping up to become the Martiniere, his word still had influence.

Ruby inclined her head regally. "I thank you all for taking the time to meet with me." For a moment she froze. Then the words returned. "I am here today with my son to request your allegiance and support for my husband Gabriel. It is time for a change in the leadership of the Martiniere Group." She paused, studying each man carefully before continuing. "You have all acknowledged receipt of the meeting call for a formal vote of confidence on Philip's leadership, and I thank you for your prompt responses. However, it is my right as Matriarch to make the case for Gabriel's proposals in advance."

Adrien snorted and rolled his eyes. "A meeting at some-place called Moondance Ranch? Really."

"You need not attend in person," Ruby said. "All you have to do is to submit your proxy to Donna. You can also attend online. The only reason why I am here is to present Gabriel's case and, hopefully, obtain your oath to support us."

"You honestly expect us to support Gabriel?" Gerard snapped. "He testified against us all those years ago."

Brandon spoke before Ruby. "My father spoke out against the imposition of mind control programming on indentured workers without their consent. It was the right thing to do then and even more so now."

"Of course you would say that, given your connections to the Indentured Freedom Coalition," Gerard said. "Someone who nearly got caught in that trap himself through poor money management might have more than a little bit of bias, wouldn't you think?"

"If I recall correctly, Brandon acquired such debt through education and helping Gabriel with his medical expenses before Gabriel's access to family funds was restored," Lucien said.

Ruby brought her scanner out of her jacket pocket before Gerard could say any more.

"Perhaps you should *listen* to what Gabriel has to say before we speak further," she said, rubbing her thumb over the emerald in her ring and stressing the *listen* with a soft tone akin to the mildest *leave it* that she and Gabe had practiced.

Gabe chuckled. *"Bet that nailed some of them. That was stronger than you probably intended, hon."*

"Umhmm," Ruby murmured back as she set the scanner on the table in front of her, observing the reactions to her tone usage.

Oh, there was no doubt that she'd been able to trigger a low-level code in those programmed to respond. Brandon, of course, showed no reaction at all. Donna-gran smirked next to her while Justine arched a brow sardonically. Charles met Artie's eyes and nodded. Gerard, Adrien and Robert looked uneasy. David raised his brows and pursed his lips thoughtfully. Pierre remained expressionless.

But it was Vincent who glowered at her the strongest. Ruby interlaced her fingers again and inclined her head slightly, allowing the slightest hint of a smile to touch her lips.

"Let's *listen* to Gabriel now," she said, snapping her fingers to play back the recording, softening the tone even more.

Rage flitted across Vincent's face at the second tone use and she had to raise her hand to cover a snicker.

"What's that about?" Gabe asked.

She left her hand over her mouth. "Vincent. That second tone usage pissed him off."

A matching chuckle from Gabe. *"Subtle but effective."*

The recording ended.

"This is *outrageous!*" Vincent bellowed, slamming fists onto the table. "He can't really expect us to—"

"He can and he is," Ruby said calmly.

Vincent pointed a forefinger at her. "And *you!* Bold as brass, wearing those jewels, claiming that title, *using those tones.* Just who do you think you are?"

"Ruby Marie Barkley. The Matriarch. Wife of Gabriel. Mother of Brandon," she said evenly.

His face twisted with scorn and that expression was *just enough* of a push for her to take it further. She had seen that look on the faces of too many blustering men over the years who thought she was a figurehead for Charlie's decisions as ranch manager. Men who had wanted to buy the ranch. Belittled her as a single woman rancher. Bullied her.

Rub it into his face.

"That is only part of who I am," she continued before Vincent could spew more words, keeping her voice level and matter-of-fact, devoid of any influencing tones except her own building anger. "I invent award-winning nanoized agricultural biobots that provide real-time tracking of plant and soil conditions down to the individual plant level. I own and operate a ranch that produces wheat, barley, and oats for a custom market requiring specific soil and chemical restriction parameters. I sell custom-raised grass-fed beef. I've actually managed to make a little bit of money doing this, which is rare for a property the size of the Double R. I have never purchased indentured contracts, but have hired local labor fairly. I'm prototyping a model high school agricultural internship program which gives local students preparation for jobs and further education." She paused, leaning forward to glare at Vincent. "Shall I go on about *who I am?* Or are you done wasting our time with this irrelevant posturing and *bullshit?*"

The last word snapped out without her using any influence other than her horse trainer voice. That earned her a further measuring look from David while his father reddened.

"Oooh. That was good, Rubes. Keep it up."

Vincent gestured toward her scanner. "All of these things are of little concern. We treat our indentureds properly here. This issue of going over contract length is not our problem. Nor do we have problems with consent for mind training."

"Actually, it *is* a problem here as well." Brandon glanced at Ruby, visibly seeking permission to speak. She nodded. He pulled up a screen. "Here are the numbers for your division's contract end dates, and the average number of days worked over contract. I also have the percentage of overall indentured workers that are affected by these restrictions." He slung copies to Gerard, David, and Vincent.

David scrolled through Brandon's worksheets faster than his father and brother. "He does have a point," he said. "Look at those numbers. But all the same, Brandon, how are we going to pay for this? Where are we going to find new employees?"

"David—" Gerard began.

David held up a hand. "Father. I'm not wedded to the indentured programs from either a financial or a moral point of view. They've outlasted their usefulness. When you start digging into the proprietary fees that PJM charges us for body mods and mind control, we're not clearing much of a profit. And given what Brandon and his colleagues have been saying in their 'casts about the problems—oh yes, I've been following them—I'm open to reform. But I want to be certain of the financials. Let's hear them out."

"Interesting," Gabe breathed. *"Better than I expected. David leans our way. I hoped so."*

"One of the reasons for the phase-out plans is that there will be a need to set up systems to switch indentureds from—well—being owned to independence, especially long-term indentureds. The idea is that already freed indentureds will help the newly freed ones," Ruby said. "In many cases they will need assistance to overcome coercive behavioral conditioning. And short-term indentureds will still be dealing with the financial issues that propelled them into indenture."

"And all that debt they've incurred?" David asked. "What about using indenture as a discouragement for people to accumulate excess debt?"

"Has the amount of debt that people carry on average lessened in the years since worldwide indenture became popular? Has the *need* for them to carry that level of debt in order to survive changed?" Ruby asked in return. "Or are we simply returning to the days of slavery and feudalism because of the financial wrecks of the past?"

David arched a single brow at her, reminding Ruby of Justine.

These Martinieres all have strong resemblances, down to behaviors.

"Very true. And how will the Martiniere Group ceasing to use indentureds change anything?"

"Change has to start somewhere. And the Martiniere Group is large enough to exert significant leadership by example." Ruby took a deep breath. "Besides. Indenture was supposed to be a *temporary* response to the problem of reduced numbers of essential workers and a collapsed economy with mounting debt. The structures we see now are far from temporary."

"Mark my words, this half-baked proposal will end up costing us money, *girl*," Vincent said.

Ruby pointed her left index finger at him, thumb resting on the emerald without invoking it. "That's quite enough. You *will* address me properly."

Vincent jerked. "You think to force me into compliance?"

"No. But I will not accept such disrespect, either. I *am* the Matriarch. You *will* respect me."

They glared at each other.

Vincent looked away first. "We risk spiraling back into the same economic nightmare as before if we do what Gabriel demands!" he blustered.

"And we're facing a similar crash now if we don't change our path!" David snapped before Ruby could say more. "Some of the tax proposals being floated will have a greater impact upon us if we hang on to our indentured contracts. Every single one focuses on a higher tax rate based on the numbers of indentured contracts we hold, to make up for the taxes that indentureds *don't* pay. Our esteemed cousin Brandon has definitely sparked up more than a little bit of controversy with his 'casts about indentured issues."

"Only if this mess continues to bubble in the US. It won't affect us."

"The taxation will."

"That's bold," Gabe whispered. *"David was never like that when we were kids. Vincent was a bully, even though he's the younger brother."*

"Um-hmm," Ruby muttered, her focus on the brothers as they glared at each other. She'd missed one exchange.

"You're a fool, David!" Vincent erupted. "You know as well as I that we can't just walk away from the research commitments we've made to Philip!" He gestured toward Donna-gran. "And look at Grandmother! Tell me that this is the same woman who could barely walk just months ago. Now she's waltzing in on Justine's arm. How does that happen, Grandmother?"

"You *will* speak respectfully to her!" Ruby snapped. "This is quite *enough.*"

Donna-gran waved it off. "That is all right, Ruby. Vincent. As you know, my conditions come and go."

"At nearly one hundred? Medical conditions don't make your face smoother. And regaining your ability to walk at your age is quite remarkable." Vincent managed to make that last comment into a sneer.

"A simple beauty treatment, nothing more." Donna-gran waved her hand again, as if dismissing an annoying fly. "But one that requires some time and recovery, along with good physical therapy. And the use of a wheelchair has been more of a convenience than absolute need."

"And we are drifting off the topic," Ruby said, hoping to steer talk away from the serum. *How much does Vincent know?* "Vincent. Tell me more about this agreement with Philip."

"I'm not telling you a damned thing!" Vincent snapped.

"It doesn't work that way, Vincent," Brandon said. He leaned forward, snapping up another screen. "Ah. Here it is. Vincent, your division is the one that apparently has a number of research agreements with PJM. Shall we go through them one at a time to see how each one would be impacted by phasing out indentureds, as opposed to risking higher taxation tied to indentured contracts held by each division? Or, for the sake of time, can we simply talk about the overall situation?"

Vincent scowled briefly at David before turning his focus to Brandon. "You have access to those files. How?"

"Is it my problem if such records are easily accessible to the public?"

"Not all of those records are public. There's proprietary material in there as well."

"Including Philip's plans for his indentured grandson," Brandon said. He shifted his gaze to Gerard. "Tell me, uncle. You hold family so dear. You know of the agreement that Saul and Philip had which resulted in the births of Joseph and my father. How do you feel about Philip knowingly encouraging his grandson's contract holders to use me as a body-modded fighter cyborg prototype?"

"That couldn't happen," Gerard said, his face paling.

Brandon didn't look away from Gerard. "Vincent. Experimental Contract number XBR2431. Describe the contract subject."

"XBR2431," Vincent repeated, snapping open his screen. "Indentured subject. Mixed race, one-quarter Hispanic male. Twenty-five years old upon contract execution by Agricultural Innovators, Inc, February 2059. Skills: video production and promotion. Significant martial arts training. Organization. Producer of...." His voice trailed off and he coughed before he continued, eyes widening. "Producer of the Superhero segment of AgInnovator 2059. Direct report to Georgy Batineau."

"That's enough," Brandon said. "And if you look up the staff of AgInnovator 2059, who best fits that description?"

Vincent's voice slowed even more. "Brandon Ramirez."

"*Ramirez.* The surname that Gabriel Martiniere took when

he went into witness protection," Brandon said. "Brandon Ramirez. Son of Gabe Ramirez. It wasn't my father's smartest move to insist on using his mother's family name as a pseudonym while keeping his first name, but I suspect at that time of his life he didn't give a damn, and later things just became too complicated. And what was the subject of the research to be conducted on contract XBR2431?"

"Kid knows me too well," Gabe muttered.

"XBR2431 to be transferred to GDV Associates research center. Objective: cyborg military prototype conversion."

The words echoed in the room as Vincent's voice faltered and the others exchanged uneasy looks.

"Don't tell me that Philip didn't know," Brandon said finally, voice low but hard. "Don't tell me it wouldn't happen. Or that you weren't aware. Vincent, whose initials are at the bottom of that proposed transfer contract from PJM to GDV Associates?"

"A full signature. Gerard Martiniere."

Silence. Then, from Gerard, his face pale and tight with fear? Anger? Both? "That's not my signature. My secretary generally signs referral contracts." He stammered further before finally speaking clearly. "I—I—I—never saw that contract. I should have because it was research. I—I—I will investigate because no. It should not have happened. I was aware of who Brandon Ramirez truly was. I would not have approved it if I had seen it. That is my mistake, and Brandon, I was wrong to be so casual in my process. My deepest regrets. I would have objected quite strongly if I had known."

"Fuucck," came from Gabe. *"Gerard screwed up."*

"There have been other family members considered to be troublesome who have simply disappeared over the past fifteen years," Justine said. "None of Brandon's status. Many of them are female. And then we get into the numbers of political activists who have just—vanished. Perhaps a debt hearing. Or imprisonment on trumped up charges which transform into indentured contracts. The indentured system is as corrupt as the system it was created to replace. It needs to end. Now."

"I have no problems with ending indenture and was leaning that way even before this meeting," David said. "And termination clauses are not an issue in our research contracts with Philip. Vincent, I ensured that we had a release clause in the boilerplate of these contracts. All the same, we need something to replace that income."

"There are possibilities," Ruby said. "Especially if you're willing to reemphasize food production."

"Oh?" David leaned back in his chair. "Originally our collaborative research programs were agricultural in intent."

"There have been problems with the technology that Philip's been willing—or able—to export," Artie said. "Durability and duration."

"The gray suits to improve harvest performance, I suppose," Ruby sighed.

Lucien shrugged. "The suit research did fit with both the beauty and body modification subsidiaries. To some degree. It's not perfect and we've been drifting more toward collaborating with Piotr's security work. *Which*," he stressed, "has been completely different from the contracts that Gerard's subsidiaries have been signing. I didn't know about this military cyborg production project. I would not have approved it."

"But you'd accept the income from it that goes into the shared Martiniere Group coffers," Robert said.

"Haven't been given cause to think that there were any problems before this information," Lucien said. "Now I won't accept it."

"All right, let's focus," Ruby said. "If there were options

other than indentured research available, you'd take advantage of them as replacement income?"

Murmurs between the family groups except for Artie and Charles; David and his brother and father. Ruby let it go on for a few minutes.

"Now's the time to throw Moondance at 'em, Rubes. Full deal."

She grunted agreement, then cleared her throat.

"Attention." She waited until they fell silent, noticing that this time it didn't take long. *They're learning to respect me.* "Moondance Microbials has several lines which could benefit from European testing and development. A larger facility and market would be beneficial to developing those product lines further."

She watched their reactions.

"That might work for some of the research subsidiaries," Marc said.

"There's also need for marketing and distribution," she said. "These microbials need to be produced on site or close to the sites where they are used and they work best when crafted for specific microclimates. Gabriel and I have discussed providing development and cultivation packages, but we just haven't had the time, finances, and staffing to put them together correctly. We'd be happy to have European cooperation in this process."

Thoughtful looks. Some nods.

"Would we be able to sign contracts today?" Charles asked.

"We need proof that you've terminated those contracts with PJM first," Ruby said. "I am sorry, but talk is easy. We require proof that you're in with us. We are not desperate and there are other prospects we can work with for European distribution. We are just offering this potential investment opportunity to the Family first—with conditions befitting the discounts you will be getting."

"*I have Statement of Intent forms ready with names and details,*" Gabe said. "*In your files now.*"

"I will be more than willing to sign Statement of Intent forms to prove our good faith, and we do have them ready," she added. "I understand that it will take time to finish the termination process." She paused. "Would this be sufficient to earn a pledge of your support?"

"Of course," Marc said.

"Not quite," David said. "Microbials—pah. That works for many of the others. But as for our division, we're going to need something more than what's available through microbials. Moondance Microbials is controlled by the Barkley-Martiniere Associates. But BMA also controls something else. What about the RubyBot?"

"What about it?"

"Would you be interested in offering exclusive European testing, marketing, and distribution rights to us?"

"We can discuss marketing and distribution, with the same caveats regarding termination of contracts with PJM as those interested in working with the microbials must agree with. I would *love* to talk marketing and distribution," Ruby said. "Testing, no. I reserve those rights exclusively for BMA. However, we can train your technicians, plus provide technicians of our own to help modify the RubyBot programming for your microclimates."

"Really," David said, leaning back in his chair. "You are reluctant to field trial it in Europe?"

"I want to keep that development process under my control," she said. "Finished RubyBots? Yes. Technicians to assess performance and report back to us about needed changes? Only under our control. There are—some complications with further developments tested off site."

"Hmmm. And the price?"

"We'll need to negotiate that. But…if it's all in the family, I'm certain we can hammer out marketing and distribution agreements which will be of interest to you—once you no longer hold contracts with PJM."

David nodded. He gestured to Vincent and Gerard, and began talking quietly.

At last he sat up. "And the gateway to such agreements will be…."

"Pledging support to Gabriel. Severing your connections with Philip."

"How do we know that Gabriel will honor the commitments you have made?" Gerard asked. "It has been many years since I have had dealings with Gabriel, and the manner of your divorce—"

Ruby raised her brows. She touched her earrings, her necklace, the brooch, and then the ring. "I am Gabriel's wife. I wear the Martiniere emeralds. Donna has pronounced me as Matriarch. His heir—" she gestured to Brandon, "—sits with me as witness. Is that not sufficient?"

"Ruby, if I may," Donna-gran said.

"Go ahead."

"Ruby has not been raised with the control words and tones. And yet she has been able to successfully manipulate the Martiniere ring's programming to affect all of us except her son, who has not undergone conditioning," Donna-gran said. "Do you honestly think she could do this if Gabriel had not put the emeralds on her? If I had not spent time training her?"

"Mother," Gerard said. "You *are* getting older, and your judg—"

"Stop right there," Donna-gran said, pointing a finger at Gerard. "Are you this much of a fool at *your* age?"

"Well, no, but...."

"Arthur. You were part of the Martiniere Ritual after Gabriel and Ruby's wedding. Was it validly executed?"

"Unquestionably yes," Artie said. "Gerard. Ruby *is* the Matriarch, and Donna *has* conveyed the title of the Martiniere on Gabriel. I would not question the validity of their word."

Gerard sighed. "All right. To what degree can you and Gabriel protect us from Philip's wrath should we go through with this process?"

"Justine?" Ruby said. "This is your area."

"Talk to me about details. We have two weeks until the formal meeting," Justine said. "Piotr and Serg are coordinating protection and support for all who sign the Statements of Intent and pledge their support to Gabriel. The Statements of Intent are the only commitments that will be public. We cannot avoid that disclosure under current law." She paused. "Remember that my father is running for President right now and these disclosures about problems with indentureds do not serve him well. You are less at risk here in Europe than Gabriel, Ruby, or Brandon are because they can influence the election. You not so much."

"Go ahead and tell them about the meeting with Tolliver. Not a lot of details, but the bare bones—and that I suspect Philip's ties."

"The risk is real," Ruby said. "Just yesterday, the private security forces of the current President, Stephen Tolliver, tried to frame Gabriel by claiming he attempted to attack the President. Gabriel had a gun pulled on him and the women with him were briefly cuffed. We have reason to believe that Philip is connected to this incident."

Now *that* made Gerard bristle. "What evidence?"

"Command codes. And I would only know those specific ones because they originated with Philip when I was growing up."

"The private security was using Martiniere command codes," Ruby said. "Gabriel had a gun to his head and a stunner to his back. He managed to talk his way out of it, because the codes were identical to ones he knew from growing up. Philip's codes."

Gerard pressed his lips together. "All right," he said finally, his voice unsteady yet resigned. "Our fates depend on the value of your word, Matriarch. I at least will sign the Statement of Intent, and pledge my support upon the ring. Philip has gone too far."

"Congratulations, my Matriarch," Gabe said softly. *"And to our son. You did it."*

CHAPTER 10

It took several more hours to go through the process of signing the statements, discussing terms and, finally, taking the oaths of the ten men. And conversations. Intense, private conversations. Gerard and David together. Gerard and David separately. Lucien. Charles and Artie. Marc.

But nothing beyond the signing and oaths with Vincent, Adrien, Pierre, or Robert. Pierre *had* engaged Brandon in a long conversation that seemed to be friendly. And Robert had huddled with David after she and David had finished their private talk.

All ten swore, though, she thought tiredly as they reentered their vehicle.

Gabe had signed out before that final step. She would call him via regular means once they were settled in Britain for the night to update him—and check in. At least this flight wasn't as long.

Still, it seemed to take forever before Ruby was curled up in a different bed, in a country estate much different from an apartment in the heart of Paris. It was almost as quiet as home. Almost.

She yawned as she called Gabe. What time was it there?

She wasn't certain and at this point she didn't care. She just wanted to talk to him.

"Hey. In bed, hmm?" he said.

"Exhausted. That was a long meeting."

"Long but productive."

"David played a role," she said. "Gerard depends a lot on him. We had some good conversations. Nothing urgent, but I spent quite a bit of time talking to them together and separately."

"David sounds reasonable from the discussion."

"He is. But he's also worried about the financials. They have a situation of their own to handle. We may be asked to help manage it—later."

"Vincent?"

"Yes. Plus Adrien and Robert. All younger brothers, restless. Gerard really laid it out for me. Robert will probably settle down, he thinks—but Vincent and Adrien have some interests that worry him. He wants to talk to you—once Philip is no longer in charge. He desperately wants to retire and hand things over to David, and David is concerned about Gerard's health. But both feel that as long as Philip has control, Gerard needs to remain in place to counter him. The same is true for Artie and Charles."

"The responsibilities of the Martiniere," Gabe sighed. "And those stepping up to take over the subsidiaries are all of our generation. No sign of involvement from others that are Brandon's age, I suppose?"

"David mentioned a daughter, but younger than Bran."

"Well, we have their commitments," Gabe said. "I'm really surprised at all ten swearing, though. Rubes. You did fantastic."

"Don't forget Bran. His taking Vincent step by step through the data to demonstrate Philip's intent didn't hurt one bit. Gerard is really shaken about Brandon's contract, and the degree of Philip's involvement with it. Now he's worried about the security within his organization. He emphasized to me that he had standing orders for all contracts like that to be submitted to him for review—and that his assistant in charge of contract processing left him back in February, after this contract had been signed."

"That's disturbing."

"He's ordered a review of everything that's come across his desk in the past year."

"Well, good. Whatever Philip had planned for Brandon is *not* the sort of thing that Gerard would like at all," Gabe said. "Gerard can be a stubborn ass, from what I remember, but he's never been evil. And if he's completely honest about not seeing Bran's contract—he has a mess to handle. All right. One meeting down, and that should have been the toughest one. And then tomorrow night we're in Denver."

"I'm looking forward to seeing you tomorrow," she said.

He grinned. "So am I. Sleep well, my Matriarch. Don't ever doubt yourself again. Yes, Bran played a big role in today's results—but he's your son, and in part your accomplishment...." A chime sounded. "What the—Rubes, I've got to take this call. Emergency frequency. I'll be right back." His image went stationary, the last position he'd been in before he pressed the hold button.

"Okay," she murmured, half-wondering what the call was, but uncertain what the nature of it could be.

"Rubes. Shit. We've got trouble." Gabe's face was tight and angry as he reappeared. "Hopefully not too bad but it's definitely a complication."

"What?" She struggled to regain alertness.

"Swait is under attack by a group of indentured."

"I'll wake Bran."

"No," Gabe said firmly. "It's under control. It's a fight

between indentureds, and Pat is already there broadcasting, running a feed to Kris at Moondance. Colin was the one who called. He had been training a troop of Freed Indentureds on site to help protect Swait's operations, in light of everything that Jeff's doing to free indentureds. His forces have body mods that haven't been inactivated yet. The attackers are modified Loyals. Supposedly the Loyals are acting on their own, led by someone calling himself Alexander Meyers, who is cyborged."

"Alexander Meyers. Now that's an interesting name. What do we know about him?" Now she was fully awake, nerves tingling.

Meyers. Connected to Mariah? Why would she have a tie to any indentured? Wait. After all, she did "help" Brandon. Sort of.

"He claims to be the child of me and Mariah," Gabe spat out. "But he's twenty-six years old, Rubes."

"No fucking way, then."

No way around it—Meyers either was lying or had been lied to. Ruby could account for just about every single move Gabe made during that era. When Meyers would have been conceived twenty-seven years ago, she and Gabe were traveling together on the Northwest regional rodeo circuit. Their competition had been cut short by Gramps's collapse in the middle of harvest. Gabe had come back to the ranch with Ruby and they had worked their butts off for the rest of the year, marrying the next summer. Then it had been a flurry of working the ranch, caring for Gramps, having Brandon, and gearing up for the first AgInnovator Superstar competition—when they still weren't slipping out to rodeos. But together, always together.

All the same, her gut tightened. It wasn't that long ago when her first reaction would have been anger at Gabe, not this response that the timing was wrong, no way could it have happened.

"You okay?" Gabe asked. "I'm sorry. Believe me, even when

I *was* screwing Mariah, I was careful as could be." He grimaced. "I might have been out of my head when we broke up but I was still sufficiently savvy not to risk leaving a passel of kids around for Philip to use as leverage against me. I was worried enough about Bran."

She made a face at the thought of Mariah. "I can't lie that it hit me in the gut," she said softly. "Even though I know the timing was wrong."

"I'm sorry. I really am." He ran his fingers through his hair. "He private messaged me and I told him I hadn't even *met* his mother until the Superstar—two years after he was born. He claims he has a DNA test which proves Martiniere descent, but he isn't specific as to parentage. Since he's indentured, we *can* access those records directly."

"I know Mariah was involved with Georgy before the Superstar because she had to disclose that. Philip was one of Georgy's early investors, so...either him, or maybe Joseph."

"Exactly. Still. Another issue to contend with. And easily disproven because neither of us left Thunder County during the probable conception times...given the birth date he provided me. We were buried in harvest and caring for your grandfather." Gabe shook his head. "I'm going to message Bran because there's no need to get him riled up tonight with a direct call. But I wanted you to be prepared, just in case they decide to go public with this."

"Got it. How's Jeff holding out?"

"Busy protecting his harvest and the labs." Gabe paused. "Beck's there, too. She's helping the Freed weaponize the Defenders to use against the Loyals if it comes to that."

"Damn." A twist she hadn't wanted to have happen. "I hate seeing the RubyBot being weaponized."

Exactly the sort of thing she had feared if Philip ever got his hands on modified RubyBots. Would she have approved this use if she were there? Hard to say—but she *had* given Gabe the authority to take such actions for just this sort of contingency months ago, when they formed Barkley-Martiniere Associates.

"I know. Beck came to me with a proposal right after you signed off from the meeting, and, well—they need it." Gabe's voice was grim. "I'm hoping to know more details in a few hours. They don't need me buzzing in with advice unless they ask for it."

Ruby sighed. "Well, if there's anyone we can trust with this, it's Beck." While Beck O'Toole was partnered romantically and professionally with Rick Keysing of AgSystems and they grew the best damn biobot stem seeds, she also had a history of political action and programming from before her indenture in Ireland. Beck had never shared details, but Ruby suspected her political past had something to do with how Beck had ended up in indenture.

Nonetheless, Beck wouldn't overstep certain boundaries in weaponizing. Not like Philip would do, and had done.

"I wouldn't have let anyone else manage weaponization of the RubyBot," Gabe said.

"Thank you." She stretched. "And now I'm wide awake again."

"I'm sorry."

"It can't be helped. And I did bring some books along. Guess now's the time to read them."

"What do you have?"

"I grabbed some Doig and Stegner from that box of your books I found in the attic."

She had wandered into the attic before packing for this trip, spurred by a faint memory of spying a box marked GABE BOOKS last winter while she was unearthing her old rodeo outfits for the Superhero competition. The box was still there, and she dragged it down to the living room, picking out a few to read as a welcome change from Gramps' old collection. Gabe had also pounced on it, exclaiming as he pored over old favorites.

"Want me to bring you more?"

She shook her head. "I have three books. I don't think I'll run out before I'm back home."

"All right." He smiled. "Now. I need to monitor this situation with Swait. You get some rest, and I'll see you tomorrow night."

"Tomorrow night," she agreed.

She climbed out of bed and pawed through her bag, finally extracting one of the Doig books. Ruby settled in to read about the denizens of Scotch Heaven, familiar and yet sufficiently different from the Ryders of Thunder County that it wasn't uncomfortably close to her experience.

―――――――

THE BRITISH BRANCH OF THE MARTINIERES *WAS* EASIER TO deal with. For one, there were fewer attendees, and women amongst the men. For another, Brandon's generation had a presence. Cousin Ken was there with his son Thomas and daughter Beth. Thomas's son Boris and Beth's daughter Karina accompanied them. Donna-gran's grandson Christopher brought his own son and daughter, Ben and Alice. It didn't take much persuasion for Thomas and Christopher to agree to the terms. But the British branch had few ties to Philip and no little resentment for the degree to which Philip and his supporters dominated the Martiniere Group.

"A marked difference," she muttered to Gabe during the signings, before the swearing. "Not just the women, but women of Brandon's generation. And they're in leadership positions."

"*Good.*"

After the signings, she was drawn off into discussions with Alice about the possibilities of coming to the Double R to do collaborative RubyBot research next spring.

And yet, by the time they clambered back into the plane to fly to Denver, she was as exhausted as she had been after meeting with the French relatives. While there were fewer issues with Philip's infiltration of their divisions, there was a strong sentiment that the British branch of the family had been passed over by Martiniere leadership in favor of other family branches for several generations. Christopher wanted to take the Group public—that and the death of his sister Kendra had driven his rebellion against Philip.

How had he survived? Justine had murmured something about *protecting Chris.*

Nonetheless, the British Martinieres were eager to collaborate.

Lots of potential for development.

But those potential projects required a meeting with Jeff Swait to make them happen and, well, now was not the time. One of the other RubyBot spinoffs they had collaborated on was the Pollinator. It was struggling in comparison to the Defender—and both Alice and Ben were interested in its prospects, as well as the possible usages of the RubyBot for forest reclamation.

Not a purpose she had envisioned—but after briefly looking at what Alice was already doing, Ruby was fascinated about the collaboration possibilities.

But that can wait.

Still, it was something positive to anticipate once Gabe was firmly in charge of the Martiniere Group. Ruby was already thinking about what more could be done with the research resources of the Group.

"Zack Worthing wasn't there," Justine said as they took off. A cousin that Ruby had met once, briefly.

Donna-gran shrugged. "His mother is not doing well. Let's not write him off yet. After all, we still have the Canadian meeting, and he flits between Canada and Britain."

"And we should have a sufficient majority already," Ruby said.

"If everyone remains true in the vote," Justine said. "I don't trust Daddy-fucking-dearest. His surrogates are likely to be following along behind us with threats and offers. Not all of these oaths are going to stand up to Daddy-poo's blandishments. Especially those of Vincent and Adrien."

"Agreed. There's enough flux that we could still end up on the wrong side of things," Ruby said. *And then there's the bit about Alexander Meyers.* She yawned. "And there's not a lot we can do about it other than locking down every vote we can find. But for now, I'm looking forward to some quiet working time." They would get into Denver around eight pm. She needed to stave off sleep as best as she could until then.

"Such as it will be," Justine said. She snapped up her screens.

Brandon already had his headphones on, screening the 'casts sent out by Kris and murmuring to her.

Ruby turned to the files she had accumulated over the past two days. David, Charles, Lucien, and Marc had all sent her proposals to review. And then there were Beth, Alice, and Ben's ideas.

When she found herself rereading paragraphs that she normally would understand on the first reading, Ruby gave up fighting the drowsiness, closed her comp, and allowed herself a brief nap.

GABE AND KRIS WAITED FOR THEM IN THE PRIVATE hangar at the small airport they came into instead of the main Denver facility. Even though they hadn't been apart that long, Ruby's heart leapt when she saw him, that slow smile spreading over his face still giving her that same old thrill.

"Things are under control at Swait's," Gabe said right away, after they had all disembarked and while security loaded their baggage into the fleet of waiting SUVs.

"How much damage?" she asked.

"Two fields contaminated—still getting the details on that. Fortunately he'd completed the harvest, but...." His voice trailed off. "The Governor ended up ordering out the National Guard to stop the fighting. Meyers is raising a fuss, claiming he was only following contract orders to recover improperly held technology."

"That body is no longer on site," Brandon protested, raising his head from kissing Kris. "That's a bullshit excuse."

Gabe chuckled. "Considering that it was in the hands of the state police to begin with...yes, that has become a bit awkward for him. About half the Loyal Indentureds are still in custody, plus one or two of the Freed that are a little hot. Pat and Colin thought it might simmer them down a little bit and— they're questionable in their reliability."

"We know there's infiltrators," Kris said. "I've been doing my best to screen out troublemakers but there's always a few."

"To be expected," Gabe continued. "Meyers has made bail —set pretty high, so I'm thinking either Philip or Mariah put up the funds. More on him later. Pat and Colin pulled back the Freeds when they got the heads up that the Guard was coming, and started sending folks away. Jeff vouched for the Freeds with the Guard, but still...it took most of the day for Kris and me to settle individual cases."

"What about Meyers?" Ruby asked.

"I pulled files," Kris said. "Running a second check for validity, but his claim that Gabe's his father? No. Not a DNA match. Joseph, however...he's Joseph's son."

"That's good news." She smiled at Gabe. "Might be disappointing for him."

"It's something," Gabe said. "I'm glad we have tomorrow before the New Dems. I'm gonna need it. And we'll still have issues. Let's talk about things midday tomorrow. I think we all need some rest, barring another urgent event. Tomorrow night will require all of us to be on alert."

And with that Gabe guided Ruby toward one of the waiting SUVs.

"We have our own place for the next two nights," he said as they settled into their seats while one of their guards drove. "I pulled rank and demanded it. I want you all to myself tonight and for as much of tomorrow as we can possibly get away with. Everyone else is going to the condo across the hallway."

"That sounds wonderful, Gabe." She snuggled into him, grateful that this back seat was a bench instead of bucket seats. For once it was just *them*, not the whole mad mess of Martinieres on the road. *Alone.* Until now she hadn't realized how nice it would be to have Gabe to herself.

If you don't count the shadows of Deidra and Janet. Without them, we wouldn't be able to do this.

His arm tightened around her. "I figured you might be pretty darn tired by now, with two days of meetings and in Europe to boot, with jet lag."

"I'm not sure I really know what time I'm at," she confessed.

"That's okay."

"Mmm." Her eyelids drooped.

It seemed just seconds before Gabe was shaking her awake. "C'mon, sleepyhead. Unfortunately we've got paparazzi."

She rolled her eyes. "Of course. When I'm tired and might end up staggering like a drunk. Just perfect." Ruby sat up and checked her hair. The bun she'd pinned it into all those ages ago back in Britain was still holding, though enough of it had fallen down around her face to appear ragged. She started to try and pat it back in place.

"Don't," Gabe said. He unfastened her seat belt for her, and eased her toward the door. Before she could step out he swept her up into his arms.

"Huh? What? Gabe!"

"Shh," he whispered into her ear. "I'm making a studly appearance here. Let's give them a show."

"Really? Come on, Gabe, don't overdo it."

"Not planning to. Just gonna carry you to the elevator. Feeling a lot stronger thanks to the serum. Now gimme a kiss and then a big smirk. We *can* have fun with this Martiniere stuff, you know. Give 'em a show."

"Oh Gabe." But she obliged, putting her arms around his neck and kissing him hard, then giggling at his leering smirk as he carried her past the gathered media, cams circling and darting around them—though none came closer than six feet. And while her primary focus was on Gabe, out of the corner of her eye she noticed that their security kept close watch on each cam.

At last they were inside and in the elevator. Gabe eased her down. She yawned again, a big one this time.

"Poor Rubes. All done in," he murmured. "But damn, lady. I'd say you more than proved yourself a capable Matriarch."

"Hope so," she said as the elevator opened.

It still took a bit of unpacking and settling in before their security moved to their stations and they were gloriously, finally, alone. By this point Ruby could barely keep her eyes open. But as she snuggled into bed, Gabe was *there*.

It was surprising how quickly his presence had become a comfort again.

And later, when they both woke in the early morning, their lovemaking, though less vigorous than when they were young, nonetheless was no less passionate.

CHAPTER 11

THIS WAS RUBY'S SECOND POLITICAL BANQUET WITHIN A couple of months, but the differences between the Real Truthers and the New Dems banquets were like night and day. And that was even before they got into the dissimilarities between their political platforms. Last time she had been nervous and alone except for Justine, marching out on a red carpet wearing the first public appearance of the Martiniere emeralds in over forty-five years—in itself a news event, since the emeralds had been rumored as lost for all that time.

Now she was part of a power couple—which in itself alternately made her want to laugh incredulously or puke with anxiety. Her? Part of the high-flying moneyed elite? She had sold horses to people like the current version of herself, not been one of them.

How things had changed since she had gone to that AgI Superhero finalist recording just about exactly nine months ago. Then she had been resistant to Brandon's encouragement that she consider reuniting with Gabe, not knowing that their son battled against being forced into indenture. That Brandon had gambled his future on the prospect of their reunion. Winning the Superhero then had only meant that she would be able to proceed to the final licensing and release of the Ruby-Bot, and have easier financial times for the ranch. Now—well, financials were not a problem, thanks to the Martiniere connection. Brandon was safe, Gabe was back in her life, and the RubyBot was launched.

Another difference between the New Dems and the Reals banquets was that instead of the tension beforehand, there had been a lively private pre-event family meal so that they didn't need to risk the possibility of mind control drugs in the food during the event.

Just because the New Dems are friendly to our cause is no reason to be complaisant, Gabe had said during dinner, with the full agreement of the others. *And after my encounter with Tolliver, I'm not inclined to make assumptions about anyone's good intentions, no matter what political label they bear. Everyone here should be operating under the anticipation that they are targets until after the family meeting on the 15th, at the earliest. That's my order to all of you, as the Martiniere.*

Gabe carried a flask of whisky in a jacket pocket and Ruby had a water bottle in her purse so they could control liquid consumption. Precautions she hadn't considered before becoming a Martiniere. Now she understood why Gabe had been so odd about his public eating and drinking habits when they first met. He had been raised amongst people who had no qualms about adulterating food and drink in order to control others—and her persuading him to drop those habits had ended up hurting them.

His hand tightened on hers as they stepped up to the red carpet for their turn in the spotlight, a column of Martinieres behind them. And that was new, having a family to brag about instead of shrink from because all the good ones had died. Brandon and Kris followed her and Gabe, then Donna-gran and Serg, Justine and Donald. And one of the British cousins,

Zack Worthing, had turned up with his son Sam, and brought up their tail.

"Gabriel Martiniere, GMR Group, Barkley-Martiniere Associates, Barkley-Martiniere-Swait Associates. AgSuperhero winner. Ruby Barkley, Barkley-Martiniere Associates, Barkley-Martiniere-Swait Associates, GMR Group. AgSuperhero winner. Miss Rodeo Oregon, third runnerup Miss Rodeo America," the announcer proclaimed as they walked down the red carpet.

"They're all looking at you, not at me," Gabe said in a stage whisper.

"They're looking at *both* of us."

Gabe had finally ditched the gray suits that had made her crazy because they washed out his skin tones—and now, in formal black tie tuxedo with the serum adding a level of energy and vitality she hadn't seen for twenty-one some years, he looked pretty darn good, if she dared say so. Ruby didn't see that much difference in her appearance, but the two days apart showed her the subtle but real changes in Gabe as the serum completed its work—mostly in his strength and the return of the catlike grace of old that Brandon also possessed.

Thank you, Deidra and Janet.

She was able to secure her old silver lucky locket underneath this dress instead of pinning the locket up in her hair, as she had been doing when wearing the Martiniere emeralds with the dress that had belonged to Gabe's mother. It had a high neckline so she could wear both necklaces without worry. Tonight she had gone for a slight curl, but otherwise left her hair down and flowing, like she had worn it for the AgI Superhero.

Except, of course, she wasn't wearing one of her show hats. Her head felt naked. She needed to figure out something else to wear on her head, some sort of fascinator or dress hat.

They had to go through a security check before entering the main reception area. Gabe's flask was allowed after a quick sniff, but the masking on the weapons they both carried held true.

Not going unarmed around Tolliver again, Gabe had also said. *Even in a public venue.*

"Gabe!" She recognized the man hailing them from pictures. Warren Davis, bane of many a Real Truthers social media campaign, financier of social reform and owner of a major media and real estate conglomerate. He claimed to have never owned an indentured contract, and had been an early advocate for indentured reform.

"Warren." They shook hands.

Warren turned to Ruby. "And I am thrilled to finally meet the famous Ruby Barkley. My trainer bought one of your horses a few years back."

"I remember. I still have her daughter and granddaughter."

Smokey was Casey's dam, and Ruby had hated to sell her. Still, she needed money that year, and Smokey's potential in cutting horse competition required more financing than Ruby could afford. The sale to Warren had been her biggest one ever. And Smokey had earned a cutting horse title, which was more than Ruby could have done with her.

"Good horse. I ride Smokey when I visit my ranch. The old lady still has a spark to her."

"As did her dam, up to her death." Sunshine had died in the winter pasture, just before the move to summer grazing this year. From all appearances Ruby suspected it was simply from old age, possibly a heart attack. Sunshine had been ancient for a horse at thirty-five. But it didn't ease the regrets when she saw only one palomino mare in the herd these days.

"Sorry to hear it." Warren paused. "There's some buzz about that indentured free-for-all on Jeff Swait's place, especially since Pat Markey was involved. Since you two are partners with him and have all those connections to Pat—what's the story?"

"Brandon's preparing a 'cast," Ruby said. "He's waiting until after tonight to release it. Long story short, it was an attempt to follow up on a threat."

"Let me guess. Philip Martiniere was the person making those threats?"

Gabe snorted. "Doesn't take rocket science to figure that one out."

"Of course not. He has been rather silent on that whole topic since then, which is interesting, given the Reals platform."

"Interesting, isn't it?" Gabe said. "Nonetheless, we're saving the dirt for Brandon's 'cast."

"Huh," Warren said, looking past them. "Now there's something else interesting. Over there with Mariah and Georgy. Isn't that the kid who was claiming to be the head of the Loyal Indentureds? The one who wouldn't shut up but kept making a bigger mess for himself? Who claims you're his dad?"

"He's *not* my kid," Gabe said. "And your people should have squelched that notion as soon as we sent notices."

"My people confirmed—sent out retractions and your official disclaimers an hour ago." Warren grinned at Gabe. "I got notices from you and Brandon. Can't overlook that."

Ruby turned to see this kid for herself. Mariah Meyers and Georgy Batineau stood near the reception area's doorway, bodies stiff, not touching, lacking their usual casual intimacy.

Has Georgy tired of sharing her with Philip?

She didn't think that was likely, despite Georgy's claim in a recent meeting with her and Gabe that Mariah sought to betray him. He had shown himself as far too willing to let bygones be bygones in the past for that to be an issue. Or was the tension between them due to this latest complication?

If so, that kid's a complication for a lot of people, not just Georgy.

She shivered as she studied the young man with Mariah and Georgy, his face half-covered with silvery metallic plaskin. Something about him set her on edge. Was it the icy blue eyes and Mariah's pale blond hair mixed with Martiniere features?

Where had he been all this time? Who had been hiding him?

Wait. She had seen Alexander with Mariah at the Super-hero finalist announcements. And he had been serving as a bodyguard the first time she'd met Philip. Only then he hadn't had the silvery plaskin over half his face.

"That's him all right," Gabe muttered. "Alexander Meyers in the flesh, so to speak. Pat's still trying to figure out how much of his cyborg is real and how much is fake. She says his behavior is too independent to be a genuine cyborg."

Warren said something but Ruby was still focused on Meyers. He had Joseph's stocky build but not the sinuous grace of Brandon or Gabe—or Justine for that matter.

Justine drifted by. "So that's my alleged nephew," she muttered. "Has Joey's look about him. Mariah does not appear at all happy. Some nerve of them bringing him here. Especially after just bailing him out after that mess at Swait's."

"Probably hope he'll rattle Pat. Or Gabe."

"That's possible."

Meyers looked toward them, and said something to Mariah and Georgy. Then he headed for them, just as Brandon and Kris joined their group.

Meyers stopped in front of Gabe and nodded his head in the barest semblance of a bow. "It's nice to finally meet you, *father.*"

Brandon stiffened. Kris elbowed him before he could speak.

"I'm not your father," Gabe said icily.

"DNA check on your indenture intake samples matches my *other* brother, Joseph, not Gabriel, you insolent pup," Justine said. "Sorry about that. You're only the Martiniere's cousin, not his eldest son." Her eyes flicked to Brandon. "Nice try, but Brandon's still the heir."

"Ah. Aunt Justine," Meyers said, with a venomous note in his voice that Ruby recognized from dealing with Mariah. "And so I meet you as well. *Our* relationship doesn't change at all, no matter who my father really is."

Justine shrugged. "Biology does not drive who I choose to have relationships with, pup. I'll thank you not to call me aunt."

Meyers winced at that comment. "I'm heartbroken," he said sarcastically. His voice sharpened. "Or do you find my indentured status offensive?"

"Say rather that I find your choice to march in lockstep with Daddy-damned-dearest to be offensive," Justine said, her voice low. "If you even have a choice in the matter. That potential lack of choice is the one thing I *might* grant you. And then again, there's the matter of your mother."

"And what's wrong with my mother?"

He's trying to pick a fight and he'll get it if he keeps poking at Justine. Need to shut this down if I can. Not the place for it.

Ruby furtively ran her thumb over the ring. "Alexander, that's quite *enough*," she said, trying a mild tone.

Meyers startled and stared at her, clearly uncomfortable. But none of the others reacted to her directed tone. Good. She was developing control. And had gained information in the process.

He's been programmed. Not surprising considering he's indentured and cyborged, but good to confirm.

Mariah swished over to join them, Georgy in tow. "Ruby.

Gabe. Justine. Warren. Are you getting acquainted with my boy?"

"It's surprising to me that you'd let him go into indenture," Ruby said.

"Alas, I had put him up for adoption and didn't know that it happened," Mariah said. "It wasn't until a few months ago that I learned about this."

That so did not ring true to Ruby. "I'm—somewhat surprised, Mariah. I would have thought that giving birth to a relative of Philip's might have been worthwhile enough to keep him around. Even if it was Joseph and not Gabe who fathered him."

Mariah scowled. "Things were complicated."

"I bet."

Huh. Was this about the time you and Philip became a thing? I wonder. Philip might not have wanted Joseph's kid underfoot. Or...

Ruby thought back to things that Mariah had said and done over the years and eyed her speculatively. It didn't make sense that Mariah would have yielded control over a potential Martiniere heir, much less acquiesced to him going into indenture. It just didn't fit who Mariah was.

"That's neither here nor there," Meyers interposed. "Cousin Brandon. I don't suppose I could persuade you to *not* produce a 'cast about the misunderstandings at Swait's, could I? I'd be willing to offer an exclusive interview on what it's really like to be cyborged. And free, while loyal to my employer."

"While the exclusivity is tempting, I don't play that kind of tradeoff game," Brandon said. "Especially after a criminal act like what happened at Swait's. And the threats to his family and employees that forced him to evacuate his people."

Meyers's eyes darted to Kris. "Ah, but aren't you concerned about how it looks to have Pat Markey involved in that riot?

Might impact your credibility should you release that 'cast. Especially since you're sleeping with her sister and enabled her contract evasion."

Kris bristled but Brandon beat her to it. "Pat was invited by Jeff. She was there with permission, Meyers. Considering that Swait had been threatened thanks to that cyborg intruding on his property, I'd say she's in the clear." He paused, his voice sharpening as he continued, fists clenching. "As for the rest of it, want to take it outside once this is over? I beat the crap out of your father. I can take care of you, cyborged or not."

God, no, Brandon.

"I'd be happy to," Meyers growled.

Gabe's hand tightened on her left one, covering the emerald before she could use a tone to make Meyers back down.

"Brandon, Alexander. That is *not* a good idea for either of you. Neither of you will benefit from the publicity. It's not happening, *period.*"

Mariah tapped on Meyers's forearm and jerked her head toward another cluster. "Alexander. We need to move on." She wrapped her hand around her son's forearm as he continued to glare at Brandon, his fists clenching, shoulders pulled back and chest thrust forward. He resisted her gentle tugs.

Brandon glanced at Gabe. "Is that an order?"

"As the Martiniere. To *both* of you," Gabe growled.

"Alexander," Mariah repeated, voice becoming shrill. "This is *not* the time or the place."

"Much as I would enjoy conversing further with family, my mother requires my attention elsewhere," Meyers said, the supercilious tone returning to his voice. "Brandon, you may want to rethink your position about that 'cast."

"Unlikely," Brandon said. "And oh. Warren, you did leak

the information I passed on about Alexander's *true* parentage to offset his claims, correct?"

Warren grinned. "As I told your father—retractions and corrections have been issued—just an hour ago. Complete with the substitution of Joseph Martiniere as father of Alexander Meyers, confirmed by DNA records."

Meyers's lips tightened and he started to turn away, just as Pat drifted over to them.

"Ah. Good to see you someplace other than a muddy field, XJM2045. Enjoying the real life?" She smiled at Meyers.

Meyers tensed. "Still showing off, XPM2142?"

Pat laughed. "I'm Freed, XJM2045. I don't need to use my slave identification any more. I'm not the one at Philip Martiniere's beck and call."

"Alexander," Mariah said curtly. "We need to move on."

Meyers shook his index finger at Pat. "This isn't over, XPM2142."

"No," Pat said, smiling. "It's not over. But you're also not on the winning side—again. Enjoy the speeches." As Meyers, Mariah, and Georgy moved away, Pat turned to face them, shaking her head. "He thought he could rattle me with my old ID. But after he tried it at Swait's, I made sure I knew his ID so I could throw it back at him. Still not convinced that his cyborging is real. His emotions are too intense for that to be the case."

"It's supposed to be real," Kris said. "The records show it was done."

"But the face part?" Pat shook her head. "Unnecessary. Garish. And it goes against every piece of preparatory training I went through with regard to cyborging. We were supposed to be unnoticeable. That metallic facial plaskin over his implants is anything but." She turned to Gabe. "Since we're among the speakers, I'd be honored if you and Ruby sat next to me."

"I suppose," Gabe said, making a face.

Warren laughed at him. "Man, do you know how many of us would *kill* to be at that head table tonight? Like it or not, you're a star right now, Gabe. Returned heir, challenging Philip, supporting indentured reform—you're making the rest of us corporate types look good."

"Wasn't exactly my primary intention to whitewash corporate leadership," Gabe said. "But if it turns out that way en route to fixing this problem, then I guess it happens. Pat, go ahead and show us where we need to be. We'll see the rest of you later." As they followed Pat, he continued in a low voice. "I stopped you because I didn't want to give Brandon an excuse to take a swing at Meyers because he was locked for a moment. That's the last thing we need."

"I was hoping to shut the whole thing down."

"Understood. That's what I took it as, but Bran's wound pretty damn tight right now, for good reason." He sighed. "Changing subject. Not happy about speaking. However, somebody dug up my contribution record to the New Dems over the years, and I could hardly say no, the way things are at the moment. Especially after Warren talked me into joining the exclusive donor club. All the same, I suspect Justine's fine hand in this one."

"It does make the Martinieres look good. A nice counter to Philip."

"I suppose," he grumped. His free hand slipped into his jacket pocket. He deftly unscrewed the top of the flask and took a swig. "Need to clear my throat after meeting that kid and keeping him and Brandon from fighting right then and there. Damn does he ever look like Joey, even with Mariah's coloring. Same temperament, too." He offered her the flask. "Want some?"

She took it, barely swallowed, then handed it back. "And

not a whisper that Mariah had a kid until now. Best-kept secret of the ages."

"That's my big question. Why does he appear out of the blue at this moment? Who raised him? Not Mariah. We'd have seen or heard of him. And for him to be a cyborged indentured? You're right. That part does not make sense. Unless he was raised in an indentured crèche."

"Either that or she's more evil than I imagined." Walking away from a child and leaving him in an indentured crèche? Ruby couldn't understand that at all.

"Unless—she was forced to give him up. But I don't see even Joseph being so—cold—as to let his own son be raised as a cyborg. Makes me wonder how many more there are out there like him," Gabe muttered. "And at what age Alexander was indentured. It's a good means to dispose of unwanted family members. Like Justine said in that meeting."

"If Gerard was put off by what happened to Brandon, what is he going to think of this business with Meyers?"

"Nothing good, though it works in our favor," Gabe said grimly. "But I'm wondering if Philip is planning to send Alexander as a proxy to that meeting. The timing of his appearance is suspicious, to say the least."

They settled into their seats next to Pat. Gabe eyed the empty water glasses.

"Dare we trust them?" he mused quietly. "No. I don't think I will."

Pat extracted a water bottle from her purse. "I'm set."

Ruby pulled her bottle out and placed it between them. Gabe discreetly handed her his flask. "Hold on to that until I've finished my speech. Just leave me something for after."

"Not a problem." She slid it into her lap, but not before taking a quick nip herself.

"Well hello there." A tall Black woman with close-cropped hair slid into the chair next to Ruby, her sleeveless white gown with irregular pink swatches accenting her elegant form. "Since that's Gabriel Martiniere, you must be Ruby Barkley. I'm Dorie Sterling. Pleased to meet you." She bowed. Ruby bowed in response.

Dorie Sterling. One of the early designers of independent projection screen comps, who had made her fortune in the production of the ubiquitous scanners and comms now used, and a major New Dems fundraiser.

"I'm pleased to meet you, Dorie," Ruby said. "We use a *lot* of your tech, especially in the field."

Dorie rolled her eyes. "I'm flattered. Gabe's told me a lot about your work on—the Double R, correct?"

"Yes."

"One of these days I need to visit you two. We might be able to cut a deal on tech—but even more importantly, if I can manage to throw my leg over a horse then I'd be in seventh heaven. It's been ages."

"You ride?"

"My grandpa was one of the Compton Cowboys. I rode in front of him during the Black Lives Matter protests. I did some rodeoing as a kid. Actually, I crossed paths with you two at one point. You and Gabe had made it to National Finals when I was just poking around in the 4D barrels, and were hotshots at the county rodeo. I remember you well. Palomino horse and red-headed rider. Not that common a combination. I was struggling with a butt-headed Paint gelding. You talked me through it."

Ruby startled. *She's that kid.* Oh yes, she remembered Dorie now. "Southern California circuit? Yeah, I remember you as well. That Paint was a stinker. He had you good and pissed, and yet you kept your cool. You didn't whale on him. You were just persistent—which was what he needed. I was impressed by your patience, especially as young as you were."

"Yeah, I'm real damn good at persistent. After that year, I discovered dressage. Surprise, surprise. He liked dressage better than barrels."

"I think we can work something out next spring," Ruby said, grinning. "Got some nice catty cowhorses."

"Dressage is more my gig these days. Getting old."

"Aren't we all," Ruby sighed. "But I have a good chestnut mare with dressage training that you might appreciate taking out of the arena." She grinned slightly. "Quarter Horse. Her yearling son's got some nice big movement and I'm cautiously optimistic about his dressage prospects."

"Ruby, are you trying to sell Dorie a horse?" Gabe said, leaning toward them. "Darn cowgirls." He shook his head, grinning.

"You knew Dorie had a horsey past," she said to him. "What did you expect?"

"I didn't expect the sales pitch for Dancer to be happening this fast."

"Dancer, hmm? Now I'm intrigued—and Gabriel, I'm enough of a horsewoman to expect it when talking to a breeder," Dorie said. "Ruby. Tell me more about this Dancer colt."

"Coming two in March," she said. "Chestnut. Social, already bigger than his fourteen-two hands sister. I'm expecting him to hit sixteen hands. Ranch raised, hillside pasture in summer."

"Ohhh. What's his breeding?"

She continued talking horses with Dorie as the food service began. Gabe and Dorie both waved their salad plates away so Ruby followed suit, glad she didn't have to look at it sitting in front of her. What she saw of the salads looked unappetizing anyway, nothing at all like the produce she raised every summer and the greens she nursed through the Double R's icy winters in the kitchen greenhouse window.

No more plates were offered after they waved away the first round. As the main course was served, Dorie got up.

"Wonderful conversation, Ruby, Gabe. I'll take you up on that invite this summer. But I have to manage this thing." She made her way to the podium and Ruby settled in for the speeches, slipping a quick sip of whisky.

The first speaker exhorted the attendees to contribute to the New Dems, citing not just Philip but the minor Realistic Republican candidate as threats to the future of the nation.

"Somebody needs to remind him that the Real Repubs haven't had a viable candidate since the twenties," Gabe whispered into her ear at one point. "Not since the Honest Repubs formed. God, he's awful. I hope I'm not this bad."

"You'll do fine," she whispered back. "It's a damn good thing they don't have me speaking. *Not* my strength while queening."

"Eh, it's why I'm not a politician." Gabe squeezed her hand. "But mostly I'm worried about someone in the crowd taking a potshot at me while I'm up there."

"They wouldn't dare to do it here, would they?"

"It wouldn't be the first time. Meyers getting in worries me. As cyborged as he's supposed to be, their detectors should have picked up on something and kept him out. I'm surprised we got through with our masked weapons, because Tolliver's here tonight. There's no excuse. That worries me."

"Maybe Mariah snuck him in," she said.

"I hope it's just something like that."

The blatherer sat down. Gabe squeezed her hand again. "Wish me luck. I'm next up."

"And now, I want to introduce you to somebody special," Dorie said as Gabe rose, standing with his hands behind his back. "Gabe Ramirez has been a good friend of the New Democratic Party ever since we split off as a separate party from the Classic Dems. Some years the money's been better than others, but no matter what, our local candidates have been able to depend on him for help of some sort or another. Imagine my very great surprise when during the AgI Superhero competition this past February, Gabe not only won in collaboration with his former wife Ruby Barkley, and Jeff Swait, but announced that he was actually Gabriel Martiniere, the rebel Martiniere heir who disappeared after his testimony about his family's involvement in mind control programming. Since then, Gabe has remarried Ruby. The two of them have actively been working with their son Brandon in organizing and taking a major role in the cause of indentured reform, amongst other things. It is my very great pleasure to introduce Gabriel Martiniere to you. Gabriel."

Gabe waited until Dorie sat back down before he advanced to the podium.

"Good to see you all," he said. "It's been a few years since I've been much more than a grain rancher with some side custom beef sales, so forgive me if I come off a bit rough. Especially compared to my son Brandon. He's the real pro."

Ruby snorted at that one as Brandon made a half-smirk, half-mortified face.

"Anyway. I've been a New Dem for a hella lot of years, both as Gabe Ramirez and Gabriel Martiniere. Like a lot of you, I've been unhappy with the pathways our nation has chosen since the Great Collapse of the late '20s. Instead of doing what is needed to strengthen the people of our nation, it's been all about how can we enrich the rich and empower the powerful."

He paused as applause broke out.

"That includes my own family heritage, I have to admit. I

spent years running from my Martiniere legacy. Avoiding it as best as I could. Engaging in political support and political action when I could, participating at the local level to effect change close to home. Like many of you and your friends who are watching us via 'cast."

Another pause.

"That changed for me this year. As most of you know from my son's 'casts, the problem of indenture became quite personal for my immediate family. I could no longer choose to duck my responsibilities in fighting the evil that indenture has become. To do that I had to return to the Martinieres, to my legacy. But to reform it, not conform to it."

Louder applause.

"Indenture is evil. It is the contemporary embodiment of the original sin of our country's past, seeking a new means to slither into our national soul and corrupt it once again. Almost two hundred years ago we fought a war in an attempt to eliminate this perversion. But here we are, with slavery existing all but in name, prettified by the title of indenture and the false promise of eventual freedom once your term is served to pay off your debt. Meanwhile children are born into indenture."

Loud roars.

"Indenture is evil. It must be banished forever from our soil. Now more than ever, we have a real choice to make next year. While we have an incumbent President, we have an even better challenger in Pat Markey. Pat has been in the ranks of the indentured. She can tell you the truth about what happens in those compounds. I encourage you to listen to what Pat has to say very carefully, and then think about who will be the better choice running against Philip Martiniere next year. Thank you very much."

As he sat down, Ruby leaned over and muttered, "Are you *sure* you aren't thinking about running for office? Because we need to talk about it if you are. I'm not a fan of the prospect." She handed him the flask.

"Fuck no," he whispered back, sipping, then heaving a huge sigh. "The Martiniere Group is going to be more than enough for me." And then he smirked. "But that doesn't mean you can't consider the notion."

"Fuck no," she echoed. "For the same reasons." She hesitated. "Besides, if I do anything above and beyond business, it would be adding horse showing back into my life."

"Mmm, you do have that Dancer colt."

She shook her head. "Thinking more about Legacy and reining. Dancer is—nice, but he doesn't fit into my program. If I had one beyond breeding Casey and eventually Legacy."

Gabe shrugged. "Get some more mares. Hell, find a stud and stand him. I know you've wanted to do this for years, talked about it when we were first together, once the RubyBot was launched. Now it is, and at some point we're going to step back to let Brandon take over. It's as good a time as any for you to lay the foundation to follow that dream."

"We'll see. Meanwhile...I need to slip out for a moment. Restroom."

"Don't go alone," he cautioned. "Take Kris or Tine."

"Kris is pregnant and will need any excuse. I'll ask her."

"Hurry back."

She slipped away from the head table and made her way to the table where family was sitting. "I'm headed to the ladies room and Gabe doesn't want me to go alone," she said quietly to Kris. "Want to join me?"

"Oh heck yes," Kris breathed back. "Brandon's being the same way." She leaned over to Brandon. "Your mother and I are stepping out for a minute. Be back soon."

"Be careful," Brandon said.

As they headed out of the restroom, Mariah entered.

Oh great, yet another scene, Ruby thought grumpily. Maybe if she didn't say anything Mariah wouldn't. *Not that she would pass up any occasion to be a bitch.*

"Ruby."

No such luck. Ruby turned to face Mariah, Kris stopping just past her. "What do you want?" Even as Ruby snapped out the words, she realized the expression on Mariah's face was distress, not the usual contempt she showed Ruby.

"Please tell Gabe thank you for breaking up the fight before it started," Mariah said quietly. "Things with Alexander are not —as they appear."

"Oh?" Despite herself Ruby was intrigued. Kris came closer.

Mariah glanced from side to side nervously. "Not enough time for the whole story. Under watch. Look. There's a plot. He's part of it but he's not willing. He's under compulsion. Do —what you can. Please. Stop him. He's been set up for this."

"Set up?" Ruby repeated.

Mariah nodded. "His programming. The cyborging. There's a conflict. Georgy found out and just told me. Oh God. I don't know how bad it's going to be but no matter what—just please. Stop Alexander and the other cyborgs. I'd much rather he dies while being stopped than what will happen if they succeed. Please."

"What the hell are you talking about?" Ruby stepped closer.

"I don't know for certain who has which target. There's four of them. One each for Tolliver, Markey, Brandon, and Gabe." Kris flinched next to Ruby. "I don't know which one Alexander's programmed for, but Philip—" her voice caught. "Georgy said the programming conflict if you use the ring to stop them could kill Alexander." Mariah gulped. "Stop him anyway. *Please.* He's—oh God, what you're seeing *is not him.*"

Ruby tapped the brooch into active mode. She hadn't thought they'd need it tonight, but she was now glad she had charged it. "Gabe?"

"Rubes, what's up? You're missing Pat."

"Danger. Mariah's warning us. Four cyborg assassins including Alexander. You, Pat, Brandon, and Tolliver are targets."

"Shit. Okay, I'll get word to Dorie right now."

"Are you talking to Gabe? Warning him?"

"Yes," Ruby said.

"Thank you. Thank you thank you thank you." Mariah blinked back tears. "Al *wants* to get out of it, but Philip's forced him into being a Loyal and there's no way, no way at all."

"There's always a way to get out," Kris said.

Mariah shook her head. "Not with the programming he's had. Get out there and stop them. Even if—" she sniffled. "Even if it kills him. He'd be the first to thank you if he could."

"Fuck," Gabe whispered. *"She's talking about Meyers?"*

"Yes," Ruby said to him.

"Tell her the warning's gone out. Brandon knows too. Dorie's alerting security and the Secret Service." A pause, then before she could say more. *"Tell her that he's a Martiniere. Tell her that we will protect him and her too, if we can."*

"Is your son part of the reason you helped Brandon avoid the indenture bounty hunters at AgI?" Kris asked before Ruby said anything.

Mariah nodded, lips tight, eyes brimming. "You'd best go. I'm going to be followed."

"All right." Ruby hesitated. "Listen. Whatever's going on—things are changing. Philip's not going to be in the same position. And—in spite of all you've done to us. This is from Gabe, direct, as the Martiniere. Alexander is a Martiniere. You're his mother. If you need help—you know where to turn. We will protect both of you if we can."

Mariah closed her eyes for a moment. "I appreciate the offer. But it may be too late. Just—just go. And stop whatever it is that's going on. *Please.*"

"All right. And thank you."

As they reentered the main hall two stern-faced brunettes brushed past Kris and Ruby. Kris halted, staring after them.

"What's up?" Ruby asked.

"Something's not right with those two. They move like gray suits, but...."

"Plaskin covering the gray suit?"

"Possibly." Kris shook her head. "She said she was going to be followed. I think we should go back."

"I need to be out there just in case—" A muffled shriek from the bathroom cut her off. They ran back down the hallway, Ruby mentally cursing her high heels with every step as Kris outpaced her.

She and Kris slammed the bathroom door open just as Mariah screamed again.

"Rubes? What the hell—"

"Don't, don't, go!" Mariah cried. She was on the floor, a bright red slap mark across her face. One of the women stood over her while the other turned to face them.

"This isn't any of your business," she snarled at Ruby and Kris.

"Looks to me like maybe it should be," Ruby said.

"Ruby don't they'll hurt you they're not what they look like!" Mariah screeched.

"Cyborged," Kris snapped. "We can deal with them."

The woman closest to them raised her fist. "I said, this isn't any of your business." The woman standing over Mariah turned to face them. She raised a weapon.

Mariah got her feet underneath her and rose shakily as her attacker took aim at Ruby.

Ruby rubbed the emerald. Would it work? *Cyborged.* It *had* to work.

"*Freeze,*" she said, pushing every bit of projection possible into the word as Mariah shoved her attacker.

Both women's eyes went dull. Kris grabbed Mariah. "Come on, let's get the hell out of here!"

Ruby swayed, momentarily dizzy, and Kris grabbed her too.

"*Ruby! God damn it, what the hell is going on?*"

"Cyborgs," she gasped as Kris drug them along. "Attacking Mariah. We've got her."

"*Shit! They're moving now, Dorie's not had time to get everyone in place.*"

"What the hell was that?" Mariah gasped. "Shots?"

Shots.

Ruby pulled away from Kris and kicked off her shoes so she could run better as people started screaming. She skidded inside the door. No one at the podium, head table, chaos...and four armed men marching menacingly toward the front, easily shoving aside the Secret Service and security people mobbing them.

Cyborged.

The slowest one with a lowered weapon had that white blond hair.

Alexander. Conflicted.

Ruby rubbed the emerald several times. Hopefully this would work again.

"*Freeze,*" she bellowed, *pushing* the tone as hard as she dared. Pain started to throb behind her left eye.

The men stopped. The three lead ones turned to face Ruby, aiming their weapons at her.

"*Stand down*," she tried again. It didn't stop that movement. "*STOP*." Her strongest tone.

A single shot. One's head exploded. The other three collapsed, two fully, a third struggling—Alexander.

"*Alexander!*" Mariah ran to Alexander, now on his knees, his mouth working but not making any sound, Kris right behind her. Ruby joined them as Mariah grabbed Alexander, his eyes wide and stunned, body jerking as he sprawled sideways. Kris shoved another woman away from Alexander.

"Stay clear!" Kris pointed at the Secret Service who were ready to pounce. "Indentured programming snafu! Stand back unless you know what you are doing!"

Gibberish spewed out of Alexander's mouth as he twitched, eyes even wider and fearful.

"Alexander, Alexander," Mariah groaned. Georgy knelt next to her, hovering, his movements hesitant.

"I tried to stop him, Mariah, I tried," he said to her.

Ruby jumped as Gabe's hand slid across her back. "What the hell do we have here?"

"Programming conflict," Justine said as she knelt by Alexander, opposite from Mariah. "Programming conflict made worse by conflicting commands and motives."

"Help him. Please," Mariah whimpered. "Oh God, please. If you can help him.... Gabe. Ruby. Please. I helped your son. Please."

"Do you know what code generation he is?" Justine asked Mariah.

She shook her head, even as Alexander gabbled random syllables faster, his body shaking more violently. "I don't even know what you're talking about."

"Pat used his ID. Worth a try," Gabe said. He crouched by Justine and took Alexander's chin in his hand to hold it steady.

"Alexander. XJM2045. Code release Foxtrot Alpha Charlie, 79300 Chamonix Lestrade Starfire. GMM authorize. Repeat."

"Code. Release. Foxtrot." Alexander writhed, his eyes fixed on Gabe. "Alpha Charlie." His body convulsed, then released. "79300," he gasped. "Chamonix." Another shudder. "Lestrade. Starfire. GMM...authorize." Another jerk, and then his body sagged, eyes closing.

Mariah gulped and pulled Alexander closer as Georgy tried to hold both of them.

"All right then," Gabe said, voice weary. "Let's get this mess straightened out someplace other than the middle of the banquet, shall we?"

CHAPTER 12

Ruby's head pounded painfully as Gabe argued with security and Secret Service. She swayed and buried her head in her hands, catching snippets of what he was saying.

"*He shot one of the damn assassins. He's disarmed. He's not a danger, hell, he's having seizures right now!*"

Someone's arm around around her shoulder, steadying her.

"You've overdone it," Donna-gran said.

"*Look, damn it, he's an indentured who has had Martiniere mind control misused on him. He needs medical help. Help that my people are qualified to provide.*"

"Head hurting?"

Ruby nodded. Even that caused pain.

"*No, my people are qualified to handle it. Yours aren't at all. For God's sake, let us get him the hell out of here, sooner the better.*"

"Here. Sugar and protein supplement mix. You need to carry this with you at all times. I didn't think you had advanced to the point that you needed it. Sorry."

Metal tube poked into her mouth. A milky gel squirted in.

"*Yes, God damn it, I'll fucking stand responsible for any future actions he takes. Look at him. He's not going anywhere on his own, and he's the only fucking survivor. Why don't you go deal with the damn bodies?"*

"Swallow," Donna-gran ordered.

"No, you're not fucking touching Ruby either. She's in no shape to talk now. She stopped them using Martiniere vocal controls, and it's just about done her in. My security will get you a full report in the morning, all right?"

Ruby swallowed, breathing fast and blinking as everything steadied around her. Their own security stood defensively around the huddle surrounding Alexander's now-limp body. Serg and Georgy stood next to Gabe. Mariah sobbed over Alexander while Justine and Kris studied a small screen projecting over his chest, occasionally poking at it.

"I may not like it, but he's a Family member and I'm responsible for him. Ownership? Hell, I don't know—wait, Georgy, you hold his paper? All right. His owner's here too."

"Slow down your breathing," Donna-gran said. "You're going to hyperventilate and pass out. Look at me. Breathe with me."

She focused on Donna-gran, the light-headedness gradually fading away. Brandon led more Martiniere security, carrying a stretcher, into the circle around Alexander.

"You okay now?"

Ruby nodded. Tiredness pulled at her, but at least the pain in her head had diminished to a dull ache and she was suddenly aware that she was barefoot. "I don't know where my shoes are."

"We'll worry about that later, all right? Shoes can be replaced."

Gabe and Georgy turned back to their group.

"All right," Gabe snapped. "We're clear. Let's get him out of here."

"You need to let go of him so we can get him on the stretcher," Justine said to Mariah.

"Where are you taking him?" Mariah whimpered.

"A safe place," Gabe said. "You and Georgy too. You're now part of this whole mess. Come on!"

Mariah released Alexander, rising shakily to her feet as Georgy steadied her. Brandon and Serg helped security ease Alexander on the stretcher. They followed security and the stretcher out.

Gabe joined Ruby, his arm replacing Donna-gran's around her shoulder. "Doing okay?"

"My head still hurts, not as bad as before," she said.

"That was a pretty damn powerful projection," Donna-gran said. "She needs rest. Gabriel, I'm going to push the last meeting back because Ruby won't be in any shape to go to Montreal tomorrow. How many days should I do it?"

"Hell, I don't know. We've got to untangle this mess further and it's not going to work for her to leave the country, even if it's just to Canada. Can we remote it?"

"I'll see what I can do."

Shoes pushed into her free hand.

"I picked them up," Kris said.

Ruby stopped to put them on, momentarily sending Gabe askew. He made an impatient noise, cutting it short when he saw what she was doing.

"Sorry, Rubes."

She straightened up, feeling somewhat steadier.

All the same, the trip back to the condos was a blur. They ended up in the bigger condo, picking up Dr. Chan from the lobby. She, Kris, Justine, Donna-gran, and Brandon disappeared into a room with Alexander. Mariah collapsed on the sofa, still sobbing. Georgy sat next to her, his arm wrapped around her shoulders.

Gabe steadied Ruby, guiding her to the big ottoman across from Mariah. He kissed Ruby after they sat, then withdrew his arm to rest both elbows on his thighs as he leaned toward Mariah. Serg and Donald sat on the sofa arms, both crossing their arms.

"Mariah. It's time to talk," Gabe said.

"Is—is he going to be all right?"

Gabe examined his hands. "I have no idea. I can't make any promises right now." He looked back up. "But between Dr. Chan and the family members back there with him, if anything can be done to save him then they will do it."

Mariah nodded, gulping for breath, dashing the tears from her eyes. "Thank you."

"Now. You know as well as I do that there was no way I could be Alexander's father. Who told him that?"

A fresh gulp of tears. "Gabe. It could have been. I—I agreed to it. Artificial insemination. It was the price to get me out of indenture. I was told you were the donor."

"What the fuck?" Gabe sat up and unhooked his tie, tossing it aside with a grimace. "Who the hell told you that?"

"Ph-Philip."

He leaned his elbows on his thighs again, shaking his head. "No. I've never donated sperm, never will. He lied to you, Mariah. So how the hell did you end up in that position?"

"My father," Mariah whispered. "Traded me to Philip when I was sixteen, to forgive his own debt. I was told if I bore a child for the Martinieres, I'd be free myself. Not true."

Brandon came into the living room and froze at Mariah's last sentence. Then he cautiously eased against the sofa arm next to Serg.

"But you've continued to work for Philip since then," Gabe said, voice gentle, persuasive, intimate. Jealousy washed over Ruby for a brief moment.

Did he talk to her like that when they slept together?

Then she dismissed the emotion. He'd talked to infant Branny like that, too. And he never had that coaxing note in his voice when he tried to talk her into something. She would have bristled even more at that—so he respected her more than Mariah.

Besides, he's mine now.

Mariah gulped. "I—I'm on a hidden indenture contract. It was the only way I could keep seeing Alexander. They took him from me at six months. If I was good, if I did what Philip wanted, I'd get to see him every three months after that." She sniffled and wiped her eyes. "How long I got to see Alexander depended on how good a girl I was." She choked. "I got a whole week with him for breaking up you and Ruby. It—he finally called me Mama at the end of it. He hadn't before. It was the real beginning for us."

"Augh," Gabe growled. He exchanged a horrified look with Ruby. She felt sick to her stomach, trying to imagine what she would have done in Mariah's place.

Not a hell of a lot different.

She had been willing to do a lot to save Branny. But this— she couldn't wrap her mind around it.

"Mariah, he's going to survive," Brandon said quietly. "He's stable now. Just came out to let you know." He rubbed his face. "But the cyborging—removing it will kill him. He'll need reprogramming before he'll be able to function at any decent level."

Mariah moaned.

"Justine's getting Dr. Caruthers in since this is more her specialty than it is Dr. Chan's," Brandon continued. "We don't know how much more function we can restore. Pat's going to come help once she gets done with the New Dems tonight. Some of that cyborging is—pretty damn old. Dad, it was a risk using those codes to stop the cyborging kill switch. If the programming had been newer, it wouldn't have worked, and might have sped up the kill factor. That's what killed the other two cyborgs—that Alexander didn't shoot."

"I thought he might have had the older codes as his base programming," Gabe said. "I didn't see many other options."

Mariah gulped. "They started the implants when he was twelve." She shuddered. "He was so proud of being chosen. Philip told Alexander that someday he would be worthy of being called a Martiniere. That if Alexander worked hard enough, let them cyborg the heck out of him, he might become Philip's heir. But Alexander had to prove himself worthy, not like Philip's failed son, not like his failed nephew." She choked and more tears ran down her cheeks. "By then I knew you were Philip's son. I—hoped that since Alexander was a year older than Brandon, that he—Philip always hinted it was possible for Alexander to be his heir."

Gabe tightened his lips and shook his head. "God damn it. God damn *him*. You know Philip was lying to you the whole damned time, didn't you?"

"I just—I didn't dare question. The one time I did, they hurt him. And sent me the vid."

"My father is a goddamned fucking psychopath," Gabe muttered. He exhaled and sat up. "All right. We need to think about the best way to fix things. Georgy. You hold Alexander's contract now, or so you said."

Georgy nodded. "Philip transferred it to me before I bailed Alexander out."

"Convenient timing. Leaves the two of you responsible if he managed to succeed tonight. So. As Alexander's contract owner, what does it take to free him?"

"Gabe, I'll sign the release now if you want. No favors asked. No payment."

"Do it." Gabe turned to Serg. "What's the status on the

report we need to submit to authorities—all of them —tomorrow?"

"I've been recording Mariah," Serg said. "I'll get a statement from Ruby and Kris, then write it up."

"All right." Gabe rubbed his face. "Contact Remy Trask. She can negotiate the legal details. Let's get Alexander's contract cancelled and see what we can do about potential charges. Brandon. Is there any chance that the authorities can question him soon?"

"Not likely," Brandon said. "He's stable now. But repairing his speech centers, his memory centers...that's a wait and see about the degree of damage that the programming conflict inflicted on him. We'll know more after Dr. Caruthers looks at him."

"Is that going to be here or someplace else?"

"We need a better facility than a condo bedroom, Dad." Brandon's lips went tight. "We need a secure location that's set up to do medical and cyborg work. Not in Denver. Not in LA. Not in Philip's home turf."

"Agreed. What kind of time frame are we looking at for him being able to speak for himself?"

"At least a week. Maybe two. If at all. The damage is bad. It was supposed to kill him."

"Mariah, Georgy. Do you have access to a secure location?" Gabe asked.

"Not one that Philip can't also reach," Georgy said.

Gabe winced. He lowered his head into his hands, rubbing his cheeks, then looking up. "This gets tough," he said finally. "I'm not going to force Ruby into saying yes to bringing him to the Double R. It's not fair to her. And I don't want to have to referee her and Mariah, or keep Mariah from Alexander. And Brandon...."

"Gabe," Mariah said, her voice finally steady. "Philip

always claimed I'd get his favor someday. But even though I swore loyalty to him—" her voice quavered and she slid onto her knees. "He never followed through. If you'll help Alexander, I'll do anything you and Ruby ask of me."

Gabe straightened up. "Will you swear loyalty to me as the Martiniere?"

"Yes," Mariah gulped.

He turned to Ruby. "Rubes." His brows raised, not needing to say more.

She spread her hands. "Gabe." She nodded. What else could she do?

Gabe looked at Brandon. "Brandon."

Brandon drew a deep breath. "I'm not real damned fond of the asshole from what I've seen of him so far, but given that he hasn't had a lot of say in what's been going on in his life, it isn't entirely his fault. And I think it's an awful lot to ask of Mom to have him and Mariah at the Double R, given all that's— happened." He gestured. "So. Moondance. That's where we'll take him. *After* these two swear loyalty to you."

"All right then." He took Ruby's left hand. "Rubes. I hate to ask, but can you do one last thing with that ring?"

She nodded and took a deep breath.

Then she rubbed the emerald and invoked the oath program in the ring.

THINGS GOT BLURRY AFTER GABE PROMPTED RUBY through the oath-swearing process for Georgy and Mariah. Her head started hurting again when she gave her statement to Serg, and even though Brandon produced another tube, it wasn't enough to stave off the continuing fatigue that pulled at her. At last Gabe swept her up in his arms.

"I'll be back," he told Serg and Brandon. "Ruby needs to sleep. The ring program's drained her."

He carried Ruby across the hall to their condo and helped her prepare for bed, finally tucking her in.

"You'll be okay by yourself for a little bit?" he asked. "I promise I'll be back as soon as I can."

"I'll be fine," she whispered. "You have things to do."

"I promise I won't be long," he whispered.

"Just get it straightened out, okay?"

"All right."

But once Gabe left, tired as her body was, her mind started spinning faster than ever. How old had Mariah been when Alexander was born? Eighteen?

What did she go through before then?

Ruby shuddered. She couldn't get rid of a sudden flash image of Brandon kneeling next to Alexander, *with the same silvery plaskin over his face.* No matter how she tried to switch her thoughts to something more cheerful, like golden Legacy galloping across the pasture in the sunshine, it always came back to that image of the two cousins, similar in features but not in coloring.

Similar in the fate their grandfather tried to engineer for them, she thought, shivering again.

What Alexander had become was what Philip had also wanted for Brandon.

What was Alexander programmed to be? A warrior like they'd planned for Brandon?

Ruby buried her head deeper in the pillow.

How many others like Alexander did Philip create?

And why?

SOME TIME LATER SHE ROUSED AS GABE EASED INTO BED.

"S'okay," he murmured. "Go back to sleep. Things are worked out."

She reached over and stroked his cheek. "How are you doing?"

He closed his eyes and shook his head. "Justine had Mariah spilling her guts when I went back over. We're both more than ready to kill our father, more than we already were."

"It's that bad."

He nodded wearily. She took him into her arms and he nestled his head in her chest, trembling.

"I knew the Family situation was bad. I knew it was fucking bad," he said without raising his head. "But—this. I feel guilty for running away, but when I said that, Donna-gran ripped me a new one. Said that Philip would have destroyed me if I had challenged him then. I needed the time to mature, to not be a Martiniere." He exhaled a deep, shuddering breath. "I think it took me too damn long to grow up. I should have—" he shook his head. "Enough of the should-haves. They don't change a damned thing. I have to move past them."

Ruby kissed his forehead, unable to find words.

He tilted his head back to smile up at her. "How are you doing? I shouldn't have left you alone, but I couldn't leave things hanging the way they were. You were out on your feet and needed to get to bed—I'm sorry."

"It's okay. I'm exhausted," she whispered. "But my brain wouldn't shut down for a while. I kept seeing Brandon with that silvery plaskin on his face. Over and over. Is that what they would have done to him?"

"I think so. Alexander's another prototype, according to Pat. And there may be more. Brandon's been able to download a bunch of Alexander's damaged cyborged files. There's one with specs for others like him." He paused. "I think Beck and

Martin should take a look at those files. The integration of biologic and cybernetic elements isn't as smooth as the Ruby-Bot. I think that's why Philip wanted the Ruby. That piece of programming that we did way back when. His people never figured it out, not like you and I did."

"Shit."

"Yeah." He leaned his head against her. "I am so, so tired, but like you, my brain can't stop. Brandon and Kris are taking Alexander et al to Moondance early tomorrow morning. Justine's going with them to run interference and make sure they're set up for medical equipment. Donna-gran's moved the Canadian meeting to virtual, in three days. She's going to the Double R with us."

"Can we swear oaths virtually?"

"No, but at this point it doesn't fucking matter. I called Gerard, Artie, Christopher, and Ken. Laid out what we've learned—Alexander, the attack at the New Dems, Philip's promises to Mariah...all of it. They're appalled, and they're the most senior family members. Together, they can force compliance on Philip. They will be at the meeting. He's finished, Ruby. The Reals are freaking out, and that's just from the New Dems broadcast. I expect they'll yank the nomination from Philip after dithering around once his connections to this attack become public—which will happen tomorrow."

"Did anyone get hurt?"

Gabe sighed. "Just ten. Indentured. Dead. Cyborged. Except for Alexander, who's a Martiniere Group property, they're registered to PJM, not the Group itself, thankfully. No one will officially say cause of death yet except for the one Alexander killed. The private observation Pat had was that they all stopped functioning after we hauled Alexander out of there. A suicide pill or an abort switch of some sort is my guess.

Oh Ruby, Ruby," he groaned. "The serum is bad enough. But this."

"I know," she whispered, her own heartsickness matching his. "Gabe. That's enough talking about this. Let's rest."

"I don't know if I can. And I just don't have the energy for what might be the best distraction. Even with the serum."

"Then let's talk about something else. Something different. You said something about maybe investing in a stud horse," she said softly. "But we'd need to get mares, too. Legacy and Casey aren't going to be enough, though I want to preserve that bloodline. I need to talk to Warren to see if he has any of Smokey's daughters."

"That'd be easy enough. None of Sunshine's other daughters?"

"Smokey was the best of them, and I'd sure like to get her sire's line back into the mix," Ruby said.

They continued murmuring to each other about horses and the goals of a potential breeding program, their words coming more and more slower, with longer pauses between one or the other speaking.

At some point Gabe nuzzled back into Ruby's chest and she rested her chin on his head, drowsing off.

AFTER A QUICK LOOK IN THE MIRROR THE NEXT MORNING as she pulled on her robe, Ruby concluded that she looked like hell. Her facial skin was drawn down tight over her cheekbones and dark circles made her eyes look bruised—a chronic redhead issue. Her freckles were pale. At least the damn headache had faded.

Gabe was already gone, his side of the bed cool. She pressed her lips together tightly, annoyed. He needed the rest, as well. Damn the man and his insistence on pushing through fatigue and illness.

As if you're any better about it, a wry part of her observed.

All the same, she wondered how long he had been up and how he managed to sneak out of bed without waking her.

I must have really been tired.

She was normally a light sleeper. As she approached the bedroom door, she heard voices—Donna-gran and Gabe—along with the welcome scent of real coffee. For a moment she considered dressing further. Then the desire for coffee overruled that one crumb of propriety.

I'm wearing pajamas, after all. Makes me decent.

And Donna-gran *had* been staying in the same apartments with her. It spoke to her foggy brain that she was thinking about this now. Ruby went through the door and directly into the kitchen.

Gabe and Donna-gran faced each other over the breakfast bar, both cradling cups. And, she noted, both still in robes and nightclothes.

"Hey, Rubes," Gabe said. "Hope we didn't wake you."

She shook her head, trying to remember where the coffee mugs were in this place. Gabe got up and guided her to the stool next to his.

"Sit. I'll get you coffee."

"Thanks."

Her head ached and her thoughts were fuzzy, just like they would be if she had spent the night drinking hard, much more than the couple of sips she had drunk from Gabe's flask. Gabe set her cup in front of her, then topped off his cup and Donna-gran's. After returning the carafe, he sat back down and put his arm around her. She leaned into him, eyes half-closed, sipping her coffee carefully.

"Brandon and the crew left for Moondance already," Gabe

said. "Serg wants us to head for the Double R this evening. We have a couple more things to clean up with the authorities, but that'll be later this afternoon. Remy wants us to wait until she gets here before you talk to them."

"How are we handling what I did with the ring?" She straightened up a little. It was getting hard to drink coffee at that angle and she needed to get it inside of her, not spill it on her and Gabe.

"We're telling them it's all Martiniere mind control woo-woo," Donna-gran said, wiggling her fingers and widening her eyes to mime *spooky stuff*. "Or words to that effect. They know a little bit about our programming for vocal control. Gabriel's reminded them that anything more than that is strictly Martiniere proprietary, trademarked material that also happens to be classified." She took a big gulp from her coffee cup. "I need to make sure that you two know the details of *that* arrangement," she muttered. "For the best interests of the family. There were things I planned to take to my grave if no good opposition arose to Philip."

"I don't know," Gabe said, staring into his cup. "After yesterday, I almost wonder. Donna-gran, what purpose is served by the Martiniere Group being set up like it is? Profit? Why the hell is it so damn important to my father that he retain control of this business, so much that he'd cyborg his relatives to keep it? Shit, if he never got another penny of income he'd still be living well for years. Power? Got to be that. It's certainly not about the Family dying out. There are enough of us to ensure survival—even in this damned era. And that doesn't count whatever games he's been playing with cyborging his descendants."

Donna-gran wrapped her hands around her mug. "The Martiniere Group started out as an aid society for family refugees after the Revolution."

"Which Revolution?" Gabe snorted.

"French, of course," Donna-gran said, fixing Gabe with a stern look. "The American branch of the family prospered in real estate and slave dealings, so they reached out to other family exiles to lend them a hand."

"The family income hasn't changed, especially when you look at the real nature of indentured contracts." Gabe said. "It's just been made pretty.

"No. It hasn't changed. But over the years the Group converted from a family aid society to a family-held business." Donna-gran sighed. "Gabriel, the fight between Philip and Saul—and how it brought about Louis's early death—meant that a small handful of us in the family have been keeping certain technology secure. The way the corporate structure is set up, it allows for sequestration of tech. Originally that was done to provide protection for Martiniere military work, especially since we have contracts with several different nations. But over the past few years, it's also allowed us to offshore things we didn't want Philip to get his hands on. Artie and to some extent Thomas and Lucien have been our best sequestration resources."

"I shouldn't be too eager to tear it all down, is what you're saying?" Gabe scowled into his coffee.

"You could take what I say to mean that," Donna-gran said.

Gabe sighed. "The American branch is going to need a lot of cleansing. I seriously do wonder what Philip intends with these cyborgs. I hope Brandon finds some clues in the files he downloaded from Alexander—and hopefully even more from Alexander himself."

Donna-gran scowled. "I suspect it's his attempt to figure out anti-aging and life extension. We won't know for certain until we see those files."

Gabe rubbed Ruby's shoulder. "Well, it's clear we're not

going to solve everything right now. I'm ready to fix some breakfast."

Ruby moaned and started to push herself up.

"No, you stay right there." Gabe said. "I think Donna-gran would have my head if I let you do anything other than sit. Besides, you look like hell."

Ruby snorted into her coffee cup. "That's what I thought when I looked in the mirror." She sipped and set it back down. "How much do we disclose about the ring, Donna-gran?"

"None of it."

"None of it?"

"You didn't do the stupid thing and wave your hand around like it was a magic wand," Donna-gran said. "You simply yelled. Augmented by the program in the ring, but they don't need to know that. The authorities *do* know that there are Martiniere mind control vocal codes but not the details of how they work. And that's what you'll tell them. No need to say any more."

"If you say so."

"It's what they know and expect from us," Donna-gran said. And then she winked at Ruby. "And that is part of the battle sometimes—showing the authorities exactly what they *expect* rather than what actually *is*."

CHAPTER 13

No place ever looked quite so sweet to Ruby as the airstrip at the Double R did on their plane's approach that evening, even after dark in a light fall drizzle with bright lights illuminating the runway. She drew a deep breath.

A week and a half to go until the big showdown.

Less than that, really, or was it? She counted down in her head. Gabe had called the family board meeting for the fifteenth on October 2nd. The 3rd, she'd been in Paris. The 4th, in Britain, and the 5th and 6th in Denver. Ten days left, and today was almost gone. So nearly nine days to go until the big blowout with Philip—unless something dramatic happened between now and then. Two more days until the virtual meeting with the Canadians.

And then what?

Much as Gabe wanted to hand over responsibility to Brandon soon, she wasn't sure how quickly that could happen. Not if he wanted to fix what appeared to be a structural problem with the Martiniere Group—with the whole world-wide process that had made indenture easy, possible, and popular.

But at least for a few days, perhaps she could settle back in here at home. As the jet eased down the runway, Ruby thought about the everyday, mundane ranch tasks that surely still needed to be done. Bringing the horse herd down to winter pasture. Securing and winterizing center pivot irrigation lines. Getting the apples that she'd been picking all summer out of cold storage to turn them into applesauce. Going over the grain harvest and shipments with Charlie. Checking in with Martin and Beck about the lab. And more.

Speaking of Beck....

Three figures stood silhouetted by the hangar lights as the pilot taxied toward it. One with short, stiff, white-blond hair— Beck. Another was Remy's partner Shannon, there to take her home. The third was Brandon.

"Were you expecting Bran to be here?" she asked Gabe.

"No, is he?" Gabe was on the other side of the plane so he couldn't see the hangar.

"I can see him. Beck's there too."

"Well, this could be interesting," Gabe muttered. "Though I think Beck's on shift for meeting us anyway."

Brandon didn't rush toward them but waited with Beck as they got off the plane.

I think that means something, but what?

"See you later," Remy said. "Can you manage to stay out of trouble for a few days, Ruby?"

"I'll try," she said.

"Don't try too hard," Remy said, grinning. "My lady expects a good vacation this year and I'm still short on giving her what she wants. But I *would* like a couple of peaceful days to catch my breath. Hey. Good luck with what's ahead. And you know how to get in touch." She gave Ruby a quick hug, then went to her wife.

"Hey," Gabe said to Brandon as they joined him and Beck. "Didn't expect you here."

"A quick run over, I'm catching your plane back to Moondance, hopped a ride with Serg over here." Brandon flipped a lock of dark hair out of his eyes. "First." He handed Gabe a chip. "Your copy of the files we've managed to download from Alexander's cyborg accesses. Barely been able to dig into them, but already there's a batch of useful information."

"Oh?"

"Alexander has five brothers. Not all from Mariah, of course. But other, unidentified, indentured mothers. All five are cyborged. Father is Joseph." He exhaled. "Carl. Daniel. Eric. Frederick. George."

"Alphabetical except for...."

Brandon nodded sharply. "I was intended for the B spot. It's in the file."

"Fuck. This has been a long time in the planning." Gabe ran his fingers through his hair nervously.

"It's in the files. But there's more, Dad." Brandon swallowed hard. "The current purpose of the cyborged is to protect a clone when they aren't serving as bodyguards. Philip's clone."

"Wait a minute," Ruby said. "Human cloning isn't possible yet—is it?"

"There's been problems with aging, physical, and mental defects," Beck said. "And it's been showing up in these clone efforts."

"Multiple attempts have been made," Brandon said. "One survived—Michael. He's five years old now. And yes. Sequential alphabetical clones. He is clone number thirteen."

Donna-gran frowned. "So pure reproductive cloning and not therapeutic?"

"It's—not clear," Brandon said. "Not yet. It may be reproductive for therapeutic purposes."

"That's inefficient," she said.

"Unless you're planning to harvest organs and blood," Beck

said harshly. "But we haven't figured that out from the files yet. Rick and Martin are working their butts off on reviewing them. I think we're pulling an all-nighter—I plan to join them once we're done here."

"Philip's raising clones to provide him with spare parts?" Ruby said, trying and failing to keep her voice level. God, that was horrible. Just when she thought she'd heard it all.

"We don't know that yet," Brandon said. "But we do know that there's a clone of Philip out there, protected by five cyborgs who are Joseph's sons."

Gabe shuddered and closed his eyes for a moment. "All right. I can see why you wanted to deliver this news personally."

Doing something about this is more than enough justification for using the serum. Thank you, Deidra and Janet, for giving us the strength to deal with this situation.

Brandon nodded curtly. "On the other side, there is some good news. Alexander's conscious. We were able to start reprogramming. He'll be functional in six days." He paused. "He wants to see both of you sooner than that. To swear loyalty to you."

"Legitimate or a trap to lure us in?" Gabe asked sharply.

"Given his reactions when he first woke—legitimate." Brandon sighed. "I had Pat assess him. When he first regained consciousness, he was very childlike. But even then, there was a strong revulsion toward Philip. As we started reprogramming his matrix, it became stronger. We've been cracking his old programming. One of the modules was a specific loyalty program to ensure that he wouldn't turn on Philip."

Gabe raised a brow. "That's interesting."

"Pat doesn't find it surprising," Brandon said.

Donna-gran heaved a heavy, sad sigh. "Philip, Philip, Philip. Louis and I fucked things up so badly with him." Her shoulders sagged. "He's chasing the anti-aging serum. This was one of our side excursions that we thought was possible, but couldn't do it. Just wasn't right. Gabriel, we have to do something about that child before Philip destroys him, because he *will* do that, I'm afraid."

"Agreed, Donna-gran. Bran. Thanks." Gabe roughly patted Brandon on his shoulder, and left his hand there. "Do we have any clues about the location of the clone and his guards?"

"Not yet." Tiredness echoed in Brandon's voice. "But we're trying. Alexander's trying. He knows that he has that knowledge, but his recall is partial. He's finding it pretty frustrating."

"You're okay with him being at your place?"

"We're finding that me being around is helpful for him," Brandon said. "I seem to facilitate his memory, such as it is. He appears to see me as—" his voice faltered. "As some sort of older brother. Dad, it's spooky. He just automatically seems to lock onto me."

"Most probably the cyborged conditioning," Donna-gran said. "You *are* the Martiniere-in-waiting, and you *were* slated to be the leader of his group. We'll need to look into the structures behind that dislike of Philip, but I suspect it's a factor of experiences he went through at Philip's hands. I can help you investigate that."

"It would be a help, Donna-gran." Brandon blinked, pushing back the errant lock of hair again. "Perhaps if you all came over in three-four days? I'll be back over here in two days for the Canadian meeting and can give you updates then."

"That sounds good," Gabe said. "Hey. You'd better get on the plane—pilots are getting close to the end of their work cycle. But thanks for getting this information to us. Take care of yourselves."

"I will." Brandon nodded. He hugged Gabe, then Ruby, then ran toward the jet.

"Sheesh," Gabe said, turning to Beck. "More issues. You're working on cracking that data? What kind of stats are they?"

"Everyday functioning, but there's a lot of other information in there," Beck said. "We can track the cyborging process, recreate how they did it. But it's taking time. The good news is that apparently there was no anticipation of the likelihood that someone other than a Martiniere would get their hands on one of the cyborged of Alexander's class. There's a lot of process notations that wouldn't be there otherwise. These cyborged indentured, to all appearances, are considered to be long-term projects, with different people working with them. High turnover. That's the seeming rationale for the detail of process notes."

"Okay," Gabe said. "Don't run yourselves into the ground, but I would like a report about what you've discovered so far tomorrow morning."

Beck nodded. "We can do that. Is there anything else?"

"Can't think of it."

"Then I'm getting back to work." She climbed into one of the waiting crawlers and drove off.

As they rode a crawler up to the house, Ruby kept turning this new information over in her head. A clone. Of Philip. Five years old. Surrounded by cyborged that apparently already had a strong dislike of his—what would be the right term for Philip? Donor? Original? Progenitor? What kind of life could that be—and what could a child raised that way become?

Even if he's not being raised for spare parts.

She shuddered. That was an entirely different level of awful.

"We have to get that kid to safety," she said to Gabe.

He nodded. "Working on it. First thing in the morning. I'm —no longer able to pull all-nighters unless it's a dire emergency. Even with the serum."

"Need help tomorrow?"

He shook his head. "Not yet. Honestly, Ruby, the best thing you could do for me right now is something that makes you happy. Rest. Recharge. You saved our butts at the New Dems and for that, I'm eternally grateful. I want you to be rested and ready in case you have to do something like that again soon. Like this upcoming meeting or—when we deal with Alexander's brothers and that clone." He sighed.

"I'm glad I can be that useful."

"More than that." He kissed her temple. "And the degree to which doing that drained you scared the crap out of me. I want you in good shape for what lies ahead."

"I'm not *that* fragile, Gabe."

"I know. But. Your presence recharges me and I don't—I want you safe. Strong. By my side. Damn, I'm suddenly very needy. But it's true. Another factor is that *one* of us has to focus on something besides the twists and turns of getting control of the Martiniere Group. Keep us on track, keep our businesses running. I did it while you were in Europe. Now it's your turn."

"All right." She really didn't want to be inside tomorrow unless the weather was stinking awful.

He smiled at the relieved tone in her voice. "I love you, Rubes."

"Me too."

THE FOLLOWING DAY BROUGHT ONE OF THOSE BRIGHT crisp, clear, and cold sunny mornings that followed an evening fall rain in Thunder County. Ruby sipped her mix of real and imitation coffee as she stared out her office window, thinking about the daily tasks ahead, sorting them out in her head. Charlie and Terri were dealing with irrigation winterization today and didn't need her help. Paperwork related to RubyBot spring orders required her review and approval, as well as other work that she'd not been able to handle while traveling. But she didn't need to do any of it first thing.

Not that she wanted to stay inside. The sky was brilliant blue, with only a couple of cloud wisps up high. The kind of day that made her impatient with being inside, that made her fidget and look away from screens.

What she *wanted* to do was ride. The horses still needed to be brought in from summer pasture and a nice day like this would make it a pleasant chore. However. It wasn't a big job, but she needed another rider, and Gabe was locked up with Martiniere business.

Unless Donna-gran would be interested?

It wasn't like it would be a complicated job. But she might still feel a bit frail for this sort of work. They could move the horses with crawlers. And maybe outside, away from potential listeners, Donna-gran would talk some more about family history.

Oh well. It was worth asking her. And if Donna-gran didn't feel like it, then there were other outside tasks that Ruby could do alone. Winterizing the garden. Checking the automatic heated stock waterers to ensure they were ready for winter operations. A host of small projects that weren't quite big enough to hand over to the high school interns (who were supposed to be in the labs anyway) or just added to the list of things that Charlie and Terri needed to manage. Or for her when she didn't want to do deskwork.

Thinking about the interns stirred a reminder.

Preliminary midterm grades due soon. Need to review the intern reports from Beck and Martin.

But not now. Ruby rolled her shoulders and went in search of Donna-gran. She sat by one of the front living room windows, ignoring the screen projected in front of her in favor of looking at the snow-dusted mountains to the south.

"It's a very pretty day," she said as Ruby came in.

"Want to get out in it? Ride a horse? The horses need to come in from summer pasture and I could use another rider. Or driver, if you'd prefer a crawler."

"Mmm." A small smile played on the corner of Donna-gran's lips. "It's been—oh, at least thirty years since I've ridden. Oh, it's tempting. But I don't know. I might embarrass myself."

"We've got some steady mounts." Pard would probably do well for Donna-gran. The big black gelding had once served as a rodeo pickup rider's mount, and had done his share of roping work. He was intelligent, calm, and quiet.

"Oh my. But I'd need riding boots."

Ruby laughed. "Boots. Helmets. Appropriate jacket for the weather, and gloves. Jeans. We've plenty of those around here."

Donna-gran grinned. "Then let's go see what fits."

After getting Donna-gran situated with riding gear, Ruby slipped into Gabe's office. He looked up from scowling at his screens, a slow smile transforming his expression as she sat on the edge of his desk. "What's up? Looks like you're dressed to ride."

"Donna-gran and I are bringing the horses in."

He glanced out his window, a regretful look crossing his face. "It's a nice day for it. Damn. I wish I could drop every-thing and go with you."

"Any luck?"

"Five possible sites for the clone and cyborged, all heavily protected." He sighed. "And doing a lot of thinking about how to proceed with all this. What has to happen when we find—and take control of—that child. And it will have to be us who does it. I talked to the authorities. They won't lift a damn finger because as a creation of the Martiniere Group laboratories, under current indenture law the kid is property, not a person. Philip can do what he damned well pleases with him as a result."

"Fuck."

Gabe nodded solemnly. "I will not let my father have him for whatever goddamn game he's playing. I don't give a shit what it looks like legally, whatever status he may claim in relationship to that child. I've already spoken to Remy about custody angles. Are you on board with me about this?"

"Completely." She pressed her lips together, looking down. "There's really no other option." In spite of what she had discussed with Justine just weeks ago, when the fear had been that Philip might have A.I. offspring with indentured women. Then the thought of caring for Philip's child hadn't been that appealing.

But that particular scenario had happened already. Alexander. His cyborged brothers.

Why only Joseph to sire them? Or has Philip been after clones and not a child of his own? Why?

"I want that kid to have a normal life—something other than what he's experiencing right now, for sure," Gabe continued, interrupting her thoughts. He started tapping his fingertips on the desk. "We can't trust him to just anyone."

"No. We can't." *Am I ready to talk about this? Not really any better time to do it, I guess.* "Unless Brandon and Kris decide to take him on."

"I—" he shook his head. "They're having a kid of their own who may have problems. I don't think it's fair to expect them to deal with this child as well."

"I've been thinking about that too."

"And I—I—it's complicated, Rubes. I don't know what whoever raises him needs to be able to handle."

"Gabe, does any parent know?"

"True. But are we the right choice?"

"We've got the resources."

Keep it up, Ruby, you'll talk yourself into it. It did make sense in far too many ways. She'd been leaning toward taking custody of the clone—the boy—*Michael.*

Michael is his name. We need to use it.

"But is that going to be enough? I don't know to what degree what's wrong with my father is biological and to what degree it's something else. I mean—there *is* something wrong with him. There has to be, to act like he does. I just—maybe I'm blind. I can't see Donna-gran raising a kid like Philip. And yet." He rubbed his face. "The more I know, the more I keep looking at myself and wondering if someday I'm going to break out with those fatal flaws."

"You're not him. Neither is Brandon."

Gabe huffed. "And that's the thing. We're different from Philip. Maybe his clone can grow up to be a different person. Maybe not. All the sources for nonhuman mammal cloning say that it's only the genotype that gets passed on, not so much temperament. All the same, God only knows what hellish crap he's already gone through."

"Hellish crap at a young age can be overcome," she said in a low, tight, voice. Yes. She knew that all too well from her own experiences.

Gabe rested one hand on her thigh. "I know. You're an example. But is it fair to ask you to deal with whatever trauma this kid has gone through?"

She placed her hand on his. "Who else can we trust? And don't minimize the hell you experienced."

"Only my teen years. And—augh, that's another issue. Can I keep myself from being reactive if he sounds too much like Philip? Because he *will* rebel. Brandon did."

"If you make yourself do it, then yes you can. Look. We

both overcame a lot. We may be better prepared than someone who hasn't gone through childhood trauma."

"But should we do it—if it turns out that he's severely traumatized, enough to be a risk? I'm sure there's other acceptable options, if we look hard enough."

Ruby chose her words carefully. "We are Michael's relatives. And even though he's a clone of your father—it's the genotype. Not necessarily the personality. We've got to keep repeating that to ourselves."

"What if he has mental issues?" Gabe said tightly.

She tightened her hand on his. "Then who better to help Michael manage it than family? I guess the real question is—are we capable of doing this? Will we be?"

"It's weird." Gabe's words came haltingly. "The thought of raising someone who is—biologically—my father. The responsibility. My own—attitudes." Now he spoke faster. "What happens if I fuck it up—and it would be me who did that, not you, you did a great job with Bran. And our health, because we're not exactly spring chickens and who knows what this damn serum does for us in the long run? How fast will we fade after five years? What about the cardiac issues?"

"I know," she said, her words coming with more confidence. "But it comes back to can we do this. I think we can. And we need to start speaking of him as *Michael*, not *the clone* or by pronouns. He is Michael. He needs to be called by his name."

"You're sure you want to do this?"

She nodded. "And ultimately, it is our responsibility, Gabe. We wanted to change things. Perhaps this is one way to do it."

That slow smile again. "Damn, Rubes, I love you and your strength." He pulled her toward him and they kissed. "Now go bring in the horses. Try not to break Donna-gran, okay? We still need her."

"She'll be up on Pard."

"All right. Go do some fun work for me, too, please. Just because I'm stuck inside juggling things doesn't mean you should be. Come back happy and smelling of horse."

"I will," she promised.

And perhaps she'd be able to pry some more information out of Donna-gran while doing it. Any clue to why Philip was so different temperamentally from his siblings would be helpful if they were going to be raising his clone.

LEGACY PINNED HER EARS AS RUBY TIGHTENED THE FRONT cinch, whipping her head around as far as the crosstie would allow to air snap at Ruby.

"Quit!" Ruby snapped, slapping Legacy's shoulder. "Geez, mare, I've barely taken up the slack."

"A little cinchy?" Donna-gran leaned against Pard's haunches. He drowsed in his crossties, head hanging low, the opposite leg from Donna-gran resting on the tip of his hoof.

"I sent her out to a trainer I thought was decent and not rough to start her last year. I was wrong. She came back cinchy. My fault, but I was just too busy to do her justice. My focus was on qualifying for the Superhero."

"Sometimes it happens," Donna-gran said.

"Also doesn't help that she's in her final heat cycle of the season, which always makes her grumpy because it's usually more intense. But her great-granddam was like this too. Get them past the initial fussiness, and they'll work their heart out." It was also still crisp and cool here in the barn—another factor.

"Gonna lunge her?"

"Mmm, no. I don't like lunging a horse in this mode." Ruby considered the options. Round pen or ride it out in the arena? Round pen didn't always work. If she could get Legacy past those first high hard bucks and into a gallop, she'd work out of it in a few circuits.

Ride it out, she decided, carefully *not* admitting to herself that she wanted to show off a little for Donna-gran. Even if she did end up eating dirt should Legacy's mood extend to some harder bucks than usual. Let her get a few bucks in, then run, and she'd settle.

Get it out and get it over with. Legacy's pattern.

"Gonna ride," Ruby said, assessing Legacy again. No, nothing unusual about her behavior. She pulled on her helmet, carefully checking the harness to ensure it was secure, then gathered up Legacy's snaffle. After Ruby slipped off her halter, the golden mare took the bit with her ears flicked back, then shook her head because Ruby didn't adjust the browband of the headstall fast enough for her satisfaction.

"Oh, I know, everything's annoying you right now," Ruby said to Legacy in a soft, soothing voice. "Want to jump out of your skin. Believe me, mare, I know how you feel. We'll both be a lot better in a few minutes." She gathered the reins up. Donna-gran moved to bridle Pard.

"Wait. I'm riding it out in the arena," Ruby said. "Not crazy enough to do it in the open. You don't need to get ready just yet, though I do want you to warm up in the arena when I'm done."

"All right. Want me to get the gate?"

Ruby shook her head. "Nah, I'll be schooling her."

As she expected, Legacy wanted to rush through the gate into the arena. Ruby made her repeat it, walking slowly. She led the golden mare to the middle of the arena. When she went to tighten the cinch, Legacy snapped again, deliberately short of Ruby's left arm.

"*Quit.*" A harder growl, punctuated by an open-hand slap

on Legacy's belly. The mare grunted in response, her ears pinned.

Oh. One of those days. Definitely the best choice to run it off. *Too much time confined in a pen. She'll be happier back in the winter pasture.*

But first, she had to *ride* Legacy.

Loop the right rein over Legacy's neck so the end hung on the left side. Loop left rein so that end hung on the right side. Take up a shorter length in the left rein, grab mane to anchor. Quick slide of left foot into stirrup, swift hop up and swing right leg over to hopefully find that stirrup fast....

Legacy exploded into a series of high, twisting bucks once Ruby's boot settled in the right stirrup.

"Yaahh! Yaahh!" Ruby urged her forward, lower legs tapping Legacy's side to encourage her to run instead of buck, giving her a long rein so she would gallop. The bucks diminished and Legacy picked up a hard, fast pace reminiscent of Sunshine's old rodeo run-ins. Ruby leaned low over Legacy's neck. Legacy *might* be faster than her great-granddam. No perspective in this arena, though, to confirm it, since it had been built after Sunshine's performance days.

Three loops of the arena, cross the center, flying lead change, and off again in the opposite direction, Legacy running hard, highblowing a rhythmic snort with each stride. Three more loops, and then Ruby sat up, shortening her reins until she had a feel of Legacy's mouth on the bit. She vibrated the inside rein, asking for a little bend, and rested her outside leg against Legacy's side to send her across the arena, squeezing the reins in the middle and switching legs to cue a flying change. Another bend, another change of lead, looping around in an oval at the end of the arena to do another three-loop serpentine.

Legacy's strides slowed, until she was cantering the serpentines quietly, her ears relaxed and twitched back to focus on Ruby, not flattened and tight in irritation. Ruby sent her down the long side of the arena, asked for a rollback in the opposite direction, then asked for it again as they reached the short end.

Halfway down the long end Ruby breathed "Whoooaaa." Legacy slid to a stop, and the light twitch of Ruby's hand was enough to send her back several feet. Another stop, and Ruby reached over to pat Legacy's neck.

"Good girl." She clucked, and Legacy ambled over to the gate, head low, on a loose rein, relaxed and temper eased after the brief run.

"That was impressive," Donna-gran said, holding a bridled Pard's reins as she opened the gate. "She's a bucker all right."

"Bucking is the occasional drawback of this bloodline," Ruby said. "But she's also a young horse. If I can get her forward, get her running, she works out of it. Eventually she'll probably be like her great-granddam where all that's needed is an occasional hard gallop around the arena to start out."

"Oh, I've had a few like those back in the day."

Ruby dismounted to hold Pard by the mounting block. After Donna-gran mounted she watched as Donna-gran rode Pard around the arena, first at a walk, then a trot, and finally a lope.

"Doesn't look bad," she finally called out. "Shouldn't need to do more than trot today. You going to be all right with it?"

"I should be able to handle it." Donna-gran rode up to Ruby, grinning. "Even though I'm going to hurt tonight. Sore muscles. But so worth it."

Ruby gave her a thumbs up and mounted Legacy.

Moving the horse herd was more of a matter of opening gates along one of the ranch roads, then getting them started for the home pasture and keeping the herd from stalling in the pastures in between. Still, it had to happen after moving the cattle down to winter pasture, since the horses were furthest out and would have to go through the cow pastures. And it easily took several hours—a morning's work.

Donna-gran rode Pard with an easy grace, quiet, just looking around her. "It's worth it to be able to ride a horse again," she said finally, after they had ridden through the next field. "I've missed riding. And the mountains—the sky—it's beautiful here. I see why you and Gabriel prefer this place for your home."

"It can be a hard life, though," Ruby said. "Fires. Storms. Long hours. Hard physical labor. Far away from a lot of resources. I'm lucky. While I lived tight, especially as a single mother, cash flow never got so bad that I couldn't find help. Sometimes it was offered, and unpaid, but...I could afford to pay Charlie and his husband Martin to help with the ranch and the lab. Not everyone could do that. Though I did have to take in bookkeeping for a few years to make ends meet."

"The ranch life seems to have done well for your son," Donna-gran said thoughtfully.

"It has." Ruby considered it further. "Brandon actually had a lot more freedom than most kids his age," she said finally. "Once he was old enough to be trusted, he and his friends went riding all over the place. And when they hit their teens, they would go out shooting and cruising around on crawlers on the place here. They'd go over to the canyons or the mountains, range over there on foot and in crawlers. He spent a lot of time outside."

"I see." Donna-gran was quiet for a few minutes. "Thought about what's going to happen with Philip's clone?"

"Gabe and I were talking about it this morning." Ruby hesitated. "We're considering taking custody of him. It's—kind of intimidating, to think about doing it, and he's the one who has to make the final call. Michael *is* his father's clone."

"That is—a challenge," Donna-gran acknowledged.

"And then there's the concern about Philip. What was different about him growing up? What would we need to watch out for?"

Donna-gran was silent for a few minutes as they approached the next field. The gate was a metal one that Ruby could open from horseback. She hung a loop of the gate chain on the hook pounded into the fence post to keep the gate open. Then she scanned the sky for raptors to give Donna-gran more time, spotting a northern harrier hawk gliding along the crest of the ridge ahead of them.

"Philip was always angry about Saul being the elder twin," Donna-gran said finally, as their horses climbed up the ridge. "I don't know why. Louis and I tried to treat all of our children the same. But Philip was born angry, and he kept on being angry. That's what really keeps coming back to me—his anger and how intense it was."

Further silence except for snorts from Legacy and Pard to clear their noses and the faint creaks of saddle leather, a quietness that lasted through the next field. They reached another gate that Ruby could open and secure from Legacy's back.

"Gerard wasn't that way," Donna-gran mused after they went through the gate. "Neither was Saul. And Peter—poor Peter. Philip manipulated him, poor boy. Set him up to cause Louis's death, or at least that's what I'll always believe. Even though it was never proven, and probably never will be."

"How did Louis die?" Ruby asked.

"An experiment gone bad. Philip and Peter were working together, and somehow the lab they were in caught fire." Donna-gran scowled. "It shouldn't have happened," she snapped, squeezing the reins tight enough that Pard raised his head in protest. "Philip knew better, that Peter wasn't ready to work at that level, and didn't correct Peter's mistake. He told me this years ago, in the middle of one of our arguments, so I'm not just guessing. Louis got Philip out, and had a fatal heart attack trying to get Peter. Saul was the Martiniere-in-waiting, and took over." She exhaled and eased her grip on the reins, patting Pard's neck.

"But if it was an accident...." Ruby's voice trailed off. No. She couldn't react. Not while on top of Legacy. No.

"It *looked* like an accident. And both Saul and Philip were privy to the knowledge that Louis was at risk of heart failure. The experiment was Philip's idea. Not Peter's, not Louis's. Philip pushed Peter into something he wasn't ready to do, because *he* wanted to do it." Donna-gran sighed. "All right. That's the other factor. Arrogance and being unwilling to admit when he was wrong. He *bragged* about it to me, and told me it was my word against his. That I would never be able to prove what he had done."

"So anger. Arrogance. Unable to admit fault—well, that last showed up enough in Brandon when he was a kid. And I've sure seen anger and unwillingness to admit mistakes in Gabe. He's much better now. Cockiness—well, that was part and parcel of riding broncs. But it never slid into arrogance, at least not that I ever saw. And Gabe now—he's still quick to anger, but if anything, he bends over backwards to admit when he's wrong."

"Gabriel is smarter than his father. But Gabriel had a tough time as a teenager. He respected Saul but not Philip, and the two of them clashed repeatedly after Saul's death. The arguments between them were—reminiscent of the fights between Saul and Philip. Philip beat Gabriel. Repeatedly. Battered him."

"He'd told me that." *One reason he had been so enraged by human trafficking and mind control.* Only she had thought it was Philip Ramirez doing the beating. And then she had seen

Gabe's *whatthehell* file, which included pictures that Justine had taken of Gabe after the worst of the beatings. He still had scars on his back from them.

Donna-gran nodded. "Getting Justine free from Philip meant Gabriel endured a horrific beating, until Gerard interfered. Philip kept his beatings of Gabriel secret. Not like it was with Saul and Philip. As Saul and Philip's battles escalated to public fistfights, we had the meeting where we hammered out the agreement that they would have to raise their brother's oldest son as their own, in the same household. Louis's brothers thought it would be a good idea, and Antoine—Artie's father—even provided the residence for Saul and Philip to share."

Ruby didn't know quite what to say.

So that was the solution? Really?

"Gabriel didn't testify until Justine was safe," Donna-gran continued. "He protected her from Joseph and Philip, even when he was in college. But again—I didn't learn about this until after the fact." She sighed. "And I wasn't well during those crucial years. So many things fell apart then."

They reached the summer pasture gate. A welcome break from the family history. Legacy whinnied as Ruby dismounted to open and secure the wire gate. She remounted as Legacy called again. This time she heard an answering nicker.

"Sounds like they're coming," she said to Donna-gran.

"Is he going to be a problem?" Donna-gran asked, taking a shorter rein as Pard raised his head, ears pricked.

"Shouldn't be." Ruby pointed to the other side of the fence. "Why don't you wait over there, and follow the herd. One mare —Star, a chestnut—has a foal at her side. The rest are young stock, retirees, broodmares, and horses we're not using. Should be ten of them. I'll lead off, then move to the side. They know the way back—we just need to keep them from wandering."

The thunder of hooves announced the arrival of the herd,

headed by the Paint mare Crystal, herd leader since Sunshine's death. Legacy's head shot up and she pranced as the herd galloped toward them. Ruby headed her back down the fence-line and to the side.

"Take 'em home, Crystal!" she yelled, just like she used to do with Sunshine. She didn't think the big chestnut and white mare understood the words, but she did know the routine and the big mare certainly knew *home*.

Donna-gran fell in behind the herd as Ruby sent Legacy to trail along the side, near Crystal. After the initial rush through the gate, the herd eased first into a trot, then walked. Ruby turned in the saddle to check on the rest of the herd and Donna-gran. All looked well, so she let herself relax and enjoy the day.

And consider what Donna-gran had said. While she already knew about Gabe's protection of Justine—and his abuse at Philip's hands—the rest of it was new.

Philip was possibly responsible for his father and brother's deaths. But was that so different from what happened to Gabe's parents? Philip was responsible for their deaths too.

The possibility of an angry child. Perhaps it *would* be better for Michael to be raised without siblings.

Remember, only the genotype is the same, she reminded herself. But what about epigenetic influence? Did that work with clones?

A possibly angry, traumatized child.

On the other hand, what kind of relationship did Michael have with the cyborged protecting him? That could affect things.

We won't know until we see him.

If they saw him. If they were able to keep Philip from harming him. After talking to Donna-gran she was convinced that Michael being in danger from Philip was a strong possibility. Focusing on keeping the herd together and moving was a welcome distraction from this new set of worries clustering in her thoughts.

Ruby was surprised to see Gabe at the back gate to the winter pasture when they reached it.

"We turned the penned horses in the field, so I thought I'd better open the gate and keep them back," he called, even as the other horses snorted, nickered, and galloped across the field to meet the main herd. "Saw your approach on the fence sensors and hustled out here."

"Thanks."

Gabe closed the gate behind Donna-gran as the horse herd spilled into the field, bucking and racing the fence line. "So how was the ride, Donna-gran?"

"Marvelous. Though I will be paying for it with sore muscles tonight."

"Worth it." Gabe raised his brows at Ruby. "Think I could take a turn? I need it. I know you've not let anyone else up on her since she came back from training."

"Don't see why not. You're not gonna rough her up."

Ruby halted Legacy and dismounted, her gut tightening at Gabe's words. What could be so bad? Or was it just that the accumulated weight of everything they were learning required a brief moment on horseback to settle? She could understand that.

Ruby adjusted the stirrup length for Gabe after he mounted, and stepped back, dismissing her other concerns momentarily in order to enjoy watching him ride Legacy. He'd come a long way in strength and regaining riding skill in the past few days.

Gabe took a shorter rein and asked Legacy to collect herself. Ruby watched as he felt the golden mare out, horse and rider assessing each other. He asked her to jog, then extend the trot, then cued a lope, taking her through a figure 8 with flying lead changes before riding her up to Ruby.

"She's more responsive than Sunshine," he said. "Smoother and lighter. You've done a good job on her, Rubes. A real pleasure to ride."

Ruby shrugged. "Go ahead and ride her to the barn. I'll walk."

Gabe half-turned in the saddle, waving Donna-gran up. "Gate duty wasn't the primary reason I was out here. There's been a lot going on this morning. Some things I need to tell you both."

"Oh?" Donna-gran said. Ruby walked between the horses as they headed for the front gate.

"Yeah. Presidential news. Tolliver announced he's not running for re-election."

Ruby whistled. "What brought that about?"

"I suspect Colin has had some *interesting* chats with him. But there's more," Gabe said as they reached the gate. Ruby scurried forward to open it, waiting for Gabe and Donna-gran to ride through.

Gabe eased Legacy around to face them after Ruby closed the gate. "The Real Truthers have pulled Philip's nomination for conduct unbecoming a presidential nominee."

"*No*," Ruby said, unbelieving. "He resigned?"

Gabe shook his head. "No. They withdrew the nomination."

"Unbelievable," Donna-gran said.

"It's confirmed," Gabe said. "They're holding a new nominating convention on the fourteenth of October."

"The day before our meeting," Ruby said.

Gabe nodded. "Philip's threatening to sue the Reals. Has filed an injunction. Request denied. Like I said, things have been happening *fast* today."

"Any word about Michael?"

Worry crossed Gabe's face. "Alexander's been able to tell us more. Brandon was here while you were gone to share what they've learned. We may have identified Michael's current location. The problem is, he's being moved from it now. Tine's following and hoping to locate him soon." He blew hard. "But the reason Brandon came over again was that he thinks they may have found the purpose Michael was supposed to serve."

"Oh?" Donna-gran pushed Pard closer.

"Yeah," Gabe said, his lips tightening. "Donor for blood transfusion. And we're not just talking a pint. Philip intends to drain the kid, given the volume discussed. Nearly killed Michael with the latest draw."

Ruby stared at Gabe, horrified, as Donna-gran gasped.

How much worse can it get?

Donna-gran moaned and shook her head. "Gabriel, you have to stop this."

"I fully intend to," Gabe said. "Whatever it takes." He exhaled. "Brandon and I have spoken to the Family. No need for the Canadian trip now. For all intents and purposes, I now possess the corporate authority of the Martiniere Group. As soon as we discover Michael's location, we can act, without needing to wait for the meeting." He exhaled again, deep, heavy, weighted. "Gerard, Artie, Ken, Christopher, and I decided, based on Alexander's records and prior precedent, that Michael is a clone created with Martiniere Group resources, not Philip's private ones," he said slowly. "As a result, Michael is legitimately a creation of the Martiniere Group. He is corporate property, not Philip's offspring, not Philip's property. As a result, I can take custody of him. And Remy confirms the legality of it."

CHAPTER 14

If Ruby had thought things were tense before, the next three days made her re-estimate that conclusion, especially since cold and drizzle followed by sleet discouraged much outside activity. She, Gabe, and Donna-gran went around their daily work, poised for *that moment* when they would need to drop everything to join the team assembling to rescue Michael. What made things worse was that none of them could directly participate in the search because they didn't have that skill set. Brandon and Kris coordinated that aspect, along with Serg and Justine.

But there was pacing the living room at various times. Arena schooling of the horses. With Gabe and Donna-gran on hand to help, Ruby started the fall groundwork to prepare Crystal's three-year-old son Flash to go under saddle in the spring. He was a big, leggy, and powerful colt she had been planning to prep for the big ranch gelding sales once he turned four. And after the fiasco with Legacy going out for training, she wasn't willing to take the risk with an outside handler. Especially now, given her Martiniere connections. Another vulnerability.

However, even training Flash didn't distract enough from the worry.

Ruby spent time in Brandon's room pulling out his old toys and preparing it for another young boy. She and Gabe set up a small bed in their room that could be screened off and private. Gramps and Granma had done it for Ruby after the deaths of her parents when she had problems sleeping. Hard to say if Michael would have the same issues—but if he did, it was ready for him.

At least Philip's appearances were such that it was unlikely he had drained Michael. Yet. But no one could tease out where Michael and his cyborged protectors had gone.

It was a relief when Brandon called to say that Alexander was finally strong enough to see them. Four days out from the meeting now. Justine flew in to pick them up, Serg beside her.

"We're going to overwhelm the poor kid with family," Ruby snarked as the corporate jet took off.

Serg snorted. "That *kid* is trained and programmed front-line security. I doubt we'll be too much for him."

"We'll see," Donna-gran said abstractly. She gazed at a screen she had popped open even before the jet had lifted off. "It is entirely possible that he *will* be overwhelmed, based on some of these psych evals Brandon's run for me. Even with the reprogramming there will be base reactions."

"What *do* you think we should expect?" Gabe asked, leaning forward, elbows on his knees.

Donna-gran scowled at her screen, scrolling through it. Finally, she looked up.

"He trusts Brandon. But not you, Gabriel. Until you win his trust—be prepared for him to resist responding to you or Ruby. He is particularly nervous about Ruby."

Gabe glanced at Ruby. "Then I guess we need to convince him of our sincerity," he said finally.

Kris met them at the airstrip and drove them up to the house.

"Not as bad as I feared," was her response to Gabe's question about how things were going with Alexander in the house. More than that was met with, "You'll see for yourself."

Gabe frowned at that, but didn't break the tense silence as the crawler climbed the hill to the main house on Moondance's ridge. When they got out and the ranch manager's border collies greeted him happily, he gave them absent-minded pats, his focus on the main house.

Ruby didn't try to distract him, her own concerns roiling as they entered the great room centered between the big house's two wings. Alexander and Brandon waited for them by the western wall of windows that looked out on yet another gray and drizzly day. Alexander sat in a straight backed chair while Brandon was in a big stuffed chair next to him. He patted Alexander's leg before standing up.

"Brought the whole crew, I see," he said.

"Unfortunately, I think that's what's required for this situation," Gabe said. He turned to face Alexander and walked up to him. "Alexander. Do you prefer for me to sit or stand?"

Alexander shrugged. "Suit yourself."

Gabe looked around and pulled a rocking chair over, setting it next to the chair Brandon had been using. "Then I'll sit." He glanced at Ruby and the others, nodding slightly to the chairs.

Ruby pulled the other rocking chair to be next to Gabe, crossing her hands over her knees so that the emerald in her ring was prominent. Alexander flinched as he glanced at it, then looked away. She intended to give him that message. After all, he *was* Mariah's son, and until she heard more directly from *him*, she was going to be cautious.

Gabe hunched over, leaning forearms on his knees, interlacing his fingers and studying them before he looked back up.

"So, we got off to a bad start," he said quietly. "Not your fault, as I understand it from Brandon."

"He's been helpful," Alexander said, body stiff and tight.

Silence fell.

Ruby let herself study Alexander in more detail. The slick metallic plaskin on the left side of his face was gone, replaced by what appeared to be actual metal. A slight difference where metal met skin suggested that the plaskin had covered the metal all along. His right arm was metal, and she thought she caught a glimpse of metal in the gap between pant cuff and slippers on his left leg.

Not hiding what he is.

"I'm glad to hear it," Gabe said finally, focusing on his fingers. He straightened back up. "All right. So here we go again. Second round. I am Gabriel Martiniere. *The* Martiniere; the head of the Family. As of three days ago, the major shareholders in the Martiniere Group have also given me preliminary control of the Group, to be confirmed and finalized on the fifteenth of October. You are Alexander Meyers, cyborged indentured, and the son of my cousin Joseph Martiniere. Not only am I your Family head, with all that means within this damn family, but as of three days ago, you are technically my property."

Surprise flashed across Alexander's face before it went blank again. "And what are your plans for your *property*, Gabriel Martiniere?"

Gabe leaned back in the chair, rocking slowly, fingers interlacing and resting in his lap. "I suppose it depends on what your intentions are. If you choose to try to assassinate President Tolliver again, then I would need to stop you by whatever means necessary." He gestured to Ruby. "That includes the control modes programmed into you which respond to Ruby."

Alexander flinched. "And other than that?"

"I don't plan to keep indentured contracts," Gabe snapped. "Wait. Let me reemphasize this further. I have absolutely no fucking interest in holding indentured contracts. As long as you don't hire yourself out as an assassin or go off on personal vendettas, your life is your own."

"I see."

"There are situations where I would appreciate your help," Gabe continued. "But your freedom is not contingent upon doing a damn thing."

"And what would these *situations* be?" Alexander asked sarcastically. "An assassination or two? Intimidation? Protection? After all, those *are* the types of *situations* I've been trained to handle."

Gabe leaned forward again, staring at his fingers once more. "There is a child," he said finally.

Alexander tightened, his hands clenching hard on the chair arms. "What do you want with him?" he snarled.

Gabe met Alexander's steady glare. "Technically, he's also my property."

"What are *you* going to do to him? After all, *technically* he's also your father."

"He is a *child*," Gabe said softly. "A *child*. Not my father. Who was brought into being through no fault of his own. And if we are going to avoid the fate that the sperm donor who is my *father* has planned for him, then we need your help."

"To do what?"

"Aren't you listening to what I say?" Gabe's voice rose in volume, irritation creeping into it. "Damn it, you're our expert. I understand that you and your brothers guard him. And if we're going to retrieve Michael—and them—safely, with as few casualties as possible, we need your advice."

As soon as Gabe said *Michael,* Alexander's demeanor changed. The grip on the chair arms loosened and he sagged in the chair.

"You said his name." An almost hopeful note in his voice.

"It *is* his name."

Alexander exhaled, the right side of his face easing slightly. "Philip never calls any of them by name. They're always number—whatever, or *it*. Never their names."

"Do any other than Michael survive?"

Alexander shook his head. "None." The word choked out of his throat, a half-moan.

"Have they all been used to replace Philip's body parts?"

"Not all." Alexander spoke haltingly. "Some—had significant health issues and didn't live past their first year. There have been four survivors of the original batch of thirteen who were able to fulfill Philip's purposes. Michael is the fourth—donor."

The wince was universal.

Gabe closed his eyes for a moment, then refocused on Alexander. "All right. We knew where Michael and your brothers were three days ago, but they've disappeared. Philip has been very public in the meantime. Is this a preparation for another—transfusion?"

Alexander shook his head. "It's not supposed to be time for it yet."

"Can it be advanced?"

"I don't know," Alexander said. "Look. A lot has gone down over the past few days. There are several locations where they could be."

Gabe rubbed his face. "All right. Will you help us find Michael? Before it's too late?"

"I will do my best," Alexander said.

"And I can trust you not to turn on me?"

"Are you going to force me to kill people? Because that's a factor in whether I trust you or not."

Gabe paused. "Why would I?"

Alexander looked down, then back up. "Your wife killed Joseph."

"Ruby is her own person. And she decided it needed to happen for my safety."

"You don't force her to be your enforcer?"

"Wait just—" Ruby started up but Gabe put a hand on her knee.

"Rubes. Let me." He shook his head, gazing at her. "Have I ever asked you to be my enforcer?"

"You're damned well capable of doing that for yourself, Gabe," she snapped. She glared at Alexander. "I'm not his puppet!"

"And I love you for that," Gabe said, shaking his head, ending with a short, sharp chuckle. "Me make Ruby do anything, Alexander? Only in my wildest dreams. She comes to her own decisions."

"Then she's the one responsible for what happened to the cyborged at the New Dems," Alexander said.

"Don't talk about me like I'm not here," Ruby retorted. "And yes. I realized that there was a need to stop you—all of you—from harming others. I had the power to do it. So I did."

"But you're not his personal attack bitch?"

She bit back the comment she wanted to make in response.

Deescalate, damn it, she told herself, remembering Donnagran's words.

He is particularly nervous about Ruby.

Well, he had reason to be nervous about her, after all. So she needed to be careful.

"I am my *own* personal attack bitch, thank you very much," she said finally. "And if you decide to assault anyone I consider to be under my protection, then yes—you will meet that side of me. Otherwise, you have no reason to fear what I can do."

"And would *you* be willing to defend and protect Michael?"

"Unequivocally yes." She gestured at Brandon. "Ask him what it was like with me as his mother. What I've done for those who are mine. Family. Friends. Once Michael comes into our hands, I will do what is needed to guard him. Heal him. Whatever is needed."

Gabe took her hand. "Alexander, Ruby and I are partners, in more ways than one. We don't always see eye-to-eye, but when it comes to indentured rights, when it comes to Michael's fate—we're in agreement. If we can manage to save Michael, then we will raise him. Not as my father's clone, but as himself, whoever Michael Martiniere chooses to be, apart from any destiny that Philip Martiniere would have forced on him."

"And my brothers and myself?"

"None of you chose your fate, if I understand the situation correctly," Gabe said. "You are the sons of my cousin Joseph. Much as I disliked him, you had as much to do with him as Michael does with Philip. As long as you don't start up your own assassination organization or something like that, we'll be fine."

"We'll be fine even though we're cyborged?"

"You're still Martinieres."

"And if I want to join Brandon's staff as one of his protectors?"

"Then he'd damned well better pay you what you're worth. But I hope you'll help us secure Michael and your brothers first."

"Can we be coded to not respond to Philip's orders?"

"Yes," Donna-gran said firmly.

Alexander's head twitched toward her. "Who are *you?* Your voice resonates within my programming structures."

"As it should," Donna-gran said. "I am Donna Martiniere, your paternal grandmother, and I helped create those original algorithms, not knowing their eventual application. Like Gabriel, Ruby, and Brandon, I am more than willing to move heaven and earth to free you. *All* of you." Her voice trembled. "Philip is my son, and I utterly abhor his atrocities. I will spend my last days doing my best to undo his legacy, and repair mine."

"Where do we begin?"

"First, you swear loyalty to Gabriel and Ruby," Donna-gran said. "That overrides your other programs."

"It depends on what that loyalty requires."

"Faithfulness," Gabe said. "A commitment to doing what is right. And the responsibility to tell any of us to go to hell if what we ask goes against your personal sense of right or wrong. No force. No coercion."

Alexander shook his head, looking down. "This sounds almost too good to be true."

"Al," Brandon said softly. Alexander jerked his head up to look at Brandon. "You trust me, right?"

"Yes." Tentative.

"Then trust my parents. They mean what they say about force or coercion."

A long pause. Then Alexander exhaled, seeming to collapse upon himself. "All right. For Michael's sake, I'll swear loyalty." His voice sharpened. "But if you ever do harm to Michael, my brothers and I will make you pay."

"I would expect no less from so loyal a guardian," Gabe said.

RUBY FLED TO THE KITCHEN AS SOON AS POSSIBLE AFTER Alexander swore loyalty. She leaned against the sink, head in her hands, making herself breathe deeply.

Just a break, she told herself. *Just a break while Donna-gran and Justine work with Alexander.* Then she'd go back.

"Ruby?" Mariah's voice.

Ruby raised her head. "Yeah."

"Everything—all right?"

Ruby gulped. "Alexander has sworn loyalty to me and Gabe. He's now acknowledged as part of the Martiniere family. If that's what you mean."

"Yeah. I guess that's what I meant." But the response lacked the usual confrontational bite from Mariah.

"So why didn't you ever tell anyone about Alexander? Years ago? Tried to get him away from Philip?"

Gabe entered the kitchen behind Mariah and froze, out of her sight.

Mariah winced. She swallowed hard, eyes widening, struggling to force words out. At last she shook her head, pointing to her throat. "I—can't."

"A compulsion," Ruby said bitterly. "Part of the mind control programs."

Gabe flinched.

Mariah nodded, biting her lip and looking down. She shuddered. "High-level. Ends only with Philip's—demise. You—can't touch it. Not all forced. Some voluntary."

Surprising that she can say that much. Or is it the case that I just need to ask the right things?

It was worth a try.

"Michael is a clone. Philip's clone. Alexander has brothers. Artificial insemination, with different mothers. Does Michael have children like Alexander has brothers?"

Mariah's eyes widened. She shook her head.

"Is there a reason?" Ruby asked.

Slow, forced speech again. "He—can't. Justine—last. Before cancer."

"Philip had cancer and it made him sterile? After Justine's birth?"

Mariah nodded. "Has."

Is that the reason for the blood transfusions?

But she couldn't make herself say that either.

Gabe sighed. He came further into the kitchen, patted Mariah's shoulder, then joined Ruby, taking her hand. "Just checking on you. I saw Mariah come in here and wanted to make sure you two weren't starting up a fight."

"Thanks."

"I'll go back now." He paused between them, giving first Ruby and then Mariah measuring looks. "Unless you need me here as a referee."

Mariah shook her head.

"All right."

Mariah waited until he was gone before she spoke again. "I just need to get this out, Ruby. Much as I want to be sorry for what I did to you and Gabe—I can't be. I just can't." She blinked and Ruby was surprised to see tears trickling down her cheeks. "Because what I did bought me that crucial week with Alexander. I can't say for sure—but I think it made a difference. And led to today. I regret what I did, but in the long run...."

"Yeah," Ruby said bitterly. Too much had gone on and— well—better Mariah be honest than lie. And perhaps Mariah was right. Without her week with Alexander at that age, he might not have turned against Philip.

But the price that Gabe and I paid. The goddamn fucking price.

"I've been listening to Alexander. What he says about the child." More tears. "It's not too late, Ruby. Alexander was the same age—when I had that lovely, marvelous week with him. Please. You and Gabe. Make all that shit I put you through worthwhile. Get Michael the hell out of Philip's hands, no matter what it takes."

Ruby raised her brows, surprised. "We'll do our best," she said.

"Thank you. Not just for freeing Alexander—but for the rest of us as well." Mariah turned to flee from the kitchen.

"Mariah."

She halted in the doorway and turned back. "What?"

"What are your plans, you and Georgy? We've four days until that meeting."

Mariah took five steps into the kitchen, hands fluttering nervously, not looking at Ruby. "Both Brandon and Alexander think that Georgy and I will be safe once the meeting's done. Then we've got to figure out how to fix the mess all this has made of our businesses." Now she looked at Ruby, scowling. "What becomes of Philip?"

"Do you care for him?"

Mariah laughed bitterly. "Did I have a choice? Hell, I don't know, Ruby! He's held my contract and Alexander's safety over my head for so long—do you know how terrified I was when Alexander showed up on my doorstep, with transfer papers naming Georgy as his new contract holder? Not knowing if Philip had a trigger control that could lead to Alexander destroying the three of us? Thinking that my son got sent back to me so he could execute us? Loving him but afraid he was more Philip's than mine? You never went through that with Brandon, thanks to *me*."

"And I thank you for that," Ruby said.

Keep it quiet. Defuse.

"I didn't want anyone else going through the hell I've been through," Mariah said bitterly. "Even you." She started to turn away, then turned back. "My involvement with Gabe was as much a hope that he could get me free from his father as it was about earning that damned week with Alexander. I almost told Gabe about his parentage then but was too cowardly to try."

"I...." Ruby's voice trailed off. She didn't know what to say.

"Even then. Even drunk as a skunk, he mourned the divorce. Leaving you."

"You and Joseph damned near manipulated him to suicide," Ruby snapped.

Mariah gulped. "*It didn't happen because I didn't finish the damn job.*"

"What?"

She swallowed hard. "I was supposed to meet Gabe that night, after he left you. If he didn't shoot himself that night when staying at that cheap motel in Grande City, I was supposed to give him another dose of psychotropics, lead him on, get him drunk and crying...and then go, because the control words I was supposed to say would push him over the edge when he woke up. I didn't dose him or say the words. I honked the horn of my car, then went to him without saying anything, and took him home. Told Philip that Gabe was really resistant and he needed more meds. Philip believed me, thank God. I was terrified that I'd just screwed everything up with Alexander." She choked. "But your son—so darling, so cute, and Gabe was so devoted to him at the AgI—I kept thinking *what if that was my son that I just made fatherless?* I couldn't do it, Ruby. I just couldn't do it."

Ruby startled, remembering Gabe's account of that event. He'd had the .45 in his hands, thinking about sticking it in his mouth and pulling the trigger.

A horn honked in the parking lot and I jumped because my next thought was that I was going to make Joseph pay if he had harmed you and Branny. Then I put everything away.

"I owe you that," she said in a low voice. "Thank you."

"He cried about losing you. And Brandon. Talking about Brandon, because as much as leaving you broke him, leaving Brandon was even harder. And it—" Mariah choked. "I kept thinking about Alexander. I—I couldn't do that to Brandon. Not to a kid that Gabe loved so much he'd leave rather than risk harm to him. It wasn't for you. It was for your son. *My* son was already screwed up. I didn't want to see that happen to Brandon."

Ruby paused, looked down at her hands, and then back up. "I appreciate it. For Brandon's sake. For Gabe. And as it turns out, for a hell of a lot more people."

"Yeah." Mariah exhaled.

"Look. The Martinieres are funny about family. Being Alexander's acknowledged mother means you're one of us." Ruby tried to smile at Mariah. "You and me both. Mothers of Martinieres."

"And?" Mariah asked, caution in her voice.

"There may be—resources to help you. Once we get this all sorted out."

"I don't want charity."

Ruby sighed. "I understand. But you of all people should know this isn't charity. We do take care of our own—and I may not like it, but you are one of our own. You're entitled to our help."

Mariah nodded. "I'll consider it."

She left.

Ruby found a glass and filled it with water.

Four more days.

And who knew how long until they found Michael?

Four more days.

CHAPTER 15

THREE MORE DAYS.

Another drizzly morning. Ruby did barn chores, and was morosely digging up carrots in the garden when Gabe yelled to her from the back porch.

"Ruby. Alexander called. Wants to talk to both of us. How soon can you be ready to call him back?"

Ruby eyed the length of the row she still had to dig and the pile of multicolored carrots.

I need a break anyway.

The carrots *were* mostly dug, with maybe a half hour's worth of work left. She could spray off what she'd harvested so far and set them on the back porch to dry, then put them in basement storage later. Yeah. She was almost at a good stopping place.

"Give me about a half hour," she answered.

"All right."

She gathered up bunches of carrots and cleaned them and her spading fork. After taking care of everything she went upstairs to change out of her wet clothing and joined Gabe in his office.

Alexander was alone when they called, standing up and somehow looking stronger than he did yesterday.

"Gabriel, Ruby. Brandon and I have managed a hack. We still don't know where Michael's current nest—that's what we call it—is. But we have a code to immobilize their loyalty oath to Philip without the same trauma I experienced. Ruby can send it to my brothers, just before we retrieve them."

"Can the same hack be done to you?" Gabe asked.

Alexander grinned humorlessly. "Brandon and I decided to reinforce my own code structures so that it *wouldn't* happen to me. That's how we discovered this backdoor, and devised a fail-safe."

"That's good."

"The one thing—Ruby needs to be in close proximity to them. And it is short-term. Otherwise we'd do it now. Needs to happen just before we move in to grab Michael, with Ruby present."

"Good job," Gabe said.

"Thanks. We're still trying to find a means to trace them through those links, but it's taking a while. Lots of blocks and diversionary paths. Brandon's working on this now. But I need integration time for my latest cyborg updates before I dive back into tracing links, so I'm the one who's making this call."

"Have you talked to your mother about blocking Philip?" Ruby asked. "I know she was worried that you were sent to kill them."

Another mirthless grin. "You immobilized that program at the banquet. A good thing. If I survived taking out Brandon at the New Dems, my next orders were to dispose of her and Georgy." The grin faded. "I—don't know how to talk to my mother about it. Should I? I—want to. But she already—that look she gives me right now...."

Gabe shrugged and looked at Ruby.

"I would tell her," she said slowly. "She needs to know."

"I—I don't know how to say it." Alexander looked down at his artificial hand, now exposed. "And...." His voice trailed off. "It hasn't been the same between us since I was sent to them. She is suspicious, and rightfully so. My programming doesn't include those modules now, but I don't know how to convince her."

Ruby sighed. "Would you like me to talk to her?"

I am the Matriarch, after all. I suppose this task falls into my realm.

Relief eased the tension in the right, non-metallic side of his face. "I would appreciate that, yes."

"I'll see if she'll speak to me."

"Thank you. That's all from us. We will let you know once we've found Michael's new nest."

"Thank you," Gabe said. As Alexander's image faded out, he focused on Ruby. "You gonna be okay with talking to Mariah?"

"Things have changed between us due to Alexander," Ruby said, trying to convince herself as well as Gabe. "But it's an ongoing dialogue. I suspect that talks like this are part of my job as the Matriarch. I'm going to do it now, then finish the carrots."

He clasped her hand. "Good luck. Let me know if you need help."

"Thanks." She got up and went to her office, sitting there staring out the window for a few moments to gather her thoughts, before she finally snapped her fingers and called Mariah.

"Ruby." Mariah appeared. She looked tired and worn as she sat at a desk, her hair back in a headband, casual clothing. Not at all the carefully styled Mariah that Ruby was accustomed to seeing.

"Mariah." Ruby drew a deep breath. "Gabe and I just finished a conversation with Alexander. About remote control codes."

Mariah tensed. "Was I right?"

Ruby nodded. "He didn't try to avoid or deny it. I just asked Alexander if he had told you that he had blocked Philip's ability to access him, that you were worried he was sent to kill you. And he answered."

Mariah crumpled, leaning her left elbow on the arm of her chair and covering her face with her hand. At last she looked up. "I wanted to be wrong," she said in a small, wavering voice. "I really wanted to be wrong. But I know Philip too damn well." Then she shuddered and straightened up. "Are we safe from him? Me and Georgy?"

"He says so. It was—supposed to happen if he survived killing Brandon. You and Georgy were next."

Mariah's face scrunched up and she shook her head. "So Philip was done with me. *Is* done with me. God! The asshole. The absolute, utter asshole. Throwing me away like everyone else in his life. Use then discard. The fucker." She continued swearing and shaking her head. At last she stopped, heaving a huge breath. "And. Alexander couldn't tell me himself."

"He is afraid to, Mariah. It really worries him that your behavior has changed toward him."

"But he told you." Bitter voice. "I've given him the chance to tell me."

"He only told me because I asked. He answered directly because I am the Matriarch, I suppose. I asked because of our conversation the other day. You have the right to know. Otherwise, I don't think he would have said one word about it." Ruby sighed. "Mariah, he really *wants* to tell you. He just doesn't know how to do it. I think he's afraid of your reaction."

Mariah looked away from Ruby, her fingers tapping on her knee. "You're *sure* that we're safe?"

"From what he said, it was one of the modules I burned out at the New Dems. Which means it's *gone*, Mariah. Doubly cancelled by Alexander swearing an oath to me and Gabe. Triply cancelled by the new safeguards he and Brandon installed, to keep Philip from regaining control of him."

"*Good*," Mariah said viciously. "Now if only we could do the same sort of thing to disable Philip."

"Unfortunately, he's not cyborged, so no kill switch for behavioral modules."

"I suppose you would have done something long before now if you did have that power," Mariah said.

"As much as I hate him for what he's done to Gabe—and that's only the beginning of what I hold against Philip? Absolutely."

"How—solid are these oaths you asked me and Georgy to take? Philip conditioned mine—" Mariah swallowed hard. "For years. It's only become slightly easier to speak since we swore to you—and you saw how I got shut down when I tried to tell you details. I thought these oaths canceled each other out."

"I'd have to talk to Donna-gran for more specifics. Why?"

"Because I have just had a sneaky, vicious idea that may require me to push the oath I swore to you and Gabe." A worried expression crossed her face. "But I still have a deep-level compulsion when it comes to Philip. And now I even doubt the validity of this idea because I have to wonder—is it my own, or is it Philip's compulsion working in me?"

"Run it by me," Ruby said. "It's probably safe if you're questioning yourself."

God, I hope I'm right.

"I need to know the limits of those oaths," Mariah said.

"Because I think that I might be able to lure the others, maybe even Philip, here before the meeting."

"Oh? How?"

"By offering him inside information. Approved by you and Gabe, of course. By suggesting that I'm already regretting the choice I made, and that I'm—" Her face twisted. "—that I'm still his *good little two-faced girl who can entice information out of anyone.* He's said that to me many times. If he thinks he can gain control of me again, he'd definitely try it."

"Hmm. That is an interesting thought." Ruby eyed Mariah. Legitimate offer or an excuse for a double-cross? *This is Mariah that you're dealing with, after all,* she reminded herself. "Let me check with Gabe. *You* might want to talk it over with Brandon and Alexander."

"I'm going to do it right now," Mariah said firmly.

"Okay. I'll talk to Gabe."

Mariah signed off. Ruby pushed herself up out of her chair. *Doesn't look like I'm going to be getting back to the carrots all that soon.* Well, she wasn't in any hurry to get wet again.

No sooner had Ruby told Gabe about Mariah's idea than Mariah called back. Brandon and Alexander were with her.

"You know, this idea of Mariah's has some possibilities," Brandon said without preliminaries. "It might give me the chance to do some further tracing."

"How safe is it?" Gabe asked.

"Philip is not going to be able to issue compulsions over a call," Brandon said. "He lacks that ability. We know that. And Al and I have come up with some further options for the call script that might make things a bit more realistic. Mariah will call from Al's bedside. He'll be powered down. We'll present it as a failure on this end, with Mariah desperate to resuscitate Al."

"And if it goes bad, I can try to piss him off so much that

he'll come here just to kill me himself," Mariah said grimly. "Or send someone to kill me."

"Are you sure this is going to work?" Ruby asked.

"We have to time it right for best effect," Mariah said. "I think we need to do it the day before the meeting, late in the afternoon, just before the Reals meet. Philip will already be focused on trying to get the Reals to reinstate his nomination. He won't have a lot of time to consider what I say—and the timing would be right for me to have second thoughts. Especially with Alexander down."

"What if he sends an assassin?" Gabe asked. "I know a little bit about how that sort of thing works, from Alvarez Armory days."

Both Brandon and Alexander grinned.

"Oh, that would be the frosting on the cake," Brandon said, rubbing his hands together gleefully.

"Bran! Don't get overconfident!" Gabe snapped. "Just because you worked on a couple of the Armory's actions doesn't mean you're the equivalent of anything Philip would send."

"Not overconfidence," Alexander said. "The probable assassin would be one of my brothers," Alexander added. "Maybe two. They'll know Michael's location. That would be better than trying to trace it down like we're doing now."

"Are you *sure* that's a good idea?" Gabe asked. "With *two* assassins, that could be problematic."

Brandon and Alexander kept smirking.

"We did a sparring session once I got back on my feet today," Alexander said. "Even with me moving at half-capacity, my assessment is that Brandon has strengths against the cyborged. He doesn't have our power and endurance—can't, he's not cyborged. However, he's quick and agile. He'll be able to hold his own." He paused. "If Brandon had been cyborged, he'd be our leader, my replacement."

"I—see," Gabe said slowly.

Ruby stifled a shiver, remembering Serg's past assessment of Brandon's fighting skills.

Brandon could go pro if he wasn't Gabe's son and in line to become the Martiniere.

Brandon turned solemn. "We need to coordinate. Once Mariah makes the call to Philip, we need to be on alert, prepared for at least one assassin. And we need to be ready to move before the meeting to recover Michael if that happens, because that's our opening." He scowled. "A thought. One way that Philip could screw us over is if he times an assassination attempt to happen right before the meeting, with plans to move Michael during the meeting."

"I need to be much more convincing, then, prod him into wanting to finish the job. He'll want to ensure Alexander is out of commission, then me and Georgy," Mariah said. "We'll need to set up some sort of response deadline where he has to act before the meeting, to give us time."

"We'll work on ideas," Brandon said.

"All right," Gabe said, running his fingers through his hair. "Get the timing down, get a script going that will convince Philip to act sooner rather than later. Keep us posted."

"We will."

They signed off.

Gabe eyed Ruby. "I think we should spend the night before the meeting at Moondance. Just in case. You and I may be old and not as agile as Brandon...but you have the mind control codes and you can take care of yourself. And I can still fight. Maybe not at Brandon's level—true for both of us—but if we have to...."

"I agree. And Justine needs to be there."

"And Serg." Gabe tapped his fingers on the desk thoughtfully. "Yes. I think that will be a sufficient greeting party for any intruding assassins. And if they don't show up?" He shrugged. "We're already present for the meeting."

"I think that's an excellent idea," Ruby said.

"Hopefully it works."

"Yes. And meanwhile...." She sighed. "Time to finish the carrot harvest."

She trudged upstairs to change back into outside work clothing.

Two more days.

A mid-morning call from Brandon, Alexander, Kris, Mariah, *and* Georgy. Donna-gran joined Ruby and Gabe in Ruby's office.

"We have it figured out," Brandon said. "Al is going to be in bed, immobilized. Mariah will call Philip, say that we're refusing to reprogram Al's structures that Ruby wiped out, that he's dying. Georgy breaks in with the news that I'm going to dissect Al to hack Philip's structures, he overheard me telling you. She begs Philip to get her out of here because we're going to feature Al's termination as part of the Martiniere Group meeting, and she's afraid for her and Georgy. Meanwhile, once she signs off, I take Al's place in the bed—"

"No," Gabe said. "*I'll* do that."

"What?" Brandon startled.

"We're coming over before you make the call. Backup—and we'll be right there if we get a traceable lead to Michael after capturing those assassins. I'll be in the bed. *You* need to be out there with the defensive force and managing comms."

Brandon pursed his lips thoughtfully. "Kris? Al? Kris was already going to be managing comms."

"I can do backup for her," Donna-gran said.

"I can help with the defense," Ruby said.

Alexander nodded. "Bran, it does give us more help. Gabriel, we also have Colin Fields on the ground with his body-modded Freed Indentureds to protect our perimeters, wielding active Defenders. Jeff Swait has sent us some more."

"All right," Brandon said thoughtfully. "Mom. I think you should be head of the group protecting Mariah and Georgy."

"Wouldn't they be in there with Alexander—or who we want them to think is Alexander?" Ruby asked.

"We will be," Mariah said. "The access links I'll pass to Philip are supposed to assume that the three of us are in one place, so that it's easier to *retrieve*—" she flashed quote marks in the air, "—the three of us."

"But we're assuming that assassination is the goal," Brandon said.

"Once we gain control of the brothers Philip sends to perform the assassination," Alexander said, "we send a 'Mission Accomplished' message to Philip and then go collect Michael."

It all seemed so simple.

Still, there was so much that could go wrong—like with Pat's extraction.

Ruby shivered.

At least this time we're all vaccinated against all variants of the G9.

ONE MORE DAY.

"You ready to go to Moondance?" Gabe asked Ruby.

She checked the garment bag that held her dress for the

meeting, a bespoke new one in Martiniere green and gold that included pockets for her lucky locket, a stunner, and a quick-access holster that concealed her .38. A derringer also clipped into the boots that went with this dress.

No more high heels or sandals.

"As ready as I'll ever be," she said.

They eyed each other. This was it. Everything they had been working toward since winning the Superhero.

Gabe nodded. Then he reached for her, pulling her close. "No matter what happens, Rubes—I couldn't have gotten this far without you. I love you."

She cupped his cheek with her right hand. "I love you, too. We'll do this, Gabe. We'll win. And then we'll settle in for the winter with the challenge of raising Michael."

He smiled. "That might prove to be simpler than the past few months."

"Or even more complex."

"Yeah. That's always possible."

They wouldn't know until they actually saw him, she reminded herself.

RUBY SHIVERED AS ALEXANDER CAREFULLY APPLIED THE plaskin to Gabe's face. Unlike Alexander's silvery cover of his cyborg parts, it mimicked Alexander's cyborg features. The likeness was uncanny—and frightening. Gabe's right hand already had plaskin applied to make it look like Alexander's.

"What do you think?" Alexander asked.

Gabe blinked his eyes. "A little uncomfortable, especially the eyelid and my mouth," he said, moving his lips slowly and carefully. "It's a good thing that I'm not supposed to be talking. How much work will it be to take off?"

"Careful peel," Justine said. She had devised the plaskin print by scanning both Gabe and Alexander's faces, then combining them. It had taken four prints to get to this stage. "All right. Stand up Gabe, and let's compare them."

Alexander and Gabe stood together. Other than hair color and the lines in Gabe's uncovered face, the resemblance was close.

"Looks good," Brandon said. "Mariah?"

"Should we try for the full-face again?" Mariah frowned. "There's just enough difference...."

"He wouldn't be lying on his back so Philip won't see his actual face, just the cyborg implants, if he chooses to look closer and you can control that, Mariah," Brandon said. "If Dad lies on his right side, with the cyborged arm and leg stretched out straight. That's what Philip will expect to see."

Justine produced a wig that matched Alexander's hair. "Now for this."

"Good thing I just had a haircut," Gabe murmured, as she carefully eased it onto him, fussing as she fit the wig over the plaskin.

"Yes," she said, stepping back, frowning thoughtfully. "All right. You'll need to keep the covers pulled up high."

"Philip would expect that," Brandon said. "Chilling of the remaining body would be one reaction to failing cyborg systems. What about infusion lines?"

"Tape them to Gabe's arm once we get him situated in bed. No thrashing around," Justine said.

"All right. I guess it's showtime, if we're all ready," Gabe said. "Everyone know their parts?" He looked around as they nodded.

"Then let's do it."

"Let me check your mics," Brandon said. He quickly inspected them, nodding. "Okay. Now I expect Philip to drop a virus load during this call. Once you make the connection, your coms get switched to a virtual simulation of our systems. Anything he does—probes, viral dumps, organizational inquiries—will be shunted off in that direction. It *should* work."

"Let's hope it does," Gabe said grimly.

"Real systems are now triple-armed," Brandon said in a matching voice. "He's good but he isn't that good. We've proven that already."

Ruby and Donna-gran exchanged an arch of brows.

Cockiness? Or confidence?

Gabe and Mariah went into Alexander's room. The first noises were of Gabe getting settled into the bed. Ruby tightened her fists, staring at the door as it closed after them.

Will this work?

"Pull up the covers a bit more," Gabe said, his voice a little scratchy over the com. "But let my hand show."

"Got it. Calling." Mariah paused. Her breathing became shallower, quicker, accompanied by gulps and half-sobs.

"Mariah." Philip's voice was flat.

"Oh God, Philip, thank God you answered, oh God I need your help," Mariah wailed. "It's Alexander. He's—" she gulped. "Oh God he's dying and they won't do anything to help him!"

"Why should I care? He's not my problem anymore. Georgy's his owner."

"Philip!" Mariah groaned. "He's my baby! He's dying!"

"You threw your lot in with Gabriel. Let *him* do something."

"That's the thing! I didn't have any choice! They dragged me and Georgy along with Alexander and they're holding me hostage here." Mariah's voice rose. "They've been keeping us drugged! Ruby threatened to kill me if I didn't come with them —oh God, Philip, it's a fucking nightmare!"

"Mariah, what the hell do you want me to do?" Philip was

clearly annoyed by now. "I'm trying to save my presidential campaign. I'm so damn close to getting that nomination back. Even if I wanted to, I *can't* drop everything to save you."

Mariah sniffled. "They won't do anything for Alexander. Not even Gabe. I *begged* him. Reminded him of what we once were to each other. I don't know what they've got planned for that meeting tomorrow but—" she choked. "—it isn't going to be pretty."

"What do you mean?" Even more annoyance.

"We're to be made examples. Of something. I don't know what."

Philip snorted. "Gabriel is too high-minded for that."

"Not Gabriel, *Brandon*. I—every time I come along people stop talking. I've overheard whispers. And Brandon just glares at me. He's threatened to beat up Georgy twice and has slapped him around. Philip, he's the one who is really in control. Not Gabriel," she repeated. "*Brandon*. Philip, he's the really scary one. He's ruthless. Just like Ruby."

Brandon smirked, then pointed at Georgy. *Now*, his lips formed.

Georgy exploded into the room, slamming the door so hard behind him that Ruby flinched. "Mariah!" he husked, trying to keep his voice to a discreet level. "We've got to get Alexander out of here now!" A pause. "Philip, for God's sake, you've got to do *something*. They're planning a dissection!"

"A dissection?" Philip's voice sharpened.

"Brandon is *pissed*," Georgy said. "I overheard him talking to Serg. He can't crack the cyborg programming so they're going to dissect Alexander before the meeting to see if they can get at him that way." He gulped. "They f-f-forced me to sign away ownership of Alexander to Gabe. And he approved what Brandon wants to do! They'll beat that code, all of them together, I'm sure of it!"

"Fuck," Philip growled. Ruby startled at how much he sounded like Gabe at that moment. "Let me try something."

Silence.

"The cyborg isn't responding."

"I *told* you that, Philip!" Mariah wailed. "They shut it all off when they couldn't break his defenses this last time."

"Don't those idiots know that shutting down the cyborg systems will kill him? And that rebooting isn't just simply flipping a switch?"

"They don't care," she moaned. "Philip, you've got to do something!"

"Why? Alexander can't tell them anything if he's dead. Why should I do one damned thing to help him?"

Shit. He's not buying it.

"Because if Alexander dies, then *I* will talk," Mariah said softly. "I'll tell them *everything* I know. Willingly. Without being tortured into it. And you too, Georgy, right?"

"Right," Georgy said, sounding less certain.

Normal for Georgy.

"How do I know you haven't already been talking to them?"

"Do you think they'd trust me?" Plaintive. "Philip, they're going to have Piotr work on me and Georgy if we don't talk. Tell them everything we've done for you over the years. You always warned me about Piotr. For God's sake, Philip. Haven't I done enough for you over the years? Helped you? If not for Alexander, then me. *Don't let them do this to me.* Or am I nothing to you?"

A heavy sigh. "Georgy. Any idea about when they're going to dissect Alexander?"

"Around midnight if they can't get him functioning. They're running one last program to see if they can access his memory."

"All right." Another sigh. "Stay with Alexander. I'll have to figure out how to get someone in there."

"I can send you links—"

"No need. I see a route."

Brandon's hands clenched and he glowered at the door.

That was too easy, Ruby thought. *Wasn't it?*

"You and Georgy stay with Alexander. Help will be there."

"When?"

"When it gets there. *Later*, Mariah. I have a nomination to save."

A moment. Then, "He's disconnected."

Ruby noticed that Brandon scanned the house systems before he opened the door. "He tried to plug in a few viruses on that call," he said as they joined Gabe and Mariah. "But they're safely isolated in the simulation. It was almost *too* responsive when he tested our vulnerabilities. Luckily the program responded with increasing resources to his probe, as it would if it were the real one and he'd discovered a breach. He downloaded the sim I prepared, though. I didn't make it easy, but he did it."

Gabe sat up in the bed. "Alexander, what do you think? How long should we have before someone shows up?"

"I'll know within a few minutes of them leaving the current nest," Alexander said, popping up a screen from his cyborged wrist. "Tentatively—I would say after eight or so—what did you put into the sim as your normal rest time, Bran?"

"Ten pm. Complete with Kris crashing earlier," Brandon said. "Mom, Mariah, just so you know. The sim shows that Mom slapped Mariah around when you came over here earlier in the week. You were careful not to leave bruises on her face, but you knocked her around pretty good. He will see that— along with my slapping of Georgy."

"You're taping us here?" Mariah asked.

Brandon shook his head. "No. But I set up a process in the sim, goes back about five days. It matches Philip's personal systems. Five day loop, recording over old material in normal circumstances unless there's an archive command. It's what he would expect to see from our security setup."

"So now it's a waiting game." Gabe's hand reached up to his face only to halt a couple of inches away. He winced and put it back down.

"Yeah," Brandon said.

THEY HAD SETTLED INTO A POKER GAME AROUND THE dining room table—*not* Texas Hold 'em but a couple of other variants with wild cards—when the projection over Alexander's wrist pinged. He laid down his cards to check it.

"Got them," he said finally. "Daniel and Eric. Okay. They're—an hour out." He looked up. "It's definitely individual assassination, not arson. That would have been George and Frederick. The three of us were training to be Philip's kill squad—when we weren't guarding Michael."

"How skilled are they?" Serg asked.

"I'm oldest and the furthest along in training," Alexander said. "If Philip just wanted to kill everyone in the house, he wouldn't have sent those two. Daniel and Eric are programmed to be precise, sneaky, and quiet."

"Okay," Brandon said. "Places, everyone. Mom."

She joined Brandon and Alexander. "Ready."

They took up their station in the bedroom with Gabe, Mariah, and Georgy, Ruby ready to act. Once Daniel and Eric were in the house itself, she would rub her ring and speak the loyalty module kill switch code. If it still functioned. If they didn't move so quickly that Brandon and

Alexander would need to fight until she could find a code to disable them.

God, she hoped this worked.

Alexander's tracker was now projected on a screen implanted into the back of his cyborged hand. She could follow their progress along with Alexander.

Daniel and Eric took the road to Moondance, not through the woods and down the ridge like she would have done if sneaking up on the house. Stopped by the center pivot line in the field below the house. Slower movement.

"*Coming up the cliffs,*" Alexander whispered into the coms.

"*Got it,*" Serg answered. "*They've shut down the alarm sims.*"

Alexander leaned over to Ruby. "They'll try to come in through the balcony and slider. Once they're on the deck, we'll do it." She nodded. He switched to coms. "*Mariah, go ahead and react when you hear them at the slider. Normal.*"

Waiting. Waiting. Waiting. Brandon and Alexander took up their positions on each side of the slider door.

The faintest rustle.

"*They're on the deck,*" Alexander whispered.

Ruby rubbed the ring. "Control module 581. AZQ019 authentication. Shut down."

Stealthy noises at the slider. Alexander pursed his lips, frowning. "*Not seeing the change. Will need to be closer. Hold until they're inside.*"

"*All right,*" she whispered, reaching for her stunner, to have it ready. Stun first if her codes wouldn't do anything. Then if that didn't work—her gun.

Guard Gabe.

If he needed to protect himself, he had to strip off that face overlay at the minimum once the assassins were inside. He had already shed the hand and leg coverings, but decided to keep the plaskin on his face—just in case.

Why had her commands worked on Alexander at the banquet but not these two?

Probably updated. Or my previous command sensitized him.

She'd figure it out later.

Scratching at the slider's lock. At least it was taking them some time to open it.

"Wh-who's there?" Mariah called, her voice quavering.

Damn, she's a good actress. But I already knew that.

"Help from the true Martiniere," a muffled voice said. "Can you open this door?"

"Don't move, Mariah," Alexander said. *"They'll grab you once they're inside. Serg?"*

"Electronically releasing slider lock after Mariah answers," Serg said.

"I'm coming," Mariah said. Brandon gestured to her to get down. She and Georgy ducked behind the bed as the slider lock clicked and the door eased open. As the first one stepped in, Ruby rubbed the ring.

"Control module 581," she said as the first one entered. "AZQ019 authentication. Shut down."

As the first person aimed his weapon at her, Brandon jumped him. Alexander wrestled with the second one.

Maybe their names, too? One last try and then it's all weapons.

She rubbed the ring again. "Daniel. Eric. Control module 581. AZQ019 authentication. SHUT DOWN."

Both cyborged invaders—but not Alexander, thankfully— froze in place. Gabe sat up, lights switching on as he did. Ruby went to him. Mariah and Georgy slowly rose from behind the bed as Serg and several members of their security team burst in the door.

"Brothers," Alexander said softly. "Immobilize control module 581. Brandon. You'll have to enter the code to finalize it. Just like you did with me."

Brandon nodded. He faced the now-frozen cyborged he had been fighting. "What is your name?" he asked, in the same soft, quiet, measured tone that Alexander had used.

"Eric," the cyborged snapped, as if it had been forced out of him.

"Eric. I am immobilizing your loyalty module, control module 581. I have done this for Alexander. Will you allow me to do this for you?"

No verbal response as Eric's left hand rose slowly, as if an invisible weight impeded its easy movement. He turned his wrist so Brandon could access his controls.

"Thank you," Brandon said, still using the quiet voice. A few quick swipes, and a screen popped up. Brandon tapped something into the screen, then released Eric's hand. "You are now free."

Eric stared at Brandon. "You are Brandon Martiniere?"

"Yes."

Eric sank to his knees in front of Brandon. "I owe you everything for my freedom. I—"

"That's enough, man," Brandon said, discomfort clearly on his face as he reached for Eric's arms. "Stand up. Cyborged or not, you're a Martiniere, just like me, just like Alexander."

As Eric stood, Brandon repeated the process with Daniel.

"Brothers," Alexander repeated.

"You live," Eric whispered, staring at him. "But we were told—"

"I know what you were told," Alexander said. "It was necessary in order to free you." He gestured toward Gabe and Ruby. "You have met the Martiniere-in-waiting. Here are the Martiniere and the Matriarch."

"But his face?" Confusion filled Daniel's voice as he frowned at Gabe. "And the hair."

"Just a moment," Gabe said as he pulled off the wig. "Ruby, can you help?"

She helped him peel off the plaskin, dropping it on the bed. Gabe walked toward the two cyborged, rubbing his face, and she followed, standing at his side as he faced them.

"Daniel. Eric," he said. "I am Gabriel Martiniere, and this is Ruby Barkley. You are the sons of my cousin Joseph, and I recognize you as Martinieres by right."

"We're cyborged," Daniel said. "Indentured, the sons of indenture. Born into indenture, doomed to live as cyborged indentured."

"You are Martinieres by right," Gabe repeated firmly. "And since I am *the* Martiniere, you are technically my property— except that I free you. Now."

"Free? How? Why?" Eric asked. "What's the catch?"

"Yes, free," Gabe said. "Officially I become the Martiniere tomorrow—but only Philip and a minority of the family will object. As for *why*—" he gestured at them. "I will not hold indentured paper, either in my name or in the name of any company I have influence over. I will not own human beings, including cyborged humans." He paused. "I will ask one favor."

"A catch after all," said Daniel.

"Michael." Both cyborged flinched. "Your brothers. I want to free them as soon as possible. Will you help us?"

"Why do you want Michael?" Eric asked suspiciously.

"Because he should live his own life and not be held hostage to—" Gabe winced. "my father's delusions of longevity."

"And what will you do with him?" Daniel's voice faltered over the word *do*.

"Ruby and I will raise him as our own son, with the awareness of who and what he is." Gabe met both cyborgeds' gaze steadily. "We will not hide his origins from him. You can visit freely with him."

A pause, an exchange of glances, and then both cyborged nodded.

"We will take you to them," Eric said. "And what of us—the brothers? Will you have need of us?"

"I have sworn loyalty to the Martiniere and the Matriarch," Alexander said. "I am employed by Brandon, to provide his security. If all of us join with Brandon, then we will be whole, as we were intended to be."

Join with Brandon? What?

"Without coercion," Brandon said. "If some of you want to work for my father Gabriel, or continue to protect Michael, that will be your choice." He swallowed. "We cannot be the force that Philip visualized. I am not cyborged, nor do I choose that for myself. But if you want to join me in the fight to keep others from indenture, to eliminate indenture, and be my protectors in this battle—I would welcome your assistance."

Daniel turned to Gabe. "I will swear loyalty to you, Gabriel, then take you to Michael and our brothers."

"As will I," Eric said.

CHAPTER 16

Michael and the remaining cyborged brothers were at an isolated location on Mt. Hood, at the end of a narrow road near the National Forest boundaries. Within an hour of getting the details from Eric and Daniel, they had loaded into two jets, heading for an airstrip on the edge of the Portland metropolitan area.

Driving rain met them as they loaded into two rental vans for the trip up Hood. Ruby leaned against Gabe, not wanting to talk as worries flitted through her thoughts. He wrapped an arm around her as they sat silently together. Waiting. Conserving their energy. Brandon and Alexander monitored the screens as Daniel drove.

"Shit!" Brandon snapped suddenly. "They're moving Michael again. Your tracker just flared, Eric." He switched to comms. "*Serg. Taking you live. May be a change. Michael is being moved.*"

"They weren't supposed to do that until we had made our way back," Eric said.

"Philip just sent a termination code," Alexander said. "Your codes are cut off. He must have figured something was hinky, damn it."

"Can we still follow them?" Gabe asked.

"We're close enough that we'll cut them off on their way to the highway," Daniel said. "Close enough that even Alexander should be able to access the tracker. His code's still viable. We checked on the plane."

"Unless they try to go through that back road over the pass," Eric said.

"They can't, Eric. It's washed out," Daniel said. "Regional notice just posted."

"Is it legitimate or a ruse?" Alexander asked.

"I don't know," Daniel said. "But we're turning off in five minutes."

It seemed like no time at all before the van careened into a left turn, speeding up a winding road that climbed quickly.

"We're getting closer," Alexander said tensely. "They're coming toward us."

"Brace yourselves," Daniel said. "They're getting close."

"*Serg. Prepare for action.*"

Daniel wheeled their van to a sudden stop crosswise on the road to block the other van. Ruby and Gabe followed the others out as they charged toward the oncoming vehicle. It screeched to a halt.

"CARL!" Alexander bellowed.

The driver of the other van hesitated. Ruby rubbed her ring.

"Carl-Frederick-George!" she yelled, before repeating an updated code that Eric had given her.

Eric opened the driver's side van door. Ruby didn't hear what he said as they ran to the side. Daniel opened the side passenger doors.

Inside, two more cyborged glared at her and Gabe but they were frozen in place. Between them, wedged protectively under the arm of one of the cyborged, was a little dark-haired boy that reminded Ruby so much of Brandon at that age that it hurt.

But he was small—oh so small for his age—and his face was drawn and tight, dark circles under his eyes, blue tinges around his nostrils and lips, skin paler than it should be. The ice blue eyes were haunted, his tense worried expression that of a child much older than five.

"I am Gabriel Martiniere," Gabe said firmly. "*The* true Martiniere. Your brothers have sworn loyalty to me and are freedmen. Release."

The little boy pressed hard against the cyborged whose arm he huddled under. The cyborged squeezed him gently. "It will be all right, Michael. We won't let them hurt you," he said softly. Then, in a harsher and challenging tone to Gabe, "What do you intend to do with him—and us?"

"Freedom," Gabe said. He knelt on the step, placing him at the same level as the frightened boy. "Michael. I am Gabriel. This is Ruby," he said in a much softer voice. "We're here to take you home with us. A real home."

Michael shrunk back even more. "I don't want to die," he whimpered. "Philip said you would kill me."

Gabe paused and Ruby eased by him, sitting closer to Michael. She took a deep breath. "Michael. We aren't going to hurt you."

"You're gonna drain my blood." He gulped. "Just like Philip does."

Ruby shook her head, her heart breaking at the fear in the little boy's face. "No." She held up her left hand, showing Michael her ring. "You see this ring?"

He nodded, a tear trickling down his cheek.

"If I make promises on it, I can't break them. I *won't* break them. I am the Matriarch of the Martinieres, and—" her voice broke at the expression on his face. "And I swear to you that we are not going to drain your blood. In fact...." She tapped up the oath program. Michael's eyes widened at the gold projection from the ring. "I promise. I will not drain your blood. I swear to act as your mother. I swear I will protect you and keep you safe, until you reach legal age. The only blood to be taken from you will be for health testing."

Gabe's hand wrapped around hers. "I will not drain your blood. I swear to act as your father. I swear as the Martiniere that I will protect you and keep you safe, until you are of legal age and can care for yourself."

The projection flashed brightly, then faded.

Michael snuffled. Then he looked up at the cyborged whose arm was around him. "George? Is it okay?"

"It's a valid oath, Michael." George looked at them. "And— Eric has commed us with what the Martiniere said to him and Daniel." He swallowed hard. "They're safe, Michael. They will take care of you."

"But I want to be with you," Michael said.

"We will swear loyalty to them," George said. "We'll see you. Go with them. They are safe."

After a moment's hesitation, Michael uncurled himself from where he had wedged himself between George and the seat. His movements were stiff and shaky, and Ruby wanted to gather him into her arms.

But from the wary look still in his eyes, she didn't think he was ready for that yet. She offered her hand for him to take. It was cold and clammy, and far too bony for a healthy child of this age, in her opinion. She delicately closed her fingers around his, guiding him down the steps. Gabe gently took his other hand and they slowly, oh so heartbreakingly slowly, walked to their van. Children weren't supposed to move so stiff and slow, as if they were arthritic.

Then they took the oaths of the remaining brothers before

loading up and speeding back to the airstrip, Michael now between her and Gabe.

Michael held himself rigid. He didn't speak until after Ruby had gently strapped him into one of the chairs on the plane.

"Where are we going?" he asked.

"For tonight and tomorrow, to a place called Moondance," she said. "Brandon—the son of me and Gabriel, the Martiniere-in-waiting—lives there." She gestured toward Brandon, who waved at Michael. "We have an important meeting tomorrow. Then we go home."

"Home?"

"To a ranch called the Double R," she said. "We have horses, cows, chickens, cats, and dogs."

Michael's face crinkled in puzzlement. "What's a horse?"

Gabe burst out with laughter that almost but not quite held a manic edge. "Oh Michael. You will learn about horses. They are big four-legged animals that carry people around, amongst other things."

"Will they eat me?"

"No. Horses eat things like grass. So do cows. But horses— ah, horses are marvelous creatures. Just wait until you watch Ruby ride one."

"Is she good?"

"The best," Gabe said, grinning at Ruby. "The very best horsewoman ever."

"Flatterer," she scoffed, even as she flushed at the compliment.

MICHAEL FELL ASLEEP AFTER TAKEOFF, WHICH GAVE RUBY and Gabe time during the brief flight to Moondance to talk to the brothers about Michael and what he knew and expected.

He had recently gone through a blood draw that had nearly killed him. His clothing was limited to pajamas and several sets of uniforms like the one he wore, a stiff black tunic and trousers that made Gabe wince. One worn stuffed bear that George carefully tucked into Michael's arms as he slept. A couple of small cars. Several picture books that Frederick identified as standard-issue indentured crèche fare, focused on the joys of serving their contract holder.

And a whole host of medicines. Sedatives for travel and when he needed to be kept quiet. Psychotropics to facilitate deep behavior programming. Chemotherapy medication to be given the week before a draw, to augment the medications Philip was already on. Besides other meds.

Frederick and George were the closest to Michael, and had the most difficulty talking about how he had been treated. The brothers had not become involved until the clones were about three years old. But the bonding seemed to be tightest with Michael, as the longest-lived of the clones.

Landing at Moondance was a welcome break from the chronicle of horrors that Michael had already undergone. He didn't rouse when they landed, so Gabe carefully carried him into the truck that took them up to the main house, big enough to carry them all instead of limiting them to multiple crawlers.

Kris, Donna-gran, and Mariah met them at the door. Donna-gran cried out at the sight of the small sleeping boy in Gabe's arms, hands covering her mouth. She turned away, shaking with tears, muffling her sobs. Brandon lingered to brief the others as Gabe and Ruby took Michael to their room.

"Should we wake him?" Gabe whispered.

"Bathroom and let's get him into pajamas."

Michael roused enough for Gabe to guide him into the bathroom while Ruby pulled a pair of pajamas out of his suitcase. She wanted to cry out as she saw how threadbare they were.

He couldn't even give the boy decent things.

But then Gabe guided Michael out of the bathroom and she had to put aside those thoughts for now. Together they got him changed and put into the small bed next to theirs that Kris and Donna-gran had prepared while they were gone. Gabe slid his arm behind her back, shaking his head, quivering against her as they watched him settle into the bedding.

"He—If I—God—If ever—" Gabe drew a deep, shuddering breath before he whispered the rest into her ear. "If I ever turn into something like my father, put me down like you would a rabid dog, Ruby. Please. *God.* Don't let me turn into him."

"I won't," she promised.

Nor will I let you become like him either, she silently promised Michael.

———

She wasn't certain how long she had been asleep when whimpers from Michael's bed woke her. Even though it had been many years since she had parented a small child, Ruby automatically rolled out of bed, crouching by Michael's bedside. She reached out and delicately stroked his forehead. Sorrowful blue eyes looked back at her as Michael sniffled.

"Are you all right?" she whispered. "Remember, I'm Ruby. I'm taking care of you."

"Are you a nurse?"

"No, honey. I'm—your new mother."

More sniffles. "Philip says I don't have a mother."

"Philip is wrong." More rage that she had to throttle back. Now was not the time for it. "You doing all right?"

"Bad dreams," he mumbled.

"Would you sit in my lap and let me rock away those bad dreams for you?" A technique she had used for Brandon when he was the same age.

He studied her, then nodded solemnly. She let herself scoop him up now and carry him to the rocker. He held himself tight, still cautious, stiff even as she rocked.

At last he looked up at her. "When is my next blood draw?"

"Oh honey. No more blood draws for you, except a tiny amount to check your health. Ever."

Blue-eyed version of Gabe measured her. "You promise."

"I promise."

He sighed and sagged against her. She rocked and rocked, stroking the side of his head and his cheek, humming softly. He tentatively put his thumb in his mouth, hesitating as if he expected her to reprimand him. She ignored it. Tension ebbed slowly from his body until she was certain he was asleep. And still she kept rocking.

Gabe padded over. "It's okay?" he whispered.

"Bad dreams," she murmured back. "I've got it."

"For tonight," he said. "My turn next time." He kissed her forehead, then went back to bed.

Ruby kept rocking, holding Michael, blinking back tears even after he had fallen asleep.

Surely something good had to come out of this horror.

Perhaps it would be this little boy.

Eventually she fell asleep while rocking, only to wake as Gabe gently extracted Michael from her arms to resettle him, then guide her to their own bed.

They woke before Michael.

"I'll stay with him," Gabe whispered. "We shouldn't let him wake alone. If you could bring me some coffee and food?"

"Sure."

She slipped quietly out of their room. Justine and Donna-gran sat at the breakfast bar, sipping coffee, untouched bowls of granola before them.

"How is he?" Donna-gran asked quickly.

"Still sleeping," Ruby said. "He had bad dreams but he let me rock him back to sleep."

Donna-gran shook her head. "He looks so...Philip never, ever looked like that as a child."

"He had a major blood draw three weeks ago and was on chemo meds for a week before," Ruby said grimly. "Who knows what kind of shape he's in health-wise? And he's terrified of blood draws."

"As he should be," Justine said, her tone matching Ruby's. "Ruby, are you two going to be able to handle raising him? If he survives for very long."

"How do parents who have kids who develop childhood cancer handle it?" Ruby groaned. "Who better to raise him? We have resources to help him. And any animosity we might have toward—his progenitor—isn't stirring. It's clear that Michael is not Philip."

Brandon ambled into the kitchen, wearing workout clothing, followed by the brothers. "Cereal in that cupboard, bowls in that one. Fruit in the fridge, and—" He paused. "Ma, you and Dad eaten yet? If Al is any judge, these guys will ravage what we have available. Need to order more supplies."

Ruby shook her head. "Just came out to get food. Michael is still sleeping, and we don't want him to wake up alone. Your dad's with him."

"Hang on then, guys. Ma, I can help you take food in."

"That would be helpful." She assembled two trays for the three of them, raising her brows as Brandon added a bowl and coffee cup for him.

"Guys, now you can dive in," he said to the brothers. "Ma, I'm going to come in and eat with the two of you—hopefully three, if Michael wakes."

"Okay."

"I'll get the door," Donna-gran said. "I—if it's possible before the meeting I'd like to meet him, too, Ruby."

She nodded. "Let's see what kind of shape he's in. I have some ideas for how to present him to the meeting, if it becomes necessary."

As Donna-gran opened the door, Ruby heard Gabe's voice, soft, quiet, saying something she couldn't make out. She and Brandon carried the trays to the small table.

"Hey," Gabe said. "Here's Ruby back with breakfast. And now you can officially meet our son Brandon. He was one of your rescuers last night, and will be a brother—sort of—to you."

Ruby turned. Gabe sat on the floor by the bed. Michael pushed himself up to a sitting position, still moving in that slow careful manner clearly meant to minimize hurting. It made her heart ache to see such a young child moving like an old man.

Brandon glided over to Michael and joined Gabe on the floor. "Hello, Michael. I'm Brandon. Son of Gabe and Ruby. Martiniere-in-waiting." He grinned. "Once you get settled in at the Double R, I can show you some cool secret stuff that they don't know about." He looked back at Ruby. "Ma, did you get rid of my toys?"

"No," Ruby said. So it was going to be a family breakfast. "I set them out for Michael, if that's all right with you."

"It is. I give all of my kid stuff to you, Michael."

Michael eyed him cautiously. "You were supposed to be

one of the brothers. Philip told me there would be a new one. He showed me your picture. But you never came."

"Yeah." Brandon sighed. "Long story there, buddy. It would not have been a good thing if I had been become one of the brothers like Philip wanted. But I'm here now, and they're with me. We worked out together this morning. They're worried about you. Now I can tell them that you're all right."

"Can I see them?" Michael asked wistfully.

"Of course," Gabe said. "But first you need to eat breakfast and get showered."

"Dad, after breakfast, we also need to talk about meeting choreography. If Philip does have the guts to show up, they want to confront him."

"No!" Michael shrieked. "Not Philip. No, no, no!"

"Hey, hey, hey," Brandon said quickly. "The brothers are here, and they will protect you. So will I. And my parents. Serg. Justine. Donna-gran. We're all here for you."

Michael's breaths came quick and fast. "He's gonna grab me back! Make the brothers take me—"

"Nope," Brandon said. "Michael. The brothers are free from his control. Thanks to my mother. We checked the codes again this morning to be sure as part of this upcoming meeting. They're free." He took a deep breath. "But we have to go through this final step. And then, one way or another—you won't see him any more."

"But-but-but he can control—"

"No he can't," Ruby said firmly, sitting on the bed next to Michael. "I won't let him. The family won't let him—and it will all be family here. We have you. You are a part of us now. Philip can't claim you."

Michael gulped, looking up at her. "You promise?"

"I promise. Let's eat breakfast and get ready for the day,"

she said. "Then there is a special person who wants to meet you."

"Who's that?"

"Donna-gran. She is—" Ruby hesitated. How best to describe Donna-gran to her son's clone? "Everybody's grandmother," she said finally. "But not what you expect from a grandmother."

Michael studied her some more. "Okay," he said finally.

"And as for you two," Ruby said, glaring at both Brandon and Gabe. "No more business over breakfast today. Understand?"

After they both nodded, she led Michael to the table.

It was a quiet meal after that.

THE FIRST ORDER OF BUSINESS AFTER BREAKFAST WAS introducing Michael to Donna-gran, something Ruby set up with her after they ate and while Gabe supervised Michael's morning routines. To her relief, he quietly reported that Michael was as proficient as one could expect from any five-year-old when it came to showering and dressing. Then Brandon and Gabe went off to talk with the brothers while Ruby took Michael to Donna-gran's room. He gazed around the great room that was being set up for the meeting later on.

"This is big," he said.

"Yes," Ruby said. "This is Moondance. Brandon lives here, and we have official Martiniere Group meetings here." *Or will have,* she amended to herself. "We have this meeting today, and then you and I and Gabe will go to our home at the Double R."

"Does Philip know we're here? Does he know this place?" he asked, in that small, tremulous voice she now recognized as his worry mode.

"Yes," she said. "He has been at Moondance before, and I don't doubt that he knows we are here." She knelt in front of him. "Just remember, Michael. We're with you. You aren't alone. We're your family. We love you. And one reason I am taking you to Donna-gran is that you need to meet her. She will keep you safe during the meeting."

His lower lip pushed out slightly—*another Brandon resonance*—and he scowled. "Why can't you and Gabe do it? Or Brandon?"

"Because we have things to do during the meeting. Gabe will be leading it, and Brandon and I will be helping him. Keeping him safe. Donna-gran's job is to keep you safe. So you need to get to know her before then. She's also someone special to you. Okay?"

She waited. He nodded.

They walked to the suite next to Brandon and Kris's. Ruby tapped once and Donna-gran opened the door. "Ruby. Michael." She bowed to him. "I am pleased to make your acquaintance, Michael." Her voice caught slightly as she studied the young boy, and Ruby thought she saw tears glimmering in her eyes.

"Pleased to make your acquaintance as well," Michael said in what was clearly a well-rehearsed response.

Donna-gran snorted. "Well, at least Philip maintained *some* standards of proper behavior." She gestured to her table, with chairs set up, paper and markers lying on it. "Why don't you come sit with me and let's talk? You may draw or color."

"Okay. Thank you." Another automatic reply, mechanically polite.

Donna-gran gestured toward the chair that had the paper and markers in front of it. "Why don't you sit there?"

Michael complied.

"Why don't you tell me a little bit about yourself, and I'll tell you something about me."

Michael shrugged. "I'm Michael. I used to live with the brothers."

Donna-gran craned her neck. "No favorite colors? Stories? Toys?"

"Philip said I don't need those things." Still reflexive, almost drone-like.

"But surely you have something favorite in your life. How about that bear I saw you with?"

Michael shrugged again and reached for a black marker. "Stuffie Bear. It belonged to John first. Then Keith, then Larry. Now me."

"John? Keith? Larry?" Ruby and Donna-gran exchanged glances.

"My befores," he said. "They're dead now. Philip drained them."

Ruby flinched at the matter-of-fact tone in Michael's voice.

"Oh." Donna-gran blinked. "Well. Michael. We are relatives."

Michael looked up, then refocused on his drawing.

"I am your mot-*grand*mother," Donna-gran said carefully.

Michael put down his marker and turned to her. "My *real* grandmother?" He then picked up a red marker and began drawing something in big, broad strokes.

Donna-gran paused, meeting Ruby's eyes, then nodded. "Yes," she said faintly. "You are my descendant."

"What do grandmothers do?" Michael put down the marker and shoved that picture aside, reaching for another piece of paper.

"Mostly spoil their grandchildren," Donna-gran said quietly. "Sometimes take care of them. If their parents allow."

"Oh. Why do I have a grandmother and my befores didn't?"

"Honey," Donna-gran said. "If I had known about your befores, I would have been there for them as well. I didn't know. None of us—knew." Her voice caught. She coughed, then looked over at Ruby. "I know Ruby has things to do. Would you mind spending some time with me? Maybe even play a game or two? I've found some games, both electronic and board."

"I don't know how to play games."

"Maybe it's time for you to start."

Michael shrugged. "Sure."

"Unless you want me to stay I'm going to go," Ruby said. "Okay, Michael?"

He shrugged. "Sure."

She stole a glance at the picture he had finished. Two stick figures, one bigger than the other. The smaller figure had something that looked like a red line coming out of one arm, running into the arm of the bigger figure. There was a knife in the hand of the smaller figure, stabbing into the bigger figure—clearly the big broad strokes in red that Michael had been drawing.

Ruby shivered.

Just how angry is Michael?

He certainly had the right to be very angry.

What did it mean for his future?

CHAPTER 17

It was time. Brandon, Kris, Justine, Michael, and Donna-gran watched as Gabe put the Martiniere emeralds on Ruby. Kathleen, the wife of the Moondance ranch manager Tim, had found some clothes for Michael to wear instead of the stiff black tunic and trousers. He now wore a pair of khaki slacks and a nice long-sleeved button-down collar blue shirt. Michael and Donna-gran would stay in her suite until it was time for them to appear. But the rest of them needed to greet the Family members on arrival.

Mariah and Georgy were also in their room. Ruby wasn't certain if they were attending the meeting or not. She had seen Mariah and Alexander talking earlier; while both still seemed stiff and formal with each other, at least they didn't *sound* like they were arguing.

"All right," Gabe said once he was finished putting the emeralds on Ruby. "Let's get this done."

They filed out, Donna-gran quickly whisking Michael into her room in the other wing of the house. Ruby noticed that the brothers followed them.

Shortly after that, the Family started arriving. Nearly everyone else was seated when Philip marched into the great room. He brushed past Ruby and Justine before they could say anything, and took a seat at the very back, arms crossed over his chest, scowling. Gabe and Brandon, up front, huddled together, glancing at Philip while they talked. Brandon moved a chair to one side of the low platform. Then he strode back to Philip. They exchanged sharp words, but Philip followed Brandon to sit in that one chair, apart from the others.

"This should be *interesting*, for certain values of the word," Justine said in Ruby's ear as the last Family members were seated.

They walked up the aisle together. Justine took a seat in the front row by two empty chairs marked RESERVED while Ruby claimed her place between Brandon and Gabe on the platform.

Philip glared stonily at her.

Gabe squeezed her hand. "It's showtime," he whispered. "Wish me luck." And then he rose and stood in the middle of the platform, facing the thirty Family members who had come to this meeting.

"Good afternoon. We all know the principals up front, but perhaps for formality's sake introductions should be necessary. I am Gabriel, informally considered to be the Martiniere, as designated by the dowager Matriarch, Donna. I have called you together to present my case for making this informal designation formal."

He turned and gestured to Brandon, then Ruby. "My son Brandon, informally the Martiniere-in-waiting. I am also asking to make this informal designation formal. My wife, Ruby Barkley, who *has* been made the Matriarch, by Donna's hand."

Gabe drew himself tighter, then turned toward Philip. "And this is Philip, once thought to be my uncle, now shown through evidence presented by Donna to be my biological father. He has served as the Martiniere for many years, but has been informally relieved of his responsibilities. He is here because by the traditions and structures of the Martiniere Group, he has a right to hear and to respond to the case for his permanent removal as the Martiniere."

"A bunch of hogwash," Philip grumbled. "I made the Martiniere Group competitive in this new era. And I'm a Presidential nominee. All of you have benefited from my tenure as Martiniere. But now you claim to have scruples about what it took to get here? Hypocrites! You happily took in all that income that *I* was responsible for creating!"

Gabe inclined his head slightly. "You will have the opportunity to speak to these accusations later. Justine, Philip's daughter, will present the reasons for removing Philip from his position." He gestured to her, then sat down.

Justine coolly, calmly, walked up to the platform. Philip's lips tightened until they were nearly invisible.

With a snap of her fingers, a projection appeared to Justine's left. They had decided to simplify the charges to five main ones.

"You have all received a list of these charges and the supporting evidence for each one. I will restate the charges but not go into detail until I am finished, if people desire more information.

"First. Philip Martiniere violated the agreement between himself and his brother Saul by causing the deaths of Saul, his wife Angelica, and their daughter Louisa."

"Lie!" Philip growled.

"Please wait until I have finished," Justine said icily, looking past Philip. "Second. Philip Martiniere further violated the agreement between himself and Saul by not acknowledging Gabriel as his son, and denying Gabriel the right to become the Martiniere upon his age of majority, as was required after his first violation of this agreement."

"You'd hand the Group over to an untried kid?" Philip snarled.

"Again, please wait," Justine said. "Third. Philip Martiniere conspired to not only manipulate his grandson, Brandon Martiniere, into a lifetime indenture contract, but intended to cyborg him, in violation of the Martiniere Group Statement of Principles enacted twenty-nine years ago."

"Limitation of free experimentation!"

Justine paused, scowling. "Daddy-poo, *shut the fuck up.*"

"Ungrateful bitch of a daughter!"

"Thank you for the compliment," she growled. "Fourth. Six instances of creation of cyborged humans under duress are *specifically* tied to Philip Martiniere, without the consent or agreement of underaged indentured. In five of these cases the indentured women who bore them were artificially inseminated without their consent. Another violation of the Statement of Principles."

"That was Joseph's doing, not mine!"

Justine ignored him. "Fifth and final. Regenerative human cloning using reproductive methodology specifically tied to Philip Martiniere, thirteen instances. One survivor of the thirteen exists. Not only a violation of the Statement of Principles but a violation of any number of international laws, rules, and regulations regarding the use of human subjects in research."

"You can't prove this!" Philip yelled. "None of it! You can't prove it. This is all bullshit! Charges cooked up by *him*—" he pointed at Gabe. "—to get control of the Group to offset his own poor financial management. And that of his son! None of this is true!"

Brandon rose. "Oh, really?" He snapped his fingers, then carefully began to peel plaskin off of the left side of his face. Silver glimmered underneath the brown plaskin, and cyborg features popped up as the covering was removed. Brandon turned to face the audience. "*This* is what my grandfather would have made of me."

Gasps as a measured tread echoed through the room while the brothers marched up the aisle, three and three. They stopped in front of the platform. Brandon stepped down from the platform as they fanned out until he stood at their head, the point of an arrowhead formation.

"*This* is what Philip sought to create. Here before you are the six sons of indenture that Philip cyborged," Brandon growled. "I was intended to stand at their head, as the son of Gabriel, leading the sons of Joseph, an enforcement squad to squelch all opposition to Philip, both within the family and outside of it. All of these men are the products of artificial insemination, with Joseph as the donor."

"Lies! All lies!"

"*Not* lies," Mariah said from the back of the room. "Alexander—my son—stands at Brandon's left."

"You too?" Philip snarled. "Betraying bitch!"

"You would have had me killed!" Mariah yelled. "All I did for you over the years, all that I thought I meant to you, and you would have had me *killed*."

"Enough!" Gabe snapped. "Thank you, Mariah."

"And this—this *cloning* accusation is hogwash!" Philip yelled.

Ruby snapped her fingers to signal Donna-gran. As Philip continued to rant, Brandon returned to his seat and the brothers took up positions next to the platform, three on each side. Donna-gran slowly, calmly led Michael from the hallway, matching his careful steps. As they walked up the aisle and Family members turned to stare at Michael, murmurs arose.

"You *didn't*." Philip stared at Michael. "You *dared*. Get that foul little piece of shit out of here!" He rose and took a step forward. Alexander and Carl blocked him. Ruby started up protectively but Gabe took her hand.

Michael stopped, breathing hard, eyes wide. "You're not gonna hurt me ever again!" he shrieked. He looked around wildly, then pointed at Ruby and Gabe. "They promised! You're not gonna hurt me. No more blood draws. I'm not gonna die like my befores did! I'll—I'll *bite* you first!"

Gabe's hand clamped down harder on Ruby's as she started to rise. Brandon and the rest of the brothers strode forward and arrayed themselves around Michael and Donna-gran.

"Sit *down*, Philip," Gabe said harshly. "Your clone Michael is under my protection. He is the product of Martiniere Group technology, and I assert guardianship over him."

"You son-of-a-bitch," Philip snarled.

Gabe jerked as if he were going to get up. It was Ruby's turn to exert pressure to keep him from rising.

"I'm your son too, and see how you treated me?" he growled finally. "Alexander. Carl. If Philip won't sit down, *make* him sit down, and *keep* him away from Michael. Thank you."

Philip momentarily resisted Carl and Alexander's pressure, then let them guide him back to his chair. He continued to glare as the rest of the brothers returned to their previous positions. Brandon and Donna-gran helped Michael sit in one of the three empty chairs in the front row. Brandon knelt and whispered something to Michael which elicited a fleeting smile, though Michael's eyes remained fixed on Philip. Then Brandon returned to his seat.

"I think the evidence speaks for itself, with the appearance of said clone," Justine said flatly. "Donna Martiniere. Are you satisfied that Michael is the clone of your son Philip?"

Donna-gran rose. "Yes. I have no doubt of that fact, and I have reviewed the DNA scans." She gestured toward Michael. "I testify on my honor as the former Matriarch that Michael is the clone of Philip." She sat, wrapping her arm reassuringly around Michael.

"Thank you. That is all." Justine returned to her seat on the other side of Michael.

Philip jumped to his feet. "False charges! All of you! After all I've done for the Group over the years. And here you are seeking to destroy me. And you...."

Alexander and Carl moved between Gabe and Philip.

"Fucking coward," Philip sneered, falling back a step. "Won't face me like a man! Like you always were, even as a boy! Choosing to run away rather than face up to consequences. You've always run, Gabriel, *always*. Gotten other people to fight your battles for you." He drew a deep breath. "You may be my biological son, but Joseph was always more of me than you will ever be! And your bitch of a wife killed him. Why isn't *she* facing charges?"

He whipped around to face the family, gesturing at Gabe wildly. "Look at him! He ran away after testifying against the Group and causing us to lose income for twelve years. He ran away from his wife and son when he thought they were threatened. Who or what is he going to run away from next? Is that what you want for the leadership of the family and the Group —a runaway? A betrayer? I've earned us a good cash flow! He's weak like the man who raised him. Adheres to principles that should have never been imposed upon us in the first place. Is that what you want? Is that who you trust?"

Artie stood. "Cash flow is not everything, Philip, if we become monsters in the process. And from the evidence, not just on these charges but concerning other things I have learned, the Martiniere Group has been complicit to a lot of monstrosities in your name. Things that the Martiniere Family should not be party to." He raised his voice. "I move that Philip

Martiniere be stripped of all authority and control of the Martiniere Group."

"I second it," Gerard said.

"All in favor?" Gabe asked.

Loud Ayes.

"Opposed?"

"No!" Philip shouted.

"I move that Gabriel Martiniere be awarded the authority and control of the Martiniere Group," Gerard said.

"Second," Artie said.

"All in favor?"

Loud Ayes.

"Opposed?"

Philip ripped his coat open to reveal a suicide vest. "If that's the way you want to have it...I'll take you all with me, and then *no one* will have the Group!"

The brothers descended upon him as icy talons gripped Ruby's gut. She wanted to grab Gabe, Brandon, and Michael, and run, but there wouldn't be enough time. She saw Donna-gran pull Michael's head to her chest, wrapping herself around him protectively.

"Defused," Alexander said, rising with the trigger in his hand.

Philip screamed. He jerked one hand free from Carl and Daniel's grasp. He grabbed something from his jacket pocket and thrust it into his mouth before either Carl or Daniel could stop him. His body tensed, then started to jerk and spasm. At last it went limp. To Ruby's relief Donna-gran kept shielding Michael so that he couldn't see it.

Brandon knelt by Philip's side, gesturing for Carl and Daniel to step back. At last he rose, turning to Gabe.

"He's gone," he said.

Mariah screamed and collapsed in the aisle.

The plaskin faded from Daniel's cyborged arm. He delicately touched Philip's mouth. A moment as he withdrew his hand. Then he looked up.

"Suicide pill. Fast-acting." A faint wisp of smoke flared from his index finger. Then the plaskin slowly filled back in.

Gabe exhaled slowly. "This is not how I wanted it to end," he said finally. "But, nonetheless, it is finished." He paused. "This is a time of mourning for the Family. Not just for what has ended but for what could have been instead over the past thirty years. I ask all of us to reflect on what we could do to prevent such perversions from happening in the future." He rubbed his face, then looked directly at Gerard. "I will not tolerate any more Philips in this family as long as I am the Martiniere. It is upon all of you, from Heads of Family, all the way down to the children, to ensure that we reach our full potential—and that also means preventing and purging the ideologies that led to Philip's actions. To begin with, I require the termination of all indentured contracts within the Martiniere Group by January 1, 2060. That includes any personal servants you may have. Work with Brandon on transition plans for your workers and operations. Are there any objections?"

Ruby studied the Family. Gerard winced, but did not speak.

"Good," Gabe said, after a long pause. "Brandon. Announce this decision on your 'cast, please. Spread this decision as wide as possible. The Martiniere Group is *finished* with indenture."

"With pleasure," Brandon said.

"Are there other concerns?"

"What about women in Family leadership roles?" Justine challenged. "Will you accept that, Gabriel?"

Gabe smiled. "You of all people should know where I stand

on this, Tine. But yes. For too long the Family has clung to outdated patriarchal structures, with the exception of the Matriarch. At this time, I authorize you, Justine, and the Matriarch, Ruby, to seek out and encourage the rise of female leaders within the family. With the aid of the dowager Matriarch, Donna." He bowed to Donna-gran.

"About time," Justine said. But she was smiling as well.

"It is a new era," Gabe said. And then he turned to look at Philip's body. "And we still have this—situation—to deal with. This meeting is over."

Ruby hurried to Mariah's side, uncertain of her reception. Mariah kept sobbing and didn't fight her off as Ruby helped her to her feet. Justine joined them as they guided her away from the others and into Georgy's arms.

Mariah may be Philip's only mourner.

Though Ruby suspected that Donna-gran, too, felt sorrow over her son's death. Even though she condemned what he had become.

THEY DIDN'T GET BACK TO THE DOUBLE R THAT NIGHT. Too much to do. Soothing family members. Informing authorities and making provisions for Philip's body. Leadership transfer technicalities. Working out the dynamics of freeing indentured workers with the assorted Family heads, along with the discussion of setting up a family foundation to help those indentureds that would need support.

And Michael. He had a meltdown caused by seeing Philip's body, not believing he was dead. Donna-gran managed most of it, along with the brothers. Ruby and Gabe both tried to steal a few minutes here and there from their work to check in with Michael. By the time they finally concluded, it was later than Ruby wanted to travel with Michael, especially after that meltdown. Better to wait until morning.

Unlike the previous afternoon, the day was bright and clear, with fresh snow on the very tops of the mountains as they flew over them. For the first time Michael behaved like Ruby would expect from a child of his age, staring out of the window and getting excited about the snow, bouncing in his seat.

If they had a site on Mt. Hood, why is he so excited about snow?

"You like snow, Michael?" she asked.

He looked away from the window. "Yes!"

"Making snow people? Snowball fights? Skiing? Snow-shoeing?"

"What's that?"

"Which one?"

"All!"

"You've never played in the snow?"

Michael shook his head.

"You'll get plenty of chances to play in the snow this winter," Ruby promised.

"Yay!" And then Michael turned his attention back to the window.

"Wow," Gabe breathed softly as he and Ruby exchanged looks. "Just—wow."

Michael kept his nose pressed against the window as they landed, staring at the mountains, the fields, even the airstrip.

As they left the plane and got into the crawlers, he was busy staring at everything and pointing.

"Is that a horse?"

"What's that machine?"

"Can I see horses?"

Gabe raised his brows at Ruby at that last question. She grinned at him.

"Sure, we can see horses."

In deference to Michael's weakened condition they had Charlie drive the crawler to the winter pasture. Gabe picked Michael up as Ruby opened the gate so they could go in the field.

"You'll see better," she heard him say.

"Horses!" she yelled.

Heads jerked up from where the horses were grazing in the far corner. Crystal started to trot toward them, followed by Legacy and then the rest of the herd. As Legacy threatened to run past her, Crystal broke into a gallop. Michael gasped as the herd thundered toward them. Ruby walked ten strides away from Gabe and Michael, to give them space.

She had no treats to give the horses, but doled out scratches as the herd swarmed around her. Gabe made his way through the herd to join her. She noticed, approvingly, that Michael was more fascinated than frightened by the mill of equine bodies around him and Gabe.

He tried to reach out to Legacy but she snorted and moved away.

"I wanna pet one," Michael said.

Ruby grabbed Crystal's mane and guided her toward Michael. Gabe showed him how to stroke Crystal's neck first, then the itchy spot under her forelock.

"Can I ride?" Michael whispered.

"Just sit," Gabe said. He raised his brows at Ruby in question.

She nodded. "Crystal's steady." Ruby placed her left hand on Crystal's nose, holding her mane with her right. "Whoa, Crystal," she said softly. The Paint mare obeyed, pinning her ears as Flash pressed near her flank, but didn't kick, just squealed.

Gabe delicately sat Michael on top of Crystal, holding him steady, ready to yank him off if needed.

Michael grinned big. Then he leaned forward to hug what he could reach of Crystal's neck.

Relief flooded through Ruby. If Michael could bond with horses so quickly—that boded well for their future.

Maybe that anger lurking within him could be calmed. He certainly deserved the chance.

APRIL, 2060

"Don't you think that perhaps you should round pen this colt first?" Gabe asked as Ruby tentatively tightened the cinch. He held Flash by the halter underneath the snaffle bridle. The colt's ears flicked back despite her care to slowly ease the latigo tighter as he played with the bit in his mouth. "He's looking pretty wound up."

Ruby shook her head. "He doesn't buck with an empty saddle," she said. "At least he hasn't so far. He may or may not buck now. But if he does, let go of the lead."

"If you say so," Gabe said, sounding unconvinced. "Mikey. Stay quiet," he said. "Don't want to set Flash off."

"All right, Gabe." Michael—now *Mikey*—leaned against the gate, quivering eagerly. Despite a winter siege of illnesses, he had still managed to shoot up six inches and fill out a little bit, and his skin was a healthy pinkish-brown from being outside regularly instead of fishbelly pale.

Ruby shook the saddle by the horn. Flash's ears flicked back hard, not yet pinned against his head but halfway there. She shook it again. His ears didn't budge.

Well, she decided. *No need to sneak a ride.* Crystal had

bucked her first few times under saddle. Now she was quiet and steady enough that Mikey could safely ride her in lessons and on short trail rides.

"I'm going for it," she said quietly. "Unless you want to."

"Nah, you'd be better at it than me. Quicker. I'm not the colt starter you are." Gabe grinned.

Ruby nodded. She delicately slid her left foot into the stirrup, weighted it, and stepped up without swinging her leg over. She had already done this with Flash without a fuss, on both sides, for multiple sessions, taking it slow because of what Ruby knew about Crystal. She had leaned over the saddle, patted his sides, everything but swing her leg over to sit.

Go for it.

She swung her leg over, inserted her right boot in the stirrup. Flash's ears pinned back harder as she gathered up the reins.

"Ready?" Gabe asked softly.

"As much as I'll ever be." She clucked softly and tapped Flash's sides with her calves as Gabe led him forward. Three steps and despite the coiled ball of muscles she felt under her, she was about ready to think that maybe, just maybe, he wouldn't be like his dam starting out.

Then he stopped dead. Wouldn't move despite the combined efforts of her and Gabe. The back underneath her tightened even more.

"Turn him loose and step back," she said softly to Gabe. "He's gonna blow and I'd just as soon not have a rope flying around. I'm going to try to get him to turn."

After Gabe had retreated to the gate, out of the way, she renewed her efforts, pulling with increasing pressure on first one rein than the other, then rocking him one way or the other, trying to make him take a step. But he remained rooted.

"C'mon, buddy," she said softly. "It's new. I know it. But you can do this."

More urging, combined with clucks. At last Flash took one step, then two...and then on three he jumped, big, his hind end popping up mixed with hops. It wasn't particularly hard to ride, not compared to what Legacy had been doing last fall. Ruby kept urging him forward. The hops and kicks slowed until he loped two strides, dropped to a trot, then walked. Ruby kept softly tapping his sides with her calves as she guided him in big circles for another five minutes.

Then he was done. She dismounted and led him over to Gabe. Flash paused for a full-body shake, making the stirrups rattle against his side. He startled for a single sideways jump, then snorted and lowered his head, chewing more on the bit.

"You big goof," Ruby said, rubbing his poll. "As if you haven't had stirrups flop against your sides plenty of times."

"I thought you were done bronkin', Ruby," Gabe teased.

"Oh, he doesn't buck as hard as Legacy used to." The golden mare now seemed to have settled into occasionally wanting to gallop hard at the beginning of a session. "And this wasn't bad. He's just new to it and not yet balanced. Couple more sessions and I bet he'll be just fine."

"Can I ride him?" Mikey asked.

"I should saaay not," Gabe said. "I won't climb on top of him just yet. My bronc riding days are *over*. And if I'm not doing it, you aren't either. Young horses need time and experienced riders."

Mikey pouted. "Can I get Smudge out now?"

Gabe looked the question at Ruby, raising his brows.

"Sure," she said as Gabe opened the gate to let them through. "Now that Flash is done."

"Yay!" Mikey tore off to the stall that had been designated as a temporary puppy kennel while Gabe and Ruby fastened the crossties to Flash's halter. Puppy whimpers and adolescent dog yips accompanied Mikey's throwing of the latch. Ruby rolled her eyes while she undid the cinch and secured the latigo and then cinch before pulling the saddle off. Gabe unbridled Flash.

Three weeks ago, a sheepish Gabe had arrived from town with a whimpering Blue Heeler pup in a carrier...*because a ranch kid needs his own dog, Ruby, and he's from a good line. I couldn't pass up the deal*, even as Ruby rolled her eyes.

She had heard this before. Shades of years earlier, when pups had followed Gabe home for infant Brandon.

But of course, Gabriel Martiniere couldn't have just one dog around, just like Gabe Ramirez could never have one dog. A week later, Gabe came back from Moondance with two half-grown border collies, out of the ones owned by the Moondance ranch manager. And now the house was strewn with dog beds and bones and chews, as well as the squabbling of *three* young dogs. It was a relief to kennel them in the barn at night on Ruby's insistence, so that she could have a quieter house in the evening.

Still, watching Mikey's big grins as the eager, roly-poly Smudge licked his face was worth the canine chaos and mess in the house.

"I hear Donna-gran's plane!" Mikey yelled. "Can I go meet her?"

"You be careful and listen to Beck," Ruby said. "And don't let the dogs knock Donna-gran down! You watch out for them!"

"Okay!" Mikey ran out of the barn, dogs at his heels. Ruby and Gabe paused to watch them run.

Gabe shook his head. "And to think we almost lost him a month ago."

"At least he bounces back fast." Ruby carried the saddle to the tack room. She suspected that Mikey's latest bout with illness was why Gabe had bought Smudge and then the collies. Viral pneumonia had turned Mikey back into the pale, tentative shadow he had been when first arriving at the Double R. It had been the third in a series of lingering illnesses that Mikey had contracted that winter. He hadn't been recovering very quickly until Gabe brought the puppy home and announced *this is your pup, Mikey, and it's your job to turn him into a good dog* as he placed the pup on Mikey's bed. *Whatcha gonna name him?*

A few slurpy puppy kisses, and Mikey's solemn, tired face had transformed into a big grin. Recovery hadn't happened immediately, but instead of silence and not eating, Mikey had started taking an interest in the world around him again.

By the time they put Flash back into the winter pasture and walked to the house, the crawlers with Mikey, Beck, Donnagran and the dogs were pulling up to the front door. Mikey peeled out first, calling to the dogs. Smudge, Cody, and Tip followed him as he moved away.

Beck helped Donna-gran out. She was using a walker.

"Damn, she's going downhill fast," Gabe muttered. "Worse than she was at Christmas."

"She warned us about that. Final dose," Ruby said. She was unsurprised—the work they had been doing with Justine had unfortunately chronicled the swift return of aging on Donnagran's body. It was one reason she had the ramp put in over part of the front steps once the winter accumulation of snow had melted. Neither she nor Justine thought that Donna-gran would make it for another year, much less the expected two years from the serum.

Could be us, soon enough.

Though all their regular lab work showed that the serum was still working in them. They'd probably get that five-year boost. And after that?

They would face that situation then. Though Ruby still worried. Sudden heart attack was one legacy of the anti-aging serum. And while her cardiac history was good, Gabe's wasn't.

Ruby stepped in to help Donna-gran up the ramp as Beck and Gabe took her suitcases. Mikey bounced eagerly at the front door as the dogs capered around him. When he opened the door for Beck and Gabe, the dogs rushed in with him.

"Dogs in the house?" Donna-gran asked, stifling a smile. "How much like Louis!"

"I'm not going to fight with *two* Martiniere men about it," Ruby said. "Though they do get kenneled in the barn at night. I draw the line at dogs in bed. Except...." Her voice faltered as they went inside, and she glanced around to ensure that Mikey was out of earshot. "Except when he was so sick and Gabe first got the puppy for Mikey. I thought we were going to lose Mikey then."

"He looks good now."

Ruby nodded. "It was a rough winter. He'd bounce back, then get sick again. Makes it hard to set up socialization opportunities with other kids because every time we did it this winter, he got sick. We're gonna try with some cousins this summer. He got along so well with them at Christmas in spite of being overwhelmed."

"Good. But even now—he is not the child that Philip was."

"Thank you," Ruby said. "We've been trying."

AUGUST, 2073

THE FUNERAL WAS ONE OF THE FEW MARTINIERE FAMILY events held at the Double R. Mike and Brandon bracketed

Ruby, holding her arms as they stood by the grave, watching the plain pine casket being lowered into it.

She couldn't cry now. There were just no more tears.

"Hey Rubes," Gabe had said that awful, awful evening when they were preparing for their thirteenth anniversary celebration. "Can you—"

She turned to see what Gabe needed as he leaned on his walker. His eyes widened and he reached for his chest, collapsing to the floor. She ran to his side. He clutched at her hand.

"Gabe!" She pressed the medic call button already knowing deep inside it was too late.

"Time—ran out. Not enough time. Love. You."

Fortunately, Mike had been there, recovering from his latest cyborg operation. He had taken care of things while she collapsed into sobs, for two days unable to do anything more than wail.

Mike and Brandon continued to support Ruby while they went back to the house. She was still getting used to Mike's cyborg elements—the procedure had needed to go beyond heart and lungs, replacing his arms because of his fragile bones. It was as yet uncertain whether his legs would also have to undergo cyborging.

The speeches at the picnic in Gabe's honor seemed to go on forever. But the one that stuck in Ruby's mind was when Mike finally rose to speak, even more than what Brandon had said.

"Gabriel Martiniere was both my son and my father," Mike started slowly. "He and Ruby didn't need to take on the job of raising the clone of his father—a man they both hated, for good reason. My progenitor was a horrible person. An awful, terrible person who killed my clone brothers just like he intended to do to me." He looked down, then back up, drawing a deep breath. "They say it's difficult for a parent to bury a child. I—sort of understand that. Gabriel was my son. But I am here to tell you that it is even worse when that child has been the father who raised you with love and encouragement. My progenitor resented his son Gabriel, and sought to kill him. If anything, he had even less regard for Gabriel than he had for me and my clone brothers, and our only purpose for existence was to extend his own life."

Mike blinked hard as tears ran down his cheeks. "I am grateful that Gabe never held that against me. That he and Ruby believed that I could be something greater than my progenitor." He choked. "I never thanked him enough for that faith in me while he was alive. Ruby, thank you for all you and Gabe have done for me. For not making me into a copy of Philip Martiniere. For letting me be Michael Martiniere, free of Philip's shadow. Thank you. *Thank you.* And thank you, Gabe, so many times over. Without your good heart and your courage, the realization of the *true* Martiniere legacy would never have come to fruition. You were the best of us all, and a standard that we all can strive to live toward."

As Brandon rose to hug Mike, clapping him on the back as he finally broke into sobs, more tears somehow blurred Ruby's eyes. This was the first time she had heard Mike say Philip's name since he had come to live with them.

Oh Gabe, she thought. *If only you realized how deep your legacy runs.*

Perhaps he had reached that realization, in his very last years.

She certainly hoped so.

But she could almost hear him say, *Rubes, it's your legacy as well.*

THE END

OUTTAKE: MARTINIERE

(*Timeline:* REALIZATION, *after the meeting where Gabe officially becomes the Martiniere*)

He couldn't sleep. Gabe stared up at the ceiling as Ruby snored softly next to him. A rare occasion that she slept so soundly. Normally Ruby was a light sleeper. But he had encouraged her to join Justine and Donna-gran for a ladies drinking session after the events of today's meeting, and from all appearances the younger women had tried to keep up with his rejuvenated, hard-drinking grandmother.

Perhaps he should have pulled rank and been the one drinking hard tonight, except that Gabe knew damned good and well it wouldn't help banish the adrenaline backflow from what had happened at the meeting. He would just be drunk and alert. Since one of them had to remain sober for Michael's sake, and it was his turn to manage night duty, he had opted out of drinking. It was only Michael's second night in their custody. Michael needed to learn that they were trustworthy.

Fortunately, both Ruby and Michael slept soundly right now. Gabe eased out of bed and softly headed for the bathroom. He splashed water on his face, a relaxation trick familiar from the sleepless nights before he had gotten back together with Ruby, then straightened up, staring at himself in the mirror.

It's done. I'm officially the Martiniere. And Philip is dead, by his own hand, and not one of ours.

That aspect did make things a bit easier for everyone. And there had been enough witnesses at the meeting to confirm that Philip had killed himself, no question about it. Hopefully that would eliminate any urge for anyone to make a martyr out of Philip—especially the Real Truthers, since he had been their Presidential candidate.

Gabe sighed and rubbed his face, then bent over to splash more water on it with cupped hands. He couldn't find it within himself to mourn his biological father. Philip Martiniere had been a cruel, manipulative man focused more on profit and power than anyone else. Philip's brother Saul had been a better father to Gabe than Philip ever could be. Saul was the man Gabe thought of as *father*, not Philip.

Thoughts of *fatherhood* sent him out of the bathroom as he heard a faint whimper. This time it was Ruby. Gabe lay down and rested a hand on her shoulder. She quieted, relaxing. He laid there, thoughts still spinning. Had he done enough to spark the first steps toward eliminating indentured staff in the Martiniere Group's holdings? It was going to take time to implement, and it was the right thing to do.

But are we doing it properly?

He hoped so.

Once he was certain that Ruby had settled back into sleep, Gabe got back up, heading for the rocking chair by the slider that led out onto the big deck. It was cold enough that he couldn't go outside without putting on more clothing, and risking waking both Ruby and Michael. But a careful tweak of the curtains let him see the moon and stars without letting in too much light to wake Michael. He settled into the chair, rocking quietly.

Sleepless nights were nothing new for Gabe here at his Moondance ranch. Had been ever since Rachel's death—what, was it a year and a half already?

Gabe rubbed his face again. Rachel. He *had* loved his second wife at the time. She was no Ruby, nor would he have expected her to be like Ruby. And after sixteen years, the fire between him and Rachel had faded.

Was it her cancer? Her family's disapproval? Or had it been the unacknowledged shadow of Ruby and the way he'd divorced her, in a misguided attempt to protect Ruby and Brandon from Philip?

Gabe tightened his lips. The divorce was another thing to hold against Philip.

And then he had met Rachel. Something clicked and for the first time in six years, since the divorce, his life felt right once more.

But there had always been a piece missing from their relationship, a lack of that quicksilver fire that had drawn him to Ruby. Rachel's battle against cancer had diminished the feelings between them—mostly a withdrawal on her part, and he had lacked the courage to try to spark whatever passion she was capable of feeling for fear of losing her.

Then that horrific night in the other primary suite at Moondance. Both of them suddenly down sick with the G9 virus. Gabe hallucinating as Rachel seized, then died in his arms.

He shuddered. He still remembered that all-too-realistic hallucinatory image of Rachel turning into Ruby, not knowing what was real and which of his wives were dying. Or if it was both of them. And then to have Ruby nearly die in his arms from the G9 just weeks ago in a macabre mirror of those damned hallucinations....

Michael whimpered. Gabe hurried to his side, before he woke Ruby.

"Michael. It's Gabe," he whispered as Michael's moans grew louder. He shook Michael to rouse him from the nightmare.

Michael's eyes flickered open.

"It's Gabe," he repeated. "You all right?"

Michael shook his head and reached for Gabe. They were making progress in bonding. He had already held Michael through a second meltdown at dinnertime, when Michael thought he had seen Philip and panicked. And Michael had been clingy at bedtime, not going to sleep until after a session of being rocked.

"Bathroom," Gabe murmured. He guided Michael to the bathroom. When he was done and hands washed, Gabe picked him up. "Bed or rocking chair?"

"Rock," Michael mumbled.

Gabe carried Michael to the rocking chair and settled in. Michael shifted in Gabe's lap until he, too, could watch the moon and stars, his thumb hesitantly drifting toward his mouth, as if he anticipated a reprimand. Gabe ignored the movement, rubbing Michael's back as he rocked. He felt Michael relax as he sucked on his thumb.

This is not what I expected my father's clone to be like.

His uncle Gerard had spoken of Philip's sneaky, bullying behavior as a child, warning Gabe to watch for it. Quiet, timid Michael was nothing like that. But Michael had also spent so much of his young life in fear, nearly dying from forced blood draws used to strengthen Philip during his cancer treatments.

Nor had Gabe expected his reaction to Michael to be so quickly protective and paternal. Taking custody of his father's clone themselves had been Ruby's idea. Gabe had agreed with her because it made the most sense, even though he had misgivings about what his response to the child would be. But he trusted her instincts and that she would call him out if he were stupid in how he treated Michael.

All of those concerns disappeared the first time Gabe set eyes on Michael—was it just yesterday? Small, clearly afraid but not willing to give into his fear in the face of someone he had been told to hate, someone he had been told wished his death. The slow, careful way that Michael moved—not right for so young a child, but between cloning artifacts and the chemotherapy he'd been subjected to before each blood draw, in Philip's belief that it would somehow supplement his own treatments—the child was frail.

All the same, there was more to Michael than what showed up at first appearance. Michael's own challenge to Philip at the meeting. *I'm not gonna die like my befores did! I'll—I'll bite you first!* The kid did not lack for nerve.

"Brave little boy," Gabe whispered. "Do you know how proud I am of you right now? That took guts to confront Philip, Michael."

Michael shifted in his arms. "You are?" he mumbled around his thumb.

"Yes," Gabe murmured. "I'm proud of you. You are brave. And Ruby and I will help you get strong as best as we can, buddy. Go to sleep, now. You're safe."

Michael snuggled closer.

This small, delicate child was not Philip. He had suffered even more from Philip than Gabe, all things considered. Gabe couldn't look at Michael and see Philip.

But it was certainly an unexpected turn of events. A year ago he had been solitary here at Moondance, struggling with his recovery from G9 and the manifestations of post-G9 syndrome. The angry behavior of Rachel's family after her death had marred his mourning. Things they had said had made him wonder about her decision to marry him, and to what degree Philip had been involved. He was a wounded old lion, hiding on his ranch and licking his wounds, without anything other than a bleak solitary future to consider.

Then the Superhero competition. Seeing Ruby again. And everything that happened since then. Oh, his life was definitely better, not just financially but emotionally. And this small boy in his arms, instead of being the curse Gabe had feared, might actually turn out to be something else.

If he survives.

Michael was tough under his fragility, however. And Gabe was more than willing to do whatever would be necessary to help him be a positive influence.

Everything Philip wasn't. You will not be another Philip, even though you're his clone, Michael. I swear it. You might be five, but you've got a better moral sense than he did. If I can make it happen, then you and Brandon will usher in a new era for the Martinieres.

He had two heirs now.

And still more thanks to my friend, mentor, and editor, Phyllis Irene Radford.

Deepest love to my husband Lew for his support.

And, as always, an appreciation for Miss Olena Chic (Mocha) for keeping me grounded when the events of 2059 and what led up to them became more real.

Afternotes, Influences, and Music

This book was written as the political scene in spring 2020 turned into an explosive nightmare...which is still happening here in August, 2020. As I said in the Afternotes for *Ascendant*, the political scene is based on my rough extrapolation of events up to August, 2020. It is entirely likely that things may be vastly different by the time you, the reader, see these words.

Or not. I have no claim to accurate foresight.

Donna-gran somewhat bullied her way into this book. I still don't know all the twists and turns and compromises that woman endorsed and supported in her roles as the Matriarch and as Louis's wife. I can't get over the impression that she has glossed over much of her past, or the degree to which her actions helped create the monster that Philip became. But she isn't talking to me about any of that, and I don't think I really want to know. Donna Martiniere is not as repentant of her past choices in the backstory of *The Martiniere Legacy* as Sarah Stephens was in *The Netwalk Sequence*, but she's a lot more slick and polished about her lack of regrets than Sarah.

Mariah Meyers is another slippery character. I knew there was more to her involvement in Ruby and Gabe's breakup than either of them knew, but it wasn't until Alexander showed up that I realized what was happening. She was whispering to me all along, though, that there was a lot more going on—until Alexander appears. Philip's death does break Mariah, while giving her the strength to evict Georgy Batineau from her life.

Ruby's weird redhead reaction to the G-9 vaccine is a known characteristic of redheads and near-redheads. We don't necessarily always react to medications and vaccinations like other people.

The Epilogue is meant to serve as a transition to the style of *The Heritage of Michael Martiniere*. I realized as I wrapped up *Realization* that I wanted to write Michael's story...but I didn't want to dedicate another trilogy to it. *Heritage* is, essentially, a collection of short pieces about Michael's youth and growth, and how he deals with the challenges of being Philip's clone. He manages to finish the job that Gabe and Brandon started, in part because, as Philip's clone, ultimately he is the only one who can so thoroughly disassemble the things that Philip did.

Musical influences:

"Wolf Totem," by the Hu, the remix with Jacoby Shaddix of Papa Roach.

"Delicate Sound of Thunder" concert, performed by Pink Floyd.

Willie Nelson.

The Martiniere Legacy

First Meetings: A Martiniere Legacy Short Story
Inheritance: The Martiniere Legacy Book One
Ascendant: The Martiniere Legacy Book Two
Realization: The Martiniere Legacy Book Three
A Belated Christmas Honeymoon: A Martiniere Legacy Short Story
The Enduring Legacy: The Martiniere Legacy Book Four

People of the Martiniere Legacy

The Heritage of Michael Martiniere: A Martiniere Legacy Novel
Broken Angel: The Lost Years of Gabriel Martiniere: A Martiniere Legacy Novel
Justine Fixes Everything: Reflections on Mortality

The Martiniere Multiverse

A Different Life: What If?
A Different Life: Now. Always. Forever.

Goddess's Honor titles currently available (chronological order):

The Goddess's Choice: A Goddess's Honor Short Story
Beyond Honor: A Goddess's Honor Novella
Exile's Honor: A Goddess's Honor Novelette
Birth of Sorrow: A Goddess's Honor Short Story
Pledges of Honor: Goddess's Honor Book One
Return to Wickmasa: A Goddess's Honor Short Story
Crown Anniversary: A Goddess's Honor Short Story
Challenges of Honor: Goddess's Honor Book Two
Cleaning House: A Goddess's Honor Outtake Story
Unexpected Alliances: A Goddess's Honor Rough Draft Outtake Story
Choices of Honor: Goddess's Honor Book Three
Judgment of Honor: Goddess's Honor Book Four

Netwalk Sequence Author Preferred 2022 Editions

Life in the Shadows: Book One
Netwalk: Book Two
Netwalker Uprising: Book Three
Netwalk's Children: Book Four
Learning in Space: Book Five
Netwalking Space: Book Six

Bright Star Fair Witches

Becoming Solo: A Bright Star Fair Witches Novella

Non-Series Titles currently available:

Alien Savvy: A Western SF Novella
Klone's Stronghold
Beating the Apocalypse
Bearing Witness

Vella Titles:

Falcon of the Martinieres (part of *Justine Fixes Everything*)

Bearing Witness (ebook release February 2022)

Beating the Apocalypse (ebook release January 2022)

A Different Life—What If? An Alternative Martiniere Legacy Novel (ebook release spring 2022)

Becoming Solo

A Different Life—Linda's Story: An Alternative Martiniere Legacy Novel

Federation Cowboy

Audiobooks Available:

Alien Savvy: A Western SF Novella

Released from other publishers:

"Queen of the Snows," in *Once Upon A Winter: A Folk and Fairy Tale Anthology*, edited by H. L. Macfarlane

"My Man Left Me, My Dog Hates Me, and There Goes My Truck," in *Black-Eyed Peas on New Year's Day: An Anthology of Hope*, edited by Shannon Page

"Lost Loves," in *All Worlds Wayfarer*

"The Wisdom of Robins," in *Whimsical Beasts: A Campcon Anthology*, edited by Joyce Reynolds-Ward

"The Cow at the End of the World," in *Well...It's Your Cow*, edited by Frog Jones

"To Plant or Pull Up Stakes," in *Pulling Up Stakes: A Campcon Anthology*, edited by Joyce Reynolds-Ward

"The Notice," in *Children of a Different Sky*, edited by Alma Alexander

ABOUT THE AUTHOR

Joyce Reynolds-Ward has been called "the best writer I've never heard of" by one reviewer. Her work includes themes of high-stakes family and political conflict, digital sentience, personal agency and control, realistic strong women, and (whenever possible) horses. She is the author of *The Netwalk Sequence* series, the *Goddess's Honor* series, and the recently released *The Martiniere Legacy* series as well as standalones *Klone's Stronghold*, *Alien Savvy*, and *Beating the Apocalypse*. Samples of her Martiniere short stories/novel in progress and her nonfiction can be found on Substack at either Speculations from the Wide Open Spaces (general, writing) or Martiniere Stories (fiction). Joyce is a Self-Published Fantasy BlogOff Semifinalist, a Writers of the Future SemiFinalist, and an Anthology Builder Finalist. She is the Secretary of the Northwest Independent Writers Association, a member of the Science Fiction and Fantasy Writers Association, and a member of Soroptimists International.

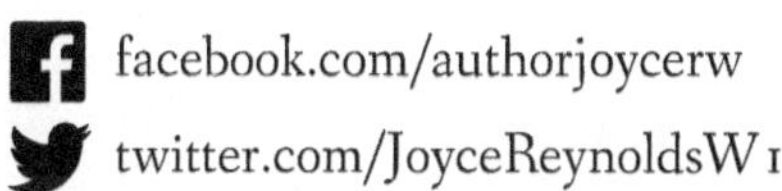